I0700800

STEALING FORBIDDEN DREAMS

A Novel

Edward L. Alban

Copyright © 2025 by Mr. Edward L. Alban

All rights reserved.

No part of this book may be reproduced in any form or by any electronic or mechanical means, including information storage and retrieval systems, without permission in writing from the publisher, except by reviewers, who may quote brief passages in a review.

This publication contains the opinions and ideas of its author. It is intended to provide helpful and informative material on the subjects addressed in the publication. The author and publisher specifically disclaim all responsibility for any liability, loss or risk, personal or otherwise, which is incurred as a consequence, directly or indirectly, of the use and application of any of the contents of this book.

WORKBOOK PRESS LLC
187 E Warm Springs Rd
Suite B285 Las Vegas NV 89119 USA

Website: https://workbookpress.com/
Hotline: 1-888-818-4856
Email: admin@workbookpress.com

Ordering Information:
Quantity sales. Special discounts are available on quantity purchases by corporations, associations, and others. For details, contact the publisher at the address above.

ISBN-13: 978-1-965732-76-2 Paperback Version
          978-1-965732-77-9 Digital Version

REV. DATE: 08/25/2025

*~To all the Maria Luisas, the Libbies,
Sashas, Imogenes, Guildas and Rams that
live in the hidden worlds of all of us.~*

TABLE OF CONTENTS

PART I: SELF KNOWLEDGE

1. KNOW THYSELF

It started with a brief exchange between Maria and a distant, oracular inner voice that exhorted her to acquire the wisdom of the ages, telling her: "Know Thyself; " to which Maria fired back with a snarky tone: "Oh yeah? Those two little words boom with roar, but exactly how does one do that? Where do I go to know myself?" The oracle then responded as it retreated, its voice fading: "Look in sleep."

This dialogue was the catalyst that launched a 10-year quest into her mind at night. And, indeed, it was in sleep that Maria ultimately found the 'self' she was looking for. Sleep, she discovered, was an echo chamber of inner voices where the defragmented elements of her own persona, her id, libido, ego, alter ego, her creative muses and her conscience came alive and held court night after night during sleep.

To this day these entities remain unseen during her conscious hours. It is only at night that they have free rein. Then they come out in human form to stage fantastic plays in her sleep. Of course, as with all humans, she forgets everything when she awakens because sleep memory seems to be allergic to the light of day. Like a mythical curse, awakening blanches out all memory and forces our mind to leave our dreams behind when we reach tomorrow. The only exceptions are the token wisps of dreams we do occasionally remember, and which constitute at most the last four minutes out of an eight-hour sleep session.

Despite sleep's memory impediment, Maria Diaz pulled off a Promethean task. She brought to light man's dark world of sleep; she found redeeming value for the heap of years in the waste bin of oblivion. How she did it, how she stole from oblivion and how she gained self-knowledge, is her strange story.

At first the elements of her persona were shy about showing themselves and Maria could hear them, but not see them. Gradually, they made themselves visible, appearing first as opaque silhouettes in black and white and eventually in full, resplendent living color. Grand as their sight was, it was nothing compared to their non-physical attributes, their vivacity, their humor, and their humanity. They became unforgettable characters. Even their jealousies and intrigues made for nightly dramas worthy of being staged. These nightly episodes gave a new dimension to Maria's existence and proved—what she had always suspected—that sleep was not a total waste.

At the center of Maria's intimate circle were the muses, her sister-like peers, each of whom pulled in her own direction. They competed for their time on the nightly stage. And some went beyond that. They tried to exert control over Maria's life. One, for example, pulled towards mathematics, and urged Maria to go for a PhD, while another pushed towards literature and dared Maria to write poetry. These two created poetry as warring oysters make pearls. Still another, her libido, thought it was high time for Maria to give up her virginity. At 26, she was past due. The Libido played tricks on Maria and aggressively pursued a critical role in Maria's existence. There were characters in authority such as her alter ego, oracles, and conscience which took various human forms and were especially influential in matters of belief and philosophy. They guided her on transcendental issues about God, about the hereafter, and about the nature of her soul on which Maria was still a babe. By the time she began writing her sleep memoirs these beliefs had solidified in her mind into a granite mountain. She knew herself. She knew what she stood for.

We all have episodes of introspection and soliloquy during sleep. And, of course, we all have dreams. But all of us forget the bulk of our night hours when we wake up. We take forgetting for granted. We accept oblivion. Maria couldn't. We do not even think about the loss. Our focus is on the conscious hours of our lives. Maria, on the other hand, railed against the colossal loss of hours, all those months and years unaccounted for by memory. No one can remember what he dreamed about a week ago, let alone five years ago. She, unlike most of us, made it her quest to salvage these hours from the waste bin of her life. She was convinced that there had to be redeeming value for so much time unaccounted for. So, she worked at it for ten years. She kept a diary and saved her dream fragments as if they were bits of tile with which she would make a big mosaic later. This enterprise led her to understand the interplay between her conscious and subconscious life and see how life asleep interphases with life awake.

Our life awake is an open book. It is tangible, well defined and documented. We have witnesses, we have data, film, videos, recordings, writings to corroborate events. Our life asleep is nebulous, insubstantial, incomplete, sketchy and impossible to repeat or corroborate. It has no witnesses. This frustrates the analysis, but it doesn't render it totally futile. Maria became very familiar with her dream characters and learned to recognize their influence during her wakeful hours. In time she learned to reconstruct the dreams behind her actions. She connected the dots.

Here is one example. We are often surprised by decisions we make in real life. We think back and ask ourselves: where did I get the gumption to do that? What possessed me? We cannot believe our actions. How we quit our job, how we broke up with someone, how we joined something, how we didn't get on a plane, how we burnt our bridges behind us. It's all beyond us. But unknown to us, or forgotten, there is a dream behind it that makes our actions perfectly clear. Maria learned to infer the nature of the dream through the snippets of memory left like recognizable tracts by her dream creatures. She came to know how they thought and what they were up to. At first, imagination –more so than memory –helped her fill in the gaps. In time, imagination and memory learned to co-ordinate better and reveal the impetus for her decisions. Deep in the night, during one of those forgotten dreams, Maria had argued with the girls at dream central and had fought tooth and nail for her principles. She thought she was right. Then she woke up and forgot all about the discussion. But when the situation materialized in the real world and demanded a decision, she suddenly realized she was wrong. She had made excuses; she had rationalized her cowardice and immediately conceded. The girls were right. So, she changed her position, making a pivotal decision of momentous consequence that changed her life. It was not until much later, when she was writing her biography, that she saw the imprint of the girls at dream central in her decision. By then she saw her life, her days and nights, her conscious and subconscious hours, as strands of time that intertwined her wakeful and sleeping hours to form the single tress of her existence. She saw how her dream sisters could push the buttons in the sinews of her soul.

Maria's desire to reconstruct her lost world of sleep became a quest. She conspired with the girls at dream central to steal the discussions, the analytical brainstorms that were not part of her dream legacy. She stole the secrets of her nights and rescued her nocturnal adventures from oblivion to share them with the world. She found the redeeming value of all her unremembered years of sleep.

Z   z   Z   z   Z   z   Z

2. AN INTERLUDE OF DARKNESS

The communication between Maria and her inner voices evolved gradually, but it picked up momentum once it got started. The next dialogue with her inner voices took place during one of those episodes when the brain engages in chatter with itself while asleep. It is not what one would call a dream but is more like the unremarkable recitatives of a long opera. Such episodes are always fodder for oblivion.   Tonight, the subject happened to be about sleep. It took place sometime around 3:30 a.m. when Maria had been asleep for hours. Suddenly, from the depth of darkness, she began to hear the unintelligible sound of female voices chattering nearby. She assumed they were strangers, women passing by the corridor outside her apartment, going to a neighbor's place. Maria ignored them, until one of the voices came closer and addressed her directly.

"Where are you, Maria? Can you describe your whereabouts?"

Maria was startled and answered as if responding to authority under oath. "I'm in bed, in my room, in my second story apartment in South Miami."

"Really now?" the voice remarked with a touch of sarcasm. "That's answering like a Girl Scout! But you left out the county and the state."

Then other female voices joined in, giggling as they came closer.

"She also left out the U.S.A.," a second voice added with a chiding tone.

"Not to mention the continent, North America," said a third voice.

"And don't forget planet Earth," chimed in a fourth voice.

"Hush you all! I told you she wasn't ready yet. You're going to wake her up. Let's give her a little more time."

Maria's body then turned and coiled in bed, pulling her sheet tightly around her while her mind dove deeper into itself, searching for a nook within oblivion in which to disappear. After a few minutes the voices resumed their questioning.

"Okay, Maria, we are back. Once again, tell us where you are. Describe what you see."

"I'm not sure… It's dark... I think I am at home in bed," she replied.

"Psssh! I can't believe this," commented the female stranger with some exasperation, "she's still not ready."

"Let me have a crack at this," another voice persisted, adding: "No, no, Maria. Your bed is where your sleeping body is. And we know where that is. But your mind and your spirit are elsewhere. Tell us where that is. Concentrate! Describe what you see behind those closed eyelids of yours."

"But that is where I am…" Maria insisted. "I am within the darkness of my closed eyes, which is in turn engulfed by the darkness of my unlit room. So, I am twice wrapped in a double darkness which lets me see nothing, absolutely nothing at all."

"This girl is too logical to be dreaming, I give up."

"Or else, she's having a most unimaginative dream, dreaming that she is where she, in fact is, in bed. How boring! I don't think she's left her moorings yet."

"Concentrate, Maria. Look around you," another voice urged. "Dark as it is, can you describe the darkness? Do you see shadows and silhouettes? Are there shades of darkness or is it all a monotone blackness? You should be envisioning the objects in your dark environment because you now have eyes like a cat that let you see in the dark. You are in a place where physical law no longer applies, where unspoken words can be understood, where meaning is carried by the atoms in the air. You are in a world governed strictly by your imagination. So, if you concentrate, you will soon see in the dark. The darkness will reveal its secrets to you."

"I will try."

Maria then mumbled incantations to herself, trying to elicit visions from the darkness. "Dark, dark, darkness," she said, "let me see what you are made of... let me cut into your fabric and examine your dark secrets. Let's see here… what lies within the flesh of darkness? Is it just more darkness? I will now pull apart your curtains, your veils and layers of black gossamer and come in. Here I come."

In a few minutes Maria had dissolved in the darkness and had become a part of it. She was aware of things without seeing them. They emitted waves that spoke to her skin directly. Objects made themselves known in non-visual terms, as if they had souls which she could perceive. She could move around them, and she could perceive their shape, she could sense their texture, their temperature. She could see in the absence of light. Above all, she had lost all fear of the dark. She had become a part of it and the feeling was one of blissful freedom and peace.

Who would have thought, she thought, that peace came in black light? But then, why not? After all, the womb is warm and dark. Who said darkness had to be sinister? She could feel thermal currents like gentle loving arms embracing her. The layers of darkness had tones of color which she learned to distinguish by their feel. The soft dark browns were distinctly warm, the grays grew less tepid, and the velvet blues were cool. And darkness changed. The dark of dreamless sleep was an evolving kaleidoscope of grays and browns, then greens and blues, like a tropic sea at dusk at different depths.

"Yes, yes, I begin to see the hidden beauty of darkness," she uttered excitedly at some point. "It is fluid, and it is so soothing. It calls me; it casts a spell on me. I want to lose myself in it and forget everything. I do not miss the light. I want to banish from my mind all sense of space and time. I want to forget addresses, maps, and co-ordinates; I want to banish the sun, the moon and the stars, computers, and clocks. I want to dissolve into the dark of infinite space, absorbing its nothingness till I cease to think, till awareness ceases to remind me of where or when, till I know nothing, till I feel embraced by oblivion. Ah, how sweet that would be. Let me descend deeper and deeper."

"We are losing her," said one of the voices. "She's going deeper. She's gonna shut us out."

"Well, let her. She needs her deep rest, poor thing. Let her have her little whiff… her little 'sniff of death,' as she calls it."

Maria then descended to the depths of her mind where all cares vanished, where memory froze, where awareness turned off, where the murmurs of her heart and the whispers of her subconscious were hushed. At that depth her mind didn't care what had passed, or what came next. She was in a stable, timeless equilibrium. She had arrived at the lowest point of consciousness at a state of hibernation where she didn't bother to have thoughts anymore—as if she knew all thoughts would be instantaneously forgotten anyway. Maria was experiencing a dark interlude of existence, a little understood episode of the night when sleep simulates the nirvana of death upon the living. The voices continued talking among themselves, but Maria could no longer hear them.

"Look at her dissolve herself in the darkness before our very eyes," one of them said. "Tomorrow, during her wakeful hours, she won't remember any of this. She will have forgotten how much she enjoyed this; she will know nothing about her bath of darkness in oblivion. All this will be a blank."

"Yeah, and she will say that sleep is a big waste."

"A stupid, senseless, costly waste. She is always harping about it."

"But only while she's awake."

"Oh, give her a break! Maria may say that, but you know that in her heart she knows sleep can't be a waste. Nature demands it. It serves a purpose."

"What purpose is that?"

"She's fuzzy about that. I once asked her about it, and she was quite embarrassed to admit she did not know. She thinks of it as a mysterious metabolic phenomenon, a molting of old cells for new cells—not something she wants to delve into. Even so, physiological necessity aside, in the big scheme of things, it's still a waste."

"How could it be a waste if she concedes it is necessary?"

"That is part of the mystery. Maria thinks the process is not very efficient. Sleep ought to multitask more. Does sleep really need to shut down everything while it does its cellular housecleaning?"

"Yes, I agree. To her, the fact that sleep uses an enormous amount of time is proof of its inefficiency. She's always asking: Why does sleep have to take so long? We sleep a third of each day, roughly eight hours on average. She is horrified when she does the arithmetic over a lifetime. At that rate, in 60 years' time, she will have slept for 20 years! That's a staggering sum! Twenty years with nothing to account for. That is a waste! Where did all those years go to?"

"It takes a mathematician like you to bring that up. You and Maria are such nerds. But your arithmetic loses sight of something very important. Think of how blissful those years of so-called waste can be. Look at her now! If you were to ask her this instant about the waste, she would ask you: what waste? Right now, she is experiencing one of the most delicious moments of her life. It is nothing short of a prelude to heaven... an aperitif of everlasting bliss. Look at her gliding lazily in the dark like a bird floating on an updraft! At this moment Maria wouldn't change where she is for anything. She is absorbed by the nothingness of it all and she is loving it. Right now, it does not matter to her one bit that sleep is unproductive. The waste is what makes it so exquisite."

"Both of you are right, but there is something else you are not taking into account. Unproductiveness aside, there is something even worse about sleep: a lack of memory, zero remembrance! What good is this bliss if she won't remember it tomorrow? The waste involved is in the forgetting! Can we say that we lived something if we cannot remember having lived it? If sleep is a coma-like experience it is no different from death. In fact, it would make sense to subtract 10 years from our age for every 30 years we live because we might as well have been dead for all those years we slept."

"God, another mathematician! It seems to me you are making

too much out of recall. Is remembering all that important?"

"Of course, it is. What good is having something if you can't remember it? Think about it, all her joys tonight, those variegated treasures of the dark, the different tones of obscurity, the velvet touch, the sense of levitation and the heavenly sense of peace, all will be forgotten. It will be as if it hadn't happened. Nature offers no explanation, no consolation for its miserliness with sleep memory. You are made queen for a night, you live it up, but you can salvage little of your precious kingdom. You can remember only the crumbs, only the dreams you have during the last four minutes before waking up. The whole thing is a most grievous injustice."

"Amen."

"Ah, yes, the curse of sleep is in forgetting. Sleep has no business mimicking death as if to give us a taste of oblivion. Death is going to provide that for an eternity no less. Why rob us of our precious hours of consciousness? It would be better if we lived up our scarce time on earth and left the sleeping for later."

"Ah, but now you're confusing death with sleep, aren't you? Death is not sleep. The similarity with sleep does not hold at all. Sleep is life. Sleep is an activity of the living; it is like a quenching of thirst, like a sating of hunger. Sleep is, after all, a bodily function..."

"Oh, really...? a bodily function? like peeing? like making doo-doo?"

"Yes, if you must, like defecating and urinating. Sleep can be just as compelling. But unlike the bladder that cries out for relief or burst, or the bowels that threaten to explode, sleep is not localized to a particular body part. Sleep is total. Your bones, your muscles, your eyes, your mind--all clamor for rest. Maybe that is why sleep requires more time... because it covers more, because it is an ablution of body and mind, of heart and soul. When you sleep, you welter in your own weariness and tend to the ills of exhaustion from the depth of your bones to your outer hide."

"What's all this talk about death and excretion? Goodness! You lost me. What's your point?"

"You must have come in late. Very simply, the dead have no bodily needs. So, don't compare death with sleep. But also, for all that bodily functions provide relief, and for all that they may be as gratifying as sleep, they need not be remembered—with the possible exception of sex which is something else altogether."

"Why shouldn't these bodily needs be remembered?"

"...Remembering sleep or other bodily functions is no panacea. It doesn't sate anything. The gratification of bodily functions is in the experience and not in their memory. You don't waste time relishing the memory of a good pee. There will be plenty more. Remembering per se quaffs nothing. As long as you're alive there will be thirsty times to come, there will be hunger again and there will be weariness. But, ah, there will also be drink, and food, and sleep. And that's what counts."

"Well, ladies, I don't think we are going to settle anything here tonight. We've touched on many subjects that have been bothering Maria lately. She still has a lot of research to do on many issues such as the metabolic processes of sleep, or the workings of the human brain during sleep, or the purpose of sleep in the big scheme of things. But she needs to go to the library on these issues because we cannot help her. She needs to do research and enlighten us all."

Z   z   z   z   z   z   Z

3. EARLY 1999

The following morning Maria got up without any recollection of the night before. She went about her business as if time had stood still during the night. At this stage of her self-analysis, Maria was not yet aware of the tricks the mind plays. While it is true that she did not remember what was said during the night, yet, paradoxically, nothing was forgotten because the thoughts expressed were really repeats, replays and echoes of ideas that were already part of Maria's legacy of long- term memory. Those thoughts had been, in fact, re-enactments of arguments that Maria had had in soliloquies during her conscious hours. Her brain at night had simply regurgitated her ideas about sleep to consolidate them into firmer convictions.

On this morning of early January Maria felt chipper. The air was charged with resolutions for new beginnings. People were out in hordes. There were joggers, skaters and cyclists packing the parks, the streets, and the sidewalks of Miami. Maria Diaz was one of those joggers. She was twenty-six years old, still single and a math teacher in a high school in south Miami. In Maria's case, she was not jogging to lose weight because she was already thin and lithesome. Nor did she drink or smoke or do drugs. Her struggle involved a problem which would not have been apparent to the casual observer: disorderly sleep habits, frequent insomnia.

To Maria, her sleep disorder was not an affliction that required medical attention; she thought of it as a bad habit which she traced back to her college years when she thrived on the free and chaotic flow of student life, staying up all night cramming for an exam, and then sleeping for the rest of the day. She had loved that pace of life and it suited her perfectly. If she could live that way again there would be no problem. But now, as a fulltime teacher inexorably confined to a rigid daytime schedule with no wiggle room, she had a problem. Her nocturnal nature made her feel like a square peg stuffed into the round hole of a day job. Even after three years of teaching she still had not adapted to her schedule, and she often went to school with as little as three hours of sleep.

Sleep control thus became a high priority for the coming year, and she wanted to gain it the right way: by discipline and perseverance, by avoiding the use of drugs and soporific syrups which, in the first place, had not worked for her in the past. She would adhere to a strict schedule; she would go to bed at the same time every night whether she was sleepy or not; she would avoid caffeine in the evening and she would forego naps during the day. That was her plan.

Meanwhile, she loaded up on scientific books and articles on sleep. She had already given up on the common pulp, the folk remedies, the warm milk, the soothing music, the reading to tire the eyes, and the myths of oneiromancers about dreams. The thought passed through her mind that perhaps she would not find solutions to her problem in books. Perhaps she would have to break new ground and conduct her own research. For good measure she started keeping a diary and taking notes. When she lay awake at night unable to sleep, she would think back and try to correlate her inability to sleep with the events of the day. Was it something she ate? Was it something she drank, like coffee or tea perhaps? And what about the full moon, did it have a bewitching effect on her? What was it about a full moon that lured her to dream awake for hours and think of love?

Dreams fascinated her. Were they a message? If so, who was sending them, and why? Sleep had become an obsession. Maria accepted the fact that sleep was necessary. But how much was indispensable? Would the amount vary by individual? And if it did, what determined how much was optimal for a person? She knew from her own experience that she could survive sleep deprivation for several days. In fact, she did that every week and often the ill effects were tolerable—until the third day. The question was: how far could she push that? Was she overdoing it?

As if the physiological considerations of sleep were not mystery enough, dreams added even more to the enigma. The emergence of the soul during sleep made sleep a Holy Grail for Maria. Her questions went beyond phrenology, neurology and psychology and led her to philosophical issues that touched on religion and life after death. Was sleep a prelude to death? Or, for that matter, did the awakening from sleep suggest an eternal continuity? Sleep and death could be mere interruptions, inflection points on an everlasting curve of consciousness.

Issues such as these led Maria to question her own beliefs about the hereafter and about God. She had always been skeptical of scripture and of religious dogma. Now sleep was intimating new perspectives. She found lines and ropes around her that led in different directions, some clear up to the sky, and she pulled them in the dark, anxious to know to what momentous beginnings, or endings, they led.

Z   z   z   z   z   z   Z

4. SLEEP RESOLUTIONS

The first few weeks into her regime of sleep-control changed nothing. Maria read at length about the workings of the human brain during sleep. She often averaged about three and a half hours of sleep per night. By the time she finally fell asleep, the women that roamed through her mind at night did not see fit to engage her in talk. They graciously left her alone so she could sleep off her weariness, giving her free pass to those peaceful interludes of darkness without dreams.

On Wednesday evenings she went to her parents' house for dinner. This Wednesday she had three consecutive days of sleep deficit. Her sleep deprivation was quite apparent to her parents. She hardly ate anything at all and after dinner she sat in front of the TV resisting sleep, struggling to keep herself awake, waging a futile battle against the inevitable. She napped for about five minutes only, and in those brief minutes her famished body feasted at a sumptuous banquet of rest. She would have slept for hours had it not been for her ubiquitous watchdog—her conscience that could break into Maria's inner sanctum and chide her for engaging in a forbidden pleasure.

"Maria," it said sternly, "at this rate you are not going to be able to sleep a wink tonight. You are blowing it! You are breaking your sleeping schedule. You can kiss your sleep resolutions goodbye!"

Maria woke up with burning pangs of guilt. A quick glance at her watch told her she had napped for about five minutes. Surely, she thought to herself, half begging forgiveness, this was too brief a nap to make a difference. Surely it would be forgiven. But in a few minutes, she succumbed to drowsiness again. She was so sleepy that even her conscience couldn't help snoozing also. She napped again for about three minutes. This time, however, her conscience woke up with a vengeance. It escalated its reproof by stinging Maria with what felt like the whip of a jelly fish, or the jolt of a lamprey that woke her up for good. Maria did not wait for another electric jolt.

She bolted from the sofa with great resolve and stomped out of the house for a breath of fresh air.

Once outside she limbered up, stretching her body in rhythmic calisthenics to shake off the sloth. Toe touches were followed by gyrations of the torso, then jumping-jacks in rhythmic hut-two cadences, then swaying motions, one after the other until she felt the vigor of rejuvenation in her blood, and she felt keenly awake, alive and interested in her surroundings. How beautiful the evening was! She absorbed the nature around her, the cool evening air, the encroaching shadows of the night, and the still unseen critters that had slept during the day and were awakening to croak and chirp in cacophonous delight to greet the fading splendor of a flamingo sky.

It was a beautiful Miami evening. Just gazing at the sky was inspiring. The night air was suffused with the redolence of the tropics, and Maria took long deep breaths, inhaling the vapors of the soil and the rich aromas of Miami's luscious flora. A gust of wind toyed with her body, swirling about her, embracing her, blowing her long black hair across her face. The ground exuded the aroma of citrus fruits and mangoes decomposing on the ground. Everything was pungent and stimulating. The land, the air and the sky touched her, each in its own way. The moonlight was playful; it darted in and out of the clouds. The palms swayed, brandishing their glossy blades as they caught the moon's silvery reflections like swords splitting the moonbeams. Now Maria was fully awake and recovered from the weariness of three consecutive nights of sleep deprivation and she felt fully reinvigorated. Her only fear was that she had pushed her luck with that snooze to the point of not being able to sleep at bedtime.

Clara, Maria's mother, came outside to see her. She had observed her daughter with great concern, noting that she had hardly touched her food during supper, and that she had dozed off intermittently while watching TV.

"Ay, Maria, *hija mia*, what's going to become of you at this rate? You don't live healthy, and you worry me. Why can't you spend the night here tonight? You could go to bed early for once. It would do you a lot of good. I don't want you driving back to your apartment short of sleep, it's not safe."

"I'll be all right, *Mami,* I'm not going yet. I'll be in good shape by the time I need to go. You'll see. And if I'm not, I'll spend the night here, I promise."

Maria was right. The calisthenics had worked wonders. Geysers of energy had spurted from the depths of her bones, giving her a reprieve from fatigue and a golden momentary euphoria. But she knew the alertness would not last long. The tide of weariness would return irrepressibly to claim its due. But, for now Maria was still under the magic of the night. She could have danced all night with the wind that still romanced her. She was in this happy state when her father came outside to check on her.

"Are you going to be all right, honey?" he asked her.

"Oh, yes, *Papi.* I'll be all right, I'm good and awake now. I am like brand new and ready to run around the block. Ah, look at those clouds, see how fast they drift away. Is this a lovely evening, or what? This is all I needed to perk me up. I am okay. You don't need to worry about me, Dad. But I should get going while the reprieve lasts."

A few minutes later they would come out again and he would escort her to her car saying: "Hope you get a good night's sleep tonight, Maria. You can't burn your candle at both ends. You got to be in good shape to face your students, you know. Going to work without sleep is just no good. You get a lot more out of life when you feel rested."

Maria nodded her head in agreement: "Yeah, Dad, tell me about it." Then she cranked the car and squirmed out of a tight parking spot on the curb into one of those narrow lanes that are typical of residential streets in North Shores where her parents lived. She made her way to Interstate-95 that took her to her apartment in South Miami, some ten miles away. As she drove, the words of her parents rang in her ears, irritating her. She could not understand how they could speak such platitudes about sleep, as if it was so easy to just close your eyes and fall asleep. Don't they know by now what a hopeless insomniac I am? "Go to bed early tonight," she said mimicking them. "Get a good night's sleep." They might as well say: "Buy yourself a lottery ticket tonight and get up a millionaire." That might be easier to do than getting a good night's rest. She could not understand how others could cross the thresholds from sleep to wakefulness and back again each day without going through the trauma that she experienced. How could they be so cheerful at 8 a.m.? And how could they be snoring so soon after going to bed? And why can't I do that? How she envied those feats! What gives them the ability to program themselves as if they were powerful humanoids? And how could she become like them and mold her existence to the mandate of the clocks?

On those nights when sleeplessness besieged her, all she could do was drift with her mind wide awake in an avalanche of time run amok. Her bed became a raft tossed about on the rapids of a wild cascading river. She had absolutely no control of her mind then. By then it would be too late to take sleeping pills. She should have taken them earlier to forestall the issue. But if she were to do that habitually, she would be hooked on soporifics and drugs, and she abhorred the thought of that. It would be preferable to suffer the malady over the cure. On such nights she would try everything to fall asleep: reading to tire her eyes, lying still in the dark, and of course, counting sheep. But it seemed that once her mind had been hijacked, nothing could be done. Sometimes she hit back by refusing to waste time idling on neutral as it were, and she engaged in something useful: working on mathematics, reading, or writing. One such night she took pen and paper, and she shot these words at her despair.

Insomnia

My bed is a rudderless ship
And I its helpless passenger
Riding out a storm of sleep denial,
Turning and tossing
Pushing buttons, pulling levers
In control panels without power.

I count sheep
While lying still in simulated coma
I mimic a catatonic state,
But all I do is dawdle
In stillness with no rest
In darkness without calm.
In silence without peace.

The night may well be a peaceful grave
For those entombed in restful sleep,
But it buries me alive.

In my despair I hear a ghastly noise.
It is the sound of my life gushing forth
In a hemorrhage of hours
Going to the gutter.

What would I give for only a little whiff,
For just a tiny little sniff
From the vial of death?
Just a half a drop to sip
For a night's worth of sleep.

What annoyed her most was that her sleeplessness was inexplicable. It came after she had done so much to prevent it. Her will seemed overpowered by mysterious forces within her that completely eluded her. Human beings are so complicated, she thought. Control of the self is a chimera. We can be masters of parts of ourselves, but helpless in others. If it isn't sleep, it is something else—diet, sex, gambling, alcohol, smoking, drugs, or bingeing. We struggle with insurgents within us in a war that is mostly private. No one around us can hear the voices arguing inside us, nor see our inner shadows fighting. People look at us and see the serene singularity of our facade, which hides our multi-faceted, complex, and warring inner reality. They cannot see the hidden plurality that fans out into factions inside us and that often rage in conflict underneath. Hidden within our collective shell is a host of entities, a community of strangers, which vie for control of our will. They exert their own wills independently, at times capriciously, and make driving body and mind in harmony an ordeal. Maria was convinced that, when it came to sleep discipline, imps within her ran wild at bedtime. If she could ever catch them, she would wring their necks. But could she ever catch her gremlins? How? That was the question! It took power to tame them, and she was beginning to doubt that she had such power. And what is the basis of that power? Is it will and discipline? Or is it drugs? She would think admiringly of those people who had complete mastery over their bodies—those Nazi officers, for example, those paragons of discipline with their Prussian punctiliousness and their Nietzschean control of mind over matter that made of their body a drivable machine. They must have been superhuman, demigods no less. How did they ever become so disciplined? And then there were those ascetics, those monks, those gurus of transcendental meditation that were able to surf on their brain's alpha waves and control their bodies almost breath by breath. How does one achieve that Zen-like state?

She would have been content with only a fraction of that power, settling gladly for just the ability to control her sleep and nothing more. How simple life would be if she could function as normal human beings who fall asleep within five minutes of turning out the light! That was the trick she wanted to master. But so far, she had failed. The only time she came close to achieving that was when she accumulated weariness over three nights of sleep deprivation. By then even her sleepless demons succumbed to extreme exhaustion. Of course, as a therapy it worked, but it was Pyrrhic. She had to pay a heavy price to achieve her goal this way. Her bed became like a devastated battlefield. Nothing was left standing–not even her restless demons. This usually occurred towards the middle of the week such as this Wednesday evening when she was tired enough to sleep straightaway. Tonight, she would sleep through all the usual outside noises that Miami could throw at her. Neither whining alarms, nor loud boom boxes driving by, nor loud chatter of rowdy neighbors could keep her awake. Tonight, even the silvery blandishments of a near full moon would fail. Maria was asleep a few minutes after turning out her light. Twenty minutes later her body was already in full repose, like an engine idling smoothly and purring gently.

Z   z   z   z   z   z   Z

5. Nocturnal Abode

Within an hour of falling asleep Maria began to dream, to see things within the womb of her sleeping mind. Had the voices asked her where she was now, she would not have said she was in bed. She would have said she was in a strange, unknown place far from her bed, far from Miami, in a strange world that was familiar and unrecognizable at the same time. In this confused and surreal world, locations mattered, but only for the drama of their symbolism. Physicality was protean and was based purely on metaphors. She was in a world where bizarre things happened, where a castle might float on the air with its lower floors over Europe and its turrets over America. This was a world fashioned either out of insubstantial remembrances, or out of the bizarre renditions of the imagination. Here the real significance of locations was in the hints of their hidden reasons.

The first thing Maria saw in this incipient stage of dreaming was a glassy, five-story building on the slope of a hill. She was on the lawn walking towards it trying to sort out what it was, because it was not a place with which she had any real connection. It was, in fact, a building she had never set foot in before. She had seen it from a distance a few years ago, from a highway and only for an instant, as her car passed through the outskirts of a distant city at 70 miles per hour. Despite the brief encounter, however, the building had made an impression on her. It had caught her eye at the time, and she had asked herself: "I wonder what that is. What goes on in there?" Then the image of the building, which had lasted in her retina for only a few brief seconds, remained behind, beyond the curve, out of sight and out of mind for years, until tonight. Now, from the deep recesses of her memory, the faint impression of that building had been dredged up to play a part in her life again.

What is this place? What am I doing here now? She asked herself. Then she heard female voices once again. One of the voices seemed to be reminding her of something.

"You were speeding through northern Virginia... It was about Alexandria, just as you approached Washington... You had thought it was the CIA, silly girl, because you had just seen signs for Langley, and you knew the CIA was at Langley. The place had seemed restricted to you, secretive in character, just the sort of place you had expected near the capital. Do you remember now? How titillated you were by all that, being there, near the capital, near the seat of world power, by its bed of secrets, in the thick of mysteries and intrigue." The voice laughed giddily and bewitchingly. Then it continued.

"Well, this is the building all right, but it is not the CIA, my sweet. It is not what you had thought, although it is a control center of sorts. It is a, what-shall-we-call-it, oh dear, a den of secrets? A lair of enigmas? A castle of riddles? Yes, yes, that's it... riddles…a mansion of riddles. Heee, hee, hee! Would you care to guess what it is? Let's give her some clues, girls. What do you say?"

"Splendid idea," answered a chorus of female voices.

"Here is your first clue, my child. It is only the plumage of a bird, not the bird," said one voice.

"Yes," another voice added, "like the turtle's carapace, or the oyster's shell, it is the habitat of the human soul..."

"It is the physical integument of your own shadow…"

"The home of your persona, the abode of all abodes…"

"The outer semblance of the self..."

"The physical site of your identity..."

"The tangible part of being..."

"The image of your ego that your mirror reflects..."

Maria convulsed in her bed, turning to the side, burying her head in her pillow, and pleading to be left alone.

"That's enough now!" said one of the voices "Let her be. She does not want to play guessing games. She's getting upset and is going to wake up. Ease up on her!"

"Yeah, you're over doing it. Cut out the mumbo jumbo."

Momentarily the inner eye of Maria's mind closed, and

everything turned to peace and darkness. It was as if her TV monitor had lost the picture. When Maria calmed down again, her visual focus gradually returned, and she saw herself on the lawn in front of the building once again. She was closer to it now. There was still no one in sight, but Maria suspected that whoever had been talking to her was still there. Without wasting more time, she addressed the invisible women.

"Hey, you out there, am I allowed to ask questions here? Would you mind telling me who you are?"

There was a moment of silence and then, matter of fact, came this straightforward two-word reply:

"Your subconscious."

"Oh, thank you," Maria said.

That was all she could muster in reaction to a description which spun a whirlwind of connotations in her mind. She repeated the words to herself... Your subconscious... Is that all? But I thought I heard several voices... Is the subconscious a collective thing then, like a chorus? If so, who conducts it?

"Don't be afraid. We are not as weird as we may sound. We were just kidding with you a minute ago. But seriously now, this is a place with which you do want to become very familiar. It is a place that all humans should know well. But they don't. Not many people are given the opportunity to visit it like you. You are very lucky, indeed. When you come in, if you do, you are going to be given the tour of tours. Many things are going to be revealed to you tonight in response to your inquiries in recent days. We are having an open house for you. You can tour this place to your heart's content and ask as many questions as you like."

Maria felt reassured by the tone and promise of those words. Her fears allayed, she became more curious, and bold. Without further ado she blurted out, "Ok, you are on. Show me. Let's go in." And she walked into the building.

The building inside was deserted but it was well lit. She walked down a long corridor on the first floor, making brief excursions into the passages that opened right and left. She was struck by the fact that although she had never been there before, she seemed to know instinctively where everything was. She had no difficulty finding the elevator, or the restroom, or the utility room, or the electrical switch room. As she came to a door, she was able to identify the room behind it before she could read the sign on the door. When she confirmed what things were she would say confidently: "Uh hum, just as I had thought, of course. At this rate, I am not going to need a guide. This place is easy." She walked clear across to the other end of the building having got the layout of the first floor in its entirety. Then she felt ready for the voices again. She hollered at them.

"Hello there. Can you hear me? I've got your number now. I think I know the answer to your riddle. I'm ready to guess what this place is. Hellooooo?"

"Yes dear. We're here. Are you ready to guess now?

"I sure am. The building is me. It's a facsimile of my body, isn't it?"

"Good heavens, you are quick."

"And accurate," another voice allowed.

Then Maria asked them: "What I can't figure out is why you've turned my body into a building."

There were whispers, like voices discussing something, trying to decide who should explain it. Then a voice addressed Maria loud and clear.

"Maria, about your question… well, to come to the point and not play games with you, we had to come up with something that would represent you, not just in outline but in sufficient detail and depth so that you could really come to know yourself. You are more than the façade you see when you look in the mirror. There are aspects of your being that you usually never see and which, frankly, if you saw them from the inside as they really are, they would gross you out, and maybe even freak you out."

"Oh, yeah," said another voice interrupting, eager to expand on the subject. "We could have gone with the real thing. We could have miniaturized you so you could enter your own body as a teeny, little microbe. We could have given you the inside view and taken you on a fantastic voyage, slip sliding through the capillaries, navigating the rapids of blood, through the mucous slime, through the plaque, the phlegm and the white, viscous smegma, hee, hee, hee."

"Enough of that," said a more somber voice. "In brief, Maria, we thought you would prefer a metaphor of your anatomy, something more pleasing than the real thing. But, of course, if you would prefer the other..."

"No, no! I would not want that," said Maria quickly. "I think it was very clever of you to dream this up. I prefer the metaphor. Thank you."

The building was a virtual dual of Maria's anatomy, a model of her physiological counterparts. When Maria heard the hum of the AC system, with its registers and ducts vibrating with the air that rushed through them she instinctively perceived it to be her respiratory system. When she saw the electrical wiring, the tubing, the network of pipes and plumbing lines, she connected in her mind with the corresponding parts in her body: her nervous system, her digestive system, and her urinary system. She was all there. Furthermore, it appeared that tonight everything was working well, everything was normal. All systems were operating without a hitch. Everything seemed to be in perfect order. She was eager to begin her in-depth tour of the place.

Z z z z z z

6. THE DOME

Even from outside the dome had caught Maria's attention. She had lingered outside admiring it, examining its bright geodesic structure whose glow seemed almost incandescent, active, as if it were alive. It had lured Maria with an irresistible pull. She told herself: "I'd love to see this up close…it's got brain written all over it. That's where I'll begin my tour."

She took the elevator to the top floor; it was one of those glass cubicles that overlooked an atrium that rose from the ground floor to the base of the dome on the sixth floor. The atrium reminded her of a Regency Hyatt hotel for its vast, bright enclosed space which gave the impression of being the great outdoors caught indoors. The gigantic hollow area with its corridors on each floor was reminiscent of a huge rib cage which emanated, as in the human body, from a vertical column that in this case was the elevator shaft. At the base of the dome on the top floor there was a circular corridor along the rim of the atrium bordered by a balustrade. Maria walked along its circumference to catch the ladder and the catwalk that led directly into the lowest lobe of the dome itself. From up close the dome seemed to be a huge diamond with passages that meandered to form a labyrinth with narrow canyons in between, like a gigantic crystal walnut or pecan. She was terrified and held tightly to the rails, going slowly, and not looking downward to avoid getting vertigo.

She could now touch the walls of the dome's compartments. These were made of an opaque glass-like material like pinkish coke-bottle glass. Its compartments hung suspended from the dome and were like a honeycomb of lobes that housed labs, work carrels, and office cubicles. In certain segments it was very confusing and difficult to tell whether the tubing turned and twisted on themselves as in a Mobius strip, or whether they fused with others. The place was daunting. As she made her way through one of the narrow passages, Maria was very careful not to step on the pipes and cables along the way. The fragility of the place made her uneasy. She had to be careful not to damage anything. She was aware that if anything went wrong, or if something broke, it was her pain. The place was not really meant for touring. It was encumbered by wires and tubing that went in and out of the cubicles.

"That's enough of this," she muttered as she turned to leave back to the lower floors. But as she pivoted, she noticed a section of the dome that was dark, abandoned, and turned off. Her sense of stewardship imposed itself and she felt obliged to check on it. "This is you, remember?" She told herself. "It behooves you to inquire in case something is wrong. After all, this is your body from dome to basement. Besides, this could well be where your problem is."

Why is that section so dark? She asked herself. Could it be a short circuit, maybe? Her sense of caring fed her curiosity and she decided to inspect it up close. There was a sign on the door that read: "Prefrontal Cortex."

If I'm not mistaken, Maria thought to herself, this is where intelligence resides, where logical thinking takes place. But how is it possible that it be turned off? Good grief! Everybody here seems to be out for lunch. She was about to ask for help when she was startled by the sound of a voice that called her from the circumferential corridor.

"Hello, there, Miss Diaz. Do you need help?" the voice asked her.

The sudden sound of a voice out of nowhere startled her and she almost lost her balance. She gripped the rail for dear life and froze in place. When she looked down and across in the direction of the voice, she saw an older gentleman wearing a white doctor's gown, balding on the top of his head and with a fringe of white hair around the sides.

"Did I startle you, Miss Diaz? I didn't mean to. Are you alright?"

"Yes, I'm okay. It's not your fault. I startle easily."

"Stay right there. I'm coming up to join you."

While she waited for the doctor to come around, she wondered how he knew her name. But that was just one more oddity out of so many in this bizarre place. She was beginning to get acclimated to the weirdness. In a few minutes the doctor showed up huffing and puffing from climbing and wiping his forehead with a handkerchief.

"Pooff! I'm a little out of breath. I shouldn't have hurried so much coming up …. How are you, Miss Diaz? I'm doctor Xk*@ w~zy$\sum$&*KpF."

Maria did not catch the name. It was long and complicated, and it did not matter for now. She would ask him later. For now, she just extended her hand, saying: "Oh, you shouldn't have hurried on my account. Thank you for coming to my rescue, Doctor. Nice to meet you."

"I've been sent to give you a guided tour. I understand you are doing research on sleep. I'll be glad to answer any questions you may have."

"Oh, that's wonderful!" Maria said, smiling broadly. "That's very kind of you. I could certainly use some help, thank you. But I wouldn't call what I'm doing 'research'. It's certainly nothing formal, nothing more than a layman's curiosity prompted by many sleepless nights. There is so much about the mind and sleep that mystify me."

"Well, you are at the right place to begin learning. This is the cradle of all your thoughts and dreams."

"Perhaps you could begin by clarifying why some of these offices are shut down. I thought this place would always be on, every part of it, with nothing shut down unless there was something wrong."

The doctor shook his head, expressing disagreement. "Well, that is not accurate. In fact, at any given time you are likely to find several areas turned off. That's the norm. Moreover, fragile as all this is, it can take a lot of abuse. I'm sure you've heard of lobotomies, not to mention surgery to remove tumors, or injury due to accidents. It is incredible how much abuse it can tolerate. Many parts of this magnificent complex can be turned off permanently without bringing on total paralysis. But what we are seeing here is something quite routine and common. Have you ever heard of 'seasonal downgrade', or 'off-peak mode'? Something like that is going on here. Take the Prefrontal Cortex over there, for example. There's no mystery in its darkness. It is dark because you're seeing it during off-hours. You should see it when it is concentrating on a math journal. Boy, that section is all lit up then, and it hums and beats like a disco bar then. Or take the Visual Cortex down there. As you can see, that is also dark and shut down. That area is crucial for vision, but only when you're awake."

"Fascinating!" Maria said with great amazement. "I am going to love this tour."

Maria was genuinely grateful for the care and solicitousness of the doctor. How kind of them to allow her to roam freely and to ask questions. How lucky for her to be getting concrete answers without any runaround. It was like a field trip to a science museum that she had visited in high school. She had learned so much on that visit and the learning experience had been effortless, delightful, and she had loved it. All learning should be like that, she had thought. Now this was turning out to be equally enjoyable and instructive.

"What puzzles me is how this shutting down comes about. Does someone issue orders to shut down the sections? Is there a foreman in charge? Also, why not leave the power on even if there is no demand? What's there to lose by leaving it on?"

"You've hit many things here, Miss Diaz. Let me take them one at a time. Let's see… Energy is a concern. It is a very important concern. They are very energy conscious here. But it isn't as if there was an Energy Czar who monitors and orders people to comply with energy conservation. Edicts and orders do not apply here. There are no echelons of power, no chains of command. There is no politics here, none whatsoever! And thank heaven for that because there is no time for such nonsense. This complex system is a paragon of synchronization and instantaneous reaction when things are working properly. You will not find such unified, concerted selfless action anywhere in the universe. If reaction time were delayed until the powers-that-be decided on a course of action, human beings wouldn't have survived. The entire complex is wired and interconnected to relay information instantly, to sound alarms when necessary and to take emergency measures reflexively, at once. The alarm system and the emergency response of this place are unparalleled.

"But complex as this place is, its workings have a simple logic and make sense. For example, when you want to go to sleep, you instinctively look for a dark, safe, and quiet place. Well, there are monitors here that take note of your intent. Once you've prepared the external environment, they relay signals to cooperate and accommodate you as much as possible internally. Your eye lids will close to shut out the world; your head will turn to one side to plug one ear and reduce noise; and parts of your mind will be shut off to prevent thinking from worrying you. Then the energy is reallocated to those areas that are needed during sleep."

The doctor had to stop talking to see what troubled Maria. Her face was anguished as if eager to interrupt him.

"Forgive me, Doctor. I had to interrupt you to ask you what goes on when things don't work. What you describe may be true in the normal case, but what about when things go wrong, and those monitors do not take note of your intent? You get in bed, you turn out your lights, but they miss your signal or ignore it. Sometimes I shout at them from the darkness in despair, but there's no one at the switch. Nothing happens. I just lie there involuntarily awake."

"It sounds like you suffer from insomnia."

"You can say that again."

"You realize, of course, that I can answer your question only in a general sense. I cannot diagnose your problem. That would have to be addressed by your physician who would need to delve into your situation, asking you many personal questions, conducting tests, and keeping an eye on developments for some time."

Maria apologized. "Yes, of course, I understand that perfectly, Doctor. I am not asking for a diagnosis of my own insomnia. I am asking about the general case. You have just explained how everything cooperates to help you achieve your aim of falling asleep. There was poetry in the simplicity and automaticity of the clockwork. My question was, and still is: what can go wrong in general?"

"Oh, yes, many things can go wrong; so many things that I don't know where to begin. There are three kinds of insomnia: transient, acute and chronic. I presume you are interested in the gravest of these, which is the chronic one. Some of the factors causing this could be stress, depression, drug addiction, alcoholism, and mental disorders. There could be a genetic, hereditary cause, or it could be hormonal. Menopause is a factor in some women."

Maria took comfort in the fact that none of those factors seemed to apply to her. She ruled them all out. "I don't think my problem is as serious as all that. But it need not detain us anymore. Please, let's continue with the tour. May I ask you another question? It's a very elementary one. How can you tell the function of each compartment? They are so alike; it's impossible to tell their function by their appearance. How do you know, for example, that that over there is the visual cortex?"

"Ah, now you've touched on something that is very dear to my heart. It is true that these compartments have no tell-tale signs that reveal their function. We've put signs on the doors exclusively for your benefit. Their shape and coloring are uniform. That is part of the mystery and wonder of this place. It divulges its secrets very sparingly. But after hundreds of years studying it, we're making progress. There are some obvious cases. I will point out some of these now. The position of things and their wiring are important. For example, take the visual cortex. That is easy because you can just follow the optic nerve coming from each eye and see where it leads to and *voila*. You can do something similar with the ear canal; just follow the ear's paraphernalia and see where it leads to."

"Of course! That is so trivial!" said Maria reproaching herself.

"Trivial?" asked the doctor, frowning and puzzled by that word.

"I'm sorry. That's math jargon for obvious," explained Maria. "When the proof of a theorem is easy and evident, we say it's trivial, meaning we should have been able to figure out the proof in seconds."

"Ah, yes," continued the doctor, "but there are other areas here about which there is nothing trivial. It has taken us years to discover their secrets. And what we have learned, we have learned the hard way by butting our heads against a wall year after year until one day by pure accident, or by pure serendipity, the mysterious lobe yielded its function to us. Of course, believe it or not, there are still areas that we do not understand fully. Let me give you an example of what I'm talking about. Once, for instance, towards the end of the 19th Century, a man suffered an awful industrial mishap. A steel rod pierced one side of his head and protruded out the other. Miraculously, he did not die. And luckily for science he lived long enough for observant doctors to examine his behavior and infer the role of the affected parts. Thus, little by little, by meticulously studying hundreds of cases such as these through the years and by recording them for posterity, we have managed to map most of the regions. I have been studying the brain all my professional life, and I don't cease to be fascinated by its workings. There is something about it that is magical, providential. There are case histories about how we came to know some of its functions that are as engaging, as fascinating, as the detective stories of Sherlock Holmes. Sometimes we have a loose end here, and a loose end there, and when we put them together, we discover worlds. Let me follow up on something else you just asked. You were baffled by the lack of activity in the visual cortex. Part of it is, indeed, turned off for obvious reasons. You've shut out all outside light while asleep, and there is nothing to process. That's what you would call trivial. But notice that part of it is not off. That section over there is also part of the Visual Cortex, but it is active even while we sleep. Look there. See those lights behind the darkened region? Why are they on? Because dreams also require light to be seen and enjoyed."

"Amazing! Fascinating!" Maria exclaimed.

"But now," the doctor continued, "you may ask: how do we know that that part which is all aglow is also part of the visual cortex? How do we know that it is the section that pertains to dreams? How would we have come by that information? You will be amazed by the answer."

"Oh, please, do tell me."

"First, I should mention that there are many ways we can detect brain activity from the outside these days. Scientists keep coming up with new methods. To name a few: we can read electric charges, we can detect blood flow through MRIs, and we can read brain waves through electroencephalograms, through positron emission tomography and other techniques that neurologists and related scientists have devised. But ultimately it comes to taking advantage of adversity also. Has it occurred to you that the blind could help shed light on our darkness? They also dream, you know. Would you be surprised to learn that blind people have helped neurologists as control subjects? Just think about the comparisons that that affords, particularly in differentiating what one sees in the real world as opposed to what one sees in dreams!"

"Gosh! That's truly fascinating. I can just imagine how productive those studies would be, and how immensely gratifying they must be for the researchers. This makes so much sense. It seems so intuitive."

"Would you say it's trivial?" asked the doctor

"Absolutely not!" replied Maria. "It's inspired!"

The doctor continued. "When analyzing the electrical signals of blind people, researchers noticed the similarity in signals—or lack of signals I should say—between them and sleeping people. Then through experimentation and measurement they could narrow down what was similar and what was different, what parts of the Primary Visual Cortex served for vision during consciousness, and what parts served during sub-consciousness, when we are asleep, but when we also see—in a manner of speaking."

Maria was beside herself with excitement. She made a humble confession and told the doctor that life sciences had never been her forte. Biology and zoology were the only courses in which she had made C's in college. And she had to drop out of zoology to avoid getting a lower grade the first time she took that course. Lately life sciences had begun to intrigue her. She found them fascinating. Then her eyes turned to another carrel that was also partly turned off.

"Well now, and this?" she said as she read the sign with the words: 'Inferior Parietal Lobe.' "This description tells me nothing."

"Some of these labels do not describe the function involved, but their location. Many of these descriptions, and this one is a good example, are strictly location identifiers. In Mathematics you have your Cartesian co-ordinate system that enables you to find any point in three-dimensional space. Well, in anatomy we also have our ways of identifying the various locations of the brain in three-dimensional space. The parietal part simply refers to this part of the cranium right here, no more and no less." This, he said as he touched the top back crown of his bald pate with his hand. "As for the 'inferior' part—well, you know what that means. That refers you downward towards the lower, back part."

"Hm, I see. Very interesting. Now tell me what it does. I'm puzzled by the fact that it seems to be made of two contiguous identical parts. One half is lit while the other is off. Why is that?"

"The story here," explained the doctor "is that these are both memory processors. Obviously, the one that happens to be turned off is the one that processes real world experiences when you're awake. Why should it be on when we are asleep, when we don't need it because the real world is turned off? But the other memory processor must be on. Do you know why? To tend to the subconscious as it processes dream experiences."

"Wow! You don't say!" exclaimed Maria excitedly. "So,

this is where the action is right now. This is awesome. I love the specificity of things, the neat order and design. But I must ask you, are things always that clear-cut between the conscious and subconscious worlds? Are real world experiences and dream experiences always that mutually exclusive in the recesses of one's memory? What happens when you are conscious but you're daydreaming? Or what happens when you are awake but remembering a dream?"

The old doctor shrugged and shook his head saying: "You may have trouble sorting through that, Miss Diaz, but these processors do not. They know! They know when their turn comes up. I suppose for some situations they both might come up. There may be a common area that they share somewhere in there. Or maybe they flicker back and forth, toggling intermittently until one wins out. Perhaps they take turns at brown outs. Who knows? What I know is that somehow, they work it out."

At this point an alarm suddenly went off. Maria panicked, thinking that the building was on fire, or under attack. Instinctively, she did what her mind urged her to do: to get out fast! So, she crashed out of the scene by breaking the membrane of her dream and opening her eyes. Her conscious mind then absorbed abruptly the light of a new setting. The scene was déjà vu. It had the reassuring familiarity of her own bedroom. Her alarm clock was crying to be petted. It was 6:45 a.m., time to get up.

Wow! Some dream, Maria told herself. But she should not have been surprised that she had dreamed that. This dream had been hatching for some time. Tonight, she had seen the spectacular gala performance in dream form of things she had read about and gleaned over several days.

There were objects in Maria's apartment which showed clearly that she had visited the topics of this dream during her conscious hours over previous days. These objects connected her hours awake with her hours asleep like footsteps to the threshold of her dreams. To judge from the material on her desk, one would have thought she was a medical student cramming for a test on the anatomy of the brain. The trail of scattered things marked the wanderings of her mind in the real world. There were medical books opened to the pages on the human brain. There were diagrams identifying the sections of the brain and there were mimeographed articles on brain function.

Z   z   z   Z   z   z   Z

7. THE BRAIN AT NIGHT

For the next few days Maria continued to read voraciously about the brain during sleep. At night she caught the echoes and reflections of what she had learned during the day in fogs of knowledge that still floated loosely in the air. It was as if sleep helped the stirrings of the day that were still percolating in her mind find a resting place.

The following night Maria picked up her dream where it had left off. She reappeared in the dome of that mysterious building where she saw Dr. Broca standing around as if he had been waiting for her.

"Hello Miss Diaz."

"Ah, Doctor, how nice to see you again. Shall we continue the tour?"

"Yes, of course. Please follow me."

They moved on, turning deeper into the labyrinth. Maria came to a section of the upper floor that was cracking with lighting; it looked like a chemistry lab, fully staffed, and busily working, with retorts and distillers boiling and condensing everywhere.

"This is the Pineal Lab," Dr. Broca said simply, as if it was something that spoke for itself. They stood together watching through a small window what was going on there. Just then, a lab technician wearing what looked like a white scuba diving outfit emerged, popping into the scene as if he had been ejected from one of the chutes coming from a lower compartment. He was rushing as he shouted orders: "Hold the adrenalin for now. Shut it off completely." Then he quickly opened valves and turned switches: "I am putting an order for another batch of Melatonin, and Serotonin. They want it pronto. Normal dosage, Stat!" Then, just as suddenly as he had shown up, he disappeared, sliding down on a metal rod (as in a fire station) to the lower floors out of sight.

Maria was thinking to herself… I wonder if he is one of those gremlins that give me so much grief falling asleep… I wonder if he is competent at his job. A little carelessness here, a little sloppiness there, and his hand might just hit me with too much adrenalin when I am trying to sleep. But then maybe the poor fellow is just a peon, carrying out orders. The real imp might be his boss. Then she approached the doctor tactfully.

"I know that you consider this to be a system of selfless and perfect cooperation. You have said that there are no echelons of power here. Tasks do not get done because someone commands them to be done. There is no politicking here. There are no jealousies among the personnel. And yet… and yet, things do go wrong at times. Maybe no one is at fault, there is no dereliction of duty, maybe no orders are disobeyed, but somehow things do go awry. For whatever reason, one section in the system drops the ball. A gland here fails to produce serotonin, say, or the delivery system fails. It's natural to inquire why and where the trouble occurs."

"Absolutely!" replied the doctor emphatically. "I have no problem with that. Systems are not always efficient. Failures do occur. All bets are off when you have deformities, or pathology, or illnesses, or genetic deficiencies, or abuses due to external causes, due to bad habits, bad diets, smoking, drug use, and what-have-you—not to mention being depressed. There are a number of causes that could impair functioning."

"I know. I know," protested Maria. "I'm aware that in extreme situations all sorts of things can be affected. But I meant in normal situations, in a healthy person like me. I don't smoke. I don't use drugs. I lead a normal life. And yet my sleep patterns are in total disarray and have been for years."

"Ah, Miss Diaz., normal… normal... You say you are normal. You say you lead a normal life. But what is normal? Who knows what normal is? Do you have a certificate of normalcy from your doctor? How do you know you're normal?"

The doctor was agitated. Maria tried to say something, but he brooked no interruption. He shushed her and continued. "No, no. Hear me out. I am not trying to cop out by lecturing you on what normal is or is not. I know what you mean to say. In a broad sense of the word, I agree with you. You are no freak. You are normal."

"Thank you, doctor."

"But within normality there can be a range of deviations and aberrations, quirks, idiosyncrasies and maladies which make you very different from other 'normal' persons. At the root of your problem may be endocrinal imbalances that could easily be treated. It could be that the production of some of the neurochemicals, which takes place down in the lower floors, is out of kilter. Your problem may arise down there, but its effects on sleep may register here. Have you seen a doctor about your problem?"

"No."

"Why not?"

"Because it's not the sort of thing that calls for a doctor. I don't feel sick. I just feel put upon by my own bad sleeping habits. I wish I were more disciplined."

The doctor was really upset now. He kept saying: "Boy, oh, boy, oh, boy, oh, boy! You've taken matters into your own hands, and you have misdiagnosed yourself and now you don't know what to do. Would you like me to help you?"

Maria was embarrassed. She didn't want to turn the tour into a personal consultation. Hesitatingly she said: "Well yes, but no…I mean, I don't want to burden you with my..."

"I am not going to examine you. This is neither the place nor the time. And I am not the doctor you should see. I am going to help you by simply giving you good advice. Go see a doctor! Start with your family physician, your general practitioner, if you have one, and let him direct you to another doctor if he can't help you. Your doctor is the only one who is qualified and better equipped than you to enter these premises and assess their performance. You need to see him and put him in control and empower him to get answers about your hormones, your thyroid. Let him run the necessary tests. If there is an imbalance, he can prescribe medicines to correct it."

"Goodness doctor, I don't know what to say. I don't think I am as sick as all that."

"Maybe I am wrong. Maybe I am jumping to conclusions, but I get the impression that something is troubling you and you don't want to see a doctor about it."

Maria mulled over his words. She had already determined that she was dealing with a candid and no-nonsense sort of old curmudgeon. While there was some truth to what he said, she was not in total agreement.

"Well yes, doctor. I do have difficulty getting to sleep. But this problem–if we can call it that–is a problem only on school nights when I have to go to work the next morning. But on weekends– when I am in control, and I can sleep late to my heart's content– there is no problem. I am in heaven then. Nor would there be any problem if I had to be in school at 11 a.m. instead of that cursed 8 o'clock in the morning. In brief, I am out of synch with the world's schedule. That's my problem. I am not sure that this is something that warrants a medical exam. Furthermore, I have had considerable testing by all sorts of specialists for one thing or another and, yes, it's all come up good and normal. I've gotten a clean bill of health. Lately, I've been trying a regime to work out my problem in my own way, changing my schedules, trying out strict discipline. But it is too early to evaluate its merits. If that does not work, if the problem continues, or worsens, then I will contemplate seeing a doctor. So, there, I hope we are all straightened out. So, let's leave it at that. Let's just go on and finish the tour."

"Suit yourself, Miss, but a doctor could save you a lot of grief."

"I think he could also give me some grief if I made too much of a deal out of this. He might put me on Prozac, or Zanax, or other soporific stuff that might make me dependent on them. Ugh. No way!"

"What do you have against those drugs?"

"That's a long story, Doctor. I am too young for them. My mother takes them, but I'm not there yet. Drugs are a slippery slope I want to avoid for now. I don't think my problems call for such measures."

They moved on, squeezing through the narrow passages between the glass compartments. Maria made a point to read the labels and signs to the various offices as she came to them. She stopped in front of one section that was scintillating with intermittent flashes as if it were weathering an electrical storm. Before she could articulate her question, the doctor answered it.

"This is the pons," he said. "This is the switch center for the so-called REM, rapid eye movement which, as you may know, is one of the manifestations of dream activity."

"Oh my, it's a virtual Christmas tree. Look at it go." Then Maria added with a twinkle: "By the looks of it, the REM tachometer must be burning up."

As the tour continued, it appeared that Maria and her guide had developed a system to expedite the process because the tour was proceeding more rapidly. Maria would see a sign with a description of the zone, and sometimes she would read it pronouncing it out loud. If the explanation was too complex, she would just tell him to skip that one, and she would move on. Sometimes she would try to guess what a particular area was about. "Don't tell me. Let me see if I can figure this one out." She would say. But if she had no idea, she would raise the palms of her hands parallel to the ceiling in a gesture of helplessness asking the doctor to please take over and explain. This was the case when she came to the limbic system.

"L-i-m-b-i-c system," she read aloud and slowly. "Might this be where we control the limbs? The arms and legs?"

"No, it's not that at all," corrected the doctor. "Don't let the word 'limb' misguide you."

"Well, you better tell me, Doctor, because the only thing I can guess is that whatever it is, it seems to be dead, kaput, unused and out of practice, or out of order. I think I see some spider webs from lack of use. What is it?"

The old doctor was embarrassed and out of words. Deep down he wanted to laugh, especially after Maria's tirade, putting down her limbic system as 'dead' and 'unused,' but he didn't want to embarrass her by laughing. Timidly, he began: "Er, the limbic system... Let me see.... How to put it? It has nothing to do with limbs. I don't know why they call it that. This is the region that imbues dreams with the fire of life, with emotions, including, of course, carnal desire, and sexual power, if you will. At times, this looms so large that it is as if it bulged in size, taking control of the whole place, not just the dome here, but the lower floors also— especially the lower floors. On those occasions it is not uncommon to have hormonal overflows from the pineal labs which trigger more overflows down below, even tremors, tsunamis, and quakes. Sexologists have hooked up couples with electrodes during coitus, for example, to examine the signals from this section and, ooh la la, the markers have gone off the margins. In fact, that section over there called the *septum* is thought to be a center for orgasms."

Maria was visibly embarrassed, blushing and clearing her throat as she tried to fade away, shrinking out of the scene. She pivoted discreetly and began moving to the next section. The old doctor quieted down and calmly followed her. When she arrived at the next section, she shook her head and made her hand gestures of helplessness indicating that he had better read the next sign also. The doctor looked and read the sign. "The Extrastriate Region," he said, reading it slowly. "Yes, oh yes, this is very important during dreams. This is the region I was telling you about earlier. It has to do with images envisioned during sleep. It is not fully understood, but we believe that this is where complex visual patterns are processed. To give you an idea of the work involved here, think of the section at police headquarters where artists try to sketch a criminal's face form a composite of witnesses' accounts. All the vivid visual imagery that is possible to be seen in dreams, including distinctive characteristics such as human faces, is developed here. This is where science and art must work together in producing credible renditions of human characteristics."

Maria was impressed and couldn't contain her emotion as she said: "This is incredible. I just can't get over the lengths they've gone to have entertainment for the sleeper. Sleep could have been a jejune and dreamless period of hibernation, a temporary death, a semi-coma where living is suspended. But the brain, it seems, felt obliged to throw in a lagniappe, to delight us with entertainment and drama while we slept. How kind! How thoughtful! How creative! But why?"

"Yes, yes. It is quite remarkable. It does speak to the grandeur of the brain. It is as if it were trying to cling to life in the darkness of sleep, bringing us its facsimile of life, its sense of the real world, creating a theater that spares nothing in the production of its plays and skits. Perhaps it is aiming for realism. Perhaps it is trying to give us our money's worth. There is a purpose in this, I am sure, a purpose that transcends physiological necessity and touches on the purpose of existence itself. Are we here to enjoy life? If so, why should we be cheated with the interruption of sleep, with a poor substitute of life—unless, of course, sleep was made first class, as joyful and rewarding as life during our conscious hours and maybe even more so in some respects."

"Bravo, Doctor! I like the way you put it. I agree. They could have thrown in token gestures, drab black and white renditions. Dreams might have been no more than a dreary mural in the dark dungeon of sleep night after night. But no, that was not good enough. The brain felt obliged to animate its dreams, to give them color and depth and sound, it had to turn them into nature's own 'Fantasia,' in splendid living cartoons. I just love it! This is so grand. That's what I find so fascinating. But do go on, Doctor! Show me more. What else do you have for me?"

"Well, there's not much more. We are almost to the end of what relates to sleep. The only other thing I can think of is the Anterior Cingulate over there." As he led her to that section, the doctor stopped for a minute, and turning back to face her, told her good-naturedly: "I think you are going to like this one also."

"I am?" Maria asked excitedly. "Oh, what's it about?

"This is where motivation, where curiosity, where interest in the surroundings during sleep are processed. You might think of it as the place where the dream director in the brain goes to work and gives it all he's got to produce scenes that grab you and engage you. This is where he turns into a puppeteer and pulls the strings of your mind. Just look at it. See how active it is now."

"Yes, indeed, it's quite alive! The Anterior Cingulate you call it…" Maria repeated the name, mumbling mnemonic codes to herself. "Think Billy Wilder, Steven Spielberg…director's chair."

They stopped the tour there and started to make their way back to the base of the dome, chatting as they walked. The doctor pointed out a couple of other areas as they came in view, but they did not bother to detour for a better look. The Thalamus, for example, was one such area they saw from a distance. The doctor explained to Maria that that section was always turned on. That was one section that could not be off, ever, because it was involved in the transmission of all signals within the brain.

When they reached the entrance where she had first come in, they stopped to say goodbye. Maria wanted to thank him warmly and profusely, in a personal way, calling him by his name which, of course, she never fully got clearly. So, inadvertently, she called him by a name that just popped into her head. The name seemed fitting now; it was the way he impressed her, as a doctor of the mind.

"It has been such a pleasure Dr. Broca. You have been most kind and helpful and you have really given me much to think about. This is truly a fascinating place. Then she clasped his hand tightly with both her hands as if to underscore her sincerity.

The doctor was thrown off balance with modest embarrassment. "It was my pleasure… My pleasure, Miss Diaz. Don't mention it. But now, tell me, where are you off to from here? Will you be leaving now, or will you continue your tour in the lower floors?"

She explained that she still had a few other places to visit although, to be sure, she was not interested in knowing everything there was to be known about that building. She snuffed out, without the slightest hesitation, the thought of inspecting the plumbing or air conditioning system. But there were still more aspects dealing with sleep–especially the production of dreams–that still intrigued her. She did not mean the hormone couriers, the electricians, the technicians, and cameramen who work within those lobes of the great dome to bring light and sounds, but the writers, the choreographers, the scene designers, and the dramatists, the people who dreamed up the dreams. She meant the creators, the manipulators of the mind, the people behind those voices she had heard.

"Is there a drama department, or a philosophy department?" she asked him. "Earlier tonight I heard several female voices. I had a sense that I was dealing with strange, secretive women who for some strange reason did not want to let themselves be seen. Imagine, therefore, my surprise and my delight when I met you. In addition to being nice, you were real, you were visible, and you were human. You turned this tour into a truly worthwhile and memorable experience for me. How I wish that those ladies—whoever they are—were like you, willing to meet me, and allow themselves to be seen as you have. I would appreciate it immensely if you could direct me to them."

"Well, this gets a little difficult for me. There's something you should know. I am different from those voices you heard. Those voices–for all that you could not see them–were a part of you, and I'm not. I am just a fill-in, an adjunct, an outside consultant. Like a character actor in a movie, like your friendly grocer, or cop on the beat, I am here as part of the scenery, like a prop, rather than as part of the plot. In fact, that is the reason that you can see me. I am here strictly as a guide, as a cicerone of the human brain in this anatomical model. My job is to guide you through the various parts, explaining the terminology and the cerebral functions like any encyclopedia, like a medical dictionary. For what I do, they could just as well have sent a robot. He could have given you the standard boilerplate tour I have given you. All that you have learned here pertains to generalized sleeping brains, to human sleep, not Maria

Diaz's brain or sleep. As I just said, you could have gotten this information from an encyclopedia, or a medical book. I think you are interested in something more personal, like a tour through your own mind, through your heart and soul. Am I making any sense? Do you understand what I am trying to tell you?"

"Yes, yes, I think you are saying that we have not really gone inside my brain, into its heart and soul. What's more, you cannot take me there. You serve merely as a guide of its parts from the outside, as a walking lexicographer of the medical terminology involved."

"Exactly. That's what I was getting at."

"You are also telling me that there are other doctors in the lower floors, like you, who could explain the various anatomical systems but only in the general case. There are urologists down there, laryngologists, ophthalmologists, and specialists of this and that. I would be able to see these specialists, but they could tell me no more and no less than what I could find for myself if I opened a medical book and read it for myself."

"Precisely! How incisive you are! Very well put."

"Well, doctor, as to the specialists down below, thanks but no thanks. I don't need lectures on the nuts and bolts of human anatomy. That is not what intrigued me about this place. Some time ago, while I was downstairs, I heard voices that invited me to come in and suggested I would see more than just this. I thought then that I would be able to go into the heart and soul of my mind. The voices made all sorts of promises. 'Come in," they said. 'We are going to open to you. We are going to reveal secrets tonight that will astound you. We are having an open house. It's as if the doors to the CIA were being open to you.' They said all that. I'm not making it up. I thought I would come face to face with my own conscience. I thought I could meet the recalcitrant part of me that refuses to march with the world's pace, in sync with when to sleep and when to work. I would have asked her: 'Why do you love the night so much? What do you have against the morning? Please be reasonable. Let me go.' I thought, also, at the very least, that those female voices would have shown themselves to me. I can't see why they must be so dramatic in communicating with me. Why all the secrecy?

"I am grateful for the tour. I really am. I am grateful to you and to the weird voices that invited me. I really appreciate it. It's been wonderful. But if that's all there is, then I have to say frankly, and I hope they overhear me, that it's not enough. This just doesn't get it. It doesn't live up to the expectations they raised. In fact, it makes me suspect that there is some sort of hoax involved here, like a loss leader, or deceptive advertising. They got me in here under false pretenses. They knew what I wanted. They could read my mind. It wasn't just this. If they think I'm going to go for more of this impersonal sort of tour through the other systems of my anatomy, they are mistaken. They can just stop their giggling like witches and their hiding in the dark like mischievous gremlins. I don't want any more anatomical tours. They should just come out and meet me or I'll just storm out of here."

"Oh come, come now, Miss Diaz," said the doctor trying to calm her. "It hasn't been all that bad. You may not have gotten quite what they promised you, but you are not leaving empty-handed. You have learned something. Besides, it's not over yet. Be patient. You may yet be satisfied. You may hear them again. So, don't do anything rash."

For his sake, Maria calmed herself and tried to be graceful through her disappointment, acknowledging that she had learned a lot, and she was truly much beholden to him for making it a pleasant tour. Still, she couldn't help feeling provoked by those voices. Something about them irritated her. Now, more than ever, as her anger subsided, she felt puzzled by them. She was morbidly curious about those voices. Who were they? Why couldn't they meet her face to face? And why did they have to be so cagey, so secretive, and so intent in playing hide and seek like mischievous little gremlins? She asked the doctor where she could go to meet them.

"It's hard to say," he began. "The problem is not where you go to meet them because one place is as good as another in this building. If you talked to them while you were outside, you could certainly talk to them here. The problem is whether they make themselves accessible. I think it's a case of don't call us, we'll call you, and I can't help you with that. The only thing I can suggest is a place where you can wait for them comfortably. I know an auditorium nearby where you can sit and wait. It is centrally located, and they are bound to show up there. Would you like me to take you there?"

"Oh, Doctor, how can I ever thank you? Of course, I would like to go there. I was so angry a few minutes ago that I was about to storm out of this dome, out of this building, and out of this silly dream. But you have prevailed, and I thank you for it. Please take me there. I have time. I'm willing to wait."

Z Z Z Z z z z

8. THE AUDITORIUM

The doctor led Maria through narrow, meandering corridors to an auditorium deep in the recesses of the dome. They did not talk much along the way, making their way single-file, squeezing through canyon-like passages full of sharp turns. They mostly muttered to themselves. The doctor mumbled something about "*sulcus* and *gyrus.*"

"What was that?" Maria asked.

"These ridges and grooves have a name. They are called *sulcus* and *gyrus.*"

Maria mumbled back: "Whatever, as long as it's not Scylla and Charybdis."

The doctor chuckled. "I can tell you know your Greek mythology, Miss Diaz. But fear not. No monsters are going to come out of these ridges."

He led Maria by the hand at times as they negotiated the passages from the thalamus down to a section of the limbic system. He was looking for a central spot like a crossroad for all traffic around and about the hippocampus and the amygdala. There was a central foyer there which connected to various meeting rooms and auditoriums. He led her into one of those.

"Well, here we are," he said as he turned on the lights in the spacious but empty auditorium. "You can wait here. Make yourself comfortable. Notice that the arm rests can be recessed back so that, if you'd like, you could lie down across several seats and take a nap."

"Thank you, Doctor. You're most kind. But I don't know about a nap."

"You know, Miss Diaz, just when I think I am beginning to know you, you surprise and baffle me. On the one hand I see you as the impetuous hot-blooded Latin who takes charge and storms out of places that displease her. On the other hand, I see you as weak and helpless—not a person in control, someone who cannot manage her sleep, who feels driven and manipulated by mischievous sleep creatures. So, when you said a minute ago that you would storm out of here, that you would call this 'whole dream off,' or words to that effect, I couldn't help wondering to myself: Could she really do that? I had to ask myself: how can a person have so much control over her dreams when she can't control her sleep?"

Maria was surprised by the sudden personal turn of the doctor's questions. He had described her at least half-right, she thought. When she gained her composure, she said: "Well, you kind of have me there, Doctor. I'll have to admit that I do have difficulty going to sleep, and I also have trouble waking up. But dreams are no problem. I could storm out of here right now. There is nothing to that at all. I would look for the nearest door, and I would just walk out. If I couldn't find the door or if I ran into hassles, I would just pull the plug on the entire proceedings by clicking my heels like Dorothy in *The Wizard of Oz*, and I would just wake up."

"Is it that easy?" asked the doctor. "Can you always pull the plug on a dream, just like that?"

"No doubt about it, I assure you, yes! I am in command where dreams are concerned. I would just open my eyes, and bingo, I would be out of here on my own bed in no time at all. I've done it before, many times. I see nothing hard about it. Anybody can do that. But why do you ask? Don't tell me that you can't do that."

"Me? Oh sure, I can do that…once in a great while. But I think I have less control in my dreams than you do. More often I ride along helplessly. For example, if I were trying to storm out of here, I would find that I couldn't. I would look for a door but could not find one. I would run in circles, seeing walls and walls, everywhere walls, without doors. Or if I did find a door, the door would lead to a closet, or it would be locked. I would then look for another door, and before I knew it, I would be led into other rooms, into other situations that would continue the dream in directions not of my choosing. The point is that the dream would continue. I would not succeed in storming out. Has that ever happened to you?"

"Has it? Gosh, at one time or another everything has happened to me in dreams. Weird things are nothing new to me. What I find remarkable is that it has happened to you. I can see that those dream witches and gremlins have gotten to you also."

"Well, I don't see the matter in terms of gremlins and little devils, as you do. Dreams are just random events that sometimes play with our emotions and give us the impression of being high drama. But they are simply disconnected scenes. They have little or no plot, no design. They just ad lib as they go along; they have no message, or purpose. Their plot, their resolution of conflicts and their denouement do not rise even to the level of a child's cartoon."

Maria disagreed with him and could hardly wait for him to stop talking so she could call him on the contradictions.

"I cannot disagree with you more now, Doctor. So, tell me: who is keeping you caged in that dream from which you are trying to wake up? Who is playing cat and mouse with you by hiding the doors, or locking them, or making them lead to closets? Who is reading your intention to get out and then actively blocking your way a la Alfred Hitchcock, revving up the anxiety, the suspense and fear by showing nothing but walls, everywhere walls without doors? Who, I ask you, your angels, or your gremlins?"

"Neither gremlins nor angels, Miss Diaz," replied Dr. Broca, "just the mind, the subconscious, your memory, and the imagination for the most part. They get caught in chaotic situations at times and they do the best they can. Of course, they have a lot of assistants which could act in ways that you would see as mischievous. For example, parts of your own personality may come out to make themselves heard, or some of your instincts may intervene. I'm talking about the id, the libido, the ego, your courage or your cowardice, your selfishness or unselfishness, your patience or impatience, your humbleness, your compassion, your generosity, or your stinginess, or your indifference. We are such complex creatures. And I haven't even mentioned your values, or your philosophies. It may all start innocently enough with the recall of a real-world experience. Then your character traits and the elements of your personality may see an opportunity to act and, boy oh boy, when they do, you are in for the joy ride, or the horror ride of your life."

Maria was nodding in agreement, adding: "I think that what you call ego and instincts are what I call imps. They run loose and act naughty during sleep. But let me ask you something, doctor. How dangerous can their antics and pranks be? Earlier tonight when we were touring the dome, clambering on those catwalks and when we were on our way here, I did think to myself: Am I being set up for a nightmare here? I was afraid of falling."

"Physical danger as such is not an issue," Dr. Broca responded. "You cannot fall any higher than your bed. Also, there is a mechanism in our nervous and muscular system called *proprioception* that protects us even when we sleep. Babies do not have this. That is why cribs have to be built specially to protect them. But this doesn't mean we are out of danger because we could encounter situations that are extremely frightening and the fear and suspense could cause problems, maybe even death. However, we also have built-in mechanisms. Your instinct of self-preservation usually kicks in and wakes you up when the danger levels get out of hand. You would probably call that instinct your guardian angel, I'm sure, but it is only a reflex action. It isn't really a case of you escaping, as much as it is a case of you being bailed out. When things get to be truly dangerous, the bubble of the bad dream bursts and you find yourself in your bed panting and gasping, but awake… unless, of course, you did die in your bed, which does happen at times."

Maria was fascinated with the old doctor. The more he talked the more human he became. She was now seeing a new facet that was more personable and friendlier than that of the lecturer on neurology.

"What you just said is fascinating," said Maria, "it brings together two subjects: death and sleep—human conditions that I have been trying to compare. They have elusive similarities that have generated a lot of myths, but they also have non-trivial connections. Now you introduce an intriguing new possibility that I hadn't thought of, namely that people could die while dreaming. It's just awesome!"

"Or not!" added the doctor emphatically, correcting her. "I was, in fact, making the opposite point: that most people probably do not die from their nightmares because they wake up in time. This conjecture is consistent with the way the brain works. The brain unflinchingly takes corrective action. Besides, for all we know, the person who died in his sleep may not have been dreaming at all. It could have been a heart attack without dreams."

"Oh, come now, Doctor, that's hard to believe, out of the blue and with no emotions involved?" Maria pressed.

"Who knows? That's the other thing about dreams: they have the last word, and they keep it to themselves. There are no witnesses. The sleeping mind is wrapped in an enigma that science will never uncover. We have come a long way at the end of the 20th century in studying sleep, whether we dream in color or just plain black and white, whether we can trick people into dreaming about certain things in sleep labs, and whether we can learn foreign languages while asleep by listening to audio tapes. But that's just superficial stuff, using the reflexes of the mind, tinkering with the nuts and bolts of the brain—no more. The mysteries of the mind are more intractable and go beyond neural mechanics. To some extent the mysteries of the mind are philosophical. I'm sure you have heard the old teaser about the tree falling in the middle of a forest. The question is: if there is no one around to see it or hear it, does the falling tree make a sound then? By the same token, what if a man is asleep alone, with no one around to monitor his sleep? Then, if a tree falls on him in the middle of his dream and nobody is there to see it, did the tree really kill him? An autopsy may reveal an aneurism, or cardiac arrest, or internal hemorrhage. But you'll never know what he was dreaming if he was dreaming at all. Unlike planes that crash, nightmares leave no black boxes."

Maria was fascinated by the discussion. "Yes, but isn't it possible that the left hand of your mind misreads what the right hand is saying, or that the signals are read wrong? Just as your body starts slipping towards a heart attack, your imagination intervenes either to take advantage of the unusual situation, or to help by frightening you into waking up. But the help is ill-advised. It exacerbates a bad situation, and you die sooner than you would have, staring Death in the face."

Dr. Broca shook his head gently, signaling his disagreement. "There you go again…looking for that tree in the middle of the forest…"

"Don't mind me. I am not disputing what you say. I am just fascinated by the subjects," Maria continued. "Death in bed triggers fascinating conjectures and juxtaposes contradictions. Who would think sleep could be so consequential? Imagine the irony! Your bed, which is supposed to be your safest haven, turns out to be your final arena. Who would think that trouble would be there, waiting for you? Think of the paraphrases to Hamlet's Soliloquy one could make: To sleep, perchance to dream, and ah, perchance to die—to die by nightmare, as it were! To sleep, and during sleep to say you fight and die, to rest forevermore. Aha, there's the twist. For in that rest of sleep what dreams may come must give us pause. Who would think that in the cradle of your safest haven, without foes, without weapons, without even a bare bodkin to bring your own quietus, you could die from fright? Thus, the bed doth make cowards of us all and turns us into inveterate insomniacs."

"You do wax poetic, Miss Diaz, and you are quite a romantic. You have just made too much out of something that is quite ordinary. Do you realize that thousands of people, if not millions, die each day in their sick beds—some in hospitals, some at home, but all in bed? It is commonplace and quite expected. But the romanticist in you had you imagining that perfectly healthy people go to bed and die from the power of a dream. This just doesn't happen."

"And the pragmatic doctor had to bring me down to earth. Thank you, Doctor. I was just kidding. I just couldn't help the parodies. But in a more serious vein, I'm fascinated by the intriguing possibilities, the ironies of fate. Bear with me a little and imagine the situations when dreams do play a crucial role. Imagine a coward who died while carrying out a heroic act, mustering the bravery that he always kept from the world, and dying nobly in his dream. Unfortunately, poor fellow, the world never learned of his final gallantry. Or you could think of someone who had been a failure at suicide before, someone who had tried it and botched it many times. But now in his sleep he finally consummated it accidentally by fantasizing about a new method and died of a heart attack even as he thought he would fail again."

"You have a vast imagination, Miss Diaz. And it is frightening. I would not want to be in one of your dreams. Now I must go. But before going I want to leave you with something else that involves death and sleep and is very, very real. You look it up. It is called **FFI** which stands for Fatal Familial Insomnia. It was discovered rather recently, in 1986, and seems to have genetic causes. A family in Italy had the gene that caused this rare insomnia. They would go days without sleep, then weeks. Their bodies would shrivel and eventually they would die from lack of sleep. One by one, a whole family perished by this phenomenon. Since then, other cases of this incredible condition have been noted around the world. Now just imagine what sort of ghouls and gremlins those afflicted with this insomnia had. Those are real harpies and lamias. When I first talked to you, I wondered if you might not suffer from this awful disease, but I ruled it out. You don't fit the pattern. Your imps are rather playful Pucks by comparison. Anyway, now I must go. You just wait here patiently for your friends, or imps, or whatever they are. And, above all, watch that imagination of yours. Who knows what dreams may come?"

Maria got up to say goodbye. They shook hands warmly. She expressed her gratitude and appreciation for all that he had done for her. He, in turn, conveyed his sincere pleasure at having met her. He had enjoyed her wild musings, the drifts of her imagination, and her penchant for thinking about the oddest connections. Then he left and she remained alone in the auditorium, waiting for those witches she had heard before, and whom she felt sure pulled the strings in her dreams and had something to do with her insomnia. Sooner or later, she would meet them, and when she did, there would be fireworks.

Dr. Broca puzzled her. He had given her so much to think about. "I wouldn't want to be in one of your dreams," she quoted him as saying. Then she added: "Where does he think he is?"

She sat uneasily there, in the twilight of consciousness, still thinking of the doctor… I suspect Dr. Broca is not who he says he is. I think he knows a lot more than he lets on. I think he knows the witches but doesn't want to get involved. For all I know, he may be a warlock himself. At first, he had tried to talk about sleep in a noncommittal way, avoiding dreams until the last, when he began to open up a bit. It's to his credit that he brought me to this auditorium, but he didn't want to stick around for the confrontation in case those gals showed up. Perhaps he is afraid of those harpies. They could eat him alive if he got out of line.

Maria began yawning in the ennui of her dream. And she did lie down across several seats as the doctor had suggested, dreaming that she was bored and that she was falling asleep, unmindful that she was already asleep.

The next morning before going to school Maria straightened her desk and picked up some of the books to return to the library. She took out the notes that she had written. Among these were the notes on the limbic system, which she had Xeroxed and in which she had written in red: "Has nothing to do with limbs." Also marked in glaring green highlighter was a Xeroxed passage on the FFI phenomenon, Fatal Familial Insomnia. That had made quite an impression on her. And, not surprisingly, there was also a highlighted area on a certain Dr. Paul Broca.

Broca (1824-1880) is most famous for his discovery of the speech production center of the brain located in the region of the frontal lobes (now known as Broca's area). He arrived at this discovery by studying the brains of patients with speech and language disorders resulting from brain injuries.

In addition, to the books and mimeograph notes on her desk, there was also a sheet next to the printer on her desk containing these verses that Maria had written earlier in the week.

Of Life, Death and Sleep

Before birth there is darkness:
The sleep of the womb.
Beyond death... more darkness:
The sleep of the tomb.
From sleep to sleep we go
As if life were a providential slip
That shone briefly for a second and then lo
Disappeared like an errant blip,
As a spark of light lost in the night.

Must human fate have such a stark finality?
Those who have faith believe life keeps on giving
And reject man's ineluctable mortality.
For them, the soul keeps on living.
But is that hopeful wishing or what?
Ah, if only I could believe that!

Penciled in her handwriting were these words. "Even in my own mind sleep is snarled and entangled with death. In all honesty, I'm not clear on this. Life in the hereafter is too facile. I can't quite swallow it. But the alternative that there is nothing is bleak and frightening. I must work on this and resolve it."

Z   z   z   z   z   z   Z

PART II: SCHOOL DAYS

9. OUTDOORS MATH

The next day was bright and sunny, and Maria could enjoy it to the fullest because for once she had had a good night of sleep. On this day she took her Geometry classes outdoors for field measurements. She showed her students how to use surveying instruments such as clinometers and sextants to measure angles. It was a field trip that the students always enjoyed, mostly because they got out of the classroom, but also because they learned practical uses of Geometry. They could apply the principles they had learned in class to perform mathematical magic, and they could measure objects that would have been too difficult, if not impossible, to measure directly. Geometry would enable them to obviate the need to climb anything, or to ford bodies of water.

The field work was a practical hands-on approach that gave students a sense for Math's relevance. They could identify their measurements with familiar objects in their environment. A hypotenuse that they themselves inferred would be more meaningful; they could identify it with objects in their own school grounds. They could look at the height of a nearby church steeple, or TV tower and relate it to the distance between the stadium's goal post and the gate. They could look at the imposingly high telephone tower and say: I took your measure from the ground to the tip-top the smart way, without ladders, without ever taking my feet off the ground.

Maria wanted her students to learn to reason, to learn to examine arguments critically, to systematically question the why of things, demanding justification for all claims. At each step of a proof, she would ask them to think of the lemma, the axiom, the theorem, the corollary or principle that would substantiate the claim and justify the statement. What gives you the right to use the measure of AB in lieu of FH, and why can you use KM as a proxy for the measure of EF? And she would not take a shrug of the shoulders for an answer, or "I don't know", or "because it works" or other such cop-outs. She would press until someone remembered the principle involved.

Sometimes the principle would be nothing more complicated than a simple unadorned truism, a gem of wisdom from antiquity such as:

"Things equal to equal things are equal to each other."

A statement such as this was one of the pieces, one of the rivets that held a logical structure together. When a student could name it and recognize its importance, Maria would beam with delight, saying: "Ah, yes. Yes! But savor that! Dwell on its beauty and simplicity. What a gem of truth it is! It sounds tautological; it seems vapid, almost highfaluting but it is a bit of golden logic from the distant past, a quintessential truth, one of the pillars of Geometry. But now tell me, who was the man that thought of that?"

By now the students knew the answer to that question because Miss Diaz had drummed his name into their heads, making Euclid almost a god for them. The simple sounding and rather tautological truism was none other than one of Euclid's Twelve Axioms, one of the gems he had given the world and posterity. Another axiom that was not technical sounding was: **the whole is equal to the sum of its parts.**"

It was not just the logic of Geometry that Maria was after. She also wanted her students to put this in historical perspective and develop an appreciation for the culture of man through the ages. She exhorted them to think of the power of seemingly simple ideas that the Greeks and the Egyptians of antiquity had developed in an age when there were no cars, no electricity, and when all their instruments were crude. Maria wanted them to appreciate the power of man's mind. What the early philosophers lacked in gadgetry they made up with thinking minds, with visions that could light up worlds. She wanted her students to appreciate the ingenuous ways that man had devised through the ages to make sense of the world. How far is the moon? And how do you go about measuring that? How could man have measured such things with his feet anchored to the earth? How, by just using the measurement of shadows cast by the sun at different latitudes, could man have inferred that the earth was round; that it was tilted on its axis; and that this tilt accounted for the seasons on earth, winter, spring, autumn. These and so many other fascinating questions Maria would research and prepare to share with her classes.

While this was fun for some students, it didn't do much for others. Those who were bored by learning, who were allergic to thinking, and who detested math were not amused. One girl groused about having to go outdoors. She was critical of everything. She found fault with Maria, with Geometry, with school, with having to think, and having to do anything she didn't feel like doing. She mumbled to another: "Why should I care how you measure this or that if I don't give a damn how wide the thing is to begin with? Who cares how far away the stupid moon is?"

Her companion couldn't agree more, adding: "I can't understand someone like her. I can't see me going to college, wasting years of my life learning all this crap about sines and cosines so I could bore kids to death in this dump. I am seriously thinking of dropping out and going into something useful like hairstyling. Now that's a job! It pays well–far more than this poor nerd here will ever make with all her schooling."

The two girls went on spitting out more insults between snickers and giggles. A third girl, who was standing nearby, was disgusted by them and was on the verge of getting violent with them but resisted her impulse and opted instead to get away from them, as far as she could. She was revolted by everything they stood for— including the way they dressed, like budding little hookers, and the way they carried on. Discreetly, she distanced herself and moved towards Maria who was on the other side of the football field. What a difference! What extremes of the female species they represented. There was Maria, handsome, elegant, classy, the smartest woman she had ever known with the demeanor, posture, and vocabulary of someone of high rank. She liked the way Maria dressed; the way she used make-up, with such inspired simplicity. But how does one become like that? Do you have to be wealthy to be like that? Do you have to come from a family of professionals? If she could ever get close enough to Miss Diaz, if she could ever get to the point that she could ask her personal questions she would be so happy. She would love to ask her what she did after school. Did she have a boyfriend? And how did she keep so trim? Does she diet, exercise, or do both? And, oh yes, where does she live? What does her father do? How hard is it for a Latin girl to make it through college? Did Maria have any difficulties with that account?

The young girl followed Maria around looking for the first opportunity to talk to her. She got in line and waited for everyone to clear out so she could talk to her idol.

"Miss Diaz, I've already turned in my measurements to my team members. They are pacing out the distances and I wanted to talk to you. I know my grades don't show it, but I'm really enjoying this Geometry more and more. I think bringing us out to measure things was a great idea. I wish we did it more often."

"Oh, thank you, Elena. I am glad you appreciate it. Thanks for telling me. But what is this about your grades? Your grades are fine. What are you talking about?"

"Cs and Bs?" the girl asked sheepishly. "Is that good?"

"Yes, of course it is! You don't need to be apologetic about yourself or your grades. You have never failed any test with me. You do your homework. You hardly ever miss class. You care, and you try."

The girl could only say to herself: "I have? Really?" She felt inches taller already! She felt gloriously absolved! Unburdened! But she still needed more assurances. "Oh, but I make such stupid mistakes on the exams. And I am not quick at picking up things in class like some of the smart students."

"Listen to me. You are as smart as they are. Don't you sell yourself short! But, yes, you could make some improvement. Now, I know you work part-time after school, and I know you are also taking other courses besides mine, but if you could put a little more time on this course you could make As and A pluses also. Could you afford to put a little more time?"

"How much more time?"

"I don't know, as much as one hour per day at first, but then after… "

Elena did not let Maria finish. "Oh, yes, yes, Miss Diaz!" she blurted out with enthusiasm. "I would love to give it a try." She was incredulous that Maria had been so nice, that it had been so easy to achieve rapport with her. The girl had feared that Maria would just listen politely but would not have volunteered to help her and would have politely brushed her off. Before leaving, she could not resist getting one more question–a personal and non-academic question.

"Ah, one more thing Miss Diaz, if I can…"

"If I may," Maria corrected her gently.

"Yes, okay, if I may… how do you keep your figure so trim and thin?"

"Hmm, I don't know. I guess it's all those *frijoles negros*, the *ceviche* and plantains that I eat."

"You eat those things, plantains and all, Miss Diaz?"

"But of course. You bet! And *chifles*, and *tostones*!"

"What are those?" Elena asked.

"Oh, yes, around here, in the Caribbean, they know them as *Mariquitas* and *pacatones*."

As Elena chuckled with joy, Maria added: "Oh and I forgot to add *maduros* also." Then they both had a good laugh over that. Elena was delighted by Maria's good nature, by her gesture of friendship and for discovering that she was one of those plantain-eating Latinos like her.

While this had been going on, the rest of the students were either taking measurements or pretending to be working. Some were horsing around, enjoying the time away from class outdoors. Maria caught sight of one of these boys who was moseying around with his hands in his pockets and wondered why he even bothered to come to school. He came so infrequently that he was hopelessly behind. He would fail her class. She had given up on him. He had failed all her tests. He was one year behind in school already and making no progress of any sort. By his age, he should have been a junior, but was still a sophomore, and failing. Maria felt uneasy around him. She did not like the way he looked at her. He, for his part, sensed her fear and liked it. She intrigued him.

There was something in an educated woman that puzzled and disturbed him, especially if she was pretty, as Maria was. Had she been homely or plain, he could have understood it. He could have told himself: that figures. By his reckoning, only women who were flawed in some respect had the need to achieve intellectually. But a pretty woman threw his logic out of kilter. He had ambivalent feelings about her. On the one hand he apotheosized her, but on the other he resented her. There had to be a flaw somewhere. He was intent on finding what that flaw was. He needed to humanize her because her brightness obfuscated him. If he thought about it much, it ended up incensing him. A rush of conflicting feelings of admiration and contempt ran through his heart. Every time he thought much about her, he ended up lusting for Maria. It was a strange way of compensating for his inadequacies. Lascivious thoughts gave him control over her by lowering her to his level. Then he could turn her from a symbol of authority to a simple woman, and he loved doing that. By diminishing her superiority and her authority, he could gain the upper hand over her. He could disarm her of all those theorems, of all those lemmas, and corollaries that he detested. They were the weapons with which she clobbered him, and he wanted to shatter them with sex.

In his mind, she had to be frigid, or something worse like a lesbian, or perhaps even a hermaphrodite, or a freak with some malady he had never heard of. Only some sort of sexual aberration could drive a woman to succeed in something as difficult and arcane as math. What a waste, he told himself as he analyzed her. She probably thinks she is too good for most men. I bet she thinks they don't measure up to her. Well, she's measuring men by the wrong yardstick. Somebody should make her understand that she is, first and above all, a woman. And he'd love to be the man for that job. He fantasized about the prospect. Perhaps there was a woman underneath the smarts after all. But he would never find out because he could never get close enough to her. Without a PhD in math, she wouldn't even give him the time of day.

About that time another student, Wally Northrop, approached him from behind slapping him on the right shoulder and flapping him with a sidekick, all at the same time.

"Hey Toro! … You had any more wet dreams about Miss Diaz lately?"

Toro squirmed out of the hold and swung back. The friend ducked. Then they horsed around and wrestled. Toro thought Wally had said that loud enough to get him in trouble. "Shut up, you dumb bastard! Watch your mouth." Wally just laughed perversely adding: "You know what? I'd just love to get my head between Miss Diaz's thighs and go (slurp!)"

"Yeah, yeah, yeah…" was Toro's response.

Toro had, indeed, related a salacious dream involving Maria to Wally some time back. That dream was fit to be framed. Wally had loved it, and Toro had enjoyed telling it at the time, even if he had some regrets on the matter later. Wally just wouldn't let up on it. He would mimic Maria, as Toro had represented her, saying: "Oh, show me the proof, Toro. I didn't know you could be so good. Ah, prove it to me. Put your QED on it."

Z   Z   z   z   z   Z   Z

10. TORO'S FANTASY

Toro did have a dream about Maria. It was inspired by the Almodóvar movie *Tie Me Up, Tie me Down,* in which a kidnapper, played by Antonio Banderas, manages to have his hostage fall in love with him. After the initial rebuffs of contempt, the young woman's resistance eventually subsided, and she succumbed to love in a few days. The plot is a real stretch, but given a good director and convincing actors, it could be pulled off on the screen. But Toro swallowed that improbable plot whole. To him it was possible. He was so immersed in the idea that he dreamed about it. Following the movie, Toro kidnapped Maria in his dream and took her to a vacant house near West Palm Beach to which he had access. However, the dream did not play as hoped for. Toro learned that dreams could take a life of their own and stray from scripts. They can take unexpected disappointing turns, even to the point of making him wish he had not dreamed that dream at all.

The hostage in his dream had a will of her own and she managed to thwart his machinations. She had control even in his dreaming mind and was not entirely his puppet. So, Toro tried to spite his subconscious by altering the misbegotten dream when he retold it. This way he could refashion his dream to his heart's content. Of course, this was no longer a dream. This was daydreaming, and daydreaming became the sport of the day where he conjured up fantasies like fake cards that enabled him to win.

He related one of these fantasies to his friend Wally. It was so improbable that even Toro himself did not believe it. But his Neanderthal friend believed it and loved it.

Toro also had another daydream which he loved even more. It was so special that he thought of it as his elite fantasy. But he kept this one to himself. Wally, he thought, was too stupid for it and wouldn't have appreciated it. In this fantasy Toro addressed a major problem that even a dreaming mind found difficult to contend with: how to seduce a woman that was so far above his head that he couldn't possibly make her look up to him. How could he lure her? What could possibly turn her on so that, even in a dream, her succumbing to him could be credible? All the things that he could think of would not work with her; and all the things that could work with her, he did not possess. Neither champagne, nor pot, nor porno videos would work with Maria. For her, only topology, vector spaces, and differential equations would work. But Toro did not have these in his bag of tricks.

Toro, however, did have a fertile imagination and he could stretch it to the point that he could make pigs fly. He knew that none of the usual hyperboles of romantic lore would work with Maria. None of the poetic nonsense about handing her the moon or parting the oceans would have any effect on her. Even a shower of rubies and pearls would bounce off from her like hail or so much water off a duck's back. The only thing that would work with her was Math-- deep, abstruse, out-of-the-mortal-park Math. So, in his elite fantasy he turned himself into a world-famous PhD mathematician, someone who surpassed Maria in all the things she admired, someone who wowed her with his superior analytical dexterity.

Supposedly, Toro, the illustrious mathematical scholar, was visiting Miami on a lecture circuit that would take him around the world. Maria had seen him at the university and had followed him around like a groupie in quest of an autograph. He picked her out from the crowd during a photo op and kindly signed the copies of some of his work that she had brought to be autographed. That had made her day. Oh, lucky girl. She was so attracted to his mind that he did not need to kidnap her. In this version of the dream, Maria came to his place of her own accord, eager and willing to do Math. He had led her on with a string, like you tease a kitten, except the string he had used was none other than "String Theory" itself. In the 1990s this was the latest fad in the circles of mathematical physics. It purported to unify the concepts that Albert Einstein himself had tried but had failed to bring together. Toro had once caught a TV show on the subject while changing channels. He had immediately thought of Maria, thinking she would like that sort of thing and eat it up. He had watched the program long enough to catch a name. He had also caught the fact that String Theory, whatever it was, was hot. Now in his dream all he had to do was just utter the words, string theory, and she would let herself be led, wherever he took her.

"What you know about String Theory, Maria?" the young Doctor Toro asked her.

"String Theory? Oh my gosh, next to nothing," admitted Maria. "I've heard about it, and I've seen papers about it, but that's all. What I saw was above my head. But I'm curious. Don't tell me you are on to that."

"Yep!" Toro-the-great-mathematician nodded, adding: "The guys that developed it are good friends of mine. We've had sessions together on the subject. Listen, I don't have too long in town. I must catch a plane for London where I'll be giving a lecture day after tomorrow. But I have some material at my hotel that I could leave with you, and if you'd like I could give you a primer on it for an hour or so. Would you be game for that?"

"Would I? I'd love nothing better," Maria gushed enthusiastically.

She came to the hotel lobby, and they chatted there for a while. But then he maneuvered her to his suite with one pretext or another. He told her that he had an important manuscript in his suite, that he had copies to give her in his safe. She was so in awe of him that she trusted him, and it was easy for him to string her along with math. She followed his promises like a child after candy, salivating, mesmerized.

Once in his room, he continued the mathematical magic. The more he demonstrated his prowess, the more in awe she was. How she looked up to him. He had reversed the intellectual pecking order. Their minds danced a mental *pas de deux* as they engaged in a mathematical tête-à-tête that took them to worlds of unimaginable dimensions. Now it was Maria who was stumped by the proofs that he expatiated. She had to interrupt him, to plead with him, and to have him go back several steps to explain again a point that had eluded her. Now it was Maria who was the student, who was running ragged behind him, unable to keep up. Now it was Maria who dropped the ball and had to apologize for her failures, begging to be given another chance. How she hated to miss a proof. Whenever she had to throw in the towel defeated by a hard proof, she always asked for another theorem to vindicate herself. He would oblige, playing the magnanimous one, and she would once again struggle hard with his trials, often crumpling one sheet of paper after another as she tried different ideas in desperation. For once, he would see her flustered, worried, sweating, and afraid of failing, trying desperately to reach what was beyond her. When she became exhausted and couldn't work on a problem anymore, she would surrender sheepishly to him. Then it was his turn to bask in the glory of superiority, enjoying the sense of power it gave him, but trying not to gloat as he corrected what she had done, complementing her here and there on her good stabs but ultimately showing her where she had failed. Maria would conk herself in the head with the palms of her hands in self-recrimination as she acknowledged her error. Then, in those problems in which she had been totally clueless, she was all eyes and ears when the master showed her how it was done, what she had failed to see. Come. Let me show you the trick to this one, he would say. And she would sit beside him, paying close attention and following his explanations full of sketches, figures and equations as he wrote them on a thick notepad.

Then, to draw her closer to him, he would write smaller, and he would warp his scribbles and symbols on purpose to make them less legible. His ploy worked, and she would be forced to get closer to him, oblivious that she was abutting against him tightly. So eager to learn was she, so enraptured by the Math and the ideas, that she thought nothing of the proximity to him. He dangled his nuggets of wisdom, and she reached for them innocently.

As she crowded next to him to read the notes, he could feel the sweet warmth of her breath on his cheek. At times they were so close that, had he turned his face ever so slightly in her direction, he could easily have found her lips and kissed her. At times he would turn his face her way but would stop short of kissing her, as if sizing up her mood and her will. He looked into her eyes searching for her heart, asking himself whether she was ready yet, whether she would rebuff his advances. As the evening passed, he determined that he was making progress, and that she was on her way. So, he continued to wow her still more. For Maria, intellectual games were intoxicating, exhilarating—and, he was convinced, they were also aphrodisiacal. Every time they finished a challenge–whether it was solving a problem or analyzing a theorem–there was great rejoicing. For her it was like reaching the peak of Mt. Everest. She would raise her arms in joy over the victory, giving high fives. Doing Math was as thrilling to her as sports, as games, or even magic. Maria would be all charged up and excited. She would sharpen her pencils, she would gather more paper and set herself up for still more.

"OK, one more. Let's prove another one," she would plead. "Let's try one of those far-reaching visions on the cutting edge of Math that you've thought up. Give me your hardest."

In his state of mind, the sound of her last request drove him mad with desire. Then he would have her read another theorem and then he would ask her: "What would you give me for proving this one, Maria?"

"Oh God, for that one? I don't know… I would give you a Nobel Prize, or a crown and a throne. I would knight you. That's a lulu."

"But you don't have those things to give, Maria. That's just pie in the sky. And even if you did have them, I wouldn't want them. I would settle for something real that is far more grandiose than all of that. It's something that only you could give here and now."

"And what would that be?"

"That would be a kiss."

"Oh, I don't know…"

Toro had good timing. Before she could harden on her

objection, he would act as if he were only joking and immediately change the subject by getting started on the math again.

"OK, here's the proof," he would begin. "Listen to this. Let X and Y be stochastically independent n by n matrices with orthogonal Eigen vectors …"

Maria would jot down his stipulations. When she was ready, she would say "Ok, got it. Go on."

He would then proceed, but he would pause along the way as if he were lost and needed her help in formulating the theorem. She would concentrate and try to help. While they were in such trances his hand would find its way to her hand. She would clutch it, as if to help him think. He would take her hand to his lips in gratitude and kiss it tenderly. Before the spell of the trance would break and she would try to remove her hand, he would say: "Aha, I got it." And then he would continue. Minutes later he would take hold of her hair gently and then move it gingerly off her face. As he stroked her hair, she sat there passively, allowing it, softening her resistance, almost daring him to do more. By now both of them had their minds on lovemaking and Math. Whereas she concentrated mostly on the math and only peripherally in lovemaking, his mind was principally in sex and only superficially, and tactically in Math.

They came to the last proof. He knew he had to work hard. This was his make-or-break, like the last match in the box with which to ignite a fire. Fortunately for him, she was dazzled by the acuity of his mind, by the depth of his vision, and she was in awe of his powers often carrying on, saying things such as: 'you are magnificent!" and 'you're absolutely brilliant!' She listened enraptured at times hugging him impulsively, squeezing his arm, holding on tightly as she discovered worlds that exist only in the nth dimension of abstraction that most mortals never see. Without benefit of drugs, save that of her own glandular secretions under a brain exalted by the psychedelic power of its own virtuosity, the world around them seemed to change, transforming the room into a spectacular space of rotating colors like an Aurora Borealis. Beams of indigo blue lights formed walls that positioned themselves between the floor of a cyan blue hyper-plane and a ceiling of moonbeams that created an ethereal atmosphere of cool blue mathematical visions. He was coming to the end of his proof, and the vistas of the looming conclusion were producing magic. The room was turning into a bright, multicolored hologram. It was as if they were inside a mirage, inside a diamond. Maria was in a Zen state. Now she cuddled willingly next to him like a purring cat. She was conquered.

The proof finished; he took his kiss. As he kissed her, he led her with his thoughts as if at last, she could read his mind through telepathy and body language, and he was telling her: Don't stop. Kiss me with all of your heart. Swallow my soul!

She paid the interest rate of her debt without objection, but she had reservations about the principal. No, no, please! She entreated as he squeezed her breasts and sucked her face and her lips.

"Maria, I love you."

"Please, this is going too fast, too far for me."

"Maria, live! Let yourself live in the physical world also! Come down to earth. The mathematical world is fine and good, but human beings are more than just mind and ideas. There are more delights on earth than the mental delights of math. We also have a heart and a soul that clamors for life inside a body eager to explode in passion. Let yourself go. Unleash the force of your desires and you will see how your flesh and blood will feel the whirlwinds of passions that are as wondrous as the mental state you have just experienced. Let me prove it to you. Please let me take you through the steps of lovemaking just as I have done with the steps of a proof. The steps of love also follow recursively one from the other like an inductive proof that leads to an inevitable, irresistible, and explosive conclusion that you must experience. That conclusion has a special name in this context. It is called an orgasm. It is like no finale, like no conclusion, like no QED and like no proof that you have ever known. Please Maria, let yourself go. Think of each advance, each hug, each little kiss, each probing into your naked parts as if they were the axioms, the postulates, the conditions and stipulations, the very steps to the portals of a universe where a thousand suns frenetically revolve around us, making us two lonely planets desperately fusing into one."

Maria was yielding more and more. She was taking an active part in the proof of the physical theorem he had postulated. That theorem had its own overwhelming sweep that was not logical but a flow of emotions in which her entire body participated. She flowed with it twisting, turning and tumbling as if carried downstream by the avalanche of a rapid. He had told her that orgasm was ten times more thrilling than clinching a mathematical proof. He had told her that that final statement at the end of proofs, QED, that final signing that gave her so much joy in class, was nothing compared to the culmination of the sexual act. She had begun to see what he meant by that. At last, she was consenting, she was volunteering for new adventures, she was begging for more unabashed incursions, anxious, desirous. In his fantasy he now saw her naked in that hologram of light, her body waving, tumbling, squirming with him amid the sparkles of the prism that surrounded them. How that woman pleaded! Oh, please Toro, Toro. Show me your QED. Prove it to me. He had thoroughly conquered her. He had succeeded in bringing out her sexual wildness. She had devoured him. He had ravished her in a multidimensional idyll of crisscrossing laser beams in outer space.

Z   z   Z   z   Z   z   Z

11. TORO'S REAL DREAM

Toro's fantasy bore no resemblance whatsoever to the original dream, the one he really had. That dream was not at all delightful, but was, in fact, thoroughly humiliating for him.

Here is what happened in the real dream. Toro had kidnapped Maria and had taken her to an isolated place where he intended to seduce her. He knew this would take time, so he was prepared to keep her for several days. The idea of rape as such was never part of his design. Deep in his heart he was revolted by the idea of raping her, but because he was a dreamer, he hoped that eventually she would consent. Even if he failed at persuasion, he believed that eventually she would consent if only to gain her freedom. Everything was going nicely for him in his dream. He had possession of her, he was in control of the situation until suddenly, somehow, she managed to gain the upper hand and to frustrate his plans.

He had taken her unconscious, drugged, bound and blindfolded to his lair, an empty secluded house near West Palm Beach. When she came to, she found herself tied spread-eagle to a bed, blindfolded but free to speak. As an added kindness she was still dressed. He fondled her gently, kissing her softly on her face, her neck. She rebuffed him the only way she could, by twisting and squirming and pleading earnestly in her helplessness: "Please, please, whoever you are, please don't hurt me."

"I have no intention of hurting you, Miss Diaz. You just relax now. This here is gonna be an act of love, not war."

Maria recognized his voice. After a pause of a few seconds in which she mulled over the advisability of pretending she did not know who he was, she decided not to play games, asserting outright: "You are Pedro Santoro, aren't you?

"Yes, Miss Diaz! Present! Err, I mean attending!"

He said that sardonically, as if he were responding to the daily roll call in class. Then he added: "Well, seeing as we are not in class anymore, we don't need to be so formal now. And, since the cat's out the bag and you know who I am, I might as well take your blindfolds off… So there! Off with that! Now you can see me."

"Thank you. I appreciate that."

Maria turned her head left and right in an effort to reach her shoulders and rub her eyes against them, but she couldn't reach them.

"Could you please untie me also so I can rub my eyes?"

"Well now, that would be a tad more difficult. I have problems with that. I don't think we are ready for that yet. I'll just have to rub your pretty eyes myself. Where do they itch? You just let me know."

"Never mind! That's fine."

"No, no, no! I insist. Here let me brush those pretty eyebrows."

"Thank you. That's enough. Now just tell me, what's all this about?"

"What do you think?"

"Is it grades? Do you want me to pass you?"

"Well now, there you go again… always thinking about school. Funny, I hadn't even thought of that. Now that you mention it, we might throw that into the package. That would be nice. I could go for that too. But no, that's not what this is about."

Maria did not want to play any cat and mouse games with him, so she cut to the chase, blurting out: "Is this about rape then?"

"Rape? Ugh, that sounds so ugly. Shame on you for bringing up such a dirty thing! Let's hope it doesn't come to that between us. You need to relax Miss Diaz. Relax… By the way, let's make ourselves more comfortable. What's your first name? It's Maria, isn't it? This is not the proper place to be calling you Miss Diaz. Now let me see, would you like a drink, Maria? I have beer; whisky, coke, and even champagne… although I think we should save the champagne for last, don't you? What would be your pleasure?"

"Nothing. I want nothing! This is so sick and stupid!"

"Oh come, Maria. That's no way to relax and be sociable."

"You are monstrous! How stupid can you get? You think you can sweeten your barbaric treatment of me by just offering me drinks–drinks that I can't even hold with my own hands because I am tied like a pig. How can you possibly think of socializing under these conditions?"

"Well, all right, I admit you have a point there. Let me think about this for a little bit before I do something I might regret. OK, let me explain the situation to you. I would like to untie your hands. I would really like to see you more friendly towards me. I would untie your hands in a flash if I thought you would behave. But make no mistake about it. I want to screw you, Maria. Oh, yes, I do. And I am gonna do it, one way or another. That's what this is about. But I want it to be sweet. I'd love it to be with your consent. If I knew I had a chance of that, I would untie you right now and shower you in champagne. But if I untie you, and you get bad ideas about escaping or rough housing with me, then it may get difficult to tie you up again. In that case I may have to get violent with you and whack you on the head just to get back to the point where we are now. So, all in all, it might be better for you if I kept you tied up. Now do you see the problem? What do you say to that, huh?"

"You are so confused. You don't even know what you want. Rape is not sex. It's violence! If sex is what you want, you are certainly going about it all wrong."

"Ah, but you are wrong there, Maria. Dead wrong! So, tell me, how could I have gotten you here in the first place? Would you have accepted my invitation for a weekend date? I don't think so. The only way we could be having this conversation is by having you just where I have you."

"You have that right. I wouldn't have come here of my own free will! But that is not the point. The point is that if sex is what you want, you could have brought a prostitute, or a willing girlfriend, or you could just masturbate yourself. All of that would be sex plain and simple. But to kidnap someone, to start so negative and expect to turn that into something positive is beyond belief. Not even in dreams."

"Whoa! Whoa! Whoa, there now! Don't start lecturing

and getting uppity with me! We are not in class now. Just so we understand each other, I could rip your clothes off right now while you are still tied to the bed. Then I could see how things go from there. I could wait and take my time till you came around. I have time. We are in no hurry. But if, after I've given you a fair chance, and after I see that we are not getting anywhere that way, then, at that point, I may just have to take my pleasure. Of course, since you probably know that I intend to go for more than one round, it may come to pass that I will untie you for round two or three because by then you might have come around to your senses and we could do it more sweetly. What do you say to that?"

"You are a disgusting animal. Beneath contempt! Do you really believe that in round two I am supposed to come around? If you do, you are more stupid and more perverted than I thought."

"My, my we are getting hot here! Well, one can always hope. Wouldn't you say?"

"Really? Let me ask you something, Toro. Are you homosexual by any chance?"

"Shit! What makes you ask a damn dumb question like that?"

"The fact that rape is rape. Even if you were a homosexual, I don't think you would want to be raped by another man. There is no pleasure in being coerced and humiliated, in being at the mercy of a stronger guy who usurps control of your body by force. And certainly, I would presume, a macho-man such as you would detest it even more, right? So, imagine how you would despair if you were tied as I am, and the thought occurred to you that the brute that was about to abuse you really believed that you might like it, that it was only a matter of time till you came around. Where does he get that idea? You would be lying here dumbfounded asking yourself: What could possibly give this beast the idea that I would be coming around and getting sweet for him after round one?"

"Shut up! Shut up, damn it! You are pissing me off; you make me sick."

"No, you disgust me. Unfortunately, I am at your mercy. But

if there is any decency left in you to grant me one request, I would ask you only this. Please tape my mouth shut. I have nothing more to say to you. And please blindfold me again so I don't have to look at your face. Finally, get it over with, but kill me first before you rape me."

Then Maria sobbed away. He stood there reeling. Her performance had simply stunned him. He was not prepared for such a reaction, so defiant, so heroic, and so full of contempt for him. Toro was thrown off balance. He didn't know what to think. She had kicked his sarcasm down his teeth, ruining his little party with a heavy dose of horse sense and reality. She had made him empathize with her; he could not avoid seeing things from her standpoint. He could feel her despair vicariously, could even sense her cold disdain. And this upset him. Suddenly, he felt a little sick–even in his dream. He felt a cold sweat, and he sensed his mouth extremely dry. He swallowed hard.

"Okay, Miss Diaz. You win. I'll untie you now. Whew! Good God, you drive a hard bargain. And you are some spunky lady. God, such talk! Rape. Murder. Homosexuality! Eeeeh ha! Yuck! Man, you do know how to put a bad face on things. You make me nervous--I think we could both use a drink."

By the time he finished saying that Maria was fully free. He started to move away, but before he did, she reached for his arm and grabbed it with both her hands in a gesture of sincere gratitude. While she pressed his arm she said: "Thank you, Toro. Thank you from the bottom of my heart... I knew you weren't as despicable as you make yourself at times. There is some decency left in you. And, yes, I would like a drink now."

"What will you have?"

"I'll take a beer. Whatever kind you have is fine."

He asked her to follow him into the living room, which was next to the kitchen. She sat in a sofa chair while he fetched the beers. There was an awkward silence. Maria looked around the room taking in her surroundings. It was an unpleasant place of tacky décor, and horrid taste. It was dingy and dirty to boot.

"Could you give me an idea of where we are? Is this Miami?"

"No. It's not. You are a little over an hour from home, a little north of West Palm Beach. Here's your beer. Cheers!"

They drank quietly, each to his thoughts.

Then Toro woke up. There was nothing more to look forward to in that dream except to carry out the chores of closing up the place, to drive her home, perhaps even to apologize. How she had ruined things for him! She had managed to take control of his dream and had effectively derailed his sexual fantasy by turning his wet-dream-to-be into an emasculating nightmare.

From that day on Maria became for Toro a powerful enigma. She exuded electricity that shocked him whenever he got too close. She was untouchable. Her intelligence, her logic, her bluntness, her demeanor, and her courage, was too much with him. He could not sort through his conflicting feelings. Now, he more admired her than desired her. Somehow, she had made him aspire to earn her heart rather than possess her body. It still irked him that she had been able to have her way in his own dream–entering his castle, as it were, where he was supposed to be king. Why, for God's sake, should she have that much control over him, even out of the classroom, in the sanctuary of his own mind! This defeat tortured him. But there was scene from this dream that was etched onto his soul. It was the look on Maria's face when she clutched his arms with her hands and thanked him from the bottom of her heart. That ineffable look in her eyes melted him and exalted him with a sense of joy and wonder. What would he give to see that look again in real life!

Z   z   Z   z   Z   z   Z

12. A Hellish School Night

That evening as Maria began to look over the students' papers, she wondered whether Wally and Toro had turned in anything. How could they have when all they did was goof off and horse around? Normally this would upset her, but considering it involved those two it did not matter. She had given up on them. In her opinion they were uneducable, especially Wally. If Maria had had any say-so on the matter, she would have expelled them from school long ago. But that option was not in her power. The only thing she could do with students of their ilk was simply to flunk them, and that she did without compunction, but at the risk of grave personal consequences for herself. Academic standards at that school were abysmal. The educational ethics were warped and perverted. Many students could not pass an exam fair and square, so they resorted to cheating and put the burden of proof on the teacher. It was futile to prosecute because the students had learned that if they raised enough of a ruckus and brought their parents, they could get away with it. They knew that in all this the teacher would get no support from the administration.

The school principal, Mildred Colson, would go through the motions, but would make it very clear where her heart was on the matter. She would just as soon throw the matter under the rug and end it all with a handshake. If the teacher insisted, she would ultimately side with the student claiming the teacher had made a mistake. She would apologize to the parents for the inconvenience, saying that it involved a young inexperienced teacher who had a lot to learn. This principal had risen to her position by spouting catchy sanctimonious platitudes. Unfortunately, she now believed her own lies and she enforced them as the law of the land. The most pernicious of her half-truths was the idea that student failure was always a reflection of teacher inadequacy. She took student failure as proof that the teacher had somehow failed.

"Our mission is to educate," she would begin simplistically, "and we have failed in that mission if our students have not learned.

If they fail, obviously they have not learned. Therefore, we have not taught them, have we?"

She thought highly of her fallacious argument as if it were cast in incontrovertible ironclad logic. She would then compound illogic with injustice by entering a bad mark on the teacher. This demerit she would produce at evaluation time. She would then lord it over the hapless teacher as she made salary recommendations and committee assignments. At that school you flunked students at your own peril.

Maria was one of the recalcitrant teachers who stood up to her and who refused to prostitute herself academically. Maria was Mildred Colson's nemesis. At first Maria had wondered to herself: what makes this woman so butt-headed? Was it naiveté or disingenuousness? Did she really believe in her own sophistry? But the more she knew her, the clearer it all became. Mildred Colson was corrupt to the bone; she was political and Machiavellian to the core and was an unscrupulous manipulator. For Colson this school was just a steppingstone to something bigger in administration, superintendent of schools, or something of that sort. In any case, Maria was too blunt and uncompromising on matters of principle to bother with political correctness. She feared reprisals, but not enough. She did what she felt was right and she expressed her mind candidly, regardless of consequences.

The word 'uneducable' was anathema to Mildred Colson's ears. The last time she heard the word she went into conniptions. She got up on her soap box and called the faculty to a special session to 'bury' that word and expel it from the school premises. As if it were that easy.

"I want you to delete the word 'uneducable' from your vocabulary. I don't care how bad you think a student is. In this school nobody is uneducable. Not on my watch. That word is unthinkable, unutterable. I don't want to hear it. We are here to educate. When we flunk our students then we have failed as teachers, and we have failed our mission."

Maria could not understand how a grown-up person could be so deluded. How she could confuse real things with the symbols and trappings: knowledge with grades, education with diplomas. How dishonest, how hypocritical, and how stupid can she be? How can she possibly think that it is that simple to distort facts with a pen? And how can she get away with it, just issuing high school diplomas to students who can hardly read, and who could not do 5th grade arithmetic? Where was the reckoning in the system, the checks and balances? Who checks on her? Where has our educational system got to at the end of the 20th Century? Would Colson also believe, by the same token, that she could make short people taller; or obese people thin; or poor people wealthy by simply issuing a fake testimonial or by making a proclamation that would right everything? Maria not only suspected that Mildred Colson really believed in the magic of her lies, but that the world was hungry for them and accepted them with gusto. It was hopeless to be honest.

It was inevitable, therefore, that the principal and Maria would clash on this and many other points of academic policy. Maria's job at that school hung tenuously in the wind. But Maria, an elitist at heart, regretted nothing. She would just as soon lose her job as pass undeserving incompetent students and be party to the mendacious game of social engineering that the principal would have her play. All the rationalizations that her principal advanced in defense of tolerance for academic slackness had more to do with politics than education. They were self-serving expediencies designed to ensure budgets and job security. Maria was appalled that schools could have sunk so low. They had turned into breeding grounds for incompetence and mediocrity, and they had turned teachers into timid hostages who engaged in egregious hypocrisy to keep their jobs.

For Maria each day at that school was becoming a horrible ordeal. Even in the best of days, something always arose to remind her that she trod over rottenness. A malodorous whiff hardly ever failed to emerge from some corner. Ironically, today had been exceptional. It had been one of those rare trouble-free days, one of those days visited by salubrious winds under a hale clean sky. She felt tired, but it was the weariness of good hard work, free of stress and disappointment. Of course, she was not aware of Toro's dreams and Wally's remarks. Had she known what those two were saying about her, it would definitely have soured her day. As it was, she could think of nothing negative about this day. Her session with Elena had been rather sweet and she remembered it as one of the bright spots of the day. It had been a good but unremarkable day. Tonight, Maria would go to bed early again, and in contentment.

But that was not to be. That evening as Maria went over the papers, she discovered a note that ruined it all for her. The note said:

Dear Miss Diaz: This here are my notes on some dangling segments, and the angles of certain masses that I took today. My conclusion is:

The heat of the meat
Is equal to the angle of the dangle
Divided by the mass of the ass.

If this ain't enough proof for you, then you just come to the parking lot after class and let me prove it to you in the backseat of my car.

The paper was nameless. Maria was livid. Her first impulse was to crumple the paper in anger and throw it in the trash, but she resisted the impulse and put the paper aside. She tried to ignore it by getting on with her work, concentrating on grading other papers, but she could not.

In addition to the nasty note, she also discovered cheating. The assignment had been one in which the students, working in teams, had to choose one of three objects whose length they had to measure. One was the height of a steeple, another was the height of a television tower, and a third was the distance between two points on opposite sides of a pond. Each team, however, had to choose their unique reference points so that their angles and the measure of their working segments would be different from those of any other team. Thus, although the same object was being measured, there was enough variation built into the exercise to allow for individuality. Most students used the Pythagorean Theorem, but that was not the only mathematical model possible. One implication of the design of this exercise was that the students could not cheat by copying what others had done. If they tried, they could easily be caught. Another implication of the exercise was that the final answer as such was not nearly as important as the work that supported that answer. To emphasize this point Maria had given them approximate ranges for the measures of all three objects to begin with.

Students cheated in the most unimaginably mindless ways possible. They seemed to be driven by a pathological compulsion to be like others, taking comfort in the idea that wrong answers wouldn't be so bad if they had a lot of company. The moral compass was totally haywire. Despite Maria's admonitions, despite her exhortations that it was better to be honest in one's work rather than accurate, many students had chosen the sucker bet. There were many similar answers with implausible figures to support them.

Maria put down those papers as if escaping from them, only to bounce back into the irritating note. The insult from that note still scorched her. How it annoyed her! Although the paper was nameless, she could only think of two suspects, Toro and Wally. It had to be them. She could picture them laughing and carrying on as they drafted the note. That incensed her all the more. She would get so worked up about it that she swore to herself that she would take action and make a federal case out of it. She would take it to Mildred Colson's office in the morning and present it as evidence... but ah, evidence of what? Had she forgotten where she was? What a joke! After thinking it over, she realized how futile it would be to try to prosecute anyone. The paper itself would prove nothing! It could not identify who had written it. And even if the culprits could be identified, nothing would be done about it. The school administration did not have the fortitude to prosecute. They would prefer to ignore it.

It was after 1 a.m. already, but Maria couldn't even think about sleep yet. The note and the papers had effectively ruined her composure. What should she do when she saw the students the next morning? Should she mention the dirty note in class? If she did, Wally and Toro would have the satisfaction of knowing that she had read it. Mission accomplished. It might even make heroes of them in the eyes of their peers. Worse yet, their prank might seem funny to the others and put ideas on their heads. She would just be inviting more notes in the future.

A second option was to not mention it at all, to carry on as if she had seen nothing and to bury it in silent disdain. Toro and Wally could assume, of course, that she had seen the note, and if that gave them any satisfaction, so be it. Her response, and her weapon, would be indifference. Rationally, she knew that this was the best option. But emotionally she simply could not muster the indifference necessary to carry it out.

Why should it matter what those two scumbags thought? Why should it bother her to know that they knew she had read the note? Maria could not put her finger on the matter, but it seemed that reading it closed a circuit of communication between her and them, a circuit that she would just as soon remain broken. It would be much better if they knew that they had missed their mark completely, that she did not even have an inkling of their machinations. For them to think that they had hit their target, that she had learned of their dirty fantasies was simply unacceptable. Maria could feel the stare of their lascivious glances on her skin like slimy invisible tentacles. It is one thing to be unaware of the presence of a spider and to go about one's business in blissful ignorance; it is quite another to learn of the spider's proximity, of its intent, and to be whipped across the face by its extending, reaching web--even if the spider didn't actually bite you.

It was around 2:30 a.m. when Maria finally hit upon a scheme that solved all her problems. She would simply announce that she was returning all the papers without a grade because, after seeing several papers from the earlier 9 o'clock class, and a few from the 11 o'clock class, she had discovered what appeared to be flagrant, reckless cheating. She was dismayed at the complete disregard for her instructions, and she had decided that there was no point in looking at any more papers and getting upset any further. So, to avoid more unpleasantness, and to make sure that they did it right she was giving them a second chance. The students could just pick up their papers. Of course, those students who had done their work conscientiously to begin with would not need to redo anything. They could just recheck their figures and turn in the same paper. She would ask, however, that these students use the time to help others who may not have understood the nature of the assignment, or who may have difficulty still with the instruments. And one more thing: she would also ask that when they turned in their papers the next time, they should have their names clearly visible on the outside. Papers without names on the outside would not be accepted. She would be checking for names first.

By this ploy she thwarted the underhanded communication that Toro and Wally had tried to have with her. They would not get the satisfaction of thinking she had even seen their note. Her plan also addressed the cheating issue in a constructive way. It was better to correct the problem by amnesty than by confrontation. Finally, her policy of requiring student's names upfront would prevent getting unsigned dirty little notes in the future.

It had been a stressful long night, but it was over. At last, she could go to bed. It was already after 3 a.m. Even so, while in bed with the lights out, she worked out the details, thinking how she would address the students and how she would execute her plan. In teaching, as in acting, timing and gestures are critical and she had to work out the details, honing in on her delivery.

She shouldn't have worried. The next day Maria's plan worked perfectly, even better than expected. A few students did grouse about having to repeat their projects, but the majority was glad to have a second chance. It turned out that many of them had never understood the assignment to begin with. After Maria went over her strictures and the students understood their purpose, they became more enthusiastic. One student suggested half facetiously that it would be nice if they could just scuttle the previous results and start from scratch. The idea received resounding approval. The class roared for it.

Maria pretended to be neutral on the matter, conveying a feigned indifference, as if it didn't matter to her. But inwardly she was ecstatic.

"I would have no objection to your suggestion," she said, "but it would have to be a majority decision. I would have to have a vote on that, and I would require at least a two-third majority in favor. Also, if a student wanted to salvage what he had done, he should be able to do so."

The vote was unanimous! So, Maria, wasting no time, just ran her hand over the papers that were piled on her desk and with one swift move swept them all into the trashcan. When she was done, she clapped her hands together as if they were cymbals glancing as they clashed. There. That's that.

Toro and Wally felt as if the rug had been pulled from under their feet and they had fallen on their butts. They saw no fireworks, no bluster of indignation. Their show had gotten rained out. The dirty little note they had planted had been ignominiously discarded before their eyes and dumped into the trashcan sight unseen. Some students rummaged through the discarded papers to salvage their work, but the majority couldn't wait to get outdoors.

A few minutes later, when the class was outside taking their measurements, Maria took a head count and noticed that Wally was missing, but she could see Toro. To her dismay, he was working with Elena who seemed to be explaining something to him. She couldn't believe what she saw, Toro paying attention and taking notes. Maria felt uneasy seeing Toro cozying up to her innocent protégé. Could he be up to something? She did not trust him. Later that day, when she had her tutoring session with Elena, she learned that Toro and Wally had had a parting of the ways, but Elena did not know why. Toro, Elena told her, really wanted to learn. He recognized that he was hopelessly behind and was embarrassed to approach Maria for help. Maria made no comment.

That evening Maria examined the student's papers and noted with great relief what a difference a day makes. The papers were much improved, and each was clearly identifiable with the student's name on the outside as she had requested. The overall quality of the student's work was most evident. She couldn't have come up with a better idea. It had been worth it. She could have a good night sleep tonight.

Z   z   Z   z   Z   z   Z

PART III: FIRST PEEKS

13. A DREAM WITHIN A DREAM

That strange building on a hill which stood as a facsimile of Maria's body began playing an important role in her perambulations through the night. It became a station, a stopover in the expanse of her sleeping mind, a place that Maria could visit again and again till it became the home of her mind at night. She came directly to the dome, materializing in the auditorium where Dr. Broca had assured her that she was bound to meet her inner voices. Night after night she came, sitting alone for hours, till often out of sheer boredom she would dream that she fell asleep.

The auditorium could be accessed by two large doors up-front. Between these doors was a dais and directly behind the dais, was a large screen for projections and video presentations. Maria would enter through one of these doors and take a seat near the front row. Tonight, however, she chose a seat on the back, on the penultimate row. It occurred to her that the auditorium could be used for some official meeting that did not concern her, and she did not want to intrude. From that position she could easily sneak out by one of the emergency-exits on the rear. But, if she chose to stay, she could see without being noticed; she could be like a bird on a perch that could fly off and vanish without attracting attention.

Tonight, she sat there alone, twiddling her thumbs and thinking about dreams. Why do we dream? Who controls the process? Is it a political process with input from various sources? Do these sources disagree about it? Do they fight like faculty at committee meetings? As the minutes passed, she became bored and began to doze off and to dream. She dreamed about a faculty meeting in the conference room of her school which had taken place several months earlier. Maria had come to the meeting early, so early that she was the only one there. It was perhaps the similarity of the situations, sitting alone waiting for people to show up, that led Maria to dream about that faculty meeting.

While Maria slept people began filing in into the auditorium at Dream Central. She could hear the noise as people shuffled their feet, as they chatted, and as they plumped down on their seats. Maria mistook these noises as not the ones at Dream Central, but that of those of her colleagues in the high school auditorium some months back. She didn't wake up and consequently she missed seeing the people that she had gone there to see.

During the high school meeting the school principal, Mildred Colson, had sat in front and center on the dais and presided. It was early in the school year, and the agenda had involved issues to which Maria could not relate, and about which she did not care one iota. It had been one of those dreadful organizational meetings about the creation and staffing of committees. There had been a lot of nominating, seconding, and voting, and carrying on. Maria could not believe with what gusto some of her colleagues participated in those meetings. They postured and acted as if those committees were of great, momentous consequence for the world at large. How Maria detested the presumptuous self-importance of those proceedings. The discussions had been insane and had lasted much too long. They had involved mostly insignificant matters, procedural issues, and picky parliamentary points that were enormously boring to Maria. Staying awake at that meeting had been sheer torture and—as it happened—it had been more than she could endure, because she had fallen dead asleep.

In her current confused state of dreaming, she pictured in her mind the flashbacks of that faculty meeting even as she heard the noises and sounds of people around her, entering the auditorium. Her senses were in different places feeding her confused information, reinforcing wrong impressions and fusing the dream in the school conference room with the dream in the auditorium. One dream plagiarized the other, confusing memories and imaginings. Because the proceedings in the school conference room bored her to tears, she wanted to escape by sleeping deeper and deeper. God, what a waste of time, she mumbled in her sleep. They do make such a fuss about nothing!

While Maria snoozed, dreaming that she was in a faculty meeting, she missed seeing the people, the denizens of her sleep world, as they came in and sat around her. These were the people that she had gone there to see, the people she had wanted to meet face to face for days, her alter egos, her conscience, her voices, the witches and imps of her own mind. They were the ones that, as Dr. Broca had promised, were bound to come sooner or later by that auditorium. Now they were there on the dais and in the seats around her, but she was missing them because she had fallen asleep, and because she was dreaming that she was elsewhere.

Because the first issues discussed in the auditorium were also procedural and involved such things as the approval of the agenda, and the approval of the minutes of the last meeting, Maria continued to think that what was happening in the auditorium was a flashback to the school auditorium. But in reality, the actual items in the auditorium's agenda had nothing to do with academic matters. The items concerned dreams, the making of dreams, the sort of thing she had been thinking about earlier. They dealt with such questions as: Who decides whether we dream or not? Who decides the subject matter of our dreams? And how is that decided? What determines whether we are able to remember our dreams the next morning or not?

The voting for the approval of the minutes proceeded smoothly, with everything being accomplished by voice vote, which was fortunate for Maria since a show of hands in her condition would have been awkward. While Maria could not grasp every word that was being said, she could get the drift of things, but as long as it concerned approval of minutes and that sort of thing, she made no great effort to pay attention.

Maria heard voices coming from very near—from the row behind her in fact. These voices did pique her curiosity; they were those of a man and a woman. The male voice was saying: "This is such a crock. I just can't see mature adults carrying on with these stupid childish games. Why can't they get to the goddamn point without all these motions? Why do they have to put everything to a vote? Shit!"

"Oh, come on, don't start griping so soon. There's a lot of good stuff coming up for discussion—if they ever get to it. Be patient...," said a female voice.

"They will never get to it. Mark my word," said the man. "I will be willing to bet you that any minute now somebody is going to object about something and that will hold things up. Then politics will start. They'll debate as to whether he is out of order or not, and before you know it the time will be piddled away on picky-picky little points."

Maria wanted to turn around and see the couple behind her and express her agreement with the sentiments of the male speaker. But she did not want to butt in on a private conversation, and above all, she did not approve of the language the man was using. By his vulgarity he did not seem to be anyone she would have wanted to support, even if she agreed with him. Besides, she found it difficult to move. She felt as though she was locked to her position. This seemed to be another of the peculiar restrictions of the state she was in, dreaming that she was asleep within another dream. She could hear, and she could think about what was happening in the world around her, but she could not see, and she could not move.

Just then somebody did object. From the front of the auditorium a man stood up calling loudly: "Madam Speaker. Madam Speaker. I wish to be recognized. Point of order."

"Go ahead, Sir."

Then Maria overheard the voice of the man sitting behind her gloat over the fact he had predicted it, saying: "Aha, you see! Here we go. What did I tell you?"

"Shhh! Hush!" shushed the female companion sternly. Then the man who had the floor began to speak.

"Madam Speaker, I would like to make a motion. I would like to resubmit for discussion the algorithm for sequencing dream priorities that I proposed at our last meeting. I have adapted some rules from Queuing Theory that should make it quite feasible."

That brought up quite an uproar. "Madam Speaker. Madam Speaker!" shouted a chorus of protesters, "He is out of order." Several people raised their hands to be recognized. Some even stood up shouting unintelligible objections. Oh, God, Maria mumbled to herself as she sank back deeper into her cocoon of sleep.

Poor Maria, she had not caught the fact that his algorithm pertained to a formula for determining the subject of the next dream. The formula was based on factors which considered recent history and old concerns. Maria was still under the impression that this was an academic meeting, and that a departmental squabble was in the making. It was obvious to her that the proponent of this measure was a mathematician and that he was pushing a pet project whose details she was not familiar with. But his proposal had unleashed pandemonium from the other departments. History, Drama, and Psychology, all had entered the fray to push their own proposals. They would not let the mathematician have it so easily. They would fight it out. The Speaker had to bang her gavel several times to regain order. When she finally managed to calm them, she asked that each of them speak calmly, one at a time. The mathematician, thinking that he still had the floor, took advantage of the quiet and began to speak again.

"It is precisely this sort of chaos that my algorithm addresses. Until we become rational and abide by a process that is fair to all, and until we implement a mechanism that takes us automatically to the agenda for tomorrow in an orderly way, we are going to waste our time each night wrangling in useless debate. What's worse, our dreams, when we do have them, will be totally independent and unrelated from each other from one day to the next. They will be what they are now: a capricious, unstructured, and inscrutable Random Walk."

The man would have said more, but he was over-ruled by the Speaker who wanted to hear from the parliamentarian on this issue. The parliamentarian, in turn, said that they were all out of order because a motion was on the floor, and it had not been seconded. But he would address the podium to consult with the Chairperson.

While this was going on, the woman behind Maria was saying: "He can't change the nature of dreams with an algorithm. Dreams are subject to the same vagaries of fate that life is. That's the way the world is…Why should dreams be any different?"

Upon hearing that, Maria became really intrigued. The meeting began to sound more about dreams than about academe. The mathematics professor had alluded to an algorithm that represented a recursive process. She had followed that pretty well, but only up to the point when the variable in question was the nightly topic of one's dreams. How can dreams be concatenated? How can they be treated as though they were a mathematical variable? Since when are dreams programmable? But although she could not quite grasp his idea, she loved the direction in which it seemed to be headed, and she found it simply fascinating! This has to be science on the cutting edge, making dreams programmable. When the woman behind her also made a reference to dreaming, that confirmed to Maria that she had not heard wrong. The mathematician was indeed talking about taming dreams by a moving average formula that incorporated recent dreams and the memory of recent real experiences. Maria found the idea exciting, even if a bit quixotic. This was all very dear to her heart. The idea of fashioning a mathematical method for the mind to control the vagaries of dreams was an idea whose time had come. It was at the vanguard of her kind of brave new world! And she loved it!

If Maria could have, she would have turned on her seat to face the woman behind her and talk to her. She would have agreed with her. Yet, she would have asked her: "But don't you think some ideas of science fiction, even if fanciful at first, can lead the way to viable practical applications eventually? What do we have to lose by letting the math professor try his algorithm?"

She was working up the nerve to do that, but the couple began talking again. The man then announced that he was leaving.

All this had been too much for him. As he picked up his things to leave, he told his companion: "I just can't take any more of this. Tell me tomorrow if these idiots decide to do anything. I'll bet you they won't!"

The chatter and discussion made it difficult for Maria to understand anything else anymore. In the confusion her mind drifted to a memory from the more distant past that took her to her college undergraduate days. During her junior year Maria had been involved very briefly with the SGA (Student Government Association). She had attended all of two meetings before resigning in disgust. It was there that she had had one of those epiphanies when one learns something significant about oneself. She had learned then that she could not stomach being in organizations of any kind. Organizations involved meetings, and meetings were inimical to her nature. She had learned that she was basically a loner, not a team player, not a committee person, and not a politician. Even from the very first, the SGA aroused ambivalent feelings within her. On the positive side, the organization gave her a sense of belonging, a sense of being useful. Everyone at those meetings was a peer: a young person and a student like her. At first, she welcomed the idea of solidarity and the sense of purpose. Then she discovered that the sense of unity evanesced on deeper contact with each individual. First to surface was the difference in disciplines. This was a minor source of alienation, but it served as a harbinger of greater differences to come. It wasn't only that the differences in discipline represented different focuses, different interests. Above all, they represented different values. This was especially true of her peers in Pre-Law, Business, and Political Science. Her peers in these disciplines seemed to be animals of a different species, ambitious creatures who lusted for power. While they were predators, she was prey. They were overzealous lawyerly types, people manipulators who thrived on everything she detested. Something in that organization gave each peer a charge that was anti-magnetic to her. The more she got to know them, the less empathy she felt with them. This brief immersion into campus politics planted a seed that made her averse to meetings, rallies, and other organizational get-togethers such as faculty meetings, and even PTA meetings. She was convinced that people changed when they got too wrapped up in their meetings. People tended to lose their humanity. They became cogs for a cause, instruments of organizations, and soldiers for agendas that transcended personal, human values. For all this, she abhorred meetings. She tried to escape them whenever she could. She was already thinking of sneaking out of this meeting when she heard the arguments and the sniping in that conference room.

The stranglehold of being asleep inside two dreams—visually imagining one while overhearing the goings on of a second dream—was also bothering Maria. Being there only halfway and not being able to move or to see the people around her was becoming unbearable. She could tolerate it no more. She had to close the school conference dream and devote all her senses to the auditorium dream. Suddenly, applying great exertion, she managed to wiggle free and open her eyes into the original dream. The lights were bright, and she had to adjust her eyes to see the people around her. The couple sitting behind her had just left their seats. Maria was morbidly curious about them. Perhaps she could still catch a glimpse of them before they left the auditorium. She turned quickly towards the rear exit and for an instant she did see them. The man, who was a step or two ahead of his female companion, had just reached the exit. Then his female companion caught up with him and disappeared from sight as well. Darn! Wonder who they were…

Then Maria looked at the rest of the people in the auditorium to see who else she might recognize. She was flabbergasted when she spotted someone whom she immediately recognized. This person's height, her slight stoop, her short hairdo, and her dress style were unmistakable. Maria had never met this lady personally—although she had seen her many times on TV, on magazine covers and, lately, spoofed on Saturday Night Live. She had become a regular butt of jokes on that show. "Oh my God!" cried Maria, when she recognized the then Attorney General of the United States, Janet Reno. "What in heaven is she doing here?"

The people were now dispersing, making their way to the exit aisles. The panel members on the dais looked incredulous at the sight of their audience leaving out of turn. The Chairperson, a look-alike of Mildred Colson, grabbed her gavel and started pounding it. "Just one minute! Just one minute here!" she shouted. Other panel members waved their arms frantically as if signaling people to return to their seats.

"Ladies and gentlemen, the meeting is not over. We have not adjourned yet. Please be kind enough to let us end this procedure in a proper manner. I know you are all anxious to go home. But the business of this body is not yet concluded. We have decided to table the discussion of the algorithm for our next meeting, which will be one week from today. You will get a memorandum by e-mail."

The chairperson had to talk fast because the people were no longer with her. Everyone was eager to leave. They were slowly inching their way out, setting in motion what would soon be a stampede to leave. It was obvious that the chairwoman could not hold the audience much longer, and she knew it. The parliamentarian who also sensed this, hurried to head off the stampede and save face. He asked the wished for question. "Is there a motion to...?" He didn't finish the question. Someone interjected: "I move we adjourn." "Is there a second?" Then the entire congregation, including Maria, answered in unison: "Second."

The shuffling turned into a fast and deliberate march towards the exits. The auditorium began clearing very quickly. Maria, still curious about the couple behind her, decided to make a run for the rear exit to catch up with them. They could answer a lot of questions for her. Who were they? And who were the rest of the people in the auditorium? Why was Janet Reno there? Maria made a desperate dash to catch up and holler at them to stop. She rushed, reaching the upper corridor that led to the exit door in a few leaps; then she dashed towards the exit door, not knowing where that door led to. She burst through it in no time. The door, it turned out, was a fire exit that opened onto a catwalk outside the building. She rushed through with such force that she nearly fell five stories to the ground. She barely caught herself at the last minute on the catwalk railing. But the shock was so great that she woke up instinctively, averting danger.

Z   Z   Z   z   Z   Z   Z

14. DREAM RECALL

Maria was sitting on her bed, panting from fright when she opened her eyes. She would have fallen five stories to the ground to certain death had she not awakened. She examined her surroundings, feeling reassured that she was safe in her own bed. The clock beside her bed displayed 5:54 in bright green digits. Normally, she would be asleep for at least another hour. She considered snoozing a little longer, but her mind wouldn't let her. The dream had crashed upon her consciousness and ideas floated around her mind like debris after an explosion. She would do well to reconstruct what she still remembered of the dream before it vanished. She remembered being in an uncomfortable situation that she could not quite describe, which was confusing, frustrating, awkward, almost to the point of bordering on torture for the mental anguish that it caused her: hearing but not seeing; teased into thinking she understood unrelated, disconnected bits of dialogue. As she rewound her memory, looking for a place to begin, Janet Reno was the first recollection to jump at her, raising the question: Why was she there?

She drew a blank at first, but as she thought of the events that led to Reno's appearance, she remembered her diatribe against lawyers. Could that putdown of lawyers have something to do with the sudden appearance of the Attorney General of the United States? It seemed plausible. In fact, Janet Reno's presence seemed to be more than a symbol. It was a rebuke for Maria's prejudicial remarks stereotyping lawyers and politicians as contemptible manipulators. A devil's advocate within Maria's mind—her conscience, no doubt—seemed to have taken issue with that and was telling her: "You are prejudiced, Maria. And you do carry on at times. Look at Janet Reno. She is a woman for whom you have expressed some admiration in the past. She is a dedicated public servant. She doesn't hog the spotlight. She doesn't grandstand. Yet, she is a lawyer and a politician to boot. I would say she debunks your stereotypes of lawyers and politicians."

Maria was almost embarrassed by the remonstrance. From her bed, she acknowledged the point with a smile and a soft-spoken *Touché*! She then continued recalling her dream. Who else was there? There was a mathematician. Maria could not remember knowing anyone like him. None of the professors she had known in college came to mind. This was a total stranger. And yet something about his demeanor and his looks made him a familiar stranger. There was something universal about him. His tall lanky frame, his sad eyes, his elongated face that ended in a pointed and silvery goatee seemed very familiar. He looked as if he had walked straight out of a painting by El Greco and she asked herself: Who is that Spaniard? Where have I seen him before? It didn't take long for Maria to make the connection and recognize him as a reincarnation of Don Quixote. But what was he doing there? Was he pleading for the impossible dream as he did in the Broadway musical *The Man of La Mancha*? Or could he be a symbol also?… But a symbol of what? Her heart had gone out to him when he explained his algorithm. Poor thing, he was trying to put order in the chaos of dreams. Perhaps Professor Quixote represented her own crusading spirit, the part of her that wanted to get all dressed up in shining armor, hop on a horse and charge against the demons of sleep and stop their shenanigans. He had questioned why the impossible had to be impossible, and he had put his finger on the cause. The trouble was the unruly nature of the denizens of the mind at night who were prima donnas. Enlisting their support was as difficult as herding cats. They were independent, ambitious and selfish. They vied for the spotlight in the subconscious theater and loved to hog the stage each night.

His algorithm would have given each of them a vote, but it would have made them fall in line to wait for their turn. Maria mused on his proposal, wondering precisely how he would do it, speculating on the details. She imagined that he would use a committee to handle the demands for the use of the time allotted for dreaming. Everybody would have a voice in dream making. De rigueur the Libido, the Id, the Ego and the Superego would be given a voice and a vote in dream making. Imagination would be overseeing all things artistic. Professor Quixote himself could handle questions of logic and scientific methodology. Conscience would be chairman. You really wouldn't need much more than that.

By this scheme Maria would not just dream mathematical dreams every night. Variety would be built in and would cover everything from the theological to the childish. Some dreams might be cartoons full of childishness and silliness; there would be comedies and tragedies, but there would also be horror shows; and there would be romances. Who knows, perhaps from time to time there could be sex. You could count on it if the Libido was part of the committee. Once the committee was in place, it would go to work pretty much as the editors of a newspaper do each night when they consider what stories make it to the front page and dominate the news the next morning. When life was normal, when there was no urgency, and when there was no controversial topic to resolve, the committee members would take items from the queue and apply an averaging process to prioritize the dream sequences. Dream time would be allotted according to a predetermined formula approved by the committee. More than likely Professor Quixote would use a Poisson probability distribution to handle the demands of the incoming dream proposals, and he would use an exponential distribution for service time–just as is used in Queuing Theory so that the backlog for dreams to be shown was kept to a minimum. Although this was a primitive sketch of what he probably had in mind, it was a start. There were many details to be nailed down yet, but the proposal–even in this primitive form–was viable. It had great promise. If only the denizens of her psyche were rational and willing to cooperate and give order a chance. How nice it would have been to talk to the quixotic mathematician at length about his scheme. She would have offered to help.

Normally at this hour, she would be blissfully asleep, but this morning she was glad to be awake because she was fascinated by looking through a window into the world of her mind that the dream had opened. This was the most provocative and intellectually stimulating dream that Maria had ever had and she was enjoying its analysis. She needed to explore further. The dream was still complex and confusing because it spoke through a language of visual metaphors and symbols which were like hieroglyphics in the murals of her mind. The mere presence of Janet Reno and Professor Quixote continued to intrigue her. Why were they there? They emitted waves, like ripples of a memory that kept on giving. The impact of the dream was still fresh, as it always is when one awakens abruptly as she had this morning. But the memory of a dream is also as fragile as the membrane of a soap bubble, and it does not last long.

She was desperately trying to transfer these images into her conscious long-term memory. Once they were etched there, they would last indefinitely. Maria chased after every wisp of dream that crossed her mind, continuing her recall. She remembered the building with its glowing crystal dome like a lighthouse over a sea of darkness. She remembered catching herself on the railing and looking at the dome of the building before her. It enlivened old memories. She saw faint fleeting images of that building, like photographs taken from below on another night, in a forgotten dream. She remembered being intrigued by the place.

There was a doctor. What was his name? It was something like Brock, or Roca. She could not quite picture him. Maria thought she had seen him on the dais, next to the chairwoman. Who was the chairwoman? Was it Mildred Colson? Heaven forbid!

Dreams are nebulous, confusing, inscrutable. And this one had been a lulu. It was getting late. Maria needed to get up and start her day, but she had one final idea that she wanted to pursue further. What if dreams are the work of a committee and the committee is often unruly and ineffective? Perhaps Professor Quixote wanted to change its bylaws. Perhaps we have dreams when the committee meetings are productive, when there is consensus and the congress of our clones finally makes a decision and presents us with a dream.

Of course, whether the dream is silly, bizarre or fantastic, whether it is about unicorns, or about UFOs, or about Prince Charming, depends on who wins the struggle for dream dominance that night. Quite possibly, there might not be any dreams that night because the entire time is whittled away arguing. Unable to reach a consensus, the entire matter would be tabled for another day, and Maria would wake up feeling as if she had been in a coma. Or it could also happen that the dream was the result of a political compromise. On such nights the dream would be disconnected, no better than a bad cartoon, just a hodge-podge of incongruous ideas--precisely what one would expect from a committee that didn't get along.

That afternoon, by strange coincidence, she went to a real faculty meeting after class. As had become her habit of late, she kept herself awake by doodling. By then the vivid images of the dream had faded. Even so, she still got faint subliminal messages from the dream that made their way inscrutably into her doodles.

Z   Z   Z   z   z   z   z

15. A Real Faculty Meeting

It was a good thing Maria took the time to analyze her double-headed dream, because dreams, although full of sound and fury while asleep, tend to disappear on tiptoes when we awaken, forever to be forgotten. Like early morning dew, dreams begin evaporating as the sun rises. Their bright images fade in the light of day. So, by that afternoon, when she attended the faculty meeting, her dream was all but gone. Only foggy vestiges kept intruding upon her consciousness in subtle enigmatic ways, as if they were parting shots from a fading specter. Some of the images emerged inexplicably, through her doodles, leaving Maria completely baffled, asking herself: why did I draw that?

Maria doodled at faculty meetings out of boredom, to keep awake, and to provide a mental buffer against the tirades of Mildred Colson. This afternoon doodling enabled her to hear, but only in muffled tones, the ranting from the dais about budgets and belt tightening, about hiring freezes, about increasing the burdens of the faculty, and about things which affected Maria, but about which she could do nothing at all. The warnings and admonitions were bad enough, but interspersed between them were the intimidating threats, which Colson delivered with great gusto. It was all too much for Maria. Her nerves were frayed to the point that for the first time Maria heard herself saying that she should start looking for another job. It was a subliminal suggestion that lasted only an instant, as if a voice within her had whispered it; it soon went out, like an errant spark, and she did not dwell upon it anymore. But the thought planted its seed.

Karen Powers, a Chemistry teacher and a good friend of Maria who usually sat next to her at faculty meetings, noticed Maria's drawing pad and winked good-naturedly as she took her seat, saying: "Oh, I see we came prepared for serious doodling today."

Maria smiled, remarking: "It's my antidote, you know. I couldn't survive these meetings without my doodles. It's either snooze or doodle."

As soon as the meeting began, Maria began sketching, fleshing out the images from her mind onto the paper. She worked deliberately, as if she knew what she wanted to convey. Karen would lean over to peek into her drawing from time to time to see what was coming. At first Maria drew a horse, but she scratched it out because it was too fat. She started a new horse on another page and made this one emaciated and skinny. This was followed by the figure of a tall, lanky man on the horse, holding a lance, wearing a distinctive 15th Century Spanish helmet.

"The Man of La Mancha?" Karen inquired, puzzled.

Maria nodded, confirming Karen's good guess.

"But why?" pleaded Karen with great curiosity.

"I'm not sure. A dream I had last night, maybe," Maria shrugged.

If Maria had thought further, she might have ventured that the sketch could have been a coded message from an arcane part of her mind which was trying to reach her consciousness on a dream frequency that was blurry and indecipherable while awake.

The meeting rambled on about various things. It was very informal. People spoke freely and under no protocol. There were reports by faculty members about their activities. The tone of the meeting was so casual that Robert's Rules of Order would have been completely out of place. All the more reason for Maria to be puzzled by the urge she felt to raise her hand and call out to Mildred Colson formally, in a most officious tone, saying: "Madam Speaker, Madam Speaker: Point of order. I wish to be recognized. Cheating is rampant in this school. Could you please tell us what you are going to do about it, if anything?"

Maria recognized the absurdity of this impulse and was embarrassed by it. Where did that come from? What in the world has come over me with this preposterous impulse? She quelled it, of course. She did not have the nerve, the chutzpah or the sarcasm for it. Whoever was prodding her in that direction should just chill out. She was not in the mood for a fight; she was too tired. The last thing she needed was to rock the boat with the subject of cheating. She bit her tongue and continued doodling. When her turn came to speak, she merely reported on her project of taking her students outdoors on a measuring field trip. She spoke briefly and eloquently on the importance of making geometry useful and relevant for her students.

"Ah, that was civil and very professional," said a voice within her, in a complimentary tone. "That was most commendable, dear… proud of you."

Only Maria heard that voice that had the warm and tender touch of maternal approval, like a gentle pat on the back of her soul. But it was not her mother. Clara would have said it in Spanish. Maria blushed outwardly and thanked the voice within her in silence as she continued to doodle. Now her pencil guided her hand mysteriously, as if trying to produce a sketch of the silhouette behind the voice. She struggled with the image. Karen was curious also and she looked over Maria's shoulder, straining to guess who Maria was trying to sketch. Unable to make it out, she finally gave up and asked Maria outright: "Who is that supposed to be?"

Maria responded silently, in writing, spelling out the name on her drawing pad: Janet Reno.

Karen frowned, unable to picture it. She was unconvinced by the drawing and made a moue of criticism as if saying: I don't think so. In any case, whether the drawing looked like Janet Reno or not, the question remained: Why Janet Reno? Where does she figure in all this? But to that question even Maria had no idea.

There were other reports. The man in charge of computers spoke to a problem which loomed large in 1999. It was "The Year Two-Thousand Problem," or Y2K for short.

"This is a very serious thing," said the computer expert with great gravity. "I kid you not. We are just living the calm before the storm now. We are enjoying the lazy rafting before the cataracts. But if we don't take the necessary measures to correct this problem, by the end of the year we are going to have chaos in banking, in transportation, in health care, in business, and in every walk of life that you can think of because computers are in everything."

"Whoa. Hold it there a minute! How do we know that this is not just the usual poppy cock of the end of an era?" the basketball coach and history teacher wanted to know. "Are you aware that at the end of every decade all sorts of nuts, all manner of end-of-the-world doomsayers and Chicken Little alarmists come out of the woodwork to predict catastrophes? This is nothing new."

"I hear you. I know where you're coming from. But this is different. There is no prank involved."

Then Karen Powers joined in, asking: "I think we've all heard about this new threat, but I am not sure that everybody understands the basis for it. As our computer expert in residence, could you please enlighten us on its cause?"

"Yes, sure… First of all, this is no hoax. It's an honest mistake, even if it is incredibly stupid. To put it simply: many computers have been mis programmed. The measure of time has been short-changed by allotting only two digits for the years. We've gotten in the bad habit of abbreviating everything, writing, say, '87, instead of 1987. This short-cut causes no problem for the first 99 years of a century, but on the last year, man, look out! In this abbreviated nomenclature the computers will be confused when the '99' rolls over to '00.' The computers' logic will not know what to make of this. They won't know whether '00' pertains to 2000 or 1900. If they take it to mean 1900, then they'll be going back in time and that's impossible. That's when the fireworks start. Some people fear that mortgages will be canceled, that contracts and depreciation schedules will expire; that machinery will shut down. Some fear that planes could fall from the sky because their dials will go kerflooey and spin out of control. Nobody wants to be flying after midnight on December 31st for fear of what might happen."

"Incredible," Karen muttered, "absolutely incredible!"

"Who woulda' thunk it!" Maria remarked. "Our technological gods have feet of clay. They have opened a Pandora's box they can't cope with."

The meeting ended shortly after that. Karen and Maria continued chatting about the Y2K snafu and other matters. Karen began by asking her: "So what do you think about this mess, Maria?"

"I am not scared by it. I think it's much ado about nothing," Maria answered with self-assurance. "Maybe it is my ignorance, or maybe it is my deep-seated skepticism, but I don't see this as a major problem. I think it is a stupid mistake aspiring to notoriety, wishing for epochal dimensions with deliriums of relevance. I would be willing to bet you that on January 1, 2000, the world will go on with nary a mishap and without a gasp or a whimper. Mark my word."

"I tend to agree with you," said Karen. "I'm not scared by it either, but I am uneasy. I feel a little preoccupied by something, I don't know what. I sense a strange disquietude, a slight anxiety over the zeitgeist of our era. But it may have nothing to do with Y2K. It may be due more to the awareness of the briefness of life as we come to the end of a millennium. I am soaked in the sadness of the end of things. While you were doodling, I, too, was drifting away. Your Man of La Mancha took me back to the early 1600s when 'Don Quixote' was written. Do you realize that it was 400 years ago? Then all this talk about the end of the century, and not to mention the end of a millennium for heaven's sake, got me thinking about the passage of time. It boggles my mind to go back 400 years. It boggles me even more when I realize that you must drop another 600 years to get to the year 1000 when this millennium began. It was then that we began putting a '1' at the start of each year, 1001, 1002, 1003, and so on till we got to the last year of the series, 1999, where we are now, and where it's all about to end. Think of it: we are at the other end of what started in the year 1000! I could almost cry. Is this silly? Am I being over sentimental?"

"No, of course not, not at all," Maria assured her. "Or, put it this way, even if you were, I am right with you. I share your sensibilities completely."

Karen continued. "I did a fast rewind through history in my mind and got to 1492 when Columbus discovered America. But after that I started drawing blanks, bigger and bigger blanks. By the time I got to the year 1000 I had absolutely nothing. Nothing at all."

"Well, they don't call it the Dark Ages for nothing, you know," Maria allowed.

"Could you name a person from the year 1000?"

"Me? Not a one!" answered Maria. "I don't think anybody could, unless he was a scholar, an expert on the arcane. And even then, he'd have very little to go on."

"This is so sad. I feel I am pulling on the end of a long rope trying to get a tug or a signal from the other end, but there is nothing there."

"If you find that disturbing, you should try the other end," said Maria, changing the subject slightly. "I went in the other direction, to the future, to 2999 and got all sorts of unnerving signals. First, I got the sense of my own death in the most unequivocal terms. No question about it, I'll be dead by then. But what about the rest of us, will man still be around then? I wasn't sure. The very doubt about man's destiny got me. I had never felt that before because I had always taken the immortality of mankind for granted. Suddenly, I got soused in the precariousness and fragility of the world."

"Oh, my God, Maria" said Karen with a nervous laughter. "After all this Weltschmerz we both need a stiff drink. But I've got to run. Let's talk again sometime. I enjoy talking to you."

"Me too, Karen… I've enjoyed this chat also. In a weird sort of way, this kind of talk is fun, like wallowing in transcendental miasma."

"Say, Maria, could you come for dinner at my house this weekend? I love for you to meet my husband and my kids."

"My weekend is open, except for tomorrow, Friday. But Saturday or Sunday is fine. I'd love to come."

"Well, Sunday then. Feel free to bring a significant other… or not. I'll talk to you tomorrow to pin down the time and give you directions."

Z   Z   z   z   z   Z   Z

16. Weekend Commitments

Thanks to Maria's doodles, but mostly due to the company of her friend Karen, the faculty meeting had been bearable, almost fun. Maria was looking forward to the dinner at Karen's on Sunday. But first she needed to decide about Friday. She had two pending commitments: one with her next-door neighbor, Gwen Wingate, and the other with her mother.

Clara had pleaded most earnestly with her daughter and was on the verge of commanding her to join her parents on a family dinner at the Valverdes. Azucena Valverde was her cousin; some of her children and grandchildren were visiting town and she wanted for the families to get together.

"We have not seen the Valverdes in such a long time," she reminded Maria. "You remember Alejandro and Silvia... don't you? They would love to see you. Your dad and I will definitely be going, but I thought I better check with you before I made a firm commitment. Can I count on you, Maria? *Por favor*, d*í que sí. Si, si, si*. (Please say yes)."

Maria had given her mother a tentative yes. It was the only response that made any sense, for if Maria said no, Clara would have wanted to know why not, and if she were not persuaded by that answer, she would have insisted until she changed the 'no' to a 'tentative yes'. So, Maria had learned that the only answer that minimized hassles with her mother when she was intent on something was a wishy-washy yes to begin with, with the implied right to wiggle out of it at the last minute.

The deal with her next-door neighbor was a blind date. Once before Maria had accepted a blind date as an act of neighborly goodwill in order to help her out, but she would not do it again. She had declined firmly, but Gwen had insisted, promising that this would be the very last time and that she would never ask her again. Maria never even hinted at giving in, but knowing Gwen, she expected she would insist again.

That last blind date had been abominably disastrous. Maria had very little in common with Gwen. They did not like the same things. Gwen for her part could not understand Maria's objections. Why should she object to playing the field when it was the best way to finding a mate and having a good time doing it? For Gwen it was all a win-win situation. Fortunately for Maria, who wanted to avoid arguing about it, the Valverde's party made it possible for her to extricate herself diplomatically.

"I have a very important family affair with my parents," she told her.

It would have been difficult for Maria to convince Gwen otherwise. The two were poles apart. Gwen could only see the surface of things, missing their depth entirely. She saw the world in simplistic, linear black and white tones. Maria could never convince Gwen that playing the field with strangers and being the merry-making bachelorette had its potential dangers also. From Maria's perspective Gwen was playing with fire and courting trouble. She was vulnerable because, for one thing, she was too eager to catch a guy, and for another because she played under the delusion that she had nothing to lose in that dating game. For Maria, blind dates–especially with Latin males–were a pain, nothing less than a tedious exercise in sex refusal. It was tiresome and demeaning. Not worth the trouble.

"Oh, I know where you're coming from, Maria. You are so right. These Latin guys act as if they are always horny. I grant you they are a pain in that score; but you can handle them, you are a big girl. I thought you liked Latin men being that you are also Latin, and that you speak the language."

Maria saw red. She was provoked by that short little spiel because it contained so many false assumptions. It seemed hopeless to argue, but she could not let it stand.

"This may come as a surprise to you, Gwen, but Latinos in the U.S. are people actually divided by a common language."

"I don't understand. I haven't the slightest of what you're talking about."

"I was trying to be funny," Maria explained. "I was paraphrasing George Bernard Shaw."

"George Bernard... who?" asked Gwen.

"Shaw. He was an Irish playwright in the early part of this century. I am sure you are familiar with one of his plays, 'Pygmalion', although you might know it better by the name of its Broadway adaptation, 'My Fair Lady.'"

"What's he got to do with Latin people?"

"Nothing. It's just that he was a very witty curmudgeon who left the world a lot of quotable bits of wisdom. The quote I alluded to pertains to the differences between the U.S. and England. He said they were two countries separated by a common language. But the idea is even more a propos to the Latinos here. Strangely enough, the fact that they speak Spanish is not a cohesive element, but a repellant. For me, it is often such an irritant that it impedes communication. I detest Spanglish, which is what so many Latinos in the U.S. speak. It's unpleasant to my ear. It's downright ugly. So, I always switch to English. It's a neutral territory where we can get past the language barrier."

"Wow, this is all new to me. I didn't know."

"Well, it's complicated. There is usually more than just language involved. There are also cultural differences. People around here go for different music; they know nothing of the music of the Andes or of the Pampas. They couldn't name more than two tangos—if that many. I have a student–Toro they call him–he is either Cuban, or Puerto Rican, or Dominican. I don't know. Whatever. The fact is that I can't stand the way he talks to me in Spanish. It's not just a question of accent... it's a matter of modality, of propriety. In Spanish he sounds disrespectful, rude, pushy, and vulgar. He uses the familiar mode, rather than the formal mode that would be appropriate for a student addressing his teacher. Ugh! But you wouldn't understand this. English does not have the familiar-formal modes that Spanish, and many other languages have."

"Gosh, Maria, you sound high-strung about this. How many languages do you speak?

"Just two, really, just English and Spanish. But I dabble in the Romance languages as well."

"Romance languages? What are those?"

"Oh, you know, Spanish, Italian, Portuguese, Rumanian, and French."

"I never heard of that. Why do they call them Romance languages?"

"Goodness, Gwen, hadn't you? All these languages derive from Latin, the language of the Roman Empire. And I am sure you've heard of that."

"Oh, yeah, sure...I've heard about that. But tell me one more thing. What do you mean by dabbling in those languages? What is it that you do?"

"I play around with the study of languages. I concentrate on Italian or French from time to time, but in a casual way, not very seriously, sort of sporadically. I go in waves. There are periods when I am enamored of everything French, or everything Italian. Then I read up on them and update my old notes. I seek out things in these languages such as movies, music, magazines, and even newspapers, until the fad wears out. I memorize the lyrics to songs in the original language, *La Vie en Rose, Arrivederci Roma* and, of course, I will listen to an opera while reading the libretto word for word. When I meet someone who speaks one of these languages, I like to summon my scanty vocabulary and try to carry on a conversation. I try to learn more."

"You know what? It just dawned on me where I screwed up with you on the last blind date. I just got you the wrong guy, that's all. What if I got you a Frenchman next time, or an Italian?

"Oh, please... "

That's the way the discussion ended earlier in the week. But just as Maria had anticipated, Gwen would not give up. She would try again and, sure enough, she did knock at her door this evening to see if she could change Maria's mind. But Gwen soon realized that when Maria said no, she meant no. She told her she was looking forward to the family dinner the next day, and as to blind dates, the answer was: not tomorrow and not ever. Period.

The rest of the evening, Maria lounged around, watching TV, reading her latest issues of Time and Vanidades, and listening to music. From time to time she wondered if she shouldn't be more proactive about meeting people—men in particular. She recognized that she was lonesome. There were days when the pain of solitude slithered like a snake and squeezed her heart. Where is Prince Charming? When is he coming? Why couldn't he hurry up and find her? Two musical pieces spoke to this issue, and both were favorites of Maria.

One was *The Man I Love* by George Gershwin. She knew the lyrics by heart and loved them as much as the music. She admired the lyricist, Ira, George's brother, as much as the composer. What a perfect fusion of poetry and music they were! She never played the song just once. It was always two or three times, and she often sang along.

> Someday he'll come along
> The man I love
> And he'll be big and strong
> The man I love
> And when he comes my way
>   I'll do my best to make him stay
>   He'll look at me and smile
>   I'll understand
>   And in a little while
>   He'll take my hand
>   And though it seems absurd
>   I know we both won't say a word.
>   And so all else above
>   I'm waiting for the man I love.

That song sent her to pine away in a sad corner of heaven every time. The other favorite was a tango, *Nunca Tuvo Novio* (She Never Had a Lover). It happened that Maria's father loved tangos, and he had quite a collection of records, tapes and CDs. She had borrowed an assortment from him. This one she had taped from a record, and she listened to it often. It touched a raw nerve; she had a great affinity to it. Her dad's collection had four versions by different artists, but the version she loved the most was by the Sexteto Mayor, with Osvaldo Berlinghieri at the piano and vocal by Raúl Lavié, recorded in the 80s. Musically, this rendition was a pianistic showpiece. It began with a long piano introduction which could have held its own by itself, even if nothing else followed. But it was followed by Lavie's mellifluous baritone voice. From the start the words drew blood, getting to the point of the matter with brutal honesty, with a remark that pierced Maria's heart: "What an old spinster you've become, without dreams, without hope."

Maria pretended not to pay attention to the lyrics. It was the music that she loved; she told herself. Ah, the music, so unbearably beautiful! She never tired of it and it always carried her off unfailingly, turning, falling, rising, and whirling to the stars and back. But the lyrics had a subliminal poignancy that she preferred not to dwell upon. For many a night the tango had cost her hours of sleep. It was more deleterious than coffee. If she heard it after 9 p.m. her soul escaped from her and would not be caged back in.

Fortunately for Maria, just when she found herself losing her footing in the maelstroms of pining for love and the melody of *Nunca Tuvo Novio*, something would come along to anchor her to the ground again. This time it was her mother, Clara, who called.

"So, Maria, are you coming or are you coming tomorrow? Which is it going to be? What shall I tell Azucena?"

"It is both, *Mami*. I am coming, I am coming."

Z   Z   Z   z   Z   Z   Z

17. LIBBY

That night Maria went to bed around 12:15 a.m. with her weekend all planned out. Poor Gwen, she would just have to fend for herself and find another companion for her discotheque soirees.

Around 2:30 a.m. Maria was dreaming already. She saw herself walking into the now familiar auditorium at Dream Central which was again empty. This time she took a seat near the front— why not? Let them come. She was ready for them. She was not going to duck out this night and she was not going to come out empty handed.

She did not have to wait long before someone showed up. Within minutes she heard footsteps down the hall. Someone was approaching and from the sound of it, the person coming was making an impression even before appearing. The sound had a distinctly feminine tone; it had the rhythmic and staccato click-click of high heels. It was followed by laughter—female, carefree, insouciant laughter. The subsequent entrance of a young woman strutting into the auditorium with aplomb and elegance left no doubt about it. Her entrance was a splash. The young starlet—that's how she impressed Maria—was followed by a dark assistant who seemed Pakistani and who immediately ran up to the projection room carrying a movie reel and other electronic gear. Maria took a measure of the elegant stranger. She seemed to be the same age and the same height as Maria, but perhaps a couple of pounds heavier. Every pound, however, was distributed differently and was squeezed tightly into scantier clothes, giving her a curvaceous and voluptuous appearance. Their hair styles were also different: the stranger had her hair up in a bun, while Maria's was loose and straight. Above all, their demeanor and posture were poles apart. Maria was reserved and unassertive while the stranger was bold, brash.

"Okay, Ram, whenever you're ready," said the young woman to her assistant as she took a seat on the front row. "Let the show begin."

Maria stood up, thinking that she was intruding, and she started to leave, apologizing, and saying: "Excuse me. I didn't know there was something scheduled here at this hour."

"No, no, no! Please don't leave. You don't have to go. You have as much right to be here as we do. It is I who should apologize for barging in. Please forgive me for not introducing myself."

The stranger stood up and made a gesture to her attendant. "Hold it a minute, Ram, please. Don't start just yet." Then she turned to Maria again, extending her hand to introduce herself, she said: "Hello, my name is Lee, but everybody just calls me Libby because my full name is Lee B. Doe... nice to meet you. As I was saying, you're most welcome to stay."

"Nice to meet you, Libby. I'm Maria Diaz."

"Maria Diaz," Libby repeated, pronouncing the name slowly. "... is that all there is to your name? Surely, there's more..."

"No, that's all there is. I don't know why you would think there should be more?"

"It's just that it sounds short and Americanized. Usually, Maria is accompanied by another name like Maria Eugenia, Maria José, or Maria Elena. You know, something Latin and sexy."

"Well, I don't know about that... But yes, there is more, now that you mention it... I was christened Maria Luisa, but nobody calls me that," Maria said shyly.

"Well, that's a shame because it's such a pretty combination. I like that... Maria Luisa... that's very classy. Don't you like it?"

"Yes, I do, the way you say it. It does have a nice ring to it. To tell you the truth, I had forgotten all about that name."

"Well, you mustn't forget that" Libby said wagging her index finger admonishingly. "You shouldn't hide your charms, you know."

Maria liked the flattery, but at the same time she felt uneasy; it threw her off balance. Something about Libby's bold, forward attitude made her a little nervous. In fact, everything about Libby seemed double edged. She carried herself well and she looked attractive, but it was not an image or a look that Maria would emulate.

Maria would not waste the time putting on as much makeup as she did, and she would not subject herself to the discomfort of such tight clothing.

"Won't you sit down?" Libby continued. "If you have time to spare, I'd love to have you see the show... Please? Won't you?"

"Thank you. I will," replied Maria. "Is it very long?"

"No, it's not too long. But it is X-rated."

Maria swallowed hard at the sound of that, but feigned composure. Because she was already committed to staying, she sat down politely. Libby then signaled to Ram, her Indian or Pakistani assistant, to start the show: "Hey, Ram. We're ready now. Go ahead! Run it, Baby!"

The lights dimmed and the screen above and behind the dais became live, absorbing Maria into a world that was about to unfold. It was a world of dreams in bright lights, in stunning colors and loud music. The credits began rolling by.

Libido Enterprises Presents
Nunca Tuvo Novio
Starring: Lee B. Doe

The movie began with an aerial view of Buenos Aires accompanied by the languorous wailing of a *bandoneon*, the Argentinean accordion which is the distinctive voice of that city. Maria felt as though she was seeing the city through the eyes of a bird as it flew over downtown, starting from the multi-lane *Avenida 9 de Julio*, alleged to be the widest avenue in the world, and going towards the intersection with *Calle Corrientes* where the tall white Obelisk stands. Although Maria had never been to Buenos Aires, she recognized the obelisk from travel posters, as it is the landmark of this great Latin American metropolis. The film, probably taken from a helicopter, took her over Palermo, one of the residential neighborhoods not far from downtown. There the camera hovered in front of a balcony on the seventh floor of a high-rise condominium, approaching it slowly, getting closer till it put the viewer on the balcony. The scene took Maria past the balcony shutters into the living room. A caption on the screen described the apartment for the viewers as "Luisa's place." The camera scanned the place all around. It was a clean and nicely decorated apartment, but it was poorly lit. The curtains were drawn, and it did not convey a warm and hale atmosphere. It was dull and somber, like the place of an elderly person or someone who was inactive, or convalescent. Looking back towards the balcony again, Maria spotted a young woman whom she had missed seeing on the first scan of the apartment. Maria assumed, correctly, that that must be Luisa.

Luisa was sitting on a reclining chair reading a book. By her profile this young woman also looked like Maria, even more so than Libby. So great was the resemblance that Maria asked herself: "What am I doing there? They say each of us has at least one clone, one identical look-alike, somewhere in the world, but I had not expected to find my double in an X-rated movie filmed in Buenos Aires." She was curious about Luisa. She wished the camera would zoom in on her so she could assess the resemblance more carefully. But, in fact, that was not to be. There was a breakdown on the projector, and the screen went glaringly white, bright and blank. Ram turned on the lights in the auditorium again.

"I'm sorry, Libby. The tape just cut," Ram cried out from the projection room. "I'll get it fixed before too long. Be patient."

Libby waved her hands above her head, signaling to Ram that it didn't matter, or that she didn't care. Then looking at Maria she said: "Sorry about that. These things happen. But how did you like it so far?"

"It was beautiful. I've never been to Buenos Aires. That is one city that absolutely fascinates me."

"That's home to me and, yes, it is beautiful, but more than that it is exciting, youthful, vibrant, fun, and very, very romantic. You must go there. May I ask you a personal question? What do you do, Maria Luisa? And do you mind if I call you that?"

"No, no. Please do. It is my name after all, even if you will be the only person in the world calling me that. As to what I do, I am a teacher. I teach math in high school: Algebra, Geometry and Trig."

"Oh, super!" said Libby ecstatically. "Well, how about that! What do you know! This is really a coincidence. Would you believe I'm also a mathematician?"

"No, actually, I wouldn't," said Maria. "I thought you were an actress."

"Well yes, I am that also, as well as a dancer, and a model. But believe it or not, I'm also a statistician. I got my undergraduate in general math at the University of Buenos Aires and got a masters in Statistics at Iowa State."

Maria was incredulous. Libby, sensing this, felt obliged to give Maria a demonstration by way of proof, and she added: "I wrote my master's thesis on methods for correcting the heteroscedasticity in multiple regression cases to ensure the conditions of the generalized Gauss-Markov theorem. Most of my research was really in Econometrics."

"Wow! But help me out with the Gauss-Markov theorem. I can't seem to recall it right now," commented Maria with genuine enthusiasm. "What was that about?"

"Okay. I'm sure you know the basic linear regression model of statistics, right?

"Yes, of course, I know that."

"Well, in the two-variable case where you are estimating only alpha and beta, the theorem states that within the set of linear unbiased estimators of these parameters, the estimator that will ensure a minimum variance is the least-squares estimator. Naturally, this can be generalized to the n-variable case, but I would need paper and pencil to articulate it in that case."

"No, no. That's not necessary. I can picture its statement in matrix form. It would be a minimization problem basically, where 'least-squares' refers to minimization of the estimation errors and entails the minimization of a quadratic form, right?"

"Bingo! Good girl!" said Libby enthusiastically. "You got it!"

"But I thought that would have been done a long time ago," observed Maria.

"The Gauss-Markov theorem, yes, of course, but not the statistical model designed to ensure compliance with its minimum variance strictures. That was my baby. As a lagniappe, I wrote a computer model to go with it."

They would have chatted longer. Maria could have talked all night on the subject. She liked what she learned about Libby more and more. She admired her multifaceted accomplishments, and she would have liked to learn more about her, but Ram came down saying that he needed to go back across town to get something. Libby also had to leave. She had just received a call from her cellular and she had to take Ram because she was driving. Libby assured Maria that they would return later, and she hoped to see her then, if she was still there. As she left, she told Maria with a wink: "Maybe I'll catch you later."

It was a few minutes past 3 a.m. when Libby left. The night was young. Maria was once again alone in the auditorium, and she did drift downward into a deep, dark interlude—one of those dark holes of existence—that lasted for several hours. Maria's consciousness was turned off until sometime shortly after 6 a.m., less than an hour before she would wake up, at which time she began to dream again. She began dreaming that she was back in the auditorium, alone this time. Libby and Ram were no longer there. Maria was sitting in front of the screen just as a movie was about to start. The lights had dimmed. The screen had just lit up and a wailing *bandoneon* began playing again. The credits were beginning to roll by:

Libido Enterprises Presents
Nunca Tuvo Novio
Starring: Lee B. Doe

The movie played exactly as before, eliciting the same reactions, invoking the same feelings, and raising the same questions as before. Maria was surprised, for example, when she caught sight of Luisa again, sitting in the living room by the balcony reading a book. She crossed her fingers, hoping the tape would not break this time so she could get a better look at Luisa and determine whether she really looked like her. She was delighted that the movie proceeded without mishap and that she finally did get a good clear shot of Luisa. There was no doubt about it. The actress in the movie was indeed a perfect look-alike, a virtual clone of Maria. The difference was that they had exaggerated certain features, turning her into a caricature of the real Maria. Luisa was meant to represent the spinster in the tango *Nunca Tuvo Novio* (She Never had a Lover). She was, therefore, a woman who lived alone, who was shy and reclusive. They had to make her slightly stooped, nerdy, plain, sad and colorless. She wore a light brown business suit that looked like a corporate uniform, her eyeglasses were old fashioned and dark rimmed. In brief, she looked like some drone in a business office.

The tango *Nunca Tuvo Novio* that inebriated Maria's soul had begun to play and it gripped Maria's heart with the force of a vise as she watched herself in the character of Luisa. She could empathize with her. This is going to be a tragedy to cry by the bucketful, Maria told herself as she watched Luisa walking across the living room into the bedroom. There was a large, wall-sized mirror by a dresser. Luisa walked past it without looking at it.

The mirror seemed to reflect Libby's image and Maria immediately recognized her. She was the pretty mathematician she had met sometime, somewhere before. She did remember that she liked her. But what was she doing there? Did she have a part in this movie also? Libby's appearance in the mirror was puzzling. Something very strange was happening. To Maria's astonishment, it appeared that what she was seeing in the mirror was not Libby's reflection, but something more incredibly bizarre. It was Libby in the flesh trapped inside the mirror. She was pushing against the glass pane, trying to get out. Maria despaired, unable to help. She wanted to get word to Luisa of Libby's plight but all she could do was squirm and writhe in her seat, moaning, moving her head as if trying to send a signal to Luisa who had walked past the mirror, unaware of Libby's image.

Then, at last, as Luisa turned to return to the living room, she noticed the image in the mirror. She thought it was her reflection at first. She looked in the mirror and then at herself, applying a comparison test. They had different poses, different motions, and even different dresses. They were not reflections of each other. They were different people.

"Oh, my God, what are you doing there? How did you get in there?"

That was the way the subtitles on the screen read, expressing what Luisa would have said had it not been a silent movie. Libby, in the meanwhile, could only shrug her shoulders, unable to speak, in a gesture of helplessness.

Luisa approached the mirror and inspected its frame to see if it could be pulled from the wall, but the mirror was flush with it—glued or nailed shut. There was nothing she could do. Then, instinctively, Luisa touched the surface of the mirror to reach Libby. As she touched the glass, the mirror turned like a revolving door, drawing Luisa inward and leaving her on the other side imprisoned inside the mirror. Now it was Libby who was out while Luisa stood trapped inside, watching Libby walking freely in the bedroom. Maria watched, stunned by the drama of her two look-alikes.

The music began again, but this time it was a tango of a different sort. It was Libby's perky, sassy, and defiant tango. Libby went around humming and dancing as she rearranged and cleaned up the place. She pulled the curtains wide open and let the sunlight flood the rooms. On the dark corners where the sun wouldn't reach, she turned on the lights. She emptied out the wilted flowers from the flower vases. As Luisa observed Libby, her mind spun up with recurring questions which appeared as subtitles on the screen.

Who are you? You, who strut like a peacock suddenly escaped from the cage of inhibitions, singing and dancing in a virtual orgasm of laughter while I watch timidly, in bondage, from the shadows. You're hauntingly familiar…I've seen you before…but I don't know where…you remind me of myself. In some ways you're uncannily like me, except…except you dress so differently, so sure of yourself, not at all shy like me! Look at you carry on and dance, so carefree! You move with such abandon, dancing a sexy soliloquy of body language that dares express what I repress, mocking propriety, making prudery out of it. God, you're peeling off your clothes. Oh my God, where is this going? And where on earth did you get that lingerie? I've never seen such strings. I would look so ridiculous in that outfit! And yet, and yet on you it is so luring, so elegant, so natural, and so sexy!

Luisa—and Maria as well—stared in awe at Libby, who was the tootsie reflection of themselves. Luisa summarized their feelings by asking one final question which she managed to stutter with earnest honesty:

"Who, who, who… just who are you? Are you the apparition of what I want to be, or the specter of what I fear to be?"

By the time Libby finished straightening and cleaning the apartment, the place had undergone a magical transformation. The light in the entire apartment was brighter and more cheerful. The tempo of the music picked up, becoming more rhythmic, more electric, and more sensual. In fact, the music was the theme song of Maria de Buenos Aires, the prostitute protagonist in Astor Piazzola's tango operetta by the same name, *Maria de Buenos Aires*. The main aria from that work starts with the strings playing a raspy, repetitive, jocose and teasing rhythm that gradually levitates a melody which soars to defiance. Libby danced it and lip-synched it as a true kindred spirit, as a sister in arms of Maria de Buenos Aires. Maria and Luisa watched admiringly Libby's show as she enacted the aria, starting with the opening lines where she introduces herself, proclaiming: "I am Maria, Maria from Buenos Aires." Then she amplifies on what that means, saying: "I am tango; I am the slum of the city; I am the night; I am fatal passion. If they should ask who I am, they'll soon know it. The women will know it because envy will tell them; the guys because they'll fall at my feet like mice in my trap."

Libby was still dancing around in her lingerie when the doorbell rang. At this point the action speeds up into a comical, vaudevillian pantomime. Music still plays, but only as background. Libby lip-synchs her lines; her acting becomes slightly exaggerated, parodying the silent era movies. As she hears the doorbell a second time, Libby throws her hands up in the air, asking: "Oh, my gosh, who is it? What shall I do?" She runs around in circles with that awkward and comical marionette stiffness of early movies. She peeks through the peep hole on the front door and sees a young man dressed in coat and tie, holding several books. Then, looking at the audience, she identifies him.

"It's Leonardo, the medical student that Luisa tutors in math."

An idea lights up inside her head and she immediately carries it out. She goes to the bathroom and comes out seconds later with a towel coiled around her head like a turban while another towel is wrapped around her body; and she answers the door, as if she had just come out of the shower.

"I'm so sorry. I must be early," Leonardo says, apologizing.

"No, no, Leonardo. I am so sorry. It is I who is running late. Please come in. You just sit right here while I go put something on. I won't be long."

Libby, pretending to be Luisa, leads Leonardo to a chair and makes him comfortable. Then she goes into the bedroom, leaving the door wide open. Leonardo sits awkwardly, leafing through the books at first, looking casually at the room around him, noticing how different it looks now—how much brighter and fresher. Then by chance he notices the mirror in the bedroom. Luisa is no longer visible inside the mirror. The mirror has lost its magic and returned to being an ordinary mirror. What Leonardo can see is Libby's reflection as she goes about the room. He sees her intermittently as she comes and goes pulling dresses out of the closet, trying to choose which one to wear. All the dresses are suits, skirt and jacket combinations; and they are all identical in every respect except for color. She holds up one of the dresses while still on its hanger in front of her and makes a moue of displeasure. She then goes in front of the mirror to see it against her body. She discards it, saying: "This won't do. This green is too drab." Then she pulls another dress and goes through the same routine, saying: "Naaah! Gray is even drabber." On the final dress she says: "Ugh! This is more of the same, but in blue. It will have to do because there is nothing else."

Leonardo is not looking at the books anymore. He has moved his chair to have a better view of the mirror. He cannot believe his eyes when he sees the towel come off her head. Her long black hair unfurls and cascades down to her shoulders; she brushes it, parting it the same way as Maria and Luisa. When she has finished with her hair, she resembles Maria more than ever. In fact, she is indistinguishable from Maria now. Leonardo cleans his glasses and wipes the sweat from his forehead. He has never seen Luisa look so gorgeous. She is still walking around with the towel wrapped around her body. Leonardo looks as if expecting her to drop it off at any time. He looks at the mirror with consuming anxiety and waits with despair. Then the actress on the screen—that is, Luisa to Leonardo, but Libby to both Luisa and Maria—does drop her last towel in a final ecdysiast act of seduction. She stands before the mirror in full view of Leonardo and in full frontal nudity for a few seconds. Her breasts are not as round and big as they appeared when Libby was dressed. In their bare untouched state, they are conical. Her body is svelte and beautiful. She is like the apparition of the goddess of love to Leonardo, a naked Venus. He is choking, gulping his own saliva as he swallows hard.

As Libby goes on walking naked in front of the mirror, pulling clothes out of the drawers, throwing bras and panties, and other garments up in the air, she calls out to Leonardo, and asks him:

"Leonardo, are you looking at the things you want me to help you with?"

Leonardo's reply flashes on the screen: "Yes, I am. I most certainly am looking at everything I want you to help me with. I'm not missing a thing. Don't rush on my account. There's more I need to see. Please, please take your time."

"Very well then."

Leonardo had been clenching his hands, rubbing his head, pulling his hair, clearing his eyes as they nearly popped out of his face as he watched a magnificent show he had not anticipated. A few minutes later Libby, (that is, Luisa to Leonardo), comes out wearing the blue skirt of the business suit and a white shirt, giving that outfit a sexiness it never had before, with the two top buttons left unbuttoned, and the sleeves rolled up by two folds.

"Luisa, you're radiant! I have never seen you look like this before, so warm, so casual. What you've done to this place is refreshing and most becoming, but what you've done to yourself is irresistible. You're stunningly beautiful today."

"Thank you. You're so gallant."

"And oh, that fragrance… and the luster of your hair. What's happening here? Are you the same Luisa? You seem so different."

"No, I'm not the same. I've changed since I last saw you. I'm dancing a new tango now. I've been working too hard. I've been missing out on life. And, I say, no more. I have turned a new chapter in my life. I have even changed my name, resurrecting the other half of my name, Maria, which was buried in my past. My full name now is Maria Luisa. Do you like it?"

"I love it. I love it as I love everything else about you today."

"Shall we celebrate then? Would you like a drink?"

"But I thought you never drank. You're full of surprises. Yes, of course, I'd love a drink. I need one desperately. Make it real cold 'cause I'm burning up."

"Well, make yourself comfortable, silly. Take off your coat and loosen up your tie."

"I don't think that would be enough. I need a cold shower."

"Well, in that case, be my guest. *Mi casa es tu casa.*"

"Even that wouldn't do it."

"Do you have a fever then? Let me see. Let me take your temperature."

She grabs the back of his head with her left hand and pulls it backwards while putting her right hand on his forehead. Her cleavage is right in front of his face. Leonardo cannot stand it anymore. He grabs her and kisses her passionately.

"I love you, Luisa. I mean Maria. I mean Maria Luisa! I adore every part of you and want you badly now. Be mine."

One thing led to another. They kissed and they embraced with abandonment. Then, in gradual steps, they proceeded to the irresistible and inevitable end. They undressed completely, and they made love as two thirsty people cavorting in the pool of an oasis after a long trek through the desert.

Maria sat in the auditorium watching the torrid love scene on the screen, seeing herself naked, entangled with Leonardo's naked body. She was so absorbed that at times she would move her head to see the screen from another angle, to catch more details and to get a better view of the sex mechanics in action. Maria was involved not only as a voyeur partaking vicariously in the lovemaking on the screen, but as an active participant who experienced everything in virtual reality, feeling what she saw on the screen in her own body. Unbeknownst to her, there was a reason why the Maria who sat in the auditorium dreaming that she was watching a movie should have felt so fully involved in it—sexually and all. She would learn later, when she woke up, that Maria, who was sleeping in bed, who was also dreaming the same dream, had taken matters into her own hand, touching herself reflexively and instinctively, and moaning and heaving with carnal pleasure. The dream was so powerful that Maria woke up from the intensity of unbearable desire. The fantasy had gone too far. She awoke finding herself hot, perspiring profusely, and with her hand on her groin, pressing hard against her wet vagina. The clock beside her bed reads 6:37. Its alarm would go off in eight minutes.

As Maria lay in bed awake, she remembered Libby's ominous words in the auditorium when she told her with a wink: "Maybe I'll catch you later." Now Maria understood the full meaning of that promise. She felt she had been tricked and manipulated into doing something that she would never do—except only in dreams. And even in dreams, only if she lost all control. Libby had been masterful in coaxing her into watching that movie, in engaging her curiosity, and in absorbing her into the scene totally.

Maria put the dream out of her mind and for the rest of the day went about her business, never thinking about it. At this point she was still not aware that Libby and Maria Luisa were really kin and part of her persona. She did not know that they were the 'witches' of her psyche that she had so badly wanted to meet face to face. She saw them as actresses, as strangers in a movie in which she had been a mere spectator. The movie had denied her any control. It hadn't even occurred to her to question the women. Instead, Maria had been swept off by a staged drama which had taken her to Buenos Aires where she had been immersed in the lyrics of tangos that had given form and life to some of its weird characters who had embroiled her in their own intrigue—including sex. It did not matter that the women resembled her. The full recognition of Libby and Maria Luisa for what they really were would come later.

z   z   z   z   Z   Z   Z

PART IV: FRIENDS AND NEIGHBORS

18. THE VALVERDES' PARTY

The Valverdes' home was in Coral Gables, one of the older and classy subdivisions in south Miami. Maria's mother was the first cousin of Azucena Valverde, the matriarch of that clan. They had not seen each other in months. The Valverde's belonged to the well-off landed gentry of Ecuador. They were people who maintained homes both in the old country and in Miami and had investments in various South American countries. They were mainly exporters and importers. Maria's family, by contrast, belonged to the professional, but less affluent middle class, and had not maintained connections with their former country. Maria's father was an accountant. He had always worked for banks and business firms. Maria's mother was a housewife.

Gwen could not have topped this party—no matter what Prince Charming she might have produced for a blind date. The Valverde's' dinner party was the kind of party that Maria idealized, and she had a lovely time. While it was true that there had been no available bachelors, that did not detract in any way from the delightful evening. In addition to the older generation, there were two young married couples and several children ranging in age from tots to teenagers. It was a family party. The food was superb; the music was eclectic, and international; the people were charming; and the conversation was intelligent, titillating and instructive. They danced and sang, and Maria loved every minute of it.

One of the women whom Maria enjoyed meeting was June Hampton-Valverde, an American married to Alejandro, a son of the host family. Maria was amazed at how well June spoke Spanish. Although she had a slight American accent, she was well spoken, quite articulate, and her Spanish flowed more easily than Maria's, showing that Maria was a little out of practice. While people milled about and chatted, a song was playing through the stereo system. June beamed at hearing it and moved closer to the speaker to hear it better.

"Oh, I've always loved this," she said, enraptured.

It was Mercedes Sosa's rendition of *Alfonsina y el Mar* (Alfonsina and the Sea). Maria had heard the song before but had never gotten the full impact of the lyrics because she had not listened attentively enough. It was about a woman, Alfonsina, who drowned in the ocean. The song describes her footprints in the sand, disappearing at the edge of the white foam, and it pictures her like a siren holding court in the bottom of the sea, writing poems there while surrounded by friendly creatures of the sea. A retinue of seahorses and sea stars revolve around her throne on a bed of corals and pearls. In the song Alfonsina requests one of her attendants to lower her lamps. She would take a nap. Then she adds: "Ah, and one more thing. If he should happen to call, please tell him I'm not in. Just say I have gone..." The song is sad, and Maria caught the lyrics word for word this time, until she, too, was swept away by the music and by the power of its poetic images. She joined June in saying: "Yes, this is truly lovely."

"You know, of course, that the song is about a real person by the same name, Alfonsina, don't you?"

"No, I didn't know that. Who was Alfonsina?"

"She was an Argentinean poetess, Alfonsina Storni, born in Switzerland of Italian extraction. Unfortunately, while still relatively young, in her early forties, she learned she had incurable cancer, and it was too much for her. She committed suicide by walking into the ocean in Mar del Plata in 1938. She left a suicide note to a friend, an editor of a newspaper, which she ended with a postscript, a reminder like that quoted in the song: 'Ah, one more thing... If he calls, just say I've gone.' Her poems are beautiful. She is one of my favorite Argentinean poets."

Thus, a spirited conversation started between Maria and June. Maria had never met an American who spoke Spanish as well as June and who knew so much about Hispanic culture. Over the course of their conversation Maria would learn how June came into that knowledge and would be astounded. June, it turned out, was a professor of Latin American literature at Catholic University; she had earned her degrees from the University of Virginia but had studied in Spain, first at Alcalá de Henares near Madrid, and then at the University of Salamanca. This accounted for her Castilian Spanish and the slight lisp that went with it. Of course, after marrying Alejandro Valverde, she had traveled all over South America as well. She had recently dropped out of teaching because she was pregnant with her second child. She and her husband lived in Washington, D.C. and were just visiting family in Miami.

Maria, who had always gravitated towards Mathematics and Physics, who had revered and preferred people in those areas, and who had felt a slight condescension towards people in linguistics, had of late felt an unprecedented awe and admiration for the humanities. June re-enforced that admiration. Maria was humbled and confided that she regretted having neglected her own culture and her Spanish language. Although she had always spoken in Spanish with her parents at home, that was only superficial and incidental talk that did not prepare her for intelligent discussion. Whenever she had to speak Spanish at a level deeper than casual conversation, she became frustrated because she became painfully aware of her limitations in her native language. Next to June, she considered herself a cripple in Spanish. June comforted her, telling her not to fret, that it was a common problem with immigrants and children of immigrants in the U.S. The second language tends to become a bastard language, always in decline and destined to be forgotten.

"It is really a sad state of affairs," continued June. "It is sad because a foreign language is really a special gift that should be nurtured and developed. Unfortunately, in many cases it comes to be regarded as something of a burden. Some children become ashamed of their parent's foreign language. We see this across all cultures; it happens to the Chinese, Vietnamese, Turkish, and Latinos. The children come to resent the foreign language as excess baggage that impedes their integration into the mainstream of American life; it makes them appear different. It embarrasses them when their parents "talk funny" in front of their American friends. Instead of feeling lucky and proud of knowing another language, they feel branded with a gift they'd just as soon not have. They do all they can to avoid using it, and they work at trying to forget it. Eventually, they do succeed in losing it and manage to forget it all."

"I think I am gradually getting there," said Maria rather meekly.

"No, you are not. You don't sound to me as though you've lost much. You have basically kept your Spanish. At your age you will never forget it. You are just a little rusty, and you may need to enrich it, but that's all. Incidentally, do you know what is sad about those children who work at losing their language and eventually succeed at it? It is that when they are older, they often regret having lost it."

"What can be done about this?"

"Well, in the case of the children, as they are growing up, it is difficult because it depends so much on the parents and on their support to instill a feeling of pride in their native culture. The trick is to be doing that while at the same time embracing American culture. People have to realize that it is not a case of either one culture or the other. It can be both. It is challenging to juggle two cultures, but it is not impossible. Now in the case of adults, such as you, whose language has eroded for lack of use it is easier to correct. First, there should be no guilt on your part. It was not your fault. You never had a formal opportunity to develop culturally. U.S. schools teach you what you need to know to succeed in American culture: English grammar, U. S. history, and American and British literature. That is as it should be. I have no problem with it. But you should be able to catch up on your own culture later. And you can. You can always go back to college and take courses in Spanish. The trouble here is that many Hispanic people are under the delusion that they already know the language and that a Spanish college course is beneath them, something for beginners, for Americans. They are wrong! Most universities offer several courses, from beginning

Spanish to literature, which cover poetry, drama, art, music, history —not just grammar and vocabulary. I teach one of these courses. It is conducted strictly in Spanish and is designed for American students in their third year of Spanish. But it is also ideal for native speakers who need exposure to Spanish culture. I always have several of those students in my classes. They get a run for their money, because they discover it isn't as easy as they had thought. I'll bet that here in Miami, with as many colleges as you have, and with such a heavy Hispanic population, that these courses are always available."

"Maybe so. I don't know because I never had the interest before."

"Have you read any Spanish or Latin American writers? For example, have you read Gabriel Garcia Marquez?"

"Yes," Maria said sheepishly, adding: "But I am ashamed to admit it, that I read him in English."

"Oh, Maria. No, no! Why did you do that?"

"Because it was faster and easier. I just wanted to have a sense of what made him so great. Frankly, he blows hot and cold with me. I liked *Chronicle of a Death Foretold*, but I did not like *One Hundred Years of Solitude*. In fact, I did not finish it."

"How I wish you could take one of my courses! We read and discuss plays, short stories, essays, and poetry. I like Garcia Marquez, though he is not a favorite of mine. My favorite is Julio Cortazar, another Argentinean, but there are so, so many more."

The women continued their conversation about Latin American literature for several more minutes. June got Maria's address and promised to send her a few books that Maria was sure to enjoy. They would have talked longer but suddenly everyone was gathering around in a circle surrounding Pepe Bellini, and his wife Silvia Valverde-Bellini. They were dancing a tango as only Argentinean professionals can dance it, with grace and elegance. It was difficult to accept that they were not professionals. Pepe was a banker, and Silvia a housewife.

That tango whetted the group's appetite for South American

music. Somebody would ask: Do you know such and such a song? If they had it, they would play it; if they didn't, they would sing it. There was always at least one person who knew every song that was named. They went through Colombian porros, Ecuadorian *pasillos* and *sanjuanitos*, Peruvian waltzes, and Chilean folk music, especially by the Chilean group Inti Illimani. But they always came back to tangos, partly because Maria was curious and asked questions about the lyrics. There were words, names and places in tango lyrics that mystified her, and this was an opportunity to ask. In one tango, for example, a man says of his old flame: "Yesterday afternoon I saw her in Florida, brooding alone, distractedly." Maria wanted to know about Florida. Is it a flowery place as the name implies? Or is it a neighborhood? What is it?"

"No, no," Pepe corrected her. "Calle Florida is the name of a street in the heart of Buenos Aires. It is an old pedestrian mall, not open to traffic, full of shops and restaurants. You are likely to see jugglers and pantomimes and to hear street musicians playing guitars and bandoneons and, of course, you will always see at least one couple dancing the tango."

"What about Corrientes 348 in the tango *A Media Luz*?" Maria asked.

"Corrientes is also a major street that cuts through downtown," Silvia told her. "In fact, it intersects the wide avenue *9 de Julio* right at the obelisk. That tango, which dates to the 1930s, made the address famous. A playboy bachelor supposedly had his apartment at Corrientes 348, which is not far from the obelisk. The tango describes his flat, how he kept it dimly lit, always ready for cocktails and love."

"The house still stands, you know," added Pepe. "In fact, it has a plaque commemorating the tango."

"Really? I remember seeing that Obelisk in a movie," Maria said, "but I cannot remember the name of the movie ..."

"You've probably seen it in several movies. It's the distinctive mark of the city, like the Eiffel Tower in Paris or the coliseum in

Rome."

Maria swore to herself then that somehow, someday soon she would make it there and when she did, she would dance the tango—maybe in Calle Florida itself. And if they asked her for her name, she would tell them it was Maria Luisa.

Z   z   z   z   z   z   Z

19. ROHYPNOL

The party at the Valverde's went on till around midnight. But Maria did not get to sleep till 3 a.m. She had enjoyed herself so much that whatever else happened on Saturday and Sunday, her quota for weekend delight had already been met. For the rest of the weekend, she could just cruise on memories of the evening which her parents had also enjoyed enormously.

Maria went to bed determined to sleep to her heart's content–till noon or later. But there was a phone call around 9:30 Saturday morning that changed the rest of her weekend. When Maria answered the phone, she recognized Gwen's voice in great distress.

"Maria, this is Gwen. Help me! Please come, Ooooh..." Then the voice broke into a ghastly moan. Maria, who was still half asleep and groggy when she answered the phone, was shocked into full awakening and rushed to Gwen's apartment. Gwen looked dreadfully sick. She had on a bathrobe that loosely draped her body, as if she had just tossed it on. She was dazed, her hair was matted, and her complexion was ashen. She moved around unable to speak, shrugging her shoulders, nodding her head, with gestures of helplessness. Maria sat her down and tried to calm her, embracing her, and rubbing her.

"I woke up there a while ago completely naked," she said feebly.

Maria looked around. The place was messy with articles of clothing strewn on the floor. One hundred questions were going through Maria's head, and she quickly prioritized what she needed to know.

"Was your blind date here last night?

Gwen gestured sheepishly that she did not know.

"Do you hurt anywhere? Would you like me to call a doctor or take you to a hospital?"

Gwen just shrugged her shoulders saying, "I don't know."

"Do you feel sick, or nauseous, or in pain? Tell me how I can help."

"I don't know."

Realizing that she was not going to get anywhere with Gwen, Maria took charge, calling 911 to ask for professional help. She informed them that she had a friend in a daze, probably drugged, who was the probable victim of a rape. They advised her to bring Gwen to the hospital. Maria helped Gwen get dressed; she put something on herself and drove to the hospital.

Through the course of the day Gwen regained her strength and her mind, but not her memory. She could only remember going to singles bar the night before, dancing and having drinks and nothing more. She did not remember leaving the place; she did not know who brought her home, how, or when. As for remembering what transpired in her apartment during the night, the memory was too vague, and she did not want to incur the pain of summoning it.

The people at the hospital–the doctor, the nurses, and the police–all acted as if this was something common; treating the case as something they were used to. They all concurred that this seemed like another case of Rohypnol abuse, but they could not classify it as such officially until they conducted more tests. Maria learned that this was the date-rape drug in vogue in Florida. It came in tablet form; it was easily crumbled to slip into a drink, any type of drink, where it readily dissolves. It takes effect quite rapidly, usually within 20 minutes, and its effects last from 8 to 12 hours, reaching its peak within the first two hours after ingestion. Because the drug is a sedative, the victims lose resistance. They do not necessarily pass out. They just lie there incapacitated, vaguely aware of what is happening to them, but unable to help themselves.

"God, this drug was just made to order for rapists," Maria noted.

"Originally, it was intended for the treatment of insomnia and presurgical sedation," allowed one of the nurses, "but then rapists hijacked it for their use. American authorities recognized the potential for mischief early on and banned it here. You cannot produce it, or distribute it in the U.S. But it is produced in Europe and Latin America, especially in Colombia. But even there, it can only be acquired legally by prescription. The college crowd here has no difficulty acquiring it. They refer to it as 'roofies' and is very popular in Florida's campuses."

Maria asked the nurse whether it was possible to determine if Gwen had been raped. The nurse rolled her eyes for a full clockwise loop, her head shaking, her face grimacing an expression that conveyed a negative response to Maria's question. Then she added:

"Man, you just don't know the professionalism of theses perverts. They've turned this crime into an art form. They've thought of everything. They leave no tracks. They use condoms to avoid being detected by their semen, and also to prevent them from catching something from the victim, just in case she happens to have AIDS or something. If they know that the victim lives alone, then they save themselves the trouble of finding a place to commit their crime; they just take her to her own place. This is one crime that stacks the cards in favor of the perps."

"That is so incredibly unfair," lamented Maria, "Surely there must be something that goes against them or in favor of the victims."

"If there is, I don't know what it is," added the policewoman. "On top of everything the drug is cheap and makes this crime quite affordable. It is cheaper than resorting to hookers. It only costs about five bucks a pop."

"I can only think of one consolation prize for the victims," added the nurse. "It is the fact that, as a rule, the victims have no memory of the assault. So, if they suffer while it is happening, at least they are spared the torture of remembering it. But then again, this benefit washes out because it also protects the rapist, as he can't be identified. Of course, if you want to consider the use of condoms as a blessing, then that can be a second consolation … At least the victim won't get pregnant, or catch his venereal disease, if he has one."

"Has anyone ever been prosecuted for this?" asked Maria.

"Uh, uh," said the policewoman nodding her head, "not that

I know of. I would guess that very few have ever been prosecuted–
and fewer still convicted. I haven't seen figures on this. It's still
fairly new. Most of the victims do not want to prosecute. It's not
worth the hassle. And you can add that as another thing in favor of
the rapist."

For the rest of the weekend Maria stayed in her apartment,
close to Gwen, calling her and dropping in from time to time. She
fixed soup and got take-outs from a nearby restaurant for both of
them. They watched TV and chatted. Maria was very tactful with
her questions. She sensed that Gwen needed help in forgetting.
Maria dispensed on her planned visit to her parents that day. As
Gwen recovered, and as she spoke more and more, it became clear
that she had made up her mind about one thing. Gwen would go
back home to Paducah, Kentucky. Life in the fast lane had proved
too wild for her.

Z   Z   Z   z   Z   Z   Z

20. GOSSIPS AND COMMENTARY

Gwen took up all of Saturday for Maria. They rested for a couple of hours after they came home from the hospital. Then Maria ordered dinner from the Pollo Tropical, a fast-food restaurant with Latin American cuisine. She got yucca, corn on the cob, grilled chicken, *macitas*—which is pork, fried Cuban style—black beans and rice, and fried ripe plantains. Maria also rented a couple of golden oldies to cheer up Gwen: "Sabrina" and "Roman Holiday"—both movies starred Audrie Hepburn, a favorite of Maria's. By the time she went back to her own apartment for the night, she had no trouble falling asleep. It had been a long day, and she was in sleep arrears.

As soon as Maria began to dream, she found herself in the auditorium once again, which had become a sort of dream central for her. But tonight, she bypassed it for a conference room nearby which was smaller and more intimate. This time she did not have to wait long for the women. Nothing would have kept them from coming, neither fire, nor flood, nor any calamity known to man. They materialized in no time at all. They had been waiting for hours for Maria to show up, anxious to gossip and discuss the day's developments. Because the conference room was poorly lit and because they were shadows, the women moved in silently and without notice. Maria could sense their presence, but only as silhouettes in the dark.

"Well, well, well, Maria," one of them began. "We've had quite a day today, haven't we? We have a lot to talk about tonight."

"Oh, Maria, we have been beside ourselves all day, watching quietly all the proceedings, but unable to intervene. We're so glad you're finally here."

Then another silhouette spoke: "Maria, I think you've been an angel to that girl. You deserve a medal. We're proud of you."

"Thank you."

"Had you warned Gwen that this might happen to her, Maria?"

"Yes, of course, although not explicitly. I had intimated it. But even I could never have anticipated Mickey in the drink. That is so low! In any case, it wouldn't have done any good even if I had spelled it out for her. She was so convinced that it was a great way to meet men and have a good time. She was determined to ignore me and prove me wrong."

"That Rohypnol is lethal, all right! It is frightening."

One of the voices came loud and strong. "If you ask me, she had it coming. She was so stupid. She thought she was so smart. She was going to have a great time playing the field while she caught herself a husband. It was all such a win-win proposition to her that she was almost cocky about it. It never occurred to her that she was playing with fire. It's unfortunate, but people like her just have to learn the hard way."

"No question about it. Gwen was courting trouble and had herself to blame for her misfortune. But what I find remarkable about this day is that Maria was truly noble for all she did today. She didn't reproach her for her naiveté, and never even hinted at any recrimination like I-told-you-so. That was quite commendable, Maria. Hear. Hear."

"I second that. Maria was true friend and good neighbor. But having said that, I think we need to shift the focus here from Gwen and Maria to the drug and to the perverts who use it. We are up against an evil menace. This drug is a rape epidemic in the making. We haven't even begun to sort through its implications. I was trying to get Maria's ear throughout the day, but to no avail. I wanted Maria to ask some questions to the nurse and the policewoman. There is so much to be done about this, and it appears that nothing is being done."

"I agree. We are past the point of lamenting the misfortunes of poor Gwen. We need to be more practical about the dangers of this drug. It's a wildfire out there. We've got to do something."

"What do you have in mind?" asked Maria. "But wait… wait before you answer that. I would like to ask you all a question first.

Who am I talking to here? Would you mind identifying yourselves, please?

"I am Sasha," said one shadow.

"And I am Libby," said another.

"Libby, really?" Maria inquired with great interest. "That sounds familiar. Have we met before?"

"At one time or another you've met all of us, Maria."

"Yes, but I think I've actually seen someone by that name."

"Well, I have appeared in films. Maybe you saw one of my pictures."

"Was it X-rated?" Maria asked.

"I'll say! She does nothing but…" said Sasha sarcastically.

"Are there others?" continued Maria, "who else is here?"

"Well, there is Maria Luisa and Ram, Mr. Random Access Memory, but he is busy in the other room now wiring memory connections."

"Would he be dark and Pakistani by any chance?" Maria asked. "I think I've seen him also."

"Yes, he is. You're very observant. And there is Imogene, also," added Sasha.

"Imogene?" Maria asked. "Who would that be?"

"Oh, you know, Imogene Natien. But she's not here right now."

"Ah, yes, with a name like that I bet she is a dream producer, or director, right?" asked Maria. "I would really like to meet her sometime. But all right, where were we? I interrupted you."

"I was saying it's a wildfire out there," said one of the shadows. "I was about to make some suggestions for you to follow up on. We need more information on the rapists. Who are they? Are they perverts, born rotten to the core, or are they as I suspect normal males who become perverts when they get access to a magic pill? That pill can tempt the best of men because it affords them a means to rape without getting caught. I can't help but wonder if all men aren't potential rapists."

"Whoa, there! I do detect a sexist bitterness there," said Libby.

"So what?"

"I think we've all been thinking along the same lines," said Maria Luisa. "The men have been at the forefront of my thoughts also. But I don't believe it would have done any good to ask the policewoman any of these questions. I think she did say—did she not? —that she knew of no prosecutions thus far. Obviously, before you can interrogate these rapists you have to capture them. So, I would pursue another tack. I would ask the policewoman this question. What—besides sitting around waiting for a brave victim to come forth and prosecute—are you doing about catching these guys? This is not an idle question. If I were police chief, I would have caught half a dozen already in sting operations. Why wait for more victims? Why not set up the rapists with police officers pretending to be victims that will turn the tables on them?"

"Oooooh, I love that! What a great idea."

"Yeah, and what about the single bars, the clubs, the places where these assaults originate? How innocent are they through all this? Don't you think they know what's going on? Why couldn't they have warnings? Why couldn't they tell the girls to guard their drinks, to keep them always covered, and to fetch the drinks themselves from the bar? They could also require that all females come in pairs, that they enforce a buddy system, that they have a female designated driver."

"You are getting ahead of yourself. None of that is going to happen until this thing explodes sky high. Somebody has to sue the single clubs, somebody has to catch a rapist and mutilate him, cutting him up into a million pieces so that the media, smelling blood, is fired up enough to expose this in a big, big way."

"Absolutely! If this were to happen to the governor's daughter, you know that would make a big splash and there'd be some action taken."

"Speaking of politicians, that reminds me that the legislatures themselves must address this issue because existing laws are probably inadequate to prosecute. What should be the penalty for possession of this drug? It may be illegal to manufacture the drug, to import it, or to distribute it. So it is with marijuana, with cocaine and what-have-you. And that hasn't stopped anything. But this drug is even worse. In my opinion, it is in the category of a weapon because—unlike drugs that are strictly self-harming—these drugs are intended to harm others. I would put it in the same category of banned weapons—poison gas, anthrax and the like. A law needs to be passed expressly and uniquely for this drug so that its mere possession is a crime. Show me a man that carries it, and I'll show you evil intent. What possible reason could someone have for the possession of this drug other than rape? There is no reason for its possession."

"These are all good questions–so good, that our good cop could not have answered them. And neither can we. We are no lawyers, or legislators."

"You are right; this is getting far out and over our heads. What we should be addressing are the ways in which Maria can do something positive in her own small way."

"Such as?"

"I don't know... maybe talking it over in school, telling your colleagues about it, maybe approaching the principal to see if she would be interested in having the policewoman, or the nurse, give a talk to the girls. Maria, let me ask you something. Would you be willing to go to Mildred Colson with this?"

"Oh God, I was afraid we would come to something like this. Count me out on that! I wouldn't mind discussing it with some colleagues and see where that leads. But Mildred Colson? No way! Unless it is reports, goals and objectives, grade distributions, and things of that sort, I have nothing to say to that woman. Next issue."

"Fine. Leave Colson out, but one way or another, the girls must be alerted, and maybe also the parents. How do you feel about that, Maria?"

"The same. In order to reach the parents, you would have to go through PTA, and in order to set that up you would have to go through Mildred Colson. No way!"

"Maria, you shock me. A while ago you seemed to be all fired up about this issue. I thought you were willing to move heaven and earth to prevent this from happening to anyone. Now you are cooling, just because you are daunted by the prospect of going to Mildred Colson. What a wuss!"

"You shock me, too. Don't you know me by now? It should come as no surprise to any of you that I am not a champion for lost causes. I am no crusader. So, don't push me on this. It won't do you any good. As you know, I reserve the right to renege on anything I promise here. And yes, I know you don't need to remind me; you can get back at me by riddling my dreams with guilt. Well, have at it. I'll be ready for you. Just don't do it tonight, please. And let me add that I will, in my own way, do something about this sometime. My concern is that this Rohypnol gets down to the high schools. I don't think it's there yet. I will talk to the senior girls, and some that I think could be vulnerable. I will talk to Elena. She worries me. I could picture her being tricked by that creep, Wally. Now there is somebody who has rape written all over his face. He and his buddy, Toro, are the types that would stop at nothing. God help us if those two should ever get a hold of this pill. But now I'm getting tired of all this. I don't mind discussing this issue in general, but I don't want to turn it into a planning session on how I am going to lead a crusade against Rohypnol. And, certainly, I don't want to make any commitments here. Why don't you all discuss it among yourselves while I sleep in peace? Maybe you can slip in your suggestions in a dream for me to consider when I wake up. How does that sound?"

"We are surprised at you, Maria. You sound as if you are getting to know the way we work around here. What sort of dream would you like to go along with that?

"I don't know... whatever. Surprise me."

"Does anybody know what time it is?"

"It is 3:47 a.m."

"We still have plenty of time to concoct something for you, Maria."

"Well, okay, but make it sweet, make it uncontroversial, and sweet. Let's not try to solve all the problems of the world in bed. Leave that for the more energetic hours."

Z   z   z   z   z   Z

21. A DREAM REMINDER

The dream makers went to work on a dream that Maria would enjoy and could take with her to her conscious hours. They tried to respect her wishes, keeping it sweet and uncomplicated. The dream would have touches from recent memory, recollections from a wonderful party with bits of wisdom and bits of nonsense as little forget-me-nots.

In her dream that Sunday morning Maria was taken back to the Valverde's party. The house had grown in her mind. It was palatial and more sumptuous than in real life. A beautiful melody was playing, and Maria floated on the air as if lifted by the music. The languor of violins swept her and carried her aloft on the strains of Bach's Air on a G-string. She felt a sublime sense of levitation, as if her soul drifted with the melody. When she passed by a window, she heard a tapping on the windowpane that broke the spell of rapture. There, outside the window, she caught a glimpse of Gwen who was trying to catch her attention, signaling her to come outside. What now? Maria thought. Maria touched down from her levitation and discreetly tiptoed out to see what it was all about.

"Hi Maria. Sorry to intrude into your party, but you must come. They got Eln up a tree. Please hurry! Follow me."

Before she could find out more about it, Gwen took off into the darkness. Maria struggled to keep up with her. What's the nature of the emergency? Where are you taking me? And who is Eln?

"Gwen, slow down, please. I can't see in this darkness, and I can't keep up with you. Who is up a tree?"

"Are you Okay, Maria? We are almost there. See up in that tree by the curb? It's Eln. Two dogs got her treed. Here, take this stick. You'll need it to help me run off those dogs."

They reached the curb and a large Banyan tree not far from a streetlamp. At the base of its trunk, two dogs barked ferociously. Maria and Gwen swung at the dogs and shooed them away. Then Maria looked up and saw a lovely helpless little kitten meowing from a limb, calling for help, and crying for mama.

"You poor baby. I'll get you down."

Maria climbed up to a bifurcation on the trunk some four feet above the ground. From there she could stretch and almost reach the kitten.

"Come on sweetie, just two more feet closer to me. Those dogs are not going to hurt you now. I promise you. Mama is here."

It was then that Maria woke up, still reaching out while holding on, still feeling full of tenderness and full of fighting spirit, ready to take on the world to save a kitten in distress. But who was that kitten? She did not have a cat. And why would it seem so familiar, as if she knew who it was? On further reflection it became so obvious. Yes, she knew that kitten. And she knew those dogs also.

z   z   z   Z   z   z   z

PART V: REVELATIONS

22. Hidden Interludes

Sunday was a lazy day. Maria canceled her dinner with Karen Powers and family. Gwen was still delicate; she felt nauseous and weak, and Maria felt it would be prudent to stand by. Not much happened throughout the day and Maria retired early.

That evening when Maria awoke within her dream, she was in the conference room of the previous night. The girls started filing into the room in silhouettes.

"Well, hello, Maria!" one of them intoned as she sat down nearby. "Here we are again."

"Hello, ladies," responded Maria, "how nice to see your dark silhouettes again. You are not just invisible voices anymore and I like that. I like that very much. We're making progress. At this rate, one would think I might be seeing you in full living color by the end of the week. Huh? What do you think?"

Maria had spoken half-jokingly, just trying them out. She was, therefore, startled, and incredulous when she heard the response: "Maybe."

"Did you say 'maybe'?" Maria pressed. "Did I hear that right?"

"Perhaps even sooner than you think," added another.

"Oh, that's wonderful!" said Maria with great delight. "I am looking forward to that. I'm dying to see you all. Any time you're ready is fine with me."

"All in due time, my pretty. All in due time," said one of the shadows in a nasal twang, sounding like a witch for old time's sake.

Maria had been reclining lazily on her chair, but she suddenly bolted and sat erect to ask: "Who was that? Who was talking just then?"

"That was the Wicked Witch of the West," someone responded.

"No, no, no! That's who she was trying to sound like. I want to know who was doing the imitation. Was it Libby, or Maria Luisa, or Imogene? Who was she?"

"It was me, Sasha. I'm known around here as Miss Sarcasm, or Miss Sassy Cut Up, but my real name is Sasha."

"But I didn't know I had it in me to be sarcastic," noted Maria.

"That's because you succeed in suppressing me when you're awake, but here I have free rein. Here, you can't keep me under wraps any more than you can keep sex out of Libby. Some of us are the ghosts of your repressed instincts who are at last free to breathe and live."

"I'm sorry, Sasha. I don't mean to be tyrannical and I'm really glad to meet you," said Maria. "I'll try not to suppress you, if you promise to behave yourself and not get me in trouble during the day."

"Well, I will try...I shall do my best to fail," said Sasha.

Everybody laughed at that.

"Well, at least you're honest. I'll keep my guard up," retorted Maria.

The banter and laughter would have continued, but there was a clanking sound, like the tapping of a spoon on a tin can to get everyone's attention.

"May I have your attention please? May I have your attention?" she said officiously. "And, oh, by the way, Maria, I am Miss Diligence, the secretary, the timekeeper, the office manager that tries to keep these discussions on track. I need to remind everyone that if there is any item from today or the last few days that they would like to have included in today's dream, they should turn in their suggestions now. Thank you."

"Oh, but today was dead," said Maria. "All I did was hold Gwen's hand until we both got tired of each other. Even the television was boring. There was very little news. The stations re-ran mostly boilerplate stuff; and, of course, being Sunday, there was a lot of sports. It was sports ad nauseum in all channels. I really don't know. I don't think this day has anything to contribute."

"Oh, by the way, speaking of dreams, did you like the dream we sent you this morning?"

"The one about the kitten Eln? Oh yes, I liked it very much, thank you," replied Maria with genuine enthusiasm. "That was very clever of you. Who thought that up?"

"The usual culprits: Imogene and Ram, with the help of their assistants of course. That was done on short notice. It was a quickie."

"It was effective though," said Maria. "I got the point and liked it."

"Back to tonight," another voice interjected. "Did we finish talking about Rohypnol?"

The reply to that question came in a loud, unanimous chorus that declared emphatically: "Absolutely! Let's not go there tonight."

"Very well, your objection is noted. Are there any suggestions for the dream tonight from further back then?"

Maria spoke up. "You know, y'all confuse me," she began. "You talk about dreaming later as if I wasn't dreaming already. Is this not a dream? What do you call this? As far as I can tell this is a dream. Anybody would call this dreaming in my book, wouldn't you? In any case, what is this business about having a dream later? I am lost. Please clarify."

There was silence. Nobody uttered a sound. It was as if Maria had blurted out that the emperor had no clothes. The women whispered among themselves. Then a silhouette came from behind and standing in front of Maria began to address the point.

"This is Imogene speaking, Maria. I will address the issue you've brought up... And no, this is not a dream. This is one of those interludes of sleep that are lost to you because it is not being recorded for later viewing. The camera is off. It is dreaming of sorts, yes; but it is... how shall I put it? ... uninteresting, routine and banal. This is like a train ride to work where nothing worth remembering happens, just strangers reading their papers or idling away the time doing crossword puzzles; or this is like the ride on the elevator on your way to the office. Unless there is an accident, there is nothing to report. Nobody ever asks you: what happened on the train on your way to work today? Or how was the elevator ride on the way to the office? People will ask you: what happened at work today? What did you do at the office? That's when the cameras are on. This is not the memorable part of your sleep session."

Imogene continued. "You could think of this as a workshop, or an in-house period of sleep when we carry out certain chores and prepare the dream that we will record and serve you later. Here, we discuss the events of the day and prepare the little skits that you will remember as dreams when you wake up. That dream time is still hours away and takes place usually within the last few minutes before awakening."

Sasha broke in and added: "It happens that sometimes you wake up suddenly in the middle of the night and you can't help remembering what you last saw. That is an accident. You get glimpses of these sessions, but you're not supposed to have them."

"You know," said Maria, "I had suspected as much. In fact, I think I can tell you when I got one of those dreams that I was not meant to have. It was that dream with Janet Reno and Professor Quixote, wasn't it?"

"Yep, that's right."

"But why not? Why so secretive? What's the problem?"

"That is a long story. There is so much you need to learn, and we have just begun. Don't rush it. We are making progress. Give us credit for trying to meet you halfway."

"Yes, I do recognize your goodwill and your efforts, and I appreciate it," added Maria. "I'm not being critical, and I don't mean to rush you. It's just that I'm in darkness about so much."

"We're aware of that, and we're working on it. Bear with us."

"May I ask you a question?" Maria continued. "Are you enjoined from taping or releasing these proceedings? Do you have orders, or what?"

"No. There are no orders as such. This is the sort of thing you should discuss with higher authorities, with people like Dr. Broca, Professor Quixote or Ram."

"You mean I can ask them about this?" asked Maria excitedly. "I can't wait! I would love to talk to them about it. In fact, if talking to them is part of the workshop, then the heck with the cartoons and skits, keep the dreams. Give me the workshops."

"Now, now, Maria. Don't you go putting down our artistic endeavors as cartoons! We put a lot of effort into our dreams, you know."

Maria apologized and gave an explanation. "I'm sorry. I didn't mean the way it sounded. It's just that I prefer the spontaneity of the intellectual discussions to dreams."

"Do you, really?" asked Imogene. "I wonder about that… would you prefer it even if you knew it is not being recorded? We do not record it because it would involve hours and hours of shoptalk, of silly inconsequential chatter. It would be such a waste. You would be bored to death if we recorded it. You would tell us spare me that, please. In any case, you could have no more than three or four minutes of that because that is the limit of sleep memory. Either way, whether workshop or dreams, you don't get much more than that."

"This is so unfair. This is awful."

"It is what it is."

"It is all so dumb!" Maria complained. "Who decrees that limitation? Who is in charge of allotting dream memory around here?"

"God, or nature, whichever you prefer. That's the way the world is. That's the way memory works. And I don't know whom you'd see to change it. You have to accept things as they are."

"Well, I still think I would opt for the discussion, especially if I could talk with Dr. Broca and Professor Quixote."

"Even if you could remember only snippets the next day? You would feel so frustrated by the truncated discussion. It wouldn't make any sense. You would rail against the torture of being teased with ideas that went nowhere and weren't concluded."

"Oh, this is horrible. You say that I can only remember minutes out of hours of sleep, that all of this is not being recorded and it will be forgotten. I will not remember you tomorrow."

"Sadly, yes."

Maria stood up and looked around. The silhouettes were still sitting around her. Finally, after some hesitation, she said to herself: What the heck, the worst they can do is to turn me down. Then she addressed them with resolve and asked them.

"Do you suppose it would be possible to turn on the lights so I could see you now? I don't see the purpose of the darkness, especially since I won't remember anything. What's the point of hiding anything then?"

Maria could hear a hubbub of whispered voices discussing as in a caucus. Then the voices quieted, and Imogene made the announcement.

"We have discussed it and have decided that you have a point. Since you can't take it with you, we agree with you: what difference would it make? So, you will be glad to know we have agreed to turn on the lights and let you see us. I warn you though, you should cover your eyes and open them gradually to protect them from the sudden light. It could be uncomfortable."

"Thank you, thank you. Oh, I do appreciate it. Don't worry about me. I'll be careful. I'll close my eyes and open them gradually... Just say when... I am ready."

Z   z   z   z   z   z   Z

23. Lights on Full Blast

The lights came on. Maria opened her eyes slowly, squinting, adjusting her pupils to the bright light. The conference room had turned into a huge prism with mirrors everywhere that replicated images several times, expanding them in reflections upon reflections that gave the illusion of a bottomless indefinite space. Maria gasped when she saw the myriad images around her. So many Marias cast reflections like optical arpeggios! As she looked in any single direction, she would find countless images unfolding in the interlocking polygons in fading perspective, like mirrors reflecting mirrors. How clever, Maria thought. I should have guessed it. This is the heart of the mind, and it is a gem, a diamond with all its facets revealed at once!

The more Maria observed, the more bewildered she became. There were so many inexplicable nuances. The images of her, though similar, could not be reflections because they were not identical. Her clones exhibited differences in the fabric and the color of their dress; or they sat in different poses; or they wore different hairdos. The view was overwhelming. Maria said aloud: "This can't be multiple reflections. It's more like multiple visions. I feel like a strange bug with a thousand eyes." She had to look down at her own lap to avoid catching that dizzying visual effect of receding mirror images that overwhelmed her senses. She turned slightly to her right in the direction of one of her clones who was conservatively dressed in the manner of an airline stewardess, with a navy-blue suit and a white blouse, like Luisa in Libby's movie. Maria, on the other hand, was wearing her white night gown. Luisa was wearing glasses, Maria was not.

Then Maria addressed the clone next to her to ask her a favor. "Luisa, or Maria Luisa, or whoever you are, would you be so kind and dim the lights again please? This is getting a little uncomfortable."

"Yes, of course. But before that, let's just get it over with so you won't have to go through this again and let me show you the rest of us."

"You mean there's more?" asked Maria incredulous.

"Oh yes, much more. I am going to drop the first tier of mirrors now so you can see everybody."

Suddenly the small chamber expanded even more, exposing an immense complex reminiscent of a sports arena, or a hangar, or an industrial warehouse. Whatever it was, it was huge and bright as a football field. There must have been thousands of people around her. Maria stood up on a stool so she could survey the multitude. Now she could see Janet Reno, Don Quixote, the Wicked Witch of the West from the Wizard of Oz, a tootsie-looking femme-fatal type with a French beret, Gwen holding a cat named Eln, Elena, two dogs, Wally, Toro, Mildred Colson, her family, and many other people she did not immediately recognize.

Stunned by the brightness, Maria gazed around panning the large crowd, briefly focusing on each person as she turned. "I am so confused. We started from a small conference room and now look at this; it has expanded beyond all credible limits, as if that were possible, as if it were elastic and could stretch itself to any length. I had expected only clones, mirror images of myself… but, oh, this is so confusing."

Professor Quixote came to help Maria get off the chair. "Come down my Dulcinea. We will explain it all to you."

"Ah, you are so chivalrous."

"Would you like to go back to the small conference room now? It is much cozier."

"Oh yes, yes, most definitely. I would. I really would," she said as she fell backward fainting. Professor Quixote caught her just in time.

Z z z Z z z Z z z

24. Denizens of the Mind at Night

Maria was escorted out of the bright super dome with her eyes smarting from the glare, her hands clasping her face, covering her eyes from the bright light. As they led her out, she could hear the remonstrance of accusing, chiding whispers around her... That was not a good idea.... I told you it would upset her....

"I'll be all right. I am okay now," Maria assured them repeatedly, apologizing at the same time. "I am sorry I put you into so much trouble."

"That's okay Maria. It was partly our fault also. We shouldn't have presented the whole shebang to you quite the way we did. We showed you more than you could cope with. We definitely mishandled it."

"Thank you for indulging me. I didn't realize I was asking for more than I could manage."

"The incredible thing is that you didn't wake up."

"Yes, isn't it?"

The other Marias found her a seat. Once again Maria settled comfortably into the twilight darkness of that cozy conference room where she had been earlier. Vision was not nearly as important as conversation without seeing her interlocutors clearly. Their silhouettes, their aura sufficed.

"Are you comfortable now, Maria?" asked Professor Quixote.

"Oh, yes. Thank you so much," replied Maria. "There is one thing I would trouble you with...Could you find Dr. Broca for me?"

"Certainly. He is making his way right now."

Maria was delighted when she felt his hand press her arm and her hand. "Hello Miss Diaz, how are you?" said Dr. Broca in a soft voice that Maria immediately recognized.

"Oh, Dr. Broca, so good to see you. I thought I had lost you. I am so glad you are here. I need you again."

Dr. Broca took a seat beside her and held her hand reassuringly.

"It's good to see you. I am glad to be of help."

"I don't know where to begin, doctor. I have a thousand questions. Just then, all those people, all those clones, those mirror images of myself, those familiar and unfamiliar faces, those strangers, and that excruciatingly bright light, they were all just overwhelming. It's as if I had peeked into the caverns of Dante and had seen a million souls on parade. Was that the population of the entire world in my brain?

"No, heavens, no!" corrected Dr. Broca. "It was, however, the entire population of your memory."

"My dream world… So big? So vast? It seems incredible that it could be assembled for inspection in a single place, not to mention that it could be gathered within the confines of my little brain."

"Yes, but remember, your mind is infinite. The chambers of your brain may be finite and small, but it can project a mindscape as boundless as the sky. That inner stadium you just saw is capable of expanding to the end of vision, if necessary, all within your head."

"Incredible!" exclaimed Maria in astonishment. "How vast the mind is. I see it, but I can't believe it."

"Yes, it is something of an overload. They should not have shown you the totality of that world the way they did, with those bright lights, with the squadrons of clones all lined up like the Russian Army on Red Square, with your eccentric characters in costumes like the patients of an insane asylum out on a fire drill. If I had been consulted, I would not have permitted raising the curtain of your mind that way. I want to be on record dissociating myself from that decision."

"All right, already. That's enough," said a female voice with some petulance. "What's done is done. Maria insisted and wouldn't have rested until she saw it all. It was bound to happen sooner or later. Now it's over with! Let's move on. Let's not turn this into a federal case."

That stirred up quite a debate. Some laughed and cheered the outspoken speaker, but others were critical for the disrespectful tone with Dr. Broca. He, for his part, apologized and managed to cool the situation. When everyone calmed down, he tuned to Maria. "As you can see, this place can get testy at times. But let's get back to your questions. What was it you wanted to ask me?"

"I wanted you to describe the people I just saw," Maria began. "Start by clarifying their nature, their numbers…their role…"

"Let me see. I don't know about the quantity. It's virtually infinite. As to their nature it consists, basically, of three parts: the population of your memory from the real world, the population from your dream experiences and the constituents of your own psyche. You can think of what you just saw as the living telephone book of all your connections. This includes friends, acquaintances, relatives, strangers and even people you don't like; in brief, people who have made an impression on you for good or ill. But I think you are more interested in that third element which is the elements of your own persona. Do you remember the gremlins and witches that you were so anxious to meet? Well, here they are! I hope you are not disappointed if they don't look like monsters."

"Oh, no, I am delighted."

"These witches and gremlins are more difficult to describe. Visually they are easy to recognize. They are all young women like you. These would be the young ladies like Libby, Sasha, Maria Luisa and the other Marias. What's difficult to describe about them is their nature and their status. They are not exactly all equal. They each have their own spheres of influence and power. Some of them are your personality traits. Still others are more basic, being personifications of your instincts, of your raw, primeval animal reflexes. They are around you ready to beat you to the punch and be the first to react to something. Others are male like me, Ram and Professor Quixote. We are your oracles and trouble shooters. Our final recourse in this environment."

The doctor looked around and whispered an aside so as not to be heard, saying: "*Some of the witches think they rank very high-- higher than muses even. They think they are goddesses, no less.*"

Then Dr. Broca resumed normal volume, saying: "I have to watch my tongue around here, mind you, so as not to step on any toes. You have seen how volatile moods can be around here. I don't want to demote anybody, but I don't want to exalt anybody either."

"Ah, Dr. Broca, it's so good to hear you again. It seems ages since we last talked in this fabulous dome. This place is fantastic. One minute it is weird, bizarre, incomprehensible, then the next minute it is so natural, so logical… so sensible. You have clarified so much for me already. I think it will take me a little time, but I'll figure things out on my own as we go along. Maybe you can tell me more about it later in your office."

"As you wish. I was about finished anyway. There is not much to add except to say that these young ladies are like contestants at a beauty pageant. In time they will define themselves by their actions and you will get to know them. You'll be able to tell Ms. Impatience from Ms. Sarcasm. You'll know Ms. Get-even, Ms. Envy, Ms. Kindness, Ms. Petulance, and Ms. Congeniality."

"Oh yes, I know a few of them already. They've already made their mark. But I would like to get to know them better. I don't mind if they are impetuous at times. I am getting used to being overpowered by them here. Of course, when I am awake and out in public, I am in total control. All in all, quite honestly, I feel privileged to have met everyone. I love the exposure to this hidden part of my life. This is so grand, so marvelous. But there is one more entity that I would like to ask you about before I let you go. What about conscience? What can you tell me about her? Is she here now?"

"Ah, yes, conscience! She is definitely complicated. She is difficult to pin down because she is a chameleon. She can take any form she likes. There is no telling how she chooses to present herself in dreams. At times, when all is right with the world, she may take an unassuming form, something ordinary like a cat purring beside you lovingly, or a faithful dog standing by his master, making no judgment, no criticism. She will make you feel a little smug even. But when she is disturbed and wants to settle a score with you, she chooses an overbearing human form. She will appear as someone above you and unimpeachable, someone with authority scowling at you, a priest, a policeman, a professor, a parent, a judge, or even the Attorney General of the United States."

Maria was beaming, laughing. "Yes, I know exactly what you mean. I have seen her. She appeared to me as Janet Reno. She really did. Oh, but do continue, Dr. Broca. I interrupted you."

"Did you see Guilt also?" Dr. Broca asked her, "because guilt is another master of disguises that follows conscience around. She is so protean that there is no telling what form she'll adopt to succeed in her mission of making you pay. She is after her pound of flesh, her due of remorse and she will extract every ounce of regret from you till she wrings you dry, and you atone. She is like a vampire after blood. She can be a buzzard hovering in circles stalking you, or a shadow you cannot shake; or a tail that you suddenly grow, that is swishing around while you are desperately trying to hide it and kick it between your legs. And then there are other complex creatures such as pride, female vanity and conceit. For such creatures there aren't enough props and costumes in the kingdom of Hollywood to accommodate them!"

Maria laughed good-naturedly. "Oh, surely you exaggerate Dr. Broca. We are not that vain. But, oh, I just thought of something! Tell me: is this ability to see the inner workings of my mind during sleep a rare experience? Or is this a common phenomenon, something everyone experiences every night?"

"At the risk of seeming equivocal, I would answer 'yes' and 'no.' It's like the tree in the forest I told you about. Do you remember?

"Vaguely. So, tell me again."

"If a tree falls in the middle of a forest and there is no one there to witness it, does the tree make a sound? How can anyone argue that it did if they weren't there? So, also, if people have dreams that they cannot remember when they wake up, how can they vouch for what they can't remember? This is a catch-22, a philosophical trap. Let me see if Professor Quixote wants to add something here. Don, would you like to add your thoughts to this question?"

"Hello, Maria," said Professor Quixote in his mellow baritone voice.

"Hello, Sir. I have been dying to talk to you ever since I heard you in that meeting where you talked about your algorithm on dream sequencing. I love to ask you about that and so many other things. Oh, this is marvelous. I love it."

"I am at your service, Maria. It will be a pleasure. But the answer to your question is a bit tricky. How common is this experience? I would conjecture that it is very common. We all hear distant voices at times, both awake and asleep. They are like intimation, hints of nebulous things. You are not the only one that comes alive in fading fleeting episodes. You probably have company, but don't make too much of that because as Dr. Broca just mentioned, we are not talking about ordinary dreams but unremembered dreams, wanderings of the mind that were not recorded and which, in any case, were doomed to be forgotten.

We know that people dream but we're not privy to those dreams. Neurologists have come up with ways to monitor brain activity during sleep. People do think during sleep. In addition, there is ample anecdotal evidence that problems get solved during sleep; that mathematicians go to bed stumped by a problem only to wake up with a solution miraculously at hand; that lost items are mysteriously found after a good night's sleep. But, at the same time make no mistake about it, the details of this nocturnal magic are lost on everyone."

Maria suddenly interrupted. "Yes, but what about the professionals who study the mind, the hypnologists, the psychologists and psychiatrists, what do they have to say about this? Would they be able to report on their own sleep experiences?"

"How? Why should they be any different? They would run into the same wall as everybody else. It is true that they are very familiar with these premises because they make it their business to study the mind. They have developed ways to observe the brain during sleep, and they can tell that something is going on, but they are not privy to other people's dreams, and they cannot remember their own. It's like they stand outside the theater knowing that a play is taking place inside, but they couldn't tell you whether it is a comedy or a tragedy. They couldn't quote dialogue. They couldn't describe the scenery. They are out of the show all together--except for the dreams that the dreamer remembers when he wakes up."

"Fascinating! But let me move on to another question now," said Maria. "Let me ask you: Why now? And why me? Why have I been allowed at this time to enter the hallowed premises of my subconscious?"

Dr. Broca picked up on the question. "We could not have kept it from you, Miss Diaz. Most people don't care about this sort of thing; but you have an inquisitive mind that won't let up, and you have been knocking at the doors so hard lately. Sooner or later, you were bound to break the barriers and walk right into the inner sanctum of your mind. Do you remember the other night in the dome when you were so intent in finding us? I had to stall you off because you weren't ready for us then, and besides, there was no time for this sort of thing that night. You had less than an hour of sleep left then. You are very thorough, very analytical, very introspective, and above all very, very persistent, Miss Diaz. This may account for the uniqueness of your situation. As to the timing, perhaps this was precipitated by the unfortunate incident of your neighbor Gwen. It got the attention of all the girls here. They were dying to get involved in that case. No army and no power known to man could have stopped them."

"That makes sense," allowed Maria. "At least, something good came out of that."

"And then there is this," added Professor Quixote. "I am reminded of a scene in Dante's Inferno where someone says: If we thought we would be stealing secrets from Providence and betraying confidences, we would be mum. But because no one ever left these premises to talk about them, we can open all doors and answer any questions you may have. Similarly, we can be open and magnanimous about these premises since we know your memory will fail you."

"Bummer!" said Maria. "I was just going to argue that I have rights to the debates and discussions that take place here. Anything I dream in my own bed, within the confines of my own skull is mine and mine to keep. I stand by that! I hope the powers-that-be here are taking note of this. I'm entitled to them and one way or another I am going to take them."

"Well, Miss Diaz, I don't think there's anything you can do about it and being defiant is not going to get you anything."

"I will still try."

"Dear Miss Diaz, there are mysteries all around us. And this is a big one! The mystery of human memory ranks so high that it is way up with the mysteries of human fate. You might as well ask: Why are humans so privileged above all other animals with the marvels of language? Why are we the only ones that can speak and write? Why can we expand our memory and add to our data base of knowledge through education? Of course, the brain is the answer to all these questions, but the brain still keeps many, many mysteries. The issues dealing with memory and intelligence are as transcendental as providential justice. This is not something that can be answered simply and briefly. But I'll be willing to wager that you will not stop trying to get answers to this. There is no stopping you. But all in due time, Miss Diaz; all in due time. Don't try to know everything at once. Perhaps the good professor can add something to this."

"Before you answer, Professor Quixote, could you each clarify your domains of concern for me?" María demanded.

z   z   z   Z   z   z   z

25. PROF. QUIXOTE AND DR. BROCA

Dr. Broca was the first to respond to Maria's question saying: "My area is neurology. I study the human brain, the functions of its various parts. I can also address questions dealing with the nature of sleep, but not from a philosophical point. I do not concern myself with questions that deal with the purpose of sleep or other transcendental issues. Don here could talk to you about that."

Then Professor Quixote spoke. "I deal with those transcendental aspects of sleep. I accept that sleep is a physiological imperative; that Nature must obey necessity, as Shakespeare put it. But then, how much sleep is enough? Is too much sleep a bad thing? Is too little sleep a good thing? If it were possible to reduce sleep without suffering significant ill-effects, should we strive for that? What exactly would we gain from sleeping less? Would we necessarily achieve more in life? Would sleeping less change the character of our lives? Could we even say that the extra hours of consciousness gained would lengthen, in some way, our life? Or, for that matter, should we lengthen sleep by hibernation for months, or even years at a time a la Rip Van Winkle, so that all in all we would live for 200 years before finally dying? Is that the way to cheat our mortal fate out of a few years? Then there are other questions which seem on first blush extraneous to sleep, but which are at the root of our beliefs in the hereafter. Do dreams give us a view of our soul in action? And is that view of our soul a preview of what we may see after death? I could go on with a thousand questions of this nature, but I'll wait my turn. Now you should continue with my colleague. It's his turn."

Maria was gushing with emotion, fascinated and delighted by these issues. She was truly enjoying the conversation. "I find this absolutely fascinating. I love it. Why couldn't I meet both of you gentlemen like this in the real world? Or why couldn't I tape this session? I know, I know. I've been told that's not possible.

Don't scowl at me for trying. It's just that this is my idea of a great dream and I so wish I could remember it. But, okay, I'll get back to my question. I was going to ask you about the nature of the representations, specifically, for example, about the use of gender. Why do we have male personifications for some things, and females for others? I can understand the clones. I can see Miss Impatience, Miss Sarcasm, and the like. The mirror images of me are easy. I can also see the symbols and metaphors such as the kitten for my protégé, Elena; Janet Reno as a surrogate for conscience, and the like. What I cannot understand are the more complex characters, such as you, in fact, Dr. Broca."

"Me? Humm, why? Because I'm male?"

"Yes, in part."

Doctor Broca paused and collected his thoughts. "Well, let's see if we can clarify this a bit. As to the gender of the characters, that should come as no surprise to you. Even someone as ignorant of biology as you, Miss Diaz, knows that all human beings have male and female chromosomes in their makeup. So, I suppose I represent a male trait of your persona. I suppose I was chosen to impart credibility and authoritativeness to the subject matter. Who better to show you the hippocampus, the limbic system, and the Anterior Cingulate, if not a doctor? Now it is true that there are female doctors and scientists. That cannot be denied. But how many of them have you known? Credibility requires that the characters be taken from your own set of expectations."

Maria was restless. "That's exactly what I had thought," she said, interrupting him. "But there is more to my question. It's just that I am having difficulty articulating it. Let me see how I can put it. It's not your gender or your age that troubles me, it's your knowledge, your being a medical doctor. I don't know how to reconcile my ignorance of medicine with your knowledge of it. How independent can our minds be? How, I ask, being a character of my dreams and, therefore, limited to the knowledge of my mind, could you know more of a subject than me? How could you know what I do not know: anatomy, physiology, and neurology? It seems to me that your medical knowledge could be no greater than my own. You cannot possibly know what I know I do not know. Does that make sense? I am so confused…"

Dr. Broca coughed trying to hide his discomfort, mumbling something like "Oh, boy! Ooh-la-la". If Maria could have seen him, she would have seen that he was embarrassed, distressed and wordless, almost to the point of puckering like an offended baby simpering, about to cry.

Maria continued. "This would make sense to me if I were told that you were not really a doctor, but an actor playing the part; that you merely appear to be one in your white lab overcoat and are appropriately aged, but all that is just for effect, to make you a symbol of authority, but in reality you know no more medicine than I do. How could you? You are part of my mind and I know I never studied medicine."

Professor Quixote broke in then. "Yes, but if you knew that he is not really a doctor, but an actor, then you would lose respect for him. He would be no more than a rag doll to you. You would feel as if you could learn nothing from him. You would tire of your dream. You would feel as empty and unchallenged as if you were playing solitaire."

Dr. Broca was swallowing hard and perspiring, wiping his forehead nervously as Maria had seen him do when he was flustered and embarrassed. Then a stern voice broke in to rescue him. It spoke with a commanding tone.

"That's enough, Maria. You are going to make poor Dr. Broca cry here in a minute. If you are wondering who I am, this is your conscience. But don't bother to turn on the light to see me, because I choose not to be seen. I am interceding here to let you know that you are only half right about your conclusions, especially as they concern Dr. Broca, whom you have just managed to denude to insignificance. Your concept of knowledge in this context is flawed. You are thinking of your mind as if it was the Universal Set, and everybody else's mind were subsets of it. No one could know more than you. The statement: 'You cannot possibly know what I know I do not know' has roar, but it is pure rhetoric and reflects your misunderstanding. In the first place, and get this straight, knowledge as such is irrelevant here. So, piff puff, throw your encyclopedias and your diplomas out the window! What matters here is Belief. You judge the world by what you believe, and you believe what we want you to believe. Belief trumps everything. So, never mind the business that Dr. Broca cannot know more than you know. You are wrong there. You are losing sight of the fact that he is not one of your clones. Not everyone you see here is necessarily just a defragmented component of Maria Diaz. Some people are real. Dr. Broca certainly is. He is here in an independent capacity. Therefore, he can know more than you, and he does. This Dr. Broca speaks Polish, and you do not. He knows surgery, anatomy, physiology, neurology, and you do not; in short, although he is in your dream, his mind is his own and he transcends the limitations of your mind. He knows infinitely more than what you know you do not know. So, now restore Dr. Broca to his previous good standing. That's all."

If Maria could have seen the old doctor now, she would have seen him standing proud, straightening his tie and pulling down his coat lapels, as if saying: "There!"

"Well, I guess you told me." Maria conceded feebly.

"Doesn't she always?" Sasha twitted amid giggles.

"I hope I didn't hurt you Dr. Broca. Please don't take it personally. I wasn't really questioning your credentials. I really didn't mean any harm with my questions. I was just confused about so much," added Maria.

"…Anything in the interest of understanding, Miss Diaz. The important thing is that you be all clear now."

Then conscience spoke again. Let me expand on the nature of the people you see here. Take Janet Reno for example, whom you have seen in these premises earlier. She was who she is, which is to say, no part of you. Some people are who they are. They are just making cameo appearances here. You wouldn't think of questioning her the way you questioned Dr. Broca, because you know Janet Reno from the real world. But you did not know Dr. Broca in the real world. You met him here and, apparently, took him to be a part of you, as Sasha and Libby are. That's why you had difficulty accepting his gender and his knowledge. Incidentally, that's also why Libby was able to wow you with her mathematical knowledge and dupe you into watching her movie. She knows as much math as you do."

"That makes sense," Maria noted. "It clears up things."

Then conscience added another disturbing observation. "The truth is that you will never really know whether Dr. Broca is or is not a real doctor because you cannot conduct tests. Dreams don't give you that much latitude. You have to flow with their intent. Actually, this is not as bad as it sounds, because you largely set the pace and direction of this flow. It works like this. We know what you want. We always do, and we try to accommodate you as much as possible. For example, we knew you wanted to get inside your mind at night and study sleep from within. That's why we came up with Dr. Broca and Professor Quixote in the first place. We looked in your database to see who you admired and who you had contempt for. And, I might add, that in the case of contempt you had battalions, my dear; but in the case of admiration, you were almost empty. Aside from Shakespeare and mathematicians, only philosophers and neurologists were your heroes. That's where Dr. Broca figured in. But the philosophers could not be of the BS-variety that blabber aphorisms that go nowhere. They had to have their feet planted firmly on the ground and know their stuff. That's why Prof. Quixote is both a mathematician and a philosopher—in addition to other things such as a poet, a composer and a polyglot."

Maria was delighted with the way things were being resolved, especially with respect to Dr. Broca. She could not contain her emotion, so she got up and approached him.

"Dr. Broca, I am so sorry for being so awkward with my questions. I wish I could have put them in a better way. I want to give you a hug."

Maria embraced the soft, shadowy bulk. The two shadows came together in the room fusing into a larger, darker lump in the twilight. After a brief pause allowing time for Maria to finish paying her respects, the secretary, Ms. Diligence, spoke.

"Well now, I suppose we move on to another subject," she said hesitantly. "And I would guess that that would be Professor Quixote's turn. But do we have enough time? As you may know, Maria has declined to have a dream this morning, but even so, her wakeup time is on the horizon."

Maria was suddenly hit by a great idea that she couldn't keep from sharing. She interrupted Miss Diligence with great excitement.

"Listen everybody! ...I've just had a great idea..." she began. "I'll tell you what. Oh, this is fantastic! I really want to know what you think about this. You have asked me before for input into the making of my dreams, right? Well, I must admit that I have been a little blasé and disinterested in it. But I want to take you up on that now. Does your offer still stand? If you are disposed to accommodate me, then I would like to put in a request. Shall I tell you what I want to dream about this morning?"

"Well yes, of course. We value your input. What's your pleasure?"

"I want a dream with everything that has transpired here tonight embedded in it. I don't care how you dress it up. It doesn't have to be in color; black and white is fine with me. You can skip the background music. You can even shorten it a bit while keeping the ideas, the arguments and counterarguments. As far as I am concerned, this is what is of value in these sleep sessions."

Conscience protested vehemently at Maria's suggestion. "Damn it, Maria. That's cheating! You know you are not supposed to take these sessions with you. You've been told about that."

"You are trying to get around the ban. That's very clever of you. But it won't work." "It can't be done."

"Why is it impossible? Maria inquired. "Who is forbidding

it? Do you have written orders? What's the problem?"

Dr. Broca stood up and said: "Boy, oh boy! I am glad this is not in my department. I am glad I don't have to answer this one. I suspect there are going to be some fireworks here. I have to go now. But before I go, just let me say one thing to you, Miss Diaz: You be cool. Stay calm."

Maria asked Dr. Broca to stay a little longer, but she could not have persuaded him to stay for anything. He was eager to get away from there and hand over the hot potato to his colleague.

z   z   Z   Z   Z   z   z

26. AN IMPOSSIBLE REQUEST

The air was tense and charged for imminent explosion. As soon as Dr. Broca left, the silhouettes started scurrying around excitedly as if they knew there was going to be a confrontation between Maria and her conscience. Conscience had called her a cheat and Maria did not like being called a cheat—not even from conscience. This was not the first time she had wrestled with her conscience. On occasions Maria had won against her because conscience tended to react too soon and be quick on the trigger. She was also too conservative. Maria did not mind taking orders as long as they were not arbitrary. But ukases without rhyme or reason she would fight, even if they came from the highest powers-that-be. With respect to this issue, they had to at least tell her what was wrong with her request.

"Ooooh, I just love a fight! I'm going to get me some popcorn and a ring-side seat," said one of the silhouettes as she rushed by

"There is no popcorn here, you idiot," shouted another.

"Oh yes, there is," cried back the first one. "It may be virtual popcorn, but it's just as good as the real thing."

Professor Quixote caught a sense of the charged atmosphere and noted the scurrying and jockeying for position to orchestrate a fight. He acted immediately, disappointing everyone by announcing loudly and firmly that he would not stand for any scuffles. His voice resonated in the chamber as he spoke.

"Okay everybody, pay attention, settle down and be quiet! There's not going to be any fighting here tonight. We are going to resolve the misunderstanding in a calm and civilized manner. If you wish to speak, wait your turn, and leave out the sass and the put-downs. Is that clear? Or we just may have to turn off the power to the whole kit and caboodle and put us all in hibernation for a while, with no dream, no workshop, no nothing. Is that clear?"

At the sound of that word, hibernation,' everyone gasped; it sent a chill up their spines. It was the dreaded word that conjured up deprivation and punishment. It meant a coma, a deathly sleep for everyone. Everybody quieted and settled down. Silence reigned in the twilight once again and Professor Quixote wasted no time in getting to the point with Maria.

"Okay, Maria, I am not sure how much you've been told about sleep memory. In any case, your request is out of line. It is the equivalent of you going to an 'All-You-Can-Eat Restaurant,' backing up a truck, and asking if you can have it 'To-Go.' That just can't be. Let me try to explain to you what's involved here. This is no ordinary run-of-the-mill dream you are having. This is much too long for that. What's more, this segment of your sleep is disconnected from your long-term memory. You won't remember any of these proceedings tomorrow because the cameras and camcorders here have very little tape, very little film."

Maria interrupted him and asked him boldly: "Well then, why can't you just find more film and tape? What's the problem?"

"I knew you would ask that. How like a child to ask for the moon and the stars. Trouble is, this is not like your world where you can just go downtown or to Walmart to get supplies. You are marooned in a barren world like the dark side of the moon. You have to go with what you have. There is no film, or tape, or paper or pencils. The only thing you have is a small receptacle for memory, a thimble's worth that can hold at most five minutes. It's like the short length of tape you have on your recording devices which is being taped and re-taped, over and over. So, even if we wanted to accommodate you by putting these proceedings in a dream, the most that we could salvage would be the last five minutes before you woke up.

"Do not confuse conscious memory with sleep memory. Sleep memory is short and in-augmentable. Conscious memory is long lasting, elastic and expandable. It grows to accept whatever you cram into it. You start feeding it in kindergarten and continue to a PhD and beyond. It can accommodate three or four foreign languages. Some people have immense memory receptacles made of steel; others have memory receptacles that are like sieves. What you must understand is that the limitations of sleep memory are imposed by nature. It's the way we are made. To put it in perspective: we cannot make the day longer than 24 hours; we cannot fly, although birds can; we cannot live under water like fish; we cannot move faster than the speed of light; we cannot make you immortal; and we cannot expand sleep memory. The small amount of memory serves us well. We were not meant to spend our lives asleep. To make something of ourselves and to succeed in life we have to work during our conscious hours. That is our arena. And that is why, on average, we are awake for two thirds of each day. We sleep for only a third.

"From your questions I gather that you think somebody is giving orders, forbidding you to transfer memories. There are no such orders. This is simply a limitation of nature."

Maria felt drained and disappointed. "I hear you. I understand what you're telling me, and I accept it reluctantly and with great reservations. It hurts me to think of the colossal waste! To think that none of this will be remembered! There must be a way! Why have any discussions then? What good does it do? I will look for a way around this curse."

The professor corrected her. "First of all, I am not so sure that these proceedings are all wasted. I do believe that in some way much of this is transferred to long term memory. How do you know, for example, that what you hear during these sessions is not an echo, a replay from your long-term memory? In that case, why tape then what you already have? Secondly, I believe that we do manage to wake up with bits and pieces of what transpires here. Over a long period of time, these distilled nuggets, these bits and pieces add up to a vision. Finally, I believe sleep memory is scarce because its purpose is more limited. Its purpose is not to foster learning or advance new knowledge. Its purpose is basically to sort, to compile and to archive what you already have. The harvesting of data, the learning, and the absorption of new knowledge occurs when you are awake, when you embrace the world with all your senses, when your eyes and ears are open and your conscious analytical valves are all open full throttle. Then it is when you need all the memory capacity you have to be at your disposal. Some night, when we have more time, I will elaborate on this."

"Thank you, Professor Quixote. I would love to know more about it. I am also sorry that my suggestion caused such a ruckus. When I asked for these proceedings to be embedded within my dreams, I was not trying to cheat. It seemed like a logical solution to me. I thought the hang-up against doing such a simple thing was due to capriciousness and bureaucracy. I didn't know how this place worked. I wasn't trying to cheat."

"I know, I know," said Professor Quixote reassuring her. "You don't need to apologize to me about that. It's been a misunderstanding. Nobody here really believes that you are a cheat, although they may carry on that way just to harass you."

Some of the shadows got up from their seats. There was a milling around of silhouettes passing by like clouds, disgruntled clouds, disappointed and grumbling clouds. One of them whined as she went by: "Just when I thought we were going to romp and have fun, the intellectuals have to spoil it all."

"It's back to sleep for us, Kiddo," said another.

"This place is getting boring," said still another.

"Wait for me. I'm coming, too."

Several of the silhouettes left the room. As Professor Quixote sat by, consoling Maria, he had a parting shot for the Marias that were walking out.

"Hey ladies, comeback! I'm not going to give you a math lecture…I promise—just a little philosophy, maybe, and that's if you behave. Geez! Look at them go."

"Well, let them go," said Maria. "Pay no attention to them. I'm looking forward to talking to you, even if I can't record it, and even if it will all be forgotten. Deep down I agree with you that it is not a waste; that something good does come of it. Somehow, in some mysterious ways we do become wiser through these unremembered experiences."

"Actually, there was nothing wrong with your request. You do take bits of these proceedings night after night. The trouble was that you wanted too much. You asked for everything, and that is definitely out of the question. But small portions, distillations of the gist of things encoded into dreams that you can keep, that's do-able and it is legal. It is done all the time."

"But isn't that like draining the ocean one tablespoon at a time?"

"So, what if it is? Don't think of how little a spoonful of water is. Think about how much it means to somebody that has none. If you had it in your power to grant one more day of life to someone who would die in the prime of his life, would you deny it on the grounds that one day was too little? Sometimes it is best to measure the gift of precious things that are given in small quantities by the potential regret of not having them at all. That regret could be immense. Those bits of dreams that you are allowed to keep can be as significant as the little tiles with which you make a mural. A tile here and a tile there, can make a magnificent picture. So, take it one night at a time, one dream at a time, one tile at a time. Record the dreams that you do remember, because those are the little tiles that over time will give you a broad view of what transpires here."

"Thank you, Professor Quixote. Thank you so much. I appreciate your good advice. I just hope the girls do a good job of distilling the essence of our discussions into my dream morsels. Maybe they will put the essence of some of these discussions in the dream nuggets they concoct for me when I wake up."

"Yes. Let's call it a night. I will be curious to see what dream the girls cook up to capture the essence of the night's proceedings. But trust me, they'll come up with something. It might be a good idea if you kept a diary of your dreams when you first get up. Pull in your net every morning from the sea of sleep and go through the catch of the night."

"Will you remind me if I forget?" Maria asked teasingly.

"Don't think that because you are far from me when you are awake that I can't reach you. I might surprise you. You just listen out for me in your wakeful hours. My voice may be faded, drowned out by the din of all your doings under the sun, but I'll come across from the dark side of the moon."

They did not discuss much more that night. The "girls," as Maria now called the silhouettes of her psyche—instead of "the witches"—had plenty to work on already. They did come up with a dream that captured the main points of the night, and it was a lulu.

ZZ   zzz   ZZ

27. DREAMS R US

That morning before awakening, Maria dreamed that she was driving at night on a road which she could not identify. There was a big billboard ahead of her that advertised a restaurant nearby. The name had a familiar ring to it, "Foods R Us," but even more intriguing was what the restaurant offered: "All You Can Eat for $18.95."

"Fancy that!" Maria thought to herself. "Wonder what they have…That price seems a little high to me. But then, considering it's all you can eat, it's probably justified." She parked her car at the entrance and went in. There was a small foyer at the entrance. Its back wall had shelves with baskets full of bread and rolls. In front of the wall was a large display counter full of pies, cakes, pastries and cookies. There was a cash register to the right of the counters, then a hostess station, and then the gateway into the dining area. One of the attendants greeted Maria and led her to a booth.

"The waitress will be right with you," the hostess told Maria as she left her comfortably situated. Then a waitress came to Maria's booth bringing her a glass of water and a menu. This waitress bore no resemblance to Maria. She was a blond, although probably dyed; she was plump; she spoke with a Southern accent and she chewed gum ungraciously, smacking her mouth in a vulgar way.

"Do you need a minute to look at the menu, Hon, or are you ready?"

"No, don't go away," said Maria, "I'm ready. I know what I want. And let's see, how to put this... I don't want to have dinner. I just want to put my $18.95 into dessert. Is that okay?"

"Oh, yes, Hon. No problem. You can have that. Do you know what kind of dessert you want?"

"Yes, cakes."

"Cakes? What kind of cakes you want?"

"All kinds."

"How many?"

"All."

"All?" asked the waitress gulping. "Let me get this straight," she continued as she put her order pad in her pocket in obvious frustration. "You want every kind of cake we got. And you want them all, is that it? Well, Honey, you don't look to me like the kind of person that has room for all that. Are you gonna eat them one slice at a time or what? I've got to see this."

"No," corrected Maria. "I want them all uncut and to-go. I've parked my car right at the front entrance. I'll just open my trunk if somebody will help me load them."

"Jesus!" exclaimed the waitress in hopeless befuddlement.

Maria could tell there was something wrong. The waitress made a face and without saying a word, she pivoted and left to consult with the manager.

Then strange things began to happen. Maria knew she was in trouble when she saw the waitress return with the Manager, a giant of a woman, who approached her with a frown, shaking her head in an accusing way. She was followed by a policeman, by the cook and other persons. Maria was suddenly surrounded by people who looked very disapprovingly at her.

"What's the big idea? You trying to be funny or something?" the manager asked her." You want all the cakes in the house to go? Is that it?"

"Well, I thought the sign said: 'All you can eat.' Isn't that right? Well, I want to eat them. I don't want them just for decoration in my house. But when I eat them is my business. What's wrong with that?"

Maria felt like an accused person on the docket, but she could not understand why. Her request made perfect sense to her. Still, she was afraid and bothered by a sense of guilt for a crime she thought she had committed but she didn't quite understand how. She felt insecure and helpless. Then the manager looked around for a higher authority and called upon a tall gentleman with stove pipe hat and a black suit and told him:

"Okay, Honest Abe, you read her the Riot Act… I mean the restaurant policy."

"Thank you, Mrs. Guilthammer," said the Lincoln look-alike as he grabbed the lapels of his coat as if preparing to orate. Then he intoned: "You can have all of the cakes you can eat on the premises all of the time. And, if you wish, you can have up to $18.95 worth of cakes to go any time. But you can't have all the cakes in the house to-go at no time. That's a no-no. No way!"

"Thank you, Mr. President," said the manager, taking control of the matter once again. "So, you want all the cakes, huh? Well, we'll give them to you one cake at a time. Here comes the first one."

Maria wanted out of this situation now. "Somehow, I think I've made a big mistake. I don't want to order anything now," she said timidly. "I changed my mind."

The waitress came carrying a big birthday cake with a lit candle. Maria could read the inscription on the cake:

**For Maria
From the Workshop
Of Dreams R Us**

The waitress put the cake in front of Maria, saying: "This one is on the house."

Then the manager said: "But wait! There's more," as she took a piece of duct-tape and stuck it across Maria's mouth, sealing it shut so that she could neither speak, nor eat. The entire restaurant broke into laughter as Maria sat there, desperately trying to scream, suffocating from being boxed in.

"You have your cake, Maria. Let's see you eat it now. Hee, hee, hee."

Maria managed to get up from the table. She pushed people aside with all her might; she broke through the crowd and got to her car. She was desperately looking for the key to start the car when she noticed that the manager and a few others had got in front of the car to prevent her from leaving.

"You forgot something. You forgot your cake," said the manager.

Just then the waitress appeared with the cake by the driver's window and as Maria turned to see it. The cake went poof! It disappeared right before her eyes. Laughter pealed from the crowd.

"Ooops! I forgot," added the waitress, "You can't take our specialties out of the premises. They self-destruct outside. Hah, hah."

"Haven't you heard? You can't have your cake and eat it, too."

There was more taunting laughter from the mob. Maria stepped on the gas and flew out of that scene, shouting: "Out of my way all of you creeps, or I'll run you over!! All of you!" As the car sped off, she woke up. She was gasping for air. The echo of scorn and ridiculing laughter was still ringing in her ears. She was glad to be out of that dream, thankful to be alive, awake, and in her own bed.

The dream haunted her that morning. It was one dream she did not enjoy remembering, but one that she felt determined to analyze because it was full of messages and symbols. She went to work right away and wrote down all the essentials of the dream into her diary. She couldn't help chuckling as she remembered the point of the dream, telling herself: How silly. Was I trying to order food for take-out in an all-you-can-eat restaurant? How ridiculous! No wonder they came after me.

The dream also brought to mind her session with Gwen a few days earlier. Maria had told a joke to Gwen on that afternoon when Gwen was recuperating from her ordeal. Maria was trying to cheer her up by telling her funny stories. The idea of ordering food to go in an all-you-can-eat restaurant was one of the wacky jokes of George Carlin, the standup comedian.

…And what of Abe Lincoln? Why was he there? Maria

recalled an eloquent quote attributed to him in connection with the power of demagogues:

"You can fool some of the people all of the time; and you can fool all of the people some of the time; but you can't fool all of the people all of the time."

How true, she thought. But what did all of that have to do with the dream? That dream was a picture puzzle. It had tantalizing pieces that seemed to connect and promised a clear vision, but which then eluded her. Parts of it had been funny, but all in all it had been a nightmare—an inscrutable and frightful experience that seemed to have an important message that she could not yet fathom.

Z   z   z   Z   z   z   Z

28. DECODING A NIGHTMARE

This dream lingered intermittently for many hours in Maria's day. In her spare moments she would go back over the notes she had written earlier when it was still fresh. Every time she found something tantalizing. Cakes stood for a forbidden fruit. It conjured up admonitions and injunctions, adages and incantations.

You can have your cake, but you can't eat it too. You can have cake sometimes; and you can eat it some of the time; but you can't have your cake and eat it all of the time.

Why was the inscription on the cake signed by The Workshop of Dreams R us? Why not signed by the restaurant involved? Could the cake be a symbol for dreams, implying I am not allowed to have all my dreams?

She went back to Abraham Lincoln's aphorism that played with the concepts of 'some' and 'all.' Maybe there were quantitative and qualitative restrictions about the number and type of dreams.

What still puzzled her was her own attitude in the dream. It seemed out of character. She could not imagine being so nervy, so inconsiderate as to demand all the cakes in the house. What would she have done with all those cakes? It didn't make sense. She could not understand her behavior. It was role playing in a drama that she had been manipulated to act out. She had been miscast in that role and should not have any guilt over it.

The following night when Maria began to dream, she found herself in the conference room at Dream Central waiting for the girls to file in. Sasha was the last one to come in, but the first to speak.

"Cakes anyone?" she asked sardonically. "They are on the house."

Maria threw a book at her, saying: "Don't make me puke. I still have indigestion from the last one."

Then Maria Luisa sat next to Maria to console her. "I really feel for you, Maria. It's awful to see the slate of your memory being erased and wiped clean before your eyes night after night. No sooner do you write something, it is gone. I think the best thing to do is to not try to connect your two worlds. Live each one independently of the other and try to enjoy them. Two thirds of your age is daylight. One third is dark night. Let it be. I, too, believe that somehow, in some mysterious way, the two worlds will manage to exchange memories over the long run."

"Thank you, Maria Luisa. That's good advice. I will try to follow it. And I do hope you are right about the osmosis of the memories."

Z   z   z   z   z   z   Z

PART VI: TRANSCENDENTAL ISSUES

29. A BLOCKBUSTER DREAM

A few weeks went by unremarkably. During sleep the girls at Dream Central exchanged their usual banter and became closer to Maria. Her real world remained mostly unchanged. She lost her next-door neighbor, Gwen, who left in February, and settled back into a safer environment in Paducah, Kentucky, in the bosom of her family. Maria had encouraged her to do that. They kept in touch by email.

Meanwhile, Maria spent more time with her friend Karen Powers. It was always fun to talk to her. They thought so much alike. On one occasion, for example, they discovered that they had both researched the same issue independently of each other. Their minds had been focused on Spain after Maria's sketch of Don Quixote at a faculty meeting and they followed on down from there. Maria first brought up the issue.

"Karen, do you remember you once asked me if I could name someone who had lived in the year 1000 AD? At the time, I had absolutely no idea. I couldn't name a single person. Well, that really bothered me. My curiosity gnawed at me, and I just had to look it up."

"Hah!" said Karen, letting out a yowl. "Isn't that a coincidence?" She, too, had been bothered by that and had researched the issue. Their research led them both to the Crusades and to El Cid, Spain's great hero in the fight against the Moors. By strange coincidence, El Cid had died in 1099 and lived 1000 years ago.

"I feel like we've resurrected someone from oblivion," said Maria.

"No, he rescued us from our ignorance of medieval history. It's like he came galloping on his horse and swept us off," said Karen. "Did you know that they made a movie about his life with Charlton Heston and Sofia Loren? ...It's called 'El Cid,' I think."

"No, I didn't know that. I'll see if I can get it at Blockbuster."

It was often like that between them. Their minds were always in sync, and it was a joy to get together because they usually learned from each other.

On the school front, Maria noticed that Elena's tutoring was making a difference. Toro was making better grades; he was coming to school more often and his attitude had improved significantly. Wally was another story. She hardly ever saw Wally, and she considered him a lost cause.

By late March, with the approach of Easter, another front flared up in Maria's life. It was religion. Her mother, Clara, led the charge there. Clara was most unhappy that Maria never went to church. This hurt her deeply; it worried her, and she could not understand it. What had she ever done to deserve such a curse? Where had she failed her daughter? Maria tried to comfort her mother. She even went to Sunday Mass with her from time to time to please her, although she hated every minute of it. Sooner or later, she would have to come out of her heretical closet and tell her mother how she really felt. But before that, she wanted to sort out things for herself. Was she really an atheist? She disliked the sound of that word and had made a rhyming pun in Spanish about it: *Ateo suena feo* (atheist sounds ugly). Perhaps there was another word that was more palatable, less jarring and that fit her beliefs as well. But what were her beliefs? Where exactly did she fit in the transcendental scheme of things? During this period, her mind drifted out of this world, reaching orbits that took her farther and farther, towards fundamental issues of faith and theology.

One evening, the subject of Maria's dream preferences came up at dream central. Someone, Miss Diligence probably, asked Maria what she would like to dream of that night. Maria was nonchalant as usual, saying that she didn't care...whatever... that they could just surprise her. But Sasha pressed the point and made it more specific.

"Maria, tell me something. Have you ever considered what your favorite dream would be? I am not just talking about tonight. I mean for all time. What, in your opinion, would constitute a memorable dream? Give me your idea for a once-in-a-lifetime-blockbuster dream. Who knows, maybe we could work on it and present it to you for a special occasion. What say you?"

Again, Maria responded with noncommittal indifference saying that she hadn't given the matter that much thought, and that she didn't particularly want to play that game. Sasha and Libby chided her for being blasé and insisted that she should be more enthusiastic. After all, they were only doing it for her benefit. They offered her some suggestions. Would she like to travel? How about Paris? Hawaii? Or would she like to go back in time? Would she like to be a teenager again or perhaps a preteen? For God's sake, Maria, do give us something to prepare. We need your input.

Finally, on this night, to the surprise of the girls, Maria changed her attitude. She apologized for her past indifference and showed them that she had something up her sleeve. She could play the dream game also.

"You want a great dream order, do you? Well, I'll give you a dream. I've got something that will throw you for a loop. You'll regret you ever bugged me about it. ... You ready?"

"No, wait!" urged Sasha. "Let me get Imogene in on this." Then she went to the door and screamed to the top of her lungs down the hall. "Imogene. Get here, pronto! Maria says she has a major blockbuster request for us. Ram, you need to be in on this also. Hurry up and come before she changes her mind."

Imogene showed up in no time, as if responding to an emergency, panting from rushing over. "Okay, what is this all about?" she asked.

"She has the blockbuster of all blockbusters," said Sasha. "She is ready to tell us her idea of her all-time favorite dream."

"Fine. I want to hear what this is," said Imogene. "Ram, please take notes."

"Oh, for heaven's sake, don't make such big a deal!" said Maria a little embarrassed. "I just finally decided to play your game. You've been urging me to come up with something for so long. You've given me so many suggestions, all of which I had to turn down because none of them hit the spot. Well, I am tired of being nonchalant and I want to give you a run for your money. Okay, here it is. I don't want to go to Paris, and I don't particularly want to go back in time. In fact, just the opposite, I want to go towards the future, but the never-never sort of future. I want something very especial. I want to test your powers of imagination and creativity. I will tell you this much about it. I want my dream to be a happy dream, colorful, maybe even a little funny without it being cartoonish. At the same time, I want you to engage my mind, to make me think without turning the dream into something abstruse and boring. Do have some philosophy if you feel inclined but go easy on it. Make it serious—even life-and-death serious—a little scary, with touches of the supernatural, but without gore, and without drifting into the macabre or into weird science fiction."

"Oh, goodness, Maria, stop. Stop! That's enough. We can't keep up with you and you're not helping. You are making it too complicated and rambling. You are going to have to be a little more specific. Could you possibly summarize it into a few words?" asked Imogene.

"Yes," replied Maria. "I can give it to you in one word, actually."

"And what, pray tell, would that one word be?" asked Sasha.

"Heaven."

"Heaven? You want us to take you to heaven?" asked a chorus of incredulous voices.

"…But aren't you an atheist?" asked Libby.

"Well, that's why…all the more reason," replied Maria. "But let's not rush to judgment about that yet. I may not be a full-blown atheist. But even if I were one, does that mean that I could not go to heaven? That's an interesting question, don't you think? That is an issue you would have to think about and resolve. Take it as my challenge to you. Show me. Convince me. Pretend that I'm from Missouri. I have to see it to believe it. Let me see what life is like beyond the beyond, beyond Jupiter and Mars. Let me see what you can do with the impossible and let me see how you can make it entertaining. You wanted a challenge, no? Well, you got one now. Ah, and one more thing. I do have a very important restriction. Your mission—if you should agree to take the assignment—is to take me there without killing me. Or, if I must die, make sure it is temporary. Got that? A t-e-m-p-o-r-a-r-y simulation of death! And make it brief and painless. That's all."

"Have no fear. If you go, we go down with you, and we don't do suicidal missions," said Imogene.

"You sure turned the tables on us with this one. This is a Lulu," said Sasha, adding, "we will definitely have to involve the big guns on this one: Dr. Broca, Professor Quixote, Janet Reno, Abe Lincoln, the works. The whole menagerie."

"Absolutely, no doubt about it, this is a big project," agreed Imogene. "I hope you are aware, Maria, that there are memory limitations. The dream cannot be too long. We may have to give it to you in installments over time."

"That's no problem. Take your time."

Z   z   z   z   z   z   Z

30. Heaven: First Take

Sometime soon after that, on the morning of Easter Sunday, the girls at dream central came up with their first dream about heaven. As in movie filming, the dream makers often had to go through repeated takes and dry runs before getting a dream right. There were always glitches. Tonight, on their first take, the girls presented their version of heaven, and it had an unexpected outcome.

The dream opened with Maria floating in the sky. All she could see in all directions—ahead, behind and above—was a baby blue sky that at times seemed azure, and at times cyan. The only exception to the blue was below where she could see an ocean of white, foamy clouds in lazy motion extending to the horizon like a carpet of soft downy fluff. Maria wondered how she had gotten there. She had no idea. It was as if she had stepped out of an airplane at 35,000 feet. To her amazement, she just hovered there as if suspended by an invisible harness, drifting ever so slowly in the air, unable to understand why she didn't plummet down.

The feeling was new; unlike anything she had ever felt. Floating on water was the nearest similar sensation, but it lacked the weightless airy sense of levitation. At first, she did not trust her feeling of suspension, and she was afraid to try anything lest she drop like a rock. With great trepidation she moved only inches at a time as she tried to understand the forces at play in this incredible world.

Fear turned to joy as she gradually discovered the new laws of physics, the strange kinetics of how steering and motion worked. It turned out that motion was governed by the power of thought and the force of will. She could descend by simply relaxing her resistance, by releasing her mental brakes and letting gravity gain and move her downward towards the clouds. She had full control of the rate of descent. It sufficed for her to think "Not so fast" and her falling speed was restrained. Moving up or sideways was equally easy. She only had to will her direction, and she was as good as heading there. Her mind quickly mastered her new powers of psychokinetic motion, and she put her body through several maneuvers, repeating them, perfecting them, till she became the master of her movements in space.

How wonderful it was! She could look upwards and think UP, and up she went. "Ah, gravity, at last I've tamed you to obey my will!" she gloated contentedly. She tried fancier locomotion. She pitched and rolled like a fish; she did pirouettes; she plunged and soared and tried every conceivable maneuver that came to her mind. She was a master of the sky, and she did it all without propellers, or jet engines, or even wings. This was better than being a bird, and better even than being an angel, unless, of course, that's what she had now become. It was all so exhilarating, so wonderful, and so fabulous to feel totally emancipated from gravity, from care, from every concern. She was a child at play. She did endless summersaults with no fear of hitting anything, with no fear of crash landing. The sky was all hers in its immensity. She felt freedom to the nth power, and she roamed totally unbounded. As she cavorted and danced in space, the strains of Domenico Modugno's song, *Nel Blu Dipinto di Blu*, (also called *Volare* by some), went through her mind and she began to live its lyrics to the letter.

> *Penso q'un sogno cosi non ritorni mai piu*
> *Mi dipingevo le mani, la facia, di blu*
> *Poi de improviso venivo dal vento rapito*
>
> *I think I'll never have a dream like this again*
> *My hands, my face were painted blue*
> *Suddenly, I was swept by the wind*

How many times she had flown to that music, but always daydreaming while awake. Now she was living the dream. Maria danced with abandon, swooning at times with the sweep of languorous melodies that carried her away until she felt a little dizzy. It was as if the various winds vied with each other to have a whirl with her. Zephyrs and gales cut into each other for a fling in the air with her. She felt she was in such demand, like the belle of the heavens' ball. "Ohhh," she sighed to her beaus, "Let me rest a bit now. This is wonderful, but it's making me giddy." Her dancing partners complied. The music turned off, the air became still, and she returned to the quiet tranquility of a blue sky on a clear and sunny day.

She dozed angelically for a few minutes, but by the time she woke up she was a little restless again. Then the calm began to pall on. Monotony set in. The quiet became disquieting and the solitude became worrisome. She turned critical. Nagging questions began to haunt her. Now what? There has to be more to this, or I'll go mad. Heaven, if that is what this is, is wonderful for its serenity, for its spaciousness, for its openness. But after a while it feels like too much of a good thing. The big blue sky is disorienting and becomes boring, a little frightening even, and its sameness becomes suffocating. Where is anything here? Where are the people? And where is time? What day is this? What time is it? Will night ever come?

The bigness of the sky began to have a strange, agoraphobic effect upon Maria. It made her feel insignificant as a mere point in an empty universe. The vast sameness was also oppressive. How does one escape from this unbounded cage, this prison of invisible walls, this bottomless trap without ceiling? She felt lost amid its nothingness. Gradually she began to feel like one condemned to a sort of torture by spaciousness, and she felt squeezed by the invisible tentacles of emptiness and lonesomeness. The experience was no longer fun.

Perhaps, she thought, this is really a special heaven meant for atheists. She could almost hear her conscience snickering and jeering at her. So, you think there is no life after death, eh? Do you still think there is no heaven and no hell? What would you call this? How is this for your atheistic concept of nothingness of the afterlife? Is it lonely enough for you? Is it empty enough? And is it silent enough, so silent that you hear yourself think? Could you take an eternity of this?

Maria kept her cool through all these unsettling, taunting questions. She tried to think of a way out of the predicament. If this is God's idea of heaven for me, then I must say He knows how to punish me. This is bordering on being torture already. Except… except, that I don't quite buy it. And God is the key. Some things don't add up. Why would He be punishing me? And would He punish me without telling me why, without a trial? It's not fair. If there is one thing we should be able to count on in heaven is justice, and I don't see it. I believe there is a flaw here. This is not God's doing. This is too sinister. I suspect that this is neither heaven nor hell, nor life after death for that matter. It's not empty enough to be death. There is entirely too much sky; there are clouds galore, there is wind, there is motion, there is coldness, there is sensation, and there is life to top it all. Yes, I think! And if I think, then I can't be dead. Descartes had it right, by gosh. This is not the inexorable nothingness I expected; this is not the sort of emptiness that an agnostic would imagine. So, what is this? I suspect this is just a bad dream, a poor attempt at imagining heaven, and I am getting tired of it. Unless something happens here soon, I'm just going to pull the plug on this bad dream and wake up. Sorry. I've had it.

Maria went for a count of five and—true to her threat—she called the bluff on her dream makers and woke up. The clock by her bed read: 6:32. She rolled in bed a couple of times; she puffed up her pillow; and she went back to sleep. Within ten minutes she was fully asleep and ready to dream again.

Meanwhile the girls at Dreams-R-Us were discussing the failed dream among themselves. One by one they were panning it. Oh, my God, that was awful! What a fiasco! This is the pits! Imogene, who had watched it from elsewhere, came barging in, furious-ready to roll heads. She was livid.

"Did we blow that dream or what? Man, what a disaster!" she said. "I want a full postmortem on this bomb. In all my years I have never seen a production as bad as this. The timing was awful! Terrible! Bad! This is the worst dream in all my life. How could we! If this were a business, heads would be rolling right now. I would fire all the ones responsible for this. I want an analysis of the failure immediately and I want suggestions to correct it. Let's consider this a very bad first draft. I will not stand for such sloppy work ever again."

Libby was the first to speak. "Well, if you ask me, I think she was kept up there far too long just twiddling her thumbs. We offered nothing for her to fall back on but blue skies. We needed people. We needed men. Handsome men. I would have represented each wind, the zephyr and the gale as a dashing prince charming-not rushing cold air sweeping her off."

"I agree... the setting was too empty, too solitary. And it dragged on too long, till heaven turned to hell, no less," said Sasha.

"Absolutely, heaven became a punishment!" said Maria Luisa.

"She was suffering, all right," commented Imogene. "That's when she put two and two together and concluded that if it's this bad, then this can't be heaven."

"It was great through the song 'Volare.' That was heaven! We should have gone right into the next scene at that time. We should have brought out the big soap bubble then. We should have added some suspense; we should have teased her and played hide and seek with the bubble so that she wondered what the bubble was as it emerged from the clouds. She would have asked: What is this? Is this a humongous whale of the sky or is it a glass zeppelin?" said Libby.

"Well, so what do we do now, then?" Sasha asked.

"I am inclined to play it again tomorrow, or in a few days, after this is forgotten. But next time we should cut into the bubble scene much sooner. Let's ask Dr. Broca and Professor Quixote what they think," said Imogene.

Professor Quixote spoke first. "Personally, I don't think it was that bad. It certainly gives her a lot to think about as it is, and that's all to the good. It all depends on what you are trying to achieve. I believe you failed because you were not in tune with Maria's mind. You have to anticipate how she'll react, and you didn't."

"Ouch, that hurts!" exclaimed Imogene. "That's the ultimate insult to our powers. I've never been so humiliated."

Prof. Quixote continued. "If you want to make it more credible for Maria, you're going to have to do your homework and learn what's in her mind. You had only one card to play about heaven, and it was the jolly-sky-diving-and-romping-around card. But she trumped you. Heaven involves other dimensions that you had not anticipated. You made it sad, both depressing and painful, by the uncommunicativeness of Providence, the monotony and the abject solitude. You forgot the fact that Maria still retains a vestige of a God who is kind and understanding. The reason she woke up out of this dream was that she couldn't picture that kind and gentle God in that hellish blue sky. He wouldn't have been so silent and so uncaring. The God she would envision is one that would have greeted her cordially at the gates of heaven. Perhaps He would have chided her a little for her lack of faith; perhaps He would have rubbed in the fact that she had been mistaken for not believing in Him. But He would have been kind and good-natured about it. He might have told her: Well Maria, as you can see, I do exist. Here I am…you were wrong! But because you meant no harm by it, and because you led a good life—better than a lot of others who professed to believe in me, I'm going to put you in a special place for a while. We will show you what that place is shortly, but for now, step right in. Welcome to heaven. Then He would have given her a hug. This is what Maria would have expected and would have understood. She would have taken her punishment willingly then and would have danced in solitude for a decade or two without complaining or waking up."

Imogene then addressed the other older statesman. "What about you, Dr. Broca, what do you think we should do?"

"It all depends on your objective. If you see your dream as

entertainment and you want to convey a joyful happy impression of heaven, then I would cut the last few minutes as you suggested and go right into the bubble scene you had planned. Keep the good times rolling! But if you want to be philosophical, thought provoking and tendentious then leave it as is. Whatever you decide, you must be aware that Maria is a tough cookie. This episode of premature awakening is likely to repeat again. Don't be surprised if it does. Her consciousness plays cat and mouse with her subconscious; it pretends to be asleep at times, allowing her subconscious to have free rein in a dream dance, but consciousness is, in fact, leading the dance. Watch out for her scrutiny. When she gets analytical, she starts tearing down the fantasies till the dream collapses."

Dr. Broca continued. "It isn't only her logic you need to worry about. Look around you. How many Marias do you see? The place is full of them, and they all want part of the action; each wants to pull in her direction, Libby up, Sasha down, and Maria Luisa straight ahead. You are not driving a one-horse surrey here, or even a troika. You are driving a team of willful fillies."

"Ah, yeah, tell me about it," said Imogene with a sigh.

"Let me make a prediction here," said Libby. "I predict that before this heavenly production is over, it is going to get mighty political around here. I can already feel the undertow."

"I agree with you," said Professor Quixote. "Let's face it, everyone here is either an agnostic or a proto atheist. No one believes in an afterlife. And yet, each one is trying to fashion a better vision of heaven than his neighbor. How can they be convincing about something they don't believe in? As soon as a vision of heaven is presented, the caustic criticism starts seeping through to undo it. 'That's not what heaven is about,' they'll say. 'If heaven were like that, then I'd just as soon stay in limbo.' Fashioning a common idea of heaven among atheists is as hopeless as having a dozen artists work together on a canvas."

"This is ridiculous!" Maria Luisa cried out. "Then why in hell are we playing this stupid game?"

Everyone chuckled to hear Maria Luisa, the quiet and normally imperturbable mathematician, sound so exasperated. Sasha responded.

"You must have been out solving theorems when we discussed this. The fact is that we asked for it, and we got ourselves into it. We kept pressing Maria to come up with a suggestion for a dream. She declined, but we insisted, and we criticized her for declining. We called her blasé, indifferent, a stick in the mud and a bad sport. Then she showed us. That's how we got into this. I must say, she was devilishly clever when she chose heaven. The situation reminds me of the story of 'The Golden Apple of Discord' from Greek mythology."

"I have only a vague recollection of that story," said Libby. "Why don't you enlighten us?"

Sasha agreed and told the story. "Eris, the goddess of discord, felt snubbed because the other gods were having a banquet and had not invited her. In retaliation, she showed up at the banquet and threw a golden apple before the three main goddesses: Hera, Athena and Aphrodite. The apple had an inscription which read, simply: 'For the Fairest.' You can just imagine the vanity and the jealousy which that inscription unleashed. Each goddess thought it was meant for her. They asked Zeus to settle the issue and tell them who was the fairest. But Zeus was no fool. He declined and, instead, he appointed Paris to decide who was the fairest. And did that ever bring out politics! Each of the goddesses tried to bribe Paris. Hera promised to make him king of Europe and Asia; Athena offered him wisdom; and Aphrodite offered him the love of the most beautiful woman in the world. Paris went for the beautiful woman and pronounced Aphrodite as the fairest. It happened that the most beautiful woman at the time was Helen of Troy. The trouble was that Helen was already married. Still, a promise is a promise. To make a long story short, this led to the great calamity of the Trojan War."

Sasha went on. "The parallel of that story to our situation is that Maria threw the gauntlet at us, and we are having difficulty coming up with a vision of heaven that doesn't step in other people's toes and is not dead-on arrival because of fatal criticisms. Good luck! Libby will want to show us that orgasms in heaven are off the Richter scale and last for decades. Maria de Buenos Aires will be having tango parties night after night with all the tango greats: Gardel, Piazzola, Troilo, and Discepolo. Maria Luisa will be in her 7th heaven raised to the aleph null power, because she will have discovered that God happens to be a mathematician. They will be solving conundrums and theorems by the ages. As for me, I can't imagine anything more heavenly than having dinner and a long interview with one of the most fascinating minds that ever wrote: Shakespeare. There are so many things I would ask him. How did he ever learn so many words? How did he know so much about Man? Oh, I just drool thinking about it."

Then Imogene had a great thought. She clapped her hands together to announce a great Eureka-moment. A marvelous idea had just flashed through her mind. "By Jove," she said excitedly, "that's it! You've just given me a great idea, Sasha. We don't have to invent one common idea of heaven to fit all atheists. We are talking about Maria here. Our Maria! We know what she likes, and she knows what we like. I will give each of you the latitude to express yourselves and present your own idea of heaven. This is the real challenge that Maria threw at us. Make heaven diverse, but make it glorious, make it inspiring, memorable, and fun. That's not impossible. We can do it. We can have Fibonacci numbers coming out of the stars and wrapping around her mind; we can have rollicking, frolicking skydiving; we can have tango parties and yes, oh yes, we can have Shakespeare also."

"Bravo! Bravo! We can't wait."

"You didn't mention love and sex. Can we have that too?" asked Libby.

"Absolutely! If it is in good taste… why not?" replied Imogene. "But let's not rush things. I think we would do well if in the next few days, we didn't serve her a dream. Let's take our time;

do our homework; and get it right next time. We need to delve more deeply into her beliefs, not only about heaven, but about death, the soul, life after death, faith and her own sort of agnosticism."

Z   z   z   z   z   Z

31. Death and Sleep

There were no dreams for the next few days, at least none to wake up with and none that Maria could remember. She was pensive during her wakeful hours, a good indication that what transpired during the night was a slog through a contemplative miasma of deep philosophy. During these days she probed deeply into her beliefs, and she matured philosophically and spiritually. Her aborted dream about heaven had triggered an avalanche of ideas that stirred in her mind at night.

On one evening during this brooding period, she delved into the distinction of death and sleep. This issue had come up in the past, but she had always shelved it to re-examine on a night of dreamless cogitation. This was the night.

Soon after she began to dream, Maria bypassed the conference room at Dream Central and went straight to the academic quarters in search of Professor Quixote. She stopped by the graduate office to make inquiries.

"Hello, Mary Dili. Could you please tell me where Prof. Quixote's office is?" Maria asked the secretary, Miss Diligence.

"His office is in Room 107, but he is in class right now."

"Really? What class is that?"

"The class is Philosophy 305, Transcendental Issues of Sleep, and it is in Room 204."

"Do you suppose he'd mind if I went in and sat in for a bit?"

"If it was any other professor" began the secretary, "and if it involved any other person, I would have my reservations, but I am sure it will be all right. Go for it."

Maria sneaked in the classroom quietly through the back door. She was eager to know what transcendental issues of sleep were about and she wanted to see Professor Quixote in action. He was still an enigma to her. She had been intrigued by him ever since she saw him expounding on the rationality of queuing theory to control dreams. She had been even more puzzled when he described his purview of expertise as being the philosophical issues of sleep. What was that about? He had told her a little, but not enough. Her curiosity had grown to a scorching intensity. She tiptoed into the room. The professor had just opened his lecture to questions from the floor, and someone had asked him to comment on the comparison of death and sleep.

"People talk as if death and sleep were comparable, death being a longer, deeper sleep. What's the basis for this?"

"Religious belief," replied Prof. Quixote without hesitation. "Those who believe in God and in an afterlife maintain that death is not an end, that life goes on. But an agnostic would tell you that the comparison has no logical validity. You cannot compare the two. They are as incomparable as a fish and a bicycle. But people can't accept death's finality. They resort to all sorts of euphemisms to camouflage its ugly reality. Instead of 'dying' they say, 'passing away' and instead of death they say, 'eternal rest.' Death is a scabrous subject that must be mollified. Our culture abounds with these similes and metaphors like *Oh, sleep, thou ape of death* from Shakespeare, or like:

> *To die, to sleep, perchance to dream.*
> *But in that sleep of death what dreams may come…?*

"Don't get me wrong, I enjoy poetry, and I love these metaphors. But they are not fact. If you remove the implicit assumptions, there can be no logical comparisons of death and sleep."

A female student asked: "What are the implicit assumptions? Could you specify them, please?"

"The soul is one assumption. Immortality is another. The simile of a voyage linking death and sleep is still another."

The young woman made a face of discomfort. "What voyage? You lost me."

"…The voyage that you take each night when you go from yesterday to today, and from today to tomorrow. Your bed is the boat that takes your tired body across that dark body of time, and you go from the shore of one day to the shore of the next. By analogy, death is the voyage that takes you from this world to the next, from mortal life to an endless tomorrow of life everlasting.

"Now you may ask: Where is the soul in all this? Popular wisdom has it that it is inside the body, biding its time, waiting for the eye lids to close. As soon as you fall asleep, the soul emerges from the body to roam freely. Off she goes, out of the body, out of the ship, flying on the wind of dreams wherever they take her: to the future, to the past, or to the kingdoms between the stars. This is one of the times during our lives when we feel incorporeal and enjoy the pleasures of a body-less existence. We may not be able to drink or eat then, but, ah, we can fly, and we can do all the impossible things that the imagination fancies. This feeds the notion that there can be life outside the body and, by extension, that there can be life beyond the body's death. It also nurtures the notion that dreams are a prelude to things to come, a taste of heaven. Immortality is a latent promise beating in our dreams.

"And there is more. As you know, this idyll of dreams and sleep comes to an end every morning when you arrive at the shore of another day. By then tomorrow has lost its futuristic patina, its lure of a distant Shangri-La. It is now jejune and déjà vu. It is just another working day. The real world intrudes and takes you back to the grind. Reluctantly you get up and get out of bed. But a few minutes later, after you have shaken off the sloth and have gotten over your resentment for being awakened, you feel stronger and younger, because while you were sleeping and dreaming, your body was performing magic on itself and reconstituting itself. Awakening is like being reborn. You feel energized, you feel much better than you did when you went to bed. The weariness is gone. As if this were not enough, there is still another subtle bonus. It is the expectation, the conviction, especially if you are young, that all this will repeat itself again and again, for years and years, for decades, and for generations. Life will keep on bubbling forth seemingly without end.

"When you are in this frame of mind, the momentum for life is unstoppable. You are predisposed emotionally to extend the virtues of sleep to death. There must be an awakening after death. There must be an eternal tomorrow. So, death is also thought to be a voyage, a crossing, but this time a crossing over a deeper, darker and more mysterious body of water, something like a pelagic darkness in which, at some point, as in sleep, your soul emerges from your body for a final time. But this time, since there is no body to return to, the soul goes on to its final destination. This final destination is the only mystery to this story. You don't know whether that destination will be heaven, hell, limbo, reincarnation, transmogrification, or purgatory. But whatever it is, you know it will be eternal. And this, ladies and gentlemen, is the framework for the analogies between death and sleep. As you can see, both are voyages—one across a river of time, the other across an ocean of ages. But in both cases, there is life again on the other shore. The soul in all this is an independent part of your being. It emerges from your body; it roams independent of the body, and it is indestructible. This is the framework that most people envision, and which sets up the similarity of death and sleep."

The professor then addressed the young woman who had asked for the clarification earlier and asked her: "Are you clear now Miss…Miss…?

"Clarina, Sir. My name is Clarina. And yes, I am clear on that part."   Maria had a sense that she knew Clarina. She reminded her of herself when she was about six years old, before her heresies, before her apostasies, before she started questioning her beliefs. Then again, Clarina also reminded her of her mother in a teenager's body. There was a resemblance there. Speaking of resemblances, Maria could not get over how much she thought like Professor Quixote. It was uncanny how much he reminded her of herself. When he spoke, she agreed with every word. His imagery about sleep struck a chord with her because it was virtually the same as in a poem, "Pelagic Voyage," that Maria had written.

Clarina continued her commentary. "The part I still don't understand, Sir, is how anyone can say that it is logically invalid to compare death to sleep. What part of this don't they get? I don't see any flaws in logic. Where is the flaw?"

"Oh, my God, she is such a babe," Maria thought. She hoped the professor would be kind to Clarina. The truth could be shattering for her. After a reasonable pause, the professor went straight to the point.

"The flaw is this. Sleep is a known fact, a known phenomenon and a known voyage. It is something that you can all account from your own known experience. Each of you has repeated this voyage from yesterday to today thousands of times through your lifetime. But death, on the other hand, is an unknown. Death is a trip which you have never taken. Furthermore, this trip is unknown not only to you, but—and get this—to the entire living world! Out of the millions and billions of people who are alive on earth today, there isn't a single person, not a one, who could tell you what death was like, because no one has ever experienced it. Neither can the dead. Out of the billions and trillions who have died, there isn't a one who can come back to talk about it, either. So, you have two facts, one a known, and the other an unknown and, at least logically, you cannot compare such unlike things."

"Yes, Sir, but for those of us who do believe in the soul and its immortality, there is no logical flaw," insisted Clarina. "The soul is independent of the body, isn't it? The soul does go on living, doesn't it? How can anyone prove that it does not?"

"Ah, now we are getting to the nitty-gritty," said the professor. "How can anyone prove that it does go on living? And what, in any case, is the soul? Is it really independent of the body? Does it go on living? How do you know that? These are the implicit assumptions that rear their heads and do mischief. We have come to the gist of the matter. But you will have to consider these issues for yourselves because I cannot go any further, at least not here and not now. For one thing, I have a plane to catch. For another, this subject gets very delicate and personal at this juncture. This discussion now scratches at the core of your basic beliefs: your belief in God, your belief in life after death and the like. And I don't want to go there. The only thing I would have you do at this point is to ponder the issue in the abstract, hypothetically, as a matter of pure logic. Assume then, for the sake of argument, that when you died everything went, body and soul. Can you see that without the belief of the soul's immortality you could not compare death and sleep? Death would not be a voyage then but an end—the end of all voyages, the end of all ends. Now, if you'll excuse me, I need to move on."

The professor left the room, and the students reluctantly followed suit—many of them puzzled and disturbed. Clarina seemed discomposed and rattled, uncomfortable in her new confusion. Maria on the other hand was curious, challenged to explore more. Her mind was restless to go where the professor had not dared to go. She wanted to look for answers, unsatisfied with the state in which the professor had left them. She felt as in those weekly TV series that leave you hanging till the next episode. The soul, the soul... she kept repeating to herself... what is the nature of the soul? What exactly is it? She decided to research the soul that very minute, so she went back to the academic office at dream central for some answers.

"Hi, Dili. It's me again. I know that Professor Quixote just left to catch a plane. Could you tell me when he will be back? I would really like to talk to him."

"I'll have to check records. I think he is going to Savannah, Georgia, today. He goes there quite a bit. Let's see. But from there he is going on vacation to Europe. Is it an emergency? What's the nature of your problem?"

"It's not an emergency. I just wish he had followed up on his lecture. He left us hanging."

"Hah, that happens more often than I care to count. You are not the first to complain about that. I think he does that deliberately sometimes, so students will think about some things on their own and research the issues. I can help you with the research. It happens that he has a lot of material on reserve in the library, things like videos of his lectures, mimeographed notes, articles, journals, etc. You need to see Ram about that. But you must see the material on the premises. You cannot take anything out."

"Oh, you don't need to tell me... I know all about that," said Maria. "You can read articles but only in the premises, you can have dreams, but you can't take them with you. I've fought those wars before. Could I trouble you with another thing? Is it possible for me to access something in my home computer from here?"

"That's possible but only in part. You only have reading rights from here. If you need to make any changes, you will have to wait till you are awake."

"No, no. I don't want to make any changes. I just want to see something I wrote once."

"You can use the computer in the other room. Just type 'My Folders' and anything you've written will come up."

"Oh, thank you Dili."

Maria sat in front of a computer and went to her folders. She opened the folder for free verses and found the following poem there.

Pelagic Voyage

There is an ocean of darkness
Between one day and the next.
It is a sea of sleep that we traverse
Night after night on sails of sheets and pillows
En route to another undiscovered island
In the archipelago of tomorrows.

When disembarking on that island-day
Tomorrow loses its futuristic glow
Becoming déjà vu like any other day.
We carry on with chores.
We work, we eat and drink, we move about

And never give a thought about sleep,
The sea that brought us there.

Until the day is spent,
Until the island burns,
Until we feel exhausted
Until the fire surrounds us, forcing us to flee.

It's then we seek the sea of sleep again
Our dark mysterious passage to salvation
Our exit from a day on fire.

We reach the shore and come to a pier,
An embarkation point to new beginnings.
It is our bedroom!
And moored to it, we spot our bed.
She is a bright and white square-rigger
About to take us to the splendor
Of yet another fresh and green tomorrow.

Maria was amazed how in sync she was with the professor. Had he read her poem? Or had she somehow plagiarized his thoughts sometime?

Perhaps she thought she would do better not to read his writings on the soul, but she should examine her own thoughts on the subject first. She could always turn to what he had written and compare notes with her own thoughts. So, she changed her strategy and opted for deep personal introspection instead. What do I believe about the soul? Is it immortal? This is the ideal place to examine these thoughts at length, here in this especial dome where I have rooms all to myself for hours, where I can think without the interruptions of real people, of street noises, of mundane distractions.

zZz   z   zZz

32. THE SOUL

The following evening Maria continued her search for her personal convictions on the nature of the soul, and it occurred to her that, surely, Ram could be of help. She walked through the corridors of her mind leading to the library that Ram oversaw. She found him busy, sorting and archiving recollections, mental souvenirs and mementos of times past. The library was immense. There were lanes and canyons of bookshelves.

"Ram, my good man, you're always at work," Maria said as she walked in. "Do you ever take a vacation or a break?"

"Nope! Not me! I'm always on the job. But I do sneak in a nap now and then. Haven't you noticed?"

"A nap…? You…? No! When…?"

"…Oh, come now! Surely, you remember. Have you forgotten the times when you were trying to recall something—the name of a person, or a place, or something that wouldn't come to your mind? At times you could almost see the image, but it came and went. So, you called me. My phone rang and rang off the wall, but there was no answer. In desperation, you started hitting your forehead with the palm of your hand, trying to shake loose the information. It was then that I woke up. It was like an earthquake here. I shouted back at you: All right, all right, I'm coming. Stop that! You're going to scramble your brains!"

Maria laughed, acknowledging with her head that she remembered. "Yes, how could I forget? You know… I had my suspicions that something was amiss then... but I didn't know just what. So that's what was going on… Of course, I remember. I'm sorry if I ruined a good dream with my knocking. Listen, Ram, I'd like to ask you a favor. Professor Quixote left us hanging the other night."

"Really…? You don't say!"

"He was discussing death, sleep and immortality…heavy stuff. Then, when he got to the nature of the human soul, which was a crucial part in the argument, he simply quit. I think he felt the subject was a little prickly for him. He preferred that the students consider the subject on their own."

"Wise man…"

"What I'd like to ask you is this: do you have something on the human soul? I would like something that is not the usual pap. I don't want psychobabble, poetic rubbish, and, above all, I don't want religious twaddle. I can get that sort of thing from the Dade County library and the local universities by the tons."

"Goodness, Maria. You've told me everything you don't want. That helps a little, but not very much. Can you focus on what you do want?"

"Oh, yes, sorry. I think I can... I'll try... Let's see…I want something fresh and original. It's got to be original. That's de rigueur. Preferably bold. I want the essence of those iconoclastic thoughts that visited my mind on several occasions, but only briefly; those shy revelations that would not linger to be scrutinized but drifted off before I had a chance to record them. I want those hesitant intimations, those timid stirrings that I swept under the rug because I wasn't ready for them, because they seemed too shocking and revolutionary and because I was too cowardly at the time. I want the progression of my own ideas on the subject. Of course, if possible, I will gladly take anything of Professor Quixote's thoughts, but only after I've read my own."

"Okay, follow me," said Ram as he led her to a carrel and sat her down in front of a monitor. He gave her a headset with earphones and told her: "Sit right here and put this on. I'll go see what soliloquies I can find."

In a few minutes, Maria heard her own voice in the earphones. Her voice sounded a little different, very young at times. It was thinking aloud, a blurting of unadulterated ideas. She was asking questions on her way to forming opinions.

"What is the soul? What does it look like? Is it a person's shadow, like a silhouette? What mirror would I look into to see it?

They don't tell you these things. The best I can make out from what they say is that the soul cannot be photographed, and it cannot be seen in a mirror because it has no substance and because it is hidden within us. We can only see it after we die."

There was a gap in the recording. When the voice resumed speaking, Maria sounded less childlike. "I wonder if all souls are alike... I wonder if they are like a puff of moisture, like a cloud-- neither tall nor short; neither pretty nor ugly, neither blond nor dark, but just pure ethereal matter invisible to living people, like the mass of a specter in the air."

On another entry, Maria sounded a little older and more confrontational. "Today, while I looked in the mirror, I couldn't help wondering: why couldn't that be the image of my soul? I am getting tired with so much abstraction, so much hocus-pocus about the soul. If the soul is as real as people claim, then I want to see mine for myself. I don't want to wait until I am dead. Why should that be necessary? I want to see it, to hear it, to feel it, in the here and now. But I can just hear the naysayers saying: 'No, no, no. You cannot see the soul. That's impossible.' Ah, but impossible in what way? Because it's all a myth? Because it doesn't exist? That is probably the truth, but they won't admit to it. Instead, they'll try to sound profound and come up with rationalizations such as: Your soul is not visible through your own eyes, but through the eyes of others. Gee, thanks! That helps a lot! That is one of the many condescending copouts they give you. I've been hearing talk such as this since my Santa Claus days. Well, I'm not a child anymore, and I am sick of runarounds."

In another soliloquy Maria was still questioning, still critical, but more mature and, paradoxically, more sentimental, slightly more romantic in her attitude towards the soul. "Today I heard yet another one of those sugary platitudes about the soul. It's still nonsense, but at least it is more palatable. It has romance and mystery added to it and goes like this: the soul is the enigma that an artist sometimes captures in a portrait. Look at Leonardo da Vinci's Mona Lisa and you will see the smiling soul of a lady known through the centuries as 'La Giaconda.' So, we are back to seeing the soul through other people's eyes. Now, in fairness, I will not deny that the soul is something real which I feel strongly and unequivocally, as if it were something trapped inside me. How silly it would be to say that crying is only the eyes spilling tears, when I know it is my soul writhing in pain. The tears are in the eye; the sorrow is in my soul. At times I feel parts of my soul so vividly that they seem like traits of my personality come alive. I could almost name them."

Then later still: "And yet, despite the keen sense of self-awareness that we all feel beneath the skin, I am not prepared to say that the soul has human form, that it is a spirit in the person's image. I've outgrown the romantic imagery of the soul. What I feel within my flesh, inside my bones and flowing in my blood, may be my soul, but it is not anthropomorphic. It is the microscopic atoms and molecules in the cells of my body. The soul's site is in the proteins and acids of our cells, in the neuron and axons of the brain. If we could see it, it would not be a pretty sight. I am most inclined to believe that the best chance of seeing a person's soul is by taking a picture of the person's DNA. That is the real paradigm of the self we call the soul."

Finally, she got to the nitty-gritty. "Looks aside, is the soul immortal? Logically that can't be! Why should it be when it is part and parcel of a very mortal, corruptible body made of blood, flesh, proteins and neurons? The only sense in which the soul can survive beyond death is through those molecules, those characteristics of the self at the cellular level that leave their track for a while. It is those miniscule prints in the semen, in the hair, in the blood, that live to tell tales that accuse the rapist or the murderer, by surviving and pointing a finger at his crime and his wickedness."

Maria was pounding the desk in obvious agreement as she heard her own recordings. She was proud of what she was hearing. "Yes, yes, yes!" Ram came to check on her.

"By the looks of it, it must be good. Is that what you were looking for?"

"Oh yes, yes, Ram. This is exactly what I was looking for. I hope never to lose it again. But tell me one thing; was I awake or asleep when you recorded this?"

"What an odd question. Why do you ask? What are you driving at?"

"I know that if I was awake when I said this, then I will be allowed to keep it. But I fear that if I was asleep, then it belongs to the kingdom of oblivion, and I cannot have it. Isn't that the way it works?"

"No. That's not the way it works. You are confused about that. These thoughts are yours to keep," he told her.

"They are? Oh, my God!"

Maria was beside herself with joy. She got up and hugged him. "Oh, thank you, thank you, Ram. You are a doll. But I don't understand. I am confused. How is this possible?"

"First of all, you articulated these thoughts on several occasions at different times. The first part was when you were about ten, the others when you were a teenager and older. Sometimes you were awake, sometimes you were asleep. In any case, your thoughts, both awake and asleep, have fused into an enduring memory on this subject. You are what you believe, and you believe what you nurture with recurring thoughts that become firmer and firmer over time. Your thoughts on the soul have now solidified into what you might call a personal credo. As such, they are part of the legacy of your long-term memory."

"The more I come here, the more I like it, but the less and less I understand it. What else do you have for me?"

"Would you like to hear Professor Quixote's take on this? It's similar to yours. You think a lot alike. But he took a different tack."

"Yes, by all means. I'd love to hear it. Now I'm ready for it."

Ram then turned on the monitor and played a video in which the professor was on a round table discussion with his colleagues.

"The soul enjoys an undeserved venerable position in the mind of man," began Professor Quixote. "This is due to much mystification in literature, in the arts, and in religion. The soul is a sort of sacred cow, and it is time we question it. I do not deny its existence, but I do not buy the usual lore about it either. Where does it reside? Is it in the heart? In the liver? My guess is in the human brain. Unfortunately, the poor human brain does not get its due. Poets have gushed too long about the heart and the soul, to the disparagement of the body. In the usual pejorative juxtaposition, the human soul is heavenly, the body mundane. During dreams the sleeping body is excess baggage, useless as a truck out of gas that the soul leaves behind while it goes off flying like Mary Poppins, like Superman, or like an angel nimble on his wings. Why bother with a truck when you can fly? It makes you feel as if you can't wait to die so you can fly like that.

"This glamorization of the soul is not only unfair but flawed. It does not give credit to the true source of the magic, which is the brain. To begin with, the heavenly nirvana that we enjoy through dreams here on earth, takes place in a body; and that body has a living brain. It is that brain that conjures up images in living color that simulates the sense of flying which makes travel through time possible. The brain serves us memories, sounds and feelings with touches of love, joy, laughter and bliss. It is this ability of the brain that comes closest to touching God's magnificence and savoring the marvel of the power that is attributed to Him. In my opinion, it is in the human brain, and not in heaven, that you would come closest to finding God. The brain is the true source of all the heavenly experiences that man enjoys on earth. Now, I will be the first to grant you one major shortcoming about the brain. The brain is downright ugly. It does not have the charisma and the ethereal aura of the soul. It's just a squiggly blob. But don't let appearances fool you, because the human brain is the creator of all the beauty conceived by man through art. And let us not forget, the brain is part of the human body.

"We feel what we feel when we dream because we are alive, because we have a brain that does its magic and regurgitates life remembered, life encapsulated in the mystery of its memory, and life simulated by the power of its imagination. The body is not just a superfluous appendage that stays behind when we dream. The body is where it happens. And the brain is making it all possible. It is wrong to dichotomize human beings in terms of body and soul. It should really be body and mind. So, what's the difference between mind and soul? The word 'mind' is a little more down to earth than 'soul' and is more reminiscent of its source, the brain. Everything about life, everything that we consider—whether feeling, knowing, perceiving and just living—takes place because of the brain and through the brain and in our body. The totality is body and mind. Diminish one in some way and you impair the quality of life. Maim the body and you may diminish your capabilities, lowering your enjoyment of life. If you become cripple, or deaf, mute, or blind, the brain can help you compensate for what you are missing, teaching your body to adapt. All I'm asking is that you recognize the importance of a healthy body on the total enjoyment of life. Similarly, injure the brain and, in spite of a healthy body, you may significantly diminish your capacity to enjoy life because you may lose your sight, your hearing, or your motor control, and you may go into a coma and turn into a vegetable.

"By the way, being in a coma is, in fact, the only instance when sleep has a similarity with death, or worse still, with hell. The annals of neurology report the incredible predicaments of people who are buried in an unresponsive, virtually dead body. There was, for instance, the case of a young woman who was involved in a car wreck and who became comatose. She could not express herself by any of the usual means. There were no sounds from her, no winking of the eyes, no tapping with a finger, no signals of any sort perceivable without instruments. It was not possible to tell whether the person could see, or hear, or think. Doctors then wired up her brain to find answers in an alternative way and discovered that the brain indeed was responsive to electrical stimulus. The woman gave evidence of awareness. Yes, she could hear, and she could understand; she could imagine and react to ideas. What her brain revealed was frightening for the dismal plight it conjured up. The young woman was asked to pretend being in a tennis court. From the waves and blood flows of the brain it could be seen that the signals and responses were the same as those of a healthy tennis player who was asked to imagine the same thing. She was asked to move about her house. The observers then saw that the areas of her brain that responded were those that would normally be activated. That poor woman was trapped in a useless body with her soul marooned somewhere in a distant place out of reach from us, out of help. She might as well have been in a desert with her truck out of gas and the wings of her soul clipped. Her predicament shatters the glamour of a living soul sans body. No one can be romantic about the free independent spirit of that soul while its body lies dormant for years. It is hard to imagine a worse living hell."

It was getting late, and Maria was drained. She left the carrel with her heart and her mind charged to surfeit, more than ready for a break. On her way out she passed by Ram's office. He was sitting on a chair inclined backwards and with his feet propped up on the desk, reading a magazine. She thanked him for all his help again and added with a wink: "Now you can take a snooze, Ram. Sweet dreams. Ciao."

Z z   z Z z   Z z

33. ATEO SUENA FEO

The following morning Maria woke up without a memory of having dreamed. It had been one of those nights entirely devoted to thinking, without dramatization. Her day was uneventful, except for the introspection and cosmic thoughts that seemed to characterize her days. Later that night, as soon as she began to dream, she went straight to the library at Dream Central and found Ram at work cataloguing and archiving thoughts.

"There he is, busy as usual--working, working, working" she said as she came in. "You should be paid triple time for all you do, Ram. I mean it. I don't know what we would ever do without you."

"You would be lost. You'd be in a fog, that's what."

"I know it. If it were up to me, I would get you some relief, an assistant or two, and I would see that you get some time off."

"Naah, I love what I do. I love tagging along with you through the dark and light, through all the wonderful places that you visit. I am there to keep them alive for you for posterity. I love sharing your joys and sorrows. My fate is to be your shadow and serve you well. But what can I help you with tonight? I bet you are after more deep philosophy tonight, aren't you? What are you looking for now?"

"Brace yourself, Ram, the a-f-t-e-r-l-i-f-e."

"Oh, that is deep—almost scary. Do you want your thoughts, or Professor Quixote's?"

"You know, I think I can save you the trouble of wasting time looking through my stuff. I don't think I have much material on this subject. I 've been too chicken to follow it through and always quit before I get too deep. So just go for Prof. Quixote's ideas on this."

"Okay, I'll see what I can find. I'll be right back."

Ram pivoted and went looking for something suitable. He was soon out of sight as he was swallowed by the labyrinth of narrow shelves upon shelves of the library. He returned in a few minutes with a VHS tape which he wagged enthusiastically before Maria, saying: "This will keep you busy. It was recorded a few years ago at a graduate seminar in statistical research. The audience is quite mature, this time—mostly PhD candidates and professors. This time Professor Quixote does not feel like he must mince his words."

"Yes, but statistical research, Ram? No, no. I think you've misunderstood me. I don't want anything statistical. I am after belief in life after death."

"That's what this is. The professor starts talking about agnosticism and atheism first, but what he is really after is examining beliefs about life in the hereafter under different conditions. He makes the point that, contrary to what many believers think, agnostics are at peace with themselves. They can look at death without fear and with great equanimity. On the other hand, he thinks some of the believers have the greatest difficulty when the end nears, because the thought of a final comeuppance after death is most unsettling—especially if they suspect they are going to hell. He is so convinced of this that he proposes it as a testable statistical hypothesis and suggests where to get the data for it."

"Wow! That does sound very interesting-this is more like it! Yes, get it for me, I can't wait to see it. It will keep me busy all night."

Maria then sat in front of the monitor and started to watch the tape. It was not a lecture; it was more like a chat with fellow intellectuals. Professor Quixote was sitting in a cushy comfortable chair, surrounded by his colleagues in the inner circle while behind them, sitting in regular chairs, were the PhD candidates. After a few introductions and other preliminaries, the Professor had the floor.

"Most people don't think much about death until they go to church or to a funeral," he began. "Death is what happens to others. It is an unpleasant subject and people don't dwell on it if they can help it. When the thought of death hits them, the first thing they think about is insurance—not just the policy with their insurance company, but especially the other kind of insurance, the eternal one. Have they paid their dues with God? Are they ready to meet their maker, or are they in default?

"The average Christian sinner who thinks he has been good has little to fear; he is not in major default and is basically ready to face his maker. He is not only guilt free, but he has another crutch that enables him to face death with serenity, his faith in God. It is a source of much comfort and solace to him, like a sedative against the fear of his mortality and like a promise of infinite bliss without end. He is beautifully set. His position seems enviable.

"But what about the atheist or the agnostic? If faith in God is the insurance for life after death, then these people are not only in default, but uninsured. You would think they would be afraid knowing, as they do, that death is an eventual certainty. How can they bear the thought of being so unprepared? The faithful pity them and cannot understand them. They rocked the boat and risked losing an eternity of peace, now they must pay the price. Poor things."

The professor then paused, smiling to himself as if remembering something amusing that had crossed his mind. "Do you know something funny? It just dawned on me that I find myself at a strange juncture now. I usually come from the other direction on this issue, showing first how happy and how content the nonbelievers are with themselves; and, curiously, how odd and loony the believers and faithful seem to them--exactly the opposite of where I am now. Let me see if I can do as well, going the other way.

"First of all, make no mistake about it… there are good people among atheists and agnostics also. Many of them are just average sinners—not perfect people, but good human beings. Because these people do not believe in God, they also do not fear Him. Their lack of faith gives them no guilt, nor—and this may surprise you—does it make them feel undeserving of heaven should there really be such a thing after all. Why should they be excluded from it if they had led good lives? Where is the justice in denying them that? But they don't dwell on this. If God should tell them when they die: 'I think it is fair to give you exactly what you expected, no more and no less. There'll be no hell for you, but also no heaven. You will get nothing, an eternity of nothingness, which is what you expected.'

That would be fine with the agnostics and atheists. They would take their lumps without rancor. It is, after all, what they expected. In brief, they really feel that they have nothing to win or to lose, even if it should turn out that there is a heaven after all."

"Nonbelievers value being at peace with themselves mentally. They insist on doing their own thinking, free from church, from dogma, from authority, from superstitious injunctions and myths. This need to think freely is so inalienable, so indispensable that they cannot imagine living a life in which they could not probe, not test and not question. Such a life would be hellish, stifling as mental slavery.

"They also insist on personal involvement with God. Of all relationships, the one between man and God should be the strongest in human bondage, more so than between offspring and parents, or between siblings, or friends, or even lovers. But this relationship should be based on continuous, clear and direct communication with God without third party intermediaries. Agnostics will not take the words of prophets, nor of the church nor other intermediaries, as the word of God. It is not the same. They break the usual three-way communication arrangement where God is on one end, the church is in the middle supposedly relaying His word, and the faithful are way out on the other end listening only to what the middlemen say. This arrangement is completely unsatisfactory to the questioners. In their opinion, it is the cause of much mischief because it sets up the people in the middle, the prelate, the ayatollahs, the prophets and the like—to act for God. The nonbelievers, for their part, cannot understand how the faithful can accept this arrangement. Talk about giving up so much, look who is talking, they'd say. The believers have given up their mind! The church does the thinking for them and that's too much! The agnostics and atheists have completely cut out this middle group. Their revolt is not so much with God as with those that pretend to speak for Him.

"Agnostics are convinced that believers don't think with their heads. Instead, they believe with their hearts, and they do not question anything. If they dared to question, they would demand an explanation for the silence and the absence of God. To the agnostics and atheists this failure in communication is untenable. They won't stand it. The faithful for their part answer that He is there even if they can't see Him or hear Him. Don't look with your eyes, they say, but think about the proof of his presence, the order of the universe, the beauty of nature in all its wonders. You can see His hand everywhere. You got to be blind not to see it.

"The atheists and agnostics respond: 'you miss the point. We, too, appreciate the wonders of nature and the magnificence of the universe and we are also very grateful. But where do we go to render our gratitude in a personal way? Since, as previously noted, personal two-way communication is all important to the nonbelievers, God's absence and silence proves frustrating. God's existence is not the issue. His absenteeism is. His silence is. Maybe He created the universe and then died. Maybe He put the ingredients together and set randomness to do the rest. As long as there is no communication, there can be no relationship.

"That's the key word: relationship! Relationship based on open communication. You don't need to point out to an adult person who never knew his father that he must have had a father. Don't tell him: look at your height; look at the color of your eyes because he would say: so, what! What matters to him is not that his eyes are blue or that he is tall because his father was. What matters to him is why did his father desert him? The man that sired him, for all he knows, never cared for him, contested his paternity, and forgot him. For that orphan bastard, creation is an insult. The real binding between father and son is built on commitment, on open communication, on solidarity, on togetherness, on relationship. That goes for God as well.

"Finally, some would think that because nonbelievers are free of religion, that they do not have a moral compass, that they are loose, reprobate, unprincipled, undependable and immoral. This is not the case. The unbelievers live by the same moral precepts, but they take them as guides to good living, not as orders. In fact, this is another peeve they have against the faithful and the church. The believers often do what they do for the wrong reason—out of fear, instead of principle or conviction. The church, for its part, exerts its control by coercing its flock, threatening them with excommunication and with hell and damnation. This point needs emphasis and I'll state it as strongly as I can. It is possible for all good people, whether believers, atheists or agnostics, to live by the golden rule, to do onto others as you would have them do onto you. It is also possible for good people, atheists and faithful alike, to live by the Ten Commandments, at least, most of them. The difference is that the good atheists abide by them, not because they fear reprisals if they break them, but because they value their virtue and wisdom. Incredible as it may seem, atheists and agnostics respect and admire Jesus Christ for what He did and what He taught; they revere him for his virtues, his message of peace, his love and devotion to man, his compassion and forbearance. It is possible to agree on fundamental values of humanity and still differ as to deities and beliefs in the hereafter. In sum, a heretic can have a clear conscience simply because he was a good human being.

"Now here is something inexplicable and repugnant that the nonbelievers could throw at the faithful: how to rationalize pedophilia, child sexual abuse and perversity on the part of the supposedly most faithful of the faithful, the clergy? This boggles the mind for the hypocrisy involved. It cheapens faith and makes a mockery of it. These perverts can fool the parishioners; they can fool their bishops, their cardinals and the Pope. But do they think they can fool God? Where is their faith? Or do they think so little of their God that they think He will forgive them? Does God not care for their victims? I could just go on and on, but I would prefer to change the subject."

One of the PhD candidates helped him with this. "Sir, I can help you change the subject. Could you please clarify the difference between an atheist and an agnostic? All night long you have been referring to them as if they were pretty much in the same camp of nonbelievers. What exactly is the difference?"

"I'm glad you brought that up. I was going to cover it sooner or later. The atheist is categorical in his denials. He asserts there is no God; there is no heaven and no hell; and there is no life after death. The soul, whatever it is, perishes with the body. It is not immortal.

"The agnostic does not think it is necessary to go that far. He doesn't deny anything. In fact, he would ask the atheist the same thing he would ask believers, which is: how do you know? How do you know that there is no life after death? How do you know what you claim to deny? The agnostic does not deny what is essentially unknowable. There may be life after death; there may be a heaven and a hell, an immortal soul, and even God, for all he knows. But, since the only way that you would ever really know this is by dying, it is unknowable here on earth and, therefore, you shouldn't deny what you cannot know. So, basically, he is in the same camp as the atheist, except he is not as adamant. He does not deny what he knows he cannot prove to be false. But he does live his life free of any commitment to what may or may not come after death."

Maria turned off the tape for a few minutes to absorb what she had heard and to personalize it. I guess I am an agnostic rather than an atheist. I still don't like the sound of the word "atheist". She switched to Spanish and articulated her feeling in that language, saying: *"Ateo suena feo"* (atheist sounds ugly). Also, she did not like the intellectual arrogance of the atheist. It seemed overkill to deny what you can't possibly know. Just don't buy it. That's all. Then she sat back on her chair and napped for a while.

zzz   Z   zzz

34. "My Credo"

While doing his errands, Ram came by Maria's carrel and found her sleeping. He tried not to disturb her and went about his chores tiptoeing quietly. But then he tripped on something and dropped the tapes he was carrying, making an awful racket, which startled Maria and woke her up.

"So sorry, Maria. How clumsy of me. I do apologize."

"Nah, don't mention it," said Maria as she got up and stretched herself.

"You know," said Ram, "I was torn between waking you up so you could go to a more comfortable place, or letting you be as you were. Now that you are awake, I am glad I tripped up. Why don't you go to the sofa in the office, and make yourself more comfortable?"

"But Ram, I am....Ah, Aha!" said Maria as if she had discovered something. "At last, I caught you in a memory lapse. You do forget things."

"Me forget? No. No way. What did I forget?"

"You forgot that I couldn't possibly be uncomfortable sleeping in that chair because my body is really at home, sleeping on its comfortable bed even as we speak."

"Hush now. You are not supposed to remember things like that while you are here. Leave such blatant reality out of these premises."

"Ah, but the point is that I did remember it and you forgot it."

"No, I didn't forget. As a matter of fact, that's the reason I decided to not wake you up. I remembered where you really were, and I knew you were comfortable. My stumble was strictly accidental."

"Oh, Ram, you're impossible. I just can't win against you."

"How far did you get with Professor Quixote's tape?"

"Through agnosticism and atheism."

"Heavy stuff, but the best is yet to come. Are you ready for more?"

"Yes, I think I can give it a go."

Maria sat in front of the monitor again and resumed playing the tape. Professor Quixote was talking.

"Another aspect of beliefs we haven't focused on is that they are changeable. People change. Atheists become believers and believers become atheists. There are forces at work that bring about these changes in humans. Sin is one of them, as are also its sequels of remorse and atonement. How many times have you heard of corrupt politicians, corporate thieves, embezzlers and unfaithful philandering preachers being 'reborn' and finding religion after they were caught? In some cases, sin serves to charge the religious batteries of the faithful—but only after they get caught."

While Maria was watching the tape, Ram was looking at Maria. She was following the professor enthusiastically, pounding the desk in approval and exclaiming things like: That's telling it! Ram approached her quietly and stood behind her then he squeezed her shoulders gently and asked her: "How is this tape? Are you getting much out of it?"

"Oh, Ram, am I? I love it! This is marvelous. I am astounded at my affinity with Professor Quixote's thinking. I hear him in rapture. I am so in sync with his mind that at times I can anticipate his very next word. It is as if he were articulating ideas, which I had thought of myself. How I wish I could take this tape with me. But I know, don't tell me, rules are rules, and material on reserve cannot be taken out of the premises."

She was astounded at Ram's response, and couldn't believe her ears when he corrected her, saying: "Well, not necessarily."

Maria bolted from the chair and stood up to look him in the face. "What? Run that by me again, please."

"It's kind of complicated…" he began hesitantly, explaining with some difficulty. "You cannot take the tape. That's true. But the ideas are already yours. You don't need the tape."

"Really? How? Tell me!" Maria said shaking his shoulders.

"Sit down. Calm yourself. Let me see how I can put it. Normally we would distill tidbits of this into your dreams. But this material would not fit well in dreams. As a matter of fact, I don't know whether you are aware of this or not, but for the last two or three nights you have not had any dreams. I told the girls not to bother with this. They would just as soon deal with something lighter. It wasn't worth their time or effort."

"Oh, Ram, you didn't! How could you? I love this!"

"Yes, I know you do. But it's too much to turn into a dream. Besides, it is not necessary. Why should the girls knock themselves out preparing something you would remember anyway? Yes, you heard right. You will remember a lot of this—not word for word as Professor Quixote expressed them, but in essence. The reason you feel so in sync with his lecture and the reason that you could anticipate his ideas so well is that you have had the same thoughts before. These transcendental issues fall into a special category, which is on a par with your knowledge of studied things such as mathematics, physics, and chemistry. It is not only their intricacy, but the keen interest you have in them. Many people put off thinking about these issues, but not you. You think about them in earnest. Should atheists be allowed in heaven if they have been good? Should atheists care if they are not allowed in? And what am I, an atheist or an agnostic? You have asked yourself these questions dozens of times. You are very committed to live by what you believe. This commitment, in turn, develops into a special wiring of your brain that involves the sturdier axons and dendrites of your long-term memory. To put it plainly and simply, you are hard-wired in a special way for these topics. You've covered all the bases that Professor Quixote covered. Sometimes it was while you were asleep, sorting and digesting recent events. Sometimes it was while you were awake, when it was triggered by something you read in a magazine or newspaper, or on TV. It could also have been when you had some of those bitter, drag-out arguments with your mother about religion.

"In fact, I can think of one instance that created quite a brainstorm for you which affected your beliefs. About a year ago you saw a documentary on the mass suicides in Jonestown, Guyana which took place on November 18, 1978. A total of 909 people were duped into drinking poison by their religious leader, Jim Jones. Do you remember that? You couldn't sleep for two days."

"Oh, God, don't bring that up. I was so sick. I was on the verge of vomiting seeing all those bloated bodies on an open field under the sun. But yes, I remember how much that made me think. I had mental marathons for hours. I swore then never to surrender any part of my mind to religion. In fact, I wrote some lines to that effect."

Ram interrupted her. "Hold it! Hold it a minute, Maria. I need to ask you something. It's important. Could you recite those lines for me now?"

"Gee, I don't know… I don't think I could do it word for word… But I could give you the gist of it, I think."

"No, I don't want the gist. I want the lines word for word."

"Oh, Ram you know I can't do that. Give me a break. Let me take a quick peek at them first."

"No. You just listen. I'll recite them for you." (He recites).

Should superstition, myth—or religion for that matter,
Announce, as they're wont to do, that they've kidnapped your soul
And that for ransom you must surrender your thinking mind.
Don't pay that ransom! You will lose both: mind and soul!
If they threaten your soul with hell and damnation
If they should call you names: heretic, pagan, infidel, or worse.
Pay no attention. Call their bluff. Slam the door on them.
Or just hang up.

"You are incredible, Ram. You are phenomenal. Even I couldn't have recited those lines as you did just then. I know I wrote them, and I remember them now, but not as well as you."

"Aha, so now perhaps you can understand better what I am trying to explain to you about your memory wiring. The lines you heard should have sounded familiar since you wrote them. Although you could not remember them word for word, you remembered the general idea, the defiance, and the importance you give the mind over the soul. It is in this sense that you will remember tonight's lecture."

Maria was in awe. "Can I ask you one more thing? What did I call those lines of verse? Do you know?"

"Don't you remember?"

"No. I went through so many titles. 'My Faith Manifesto' was one. 'This I believe,' was another and there were a couple of others. I can't remember what I ended up with."

"You called it: 'My Credo.'"

Maria kept shaking her head in disbelief at the wonder of Ram's infallible memory. But it was getting late. Ram asked her how far she had got on the tape, which Maria had left on pause. She now rewound it a few turns to catch a drift of where she was, but then she saw something that had aroused her curiosity. There was a person among the PhD candidates whom she thought she could recognize, but she could not get a clear view of him. She thought it was Kenneth Flynn, a classmate from undergraduate days on whom she had had a terrible crush.

"Ram, as a man who remembers everything and who seems to know so much, could you tell me where and when this tape was recorded?"

"At the University of Georgia, a couple of years ago. Why do you ask?"

"I thought I recognized an old flame."

"Kenneth Flynn?"

"Yes! How did you know? Never mind. Scratch that. I don't think there is a page of my history that you do not remember. I wonder what happened to him."

"Now that I don't know! But it is getting late, my Sweet. I don't think you'll have time for the last part of the lecture. Why don't we leave it for tomorrow, okay? Little vampires need to get to their tombs."

Maria retorted: "This little vampire needs to get up to go to work. Thank God tomorrow is Friday."

Z Z   z z z   Z Z

35. HELL, THE MERCURIAL

On Friday, neither Elena nor Toro nor Wally were at school. Maria noted their absence with increasing concern. She was beginning to fear that something ugly might be afoot.

Aside from that, it was a slow day. That evening she had dinner at the Powers. Karen Powers, the chemistry teacher, had become her closest colleague and dear friend. She always enjoyed her company. After a lovely evening, Maria turned in around midnight.

When her mind opened to dreams, Maria saw herself returning to the library at Dream Central looking for Ram, but Ram was not at the counter. Maria waited for a few minutes, and then she began to call for him teasingly, singing her calls to the tune of "Frere Jacques."

"Ram? Are you here?" There was no answer. "*Frere Ram, Frere Ram, Ou est vous? Dormez vous? Sonnez la matina. Sonnez la matina. Ding, dang, dong.*"

Just then he appeared from behind one of the shelves as if he had been playing peek-a-boo.

"Tah dah!" he blared. "Here I am wide awake. I'd bet you thought I was napping, didn't you? But I fooled you. I was ordering thoughts and memories, putting them in the right place. I could swear that there are gremlins and ghosts around here that move things. Or else, things have a life of their own and go visiting other shelves."

Maria concurred, musing about the place. "Now that you mention it, this place does have a rather spooky ambience."

"Would you like to finish viewing the tape? It is right at the place where you left it. It's the one where the professor was talking about faith and belief in the afterlife."

"Thank you, thank you, Ram. That's the one. Let's see where that goes." Maria then sat in front of the monitor and resumed listening to Professor Quixote.

"I want to share with you an idea that has intrigued me for some time. It is the elasticity of faith, especially under dire circumstances. To illustrate, suppose we have an individual who believes in divine justice; that is, he was raised to believe that you will go to heaven if you are good; and you will go to hell if you are bad. And let us suppose further that this individual knows, based on how bad he has been, that he would be going to hell. The question is: how stable is his belief when he thinks his own death is near? As an interesting aside, note that this question can be investigated statistically. All you have to do is to visit a hospice, or better yet death row in a maximum-security penitentiary to find a mother lode of cases. Think of how much you could glean from that. First, you could poll the condemned inmates about divine justice. That would give you the proportion of that population that believes in heaven and hell, which is an interesting statistical parameter. Then you could compare this parameter to the rest of the larger, non-criminal population and see how it fares. I think this could be a great source for sociological and psychological research.

"Don't be alarmed to find surprises though. The matter is not simple, or static. I would suspect it is complex and unstable. There may be a certain psychological dynamic, a certain defense mechanism that causes belief to change. Keep in mind that the individuals in question have been through a lot; they've been caught in their crimes; they've been tried and convicted; and they have been sentenced. They find themselves trapped in a dead end with death as the only way out. However, hope springs eternal in humans. Remember, these convicts typically appeal their sentences to the end; they study the law books looking for escape clauses and try every trick to protract the process. Even when everything has failed, they still don't give up. They keep their hope clear up to the execution day when the governor might sign a stay of execution, or the Supreme Court at the last minute may order a commutation of their sentence. The hope for a *deus ex-machina* is not extinguished till the last minute. What you need to consider is that if they are still trying to work the man-made system of justice to the very end, imagine how they feel about the providential system. Do they feel like they can work that also?

"This is where the elasticity of faith comes into play, changing beliefs over time. Bad Christians would become better Christians; non-believers could become believers; and believers could go atheistic. Don't be surprised to learn that it could go both ways. Time plays a critical role here and your analysis would need to take that into account.

"Some would argue that most of these sinners do not believe in divine justice, for if they had been true believers to begin with, they wouldn't have been such rotten criminals. Well, that sounds like a hypothesis to me and all I have to say about it is test it.

"There are hypotheses and hypotheses. This situation is ripe with hypotheses ready for the picking. I don't think this phenomenon has been investigated. Here is another interesting issue to research. Would you expect the proportion of those who change from non-believers to believers to be less than, equal to, or greater than the proportion of believers who change to non-believers? It is tempting to think that there would be more converts to Christianity. The Christian Faith does have two things going for it: the mercy of providence and the redeeming power of atonement. These are good selling points. I could see how condemned men could be persuaded by them. By the time they are to be executed, they would have changed so completely that some of them would be ardently devout, blindly faithful and, as they like to say, reborn. Some would feel that they have already paid for their crimes in good part and will have earned the right to go at least to purgatory. In their heart of hearts, these men would not contemplate going to hell, especially if they've been in death row for long. The time they have already served; the good deeds they've performed while in jail; their repentance and their devotion and fervent prayers would save them from hell in their minds. In their hearts they would be convinced that they will not burn forever.

"But what do the agnostics and nonbelievers have? Where could they find refuge? What lure does disbelief offer them? Who can they pray to? Just when you think that they have nothing, I must tell you that there are times when nothing is, actually, something. Nonbelievers may not have the promises of heaven, but by the same token they don't have the threat of hell either. There is peace in the thought that there is nothing after death. There is no gain, but also no pain. And this is something.

"I do not believe that it is possible to predict a priori one way or the other who would change how. There are other factors at play that could influence the decision. What I do emphasize is that in this desperate predicament, any man would seek escape. If he could not escape from prison, then at least, maybe, he could escape from the curse of hell. But how? Believe it or not, the escape from hell is easier than the escape from prison. It is well within his power; it is entirely up to him because hell is only in his mind. There are no concrete walls to climb. All he would have to do is to sweep off the webs of faith that religion has woven around his mind. When he has cleared his mind of them, he would be at peace with his new vision of death. Death would be the end of ends with nothing after it: with no God, no heaven and no hell. By extirpating religious beliefs, the man would find that death would have lost its bite because hell itself would have been defanged. And so, like the criminal who found peace and freedom from hell by becoming a devout believer, this nonbeliever also, would not spend his last days thinking that he was going to hell."

"All roads lead to Rome. The two men we just considered came to the same ultimate belief by entirely different routes: one by embracing religion, the other by rejecting it. Yet, both eliminated the threat of hell from their minds and from their futures. I would suspect that all men on death row gravitate towards a belief in the afterlife that, in one way or another, gets rid of hell. It is almost contrary to human nature to accept eternal doom with equanimity. And I would suggest, therefore, that this is at the core of what needs to be investigated statistically."

At that point, several hands went up. Professor Quixote recognized one at random and it happened to be Kenneth Flynn. When Maria recognized him, she was aware that after all these years her heart still throbbed for him. He had been her Prince Charming during her senior year.

"Sir, I have a dozen questions about the design of the questionnaire and the statistical model to research these issues," began Kenneth. "I agree completely that time would be a critical conditioning factor. But I will leave these questions until after class so as not to change the subject. What I would like to ask you now, if you forgive me for being personal, is: What do you believe? Do you believe in God, in divine justice, or in an afterlife? And if you don't, could you then tell us what your notion of the afterlife is."

There was quite a hubbub in the room. Some people grumbled at the impertinent question. Others cheered him quietly for having the nerve to ask what was on everybody's mind. Maria thought: "Gosh, that's not quite the way I would have put it, but I am glad he asked it."

A professor got up and, grabbing at the lapels of his coat with his hands, intoned firmly: "Don't answer that, Professor Quixote. You don't have to answer that if you don't want to. You're not on trial here. You have a right to keep your personal beliefs private." The man was the personification of Abraham Lincoln and Maria was not surprised to see him interjecting his objections as he did. Lately, it seemed, Maria's conscience had taken a liking to Lincoln and was using his persona more often than Janet Reno's.

"Calm down all of you," said Professor Quixote confidently. "Thank you, Mr. President, but I can handle this. I am not offended in the least by the question. What's more, I've been expecting it. It never fails. Discussions of this nature cannot be kept in the abstract. You can't hide behind privacy laws because inquiring minds are desperate to break through them and put you on the spot. The discussion is bound to be personal. So, take notes if you want as I pour out the story of my life and reveal anything else that might be pertinent. Here goes. I have been an agnostic ever since I can remember. I can honestly tell you that I played hooky from church long before I played hooky from elementary school. By age seven I was a doubting Thomas, but at twelve I was a hard core and hard-boiled nonbeliever. I had it absolutely all worked out. And I had lost absolutely all fear of God. Heaven went with Santa Claus. And let's see…have I left something out? What else? Oh, yes, I've asked to be cremated with no service of any kind when I die. I love pork and I am uncircumcised, thank God! There! I hope we've cleared the air. Will that do?"

The young man responded: "Yes, Sir. I meant no offense. I apologize for the impertinence, but there comes a point when people need to take positions and speak from their own personal convictions. I was glad to hear you say that you expected it. Now, if you will, please clarify the beliefs of someone who considers death to be an end. I just can't picture that. Also, I don't understand the position of the agnostic. He claims not to know what will happen after death; yet he denies what others believe could happen. Why should the agnostic's denial be more definitive than the other's belief?"

The professor corrected him. "You have misrepresented the position of the agnostic. What you say is not accurate. The agnostic does not deny anything. I would prefer to say that the agnostic does not accept as true what others believe. He does not sup at their table of beliefs. For all he knows, there may be a God, a heaven and a hell. What matters to him is the conduct of his life on this earth. He wants to live his life free of the promise or the threat of what may or may not happen in another world."

Flynn was still puzzled. "What does he make of the fact that the whole world speaks practically in one voice about this. I mean the millions of Christians, Jews and Muslims. They all say there is a God. These beliefs have been passed on for thousands of years. Who is he to question them?"

The professor responded calmly. "Your last comment about the overwhelming number of believers reminds me of the fallacy of large numbers encapsulated by this saying: 'Eat excrement; feast on feces because a thousand million flies couldn't possibly be all wrong.'

There was loud laughter in the room. When everyone quieted again, the professor continued. "Now, as to your question of who does he think he is? There is a simple answer: he thinks he is his own man and his own Prophet. Who else, if not himself, should he be to settle his own beliefs? But amazingly—and this is what astounds the agnostic—millions of people entrust their theological analysis to others and basically abdicate from their responsibility to reckon with God rationally for themselves.

"As if this were not bad enough, the agnostic then asks himself: and to whom do believers entrust their analysis? And the answer is: to antiquity, which brings us to the final point in your question. Well, antiquity is part of the problem. The agnostic takes the Bible as early literary fiction, not as history, and certainly not as the word of God."

The discussion was turning into a match between Professor Quixote and Kenneth Flynn. Each shot back in a volley of questions and answers. Flynn was not being argumentative. He was simply curious. He had never met someone who thought like Professor Quixote and who refused so much of the world's cherished beliefs. This was all quite an education for him.

Professor Quixote then asked him to let him finish because they would never get anywhere one question at a time. "Let me drop the third person and speak bluntly for myself now. Here is the crux of the matter. God presents an insuperable difficulty for me because of his silence. His existence is not a problem. His silence is. Silence frustrates all communication and prevents forging any sort of relationship. Ah, you say, but His word has come down from the ages in scripture. Well, that's not the same thing. That is not communication at all. That is just reading pages in a book, pages that cannot hear you, and cannot answer back. Moreover, the words in all the holy books were written by man, by intermediaries—not by God. To compound matters, even the writers of these words themselves are dead by now, so I cannot ask them about what they thought they saw, or what they thought they heard. Finally, whoever those writers might have been, I simply cannot trust them. I have very little in common with them intellectually. They lived in a world thousands of years ago that is much, much different from mine. It was a world when the earth was thought to be flat, when science was nonexistent, when Physics, Chemistry or Biology had not yet been invented, when the thought processes of man were still very raw and rudimentary. Thanks, but no thanks. I will do my own thinking.

"Agnosticism is not easy. There is no romance in it. No fairy tale. The truths you live by must be hewn the hard way, by constant and tedious examination and you must let them age like tight shoes. You must wear them till they quit hurting and feel comfortable. Take, for example, the question that you asked earlier about the agnostic's concept of death. I believe death takes away everything. Everything ends. Everything is gone. The world. The universe. All is lost. You become blind, deaf, mute, and unfeeling all at once. Picture that and you picture death. You enter the end of ends which is nothingness forever. What does a rock think? What does dust feel? Nothing! And that's what we all turn into. This is hard for people to accept, even for an agnostic. You must mature into that belief, but in time you do learn to accept it and, strangely enough, when you accept it, it enriches your life. You only live once, so make the most of each hour, each minute. As an older person, I accept the fact that good things must come to an end and that nothing is forever. I accept it with gratitude, without rancor."

The tape ended there. Maria sat pensive for a while staring at the blank monitor. Then Ram came and interrupted her trance. He turned off the monitor and told her: "You need to take a nap my pretty."

"It will take me a while to digest all this," said Maria. "But I am in no hurry. I see differences between me and Prof Quixote, but it is just what you would expect. It's not disagreement as much as comfort with one's beliefs. He is surer of himself and more comfortable with his beliefs because he is older. He has matured into his agnosticism. I am just a little chic, not long out of my shell, running circles around a mother hen that wants to corral me and re-hatch me into a bird of a different feather."

"Go on. Get some rest, my sweet," said Ram.

Maria then walked to a special nook in the library where she could get away from it all. She plumped down on a soft sofa and blanked out.

Z   z Z   z Z   z Z

36. DREAMS AS THE POLLINATING SEEDS OF IDEAS

After Maria fell asleep in the library lounge, Ram went to see the girls at the dream workshop to remind them that Maria had not had a take-home dream in several days. If Professor Quixote knew that, he would have a fit. Ram urged them to come up with something for tonight. The girls were eager to comply, but they were all out of ideas. The subject matter was not very promising. Happily, someone came up with the idea of a pictorial presentation, as in an art show and the idea was an instant hit.

"I like that…it has definite possibilities," said Imogene Natien, the director of productions at the dream works. "Thank you, Azucena. I really like your idea. We'll get to work on it immediately. First, let me call Professor Quixote and see what he thinks.

"Don, Imogene here. I have you on speaker phone. Maria has not had a dream to wake up with for several days. She needs to have one tonight, but we're having trouble with your lecture on hell and faith. We are thinking of something brief like a visit to the Louvre, a pictorial dream, maybe."

"Absolutely!" was Professor Quixote's unflinching response. "Whatever you do, be sure she has a dream today. I don't care what it is. Your pictorial idea sounds good to me. Go for it. Just don't try to make it a masterpiece. The important thing is that we plant a seed every day, that there'd be something in her conscious mind to grow roots and make connections with her world of sleep. You just plant the seed like a bee pollinating, or a diadromous salmon spawning from the salty sea of sleep to the sweet rivers of the conscious world. Time and nature will do the rest."

"Okay, thank you, Don. You can tell us more later. We're pressed for time right now. We must start working on the dream. Thanks a bunch," said Imogene as she started to hang up. But he interrupted her again.

"One more thing, Imogene, please, listen. This is important. Be sure and put something zappy in the dream. Put a sweet little something—a hook or a magnet—that will lure her back to analyze the dream. This weighty lecture needs a little zap. Otherwise, she'll forget it all and your work will be for nothing."

"Okay, okay, Don… We'll do," said Imogene as she hung up. Then facing her crew, she added: "He is good, but sometimes you just have to cut him off. Okay, ladies, let's get to work."

"But what about the hook?" Azucena asked. "I have no idea about that."

"We'll think of something. For now, forget about it."

Ram, who had been listening, came up with an idea. "Put Kenneth Flynn in it. That will be your hook."

"Who is he?"

"An old flame."

"Man, you got it! That'll work!"

The girls went to work on the dream, and the result was a visit to an art museum, as big as the Louvre. Maria was walking through the galleries looking at pictures at an exhibition. She came to a room with two large paintings in series; they were triptychs that took up two walls of the room.

On the first wall, the triptych was entitled "The Believer." Its first frame showed a prison cell. Two men were kneeling side by side in fervent prayer: one was a condemned man, and the other a priest. The cell is all aglow, tinged with a red hue because of the incandescent window behind the men. A fire seems to be raging just outside the window, its flames lash at the window frames like angry, hungry snake tongues. The second frame shows the condemned man on a gurney fitted with intravenous tubes and strapped in place. The priest is kneeling beside him in prayer. The fire behind the window has abated, but it is still reddish. There is only a narrow band of blue sky on the upper fringe of the window. The third frame of the first triptych shows the priest no longer kneeling but standing beside the corpse on the gurney and waving at the retreating soul of the executed man, which is going out the window. The window is mostly blue now. There is only a strip of faded orange in its lower fringe. Maria looked back at the previous frames and caught the changes in the window and the point of the painting. The window held the key to the triptych. The fires of hell seemed to cool through atonement, revealing more and more sky on the window. The priest seemed to sense this. He had a contented expression on his face on the last frame like a final remark of 'mission accomplished.' Maria, herself, commented: "Well, it seems that prayer, faith and repentance have cooled the fires of hell here. There's the idea of an implied purgatory here. Hum, very interesting."

Then she began looking at the next wall of the exhibition room. The triptych there was called "The Agnostic." The first frame showed the same jail cell as before, except for one significant omission: there was no window, just a hard concrete-block wall. Also, this time the priest was pleading with the prisoner who had his back to him and who had plugged his ears with his hands to shut out the priest's words. He wanted no part of what the priest was selling. In the second frame, the prisoner is seen fastened to the gurney. A policeman is blocking the priest, not allowing him to approach the condemned man. In the last frame we see the dead body of the condemned man on the gurney. This time there is no soul leaving the body. The priest is seen returning, walking away from the execution room with a sad look on his face.

"No blue skies here," said Maria, "no heaven, but then also no fire from hell. And no soul either. This is all so stark it is unpleasant." Maria then turned to go to the main gallery of the museum and see more pleasant things, mumbling to herself: "This is definitely not my cup of tea." She was eager to get away from there. She had had enough philosophical art for one day.

When she reached the main concourse of the gallery, she spotted Prof. Quixote in the distance, surrounded by several students. What a coincidence to find him here. He was engaged in a very intense discussion with someone who seemed familiar. As she focused on the stranger, she recognized him, and the surprise exhilarated her. Her heart thumped wildly; her blood flowed faster. It was Kenneth Flynn. "Ken? Here? Oh, my God!"

After five years Ken stirred old emotions that she had thought were dead. The vision of his image had rekindled an old flame. She ran anxiously and excited towards the group. She wanted to shout, but she could not. The professor and his entourage had turned a corner. She followed them, shouting in her heart as hard as she could: "Ken! Ken! Please wait. It's Maria." The distances in this museum were enormous. When she reached the corner, she looked in all directions, but she had lost them. She walked a few more steps feeling dejected and hopeless. She woke up as if to spite her bad luck. What was the point of lingering there, wallowing in disappointment? But the image of Kenneth Flynn had been planted indelibly in her mind, and she wanted to preserve it. He was the catalytic fleeting bit of memory, the bait that held her mind to those triptychs that she would just as soon forget. What was Ken discussing with Professor Quixote? Surely, they would have seen the same triptychs. Could they have been discussing life and death, or belief in the afterlife? Or could they have been discussing capital punishment? Capital punishment was most unlikely. If they were discussing it, it would not be from a legal or political point of view, but from a philosophical perspective. The seed had sprouted roots.

Z   Z   Z   Z   z   z   z

PART VII: DISENTANGLEMENTS

37. ANOTHER TROUBLED SATURDAY

It was now the morning of Saturday, April 17, 1999. Maria had gotten up relatively early to do the chores that she usually did on weekends—laundry, sweeping, and dusting. While she worked, she often put on a tape. Today she picked one at random that, it so happened, had the song "The Man I Love," one of her all-time favorites. She went about her work, listening to the tape, not even aware that her favorite song would be coming up. But when she heard the song, the world stopped. She had to hear it.

That song was a call to daydream; it inspired her; it coiled around her heart every time. Strangely, for all that the song described the man as being "big and strong," her vision of the man was not clear. He had to be intelligent, yes; that was for sure. But given that, he could be of any type. She rather liked him as an indescribable sort, as an elusive mirage that changed from one time to the next from blond to dark, that was as vague as 'nobody in particular,' and as indefinite as 'no one I know.' This morning, however, she had seen him more clearly defined when she had caught a glimpse of him in a museum. The combination of the song and his cameo appearance in the dream had turned the morning into an interlude of bliss under the sun. Her world was flavored with an indescribable sweetness, like a lingering dream that did not want to vanish in the light of day.

Her happy daydream state would have lasted longer had it not been for a phone call she received around 10 a.m. Elena had called her from a hospital in West Palm Beach to inform her that she had been beaten and stabbed in an attempted rape but was now out of danger. Toro, who had also been brought to the hospital with her by ambulance, was in guarded condition and had been in intensive care. Maria took the address of the hospital; she called her parents to cancel plans and let them know where she was going. She did not have a cell phone in those days, or she would have been talking to Elena as she drove, asking her Why? How? When? Where exactly in

West Palm Beach? What was she doing there? What did Toro have to do with it? Maria was inundated with questions.

The attack took place last Thursday afternoon after school. Wally Northrop, knowing that Toro had some business to attend to, had taken advantage of his absence to put into action a sinister plan. Wally had persuaded Elena to get in the car with him under false pretense and he had taken her to a house on the outskirts of West Palm Beach. His line had been that, supposedly, several students were involved in a surprise party to honor Maria. Toro had gone to get her a gift, an expensive Math book that all students would need to contribute for. Could he count on her support for maybe five or ten dollars? Elena agreed graciously. Also, it was not widely disseminated because it was a surprise party. That was the reason Elena might not have heard anything about it. It was very important that students should come on short notice. Could he count on her for that? Elena, of course, would have done anything for Maria.

The plot for a kidnap and rape had been hatching ever since Toro confided to Wally his sexual fantasy about Maria some weeks earlier. Wally had loved that dream and wanted to carry it out. The dream had taken place in a run-down house in West Palm Beach which belonged to some relatives of his who were away most of the time. Toro and Wally used it for weekend parties from time to time. Toro's dream grew into a quest in Wally's mind. He obsessed about making it come true. Initially, the target was Maria, not Elena.

Toro became sick of the idea and told Wally so. He regretted he ever mentioned that dream. Unfortunately, Toro could not undo what he had planted in Wally's mind. Toro's dream had awakened a monster in Wally, and now the monster demanded to be fed the real thing.

Toro tried to talk sense into Wally. He told him that he did not think of Maria that way anymore, that he did not lust for her. But Wally thought he was lying and did not believe him. Toro insisted that he was not capable of raping anybody. He wanted no part of that. Wally persisted. That dream was ripe for the picking, he said.

Why not give it a try? They had the means; it was so easy; it was so doable. The two had drifted apart so much that they were strangers to each other; they could not communicate anymore. Toro was disgusted by Wally and wanted to have nothing to do with him. A few days earlier, they had come to blows over the issue. It was then that Wally changed his plans for an easier prey that he could handle without the help of Toro. In addition, he thought Toro and Elena were getting chummy and his plan had the added bonus of revenge against Toro.

Wally never heard the real dream that Toro had, the dream in which Maria gained the upper hand and humiliated him. But even if he had, he would not have reacted as Toro reacted. It changed Toro. It had an appreciable impact on his life. It pointed him towards loftier directions. He saw the value of getting an education and striving for decency. Maria became like a Goddess for Toro. He admired her. He would do everything in his power to aspire for a woman like her. He revered her.

Wally, on the other hand, had remained mired in the gutter of the dream's perversity. For him, the dream was just a blueprint for evil.

The chasm between Toro and Wally had torn all bonds of friendship. Toro had thought of straightening out the whole sordid business by telling Wally the truth about the real dream once and for all. He had not raped Maria because Maria had turned the tables on him. Somehow, she had managed to make goodness triumph over evil. She had exuded strength, firmness and valor in the face of danger; she had thrown contempt at his lechery, and she had made him empathize with her by appealing to his better half and by making him think like a responsible adult. Rape was not sex; she had told him; rape was violence that could lead to murder. Are you willing to go that far for your jollies? Maria had made him think and reckon with reality, and she had done it with such class, with such nobility that she had transformed Toro, inspiring him in a way that neither prayer, nor art, nor poetry had ever done for him before.

There was a scene from that dream that he cherished as one of the most exalted moments in his life. He would remember it always as a source of inspiration. It occurred right after he untied Maria. He expected her to bolt free, to put a distance between them. Instead, he was surprised by what she did. Maria's first use of her free hands was for a gesture of gratitude. She clutched Toro's arm with both her hands. He was startled at first, but as she pressed his arm, he felt beautiful sentiments he had not felt before that were more than just gratitude. The squeeze of her hands conveyed a charge of approval, of praise, of encouragement, and maybe even admiration. The experience had an exalting effect. He felt cleansed, purified, blessed by her spontaneous gesture. But Wally would not have recognized the noble qualities that Toro described. He wasn't worth an explanation.

Elena waited anxiously in her hospital room, looking at the clock and counting the minutes. Even so, despite her anxious expectation, she was incredulous when Maria walked into her room. Elena thought she saw a vision. Her eyes filled with tears of sheer joy. What a thrill it was to see Maria there, in her room, away from class, not as a teacher, but as a friend. It made all that she had been through seem worth it. At first the two women hugged, without saying a word. Elena sobbed on Maria's shoulder. Then Elena talked and talked and told her everything she knew.

Elena had been so thrilled at the idea of being at a party with Maria that she got in Wally's car eagerly and absent-mindedly. She had swallowed his lies, hook, line and sinker. She began to feel uneasy only when she realized how far away the party was. It didn't seem right. Her fears intensified when she saw the house, empty, cluttered, dirty and solitary. But Wally continued to assure her that everyone would show up in ten minutes and she continued to have hopes. In the meanwhile, he insisted that she should relax and have a drink. He fixed her a gin and tonic that could have choked a horse with ninety percent gin. It tasted like liquid fire, and she spit it out. Then it went downhill from that point. She wanted to get out of there and tried to escape, but he blocked and overpowered her. She got away from his grip, and the chase and rough house began. She battled with him for almost an hour, a period that seemed like an eternity. Then Toro arrived.

Toro had passed by Maria's office a few minutes after 3 p.m. and had noticed that Elena was not there. Maria was alone. Elena's absence seemed odd and was most disturbing to him. He then inquired of some kids who were milling around the school grounds if they had seen Elena and was told that they had seen her leave with Wally. She had gotten in his car and the two had driven off somewhere. Toro smelled trouble immediately and took off for the raunchy house in West Palm Beach at warp speed. His suspicions were confirmed when he saw Wally's car on the driveway.

On his way into the house, Toro had enough presence of mind to open his trunk and get a crowbar, which came in handy eventually. He found them on the floor still struggling. Elena had put up quite a fight and had paid dearly for it, but at least she was still alive, and virgin. He had punched her on the face several times, breaking a tooth, cutting her lips, breaking her nose, and giving her a black eye. Her clothes were in tatters. She had given back as bad as she got, punching him, scratching him and even biting him. But in the end, she had to stop resisting when he escalated the fight by pulling a knife on her and threatening to kill her. She had no doubts that he could go that far. He was an animal.

Luckily for Elena, a female deus ex machina was looking after her and gave her a reprise from her tribulations. She never thought this would ever come in handy, but it did. She was having her period. When Wally discovered this, he felt as if the devil had cheated him. He screamed like a wounded pig in anger and disgust. Elena thanked her lucky stars and for a few minutes, she thought she had been saved. But the reprise didn't last long. He then decided he would sodomize her. The struggle started anew. He grabbed her hair, wrapping it around his right hand while he held the knife to her exposed neck. But it was all half-hearted now. They were both tired.

He tried but could not. It was more difficult to consummate than he had ever imagined. To make matters worse, Elena was helped again—this time by a male deus ex machina. Wally's penis was erect but not hard enough; it was flaccid and wimpy. He pounded the floor with his bare hands, shouting obscenities. "God damn it, fuck it, shit!" He shouted it over and over. Then, as Elena started to move, he growled at her, halting her: "Stay put, Bitch. We ain't through here yet."

Who knows what else Wally might have had in mind then? But Toro came in just then, before Wally could implement another perverse scheme.

"Drop that crowbar or I'll slash her throat," Wally commanded when he saw Toro barge in. Toro thought about it for a moment but soon complied.

"Okay. I put it down, but you let her go."

There was no reply from Wally; he moved the knife away from her neck while he thought about what he would do next. Elena bolted away from him. It was then that Wally slashed her in the back. Fortunately, it was not a deep stab, but a long superficial gash that cut no vital parts or organs. At least now she was free from his grip, and it gave Toro a chance to come into play. Toro came in with a mighty kick to Wally's lower back. But it was not an incapacitating kick. Before Toro could follow up with other blows, Wally managed to stab Toro in the left calf. Toro quickly grabbed the hand that held the knife and the two struggled on the floor, until Toro managed to disarm Wally and throw the knife to the side. Then, with the weapon out of the way, he stood up and lifted Wally to his feet so he could beat him and punish him for all he deserved.

Toro was overconfident. He pummeled Wally out of anger, to punish him, or to teach him a lesson, but not to subdue him. In one of those openings between blows when Wally had a chance, he managed to get hold of the knife again and came back swinging. This time he backed Toro up to the wall and began stabbing him wherever he could, in the arms, in the shoulder, in the stomach with quick jabs. He could have killed him. Toro was weakened and could not defend himself well anymore from the multiple cuts. Wally was raising his hand for a final stab, when out of the blue came a thump that missed his head, but hit him on the shoulder, breaking his clavicle. Elena had grabbed the crowbar and had come down on Wally with all her might. She followed with another blow aimed at his face which Wally blocked with his arm. As Toro took the crowbar, Wally turned and ran out of the house.

"There's a phone in the kitchen. Call 911," Toro instructed Elena.

Elena rushed to make the call as Toro held his belly to keep from bleeding to death. He had bled quite a lot already. While they waited for the ambulance to arrive, Elena brought towels and pillowcases, anything she could find, to tie around his calf and to compress the wounds in his belly. Eventually, before reaching the hospital, Toro passed out. At the hospital he had to have a blood transfusion.

"Poor child, how terrible what you've been put through," said Maria as she held Elena's hand. "This is truly awful. The strange thing is that I thought Toro was the one who had attacked you. For some time, I had wanted to warn you about him because, somehow, I didn't trust him. Now I learn that he saved you. I hadn't even thought about the other one, the real monster."

"Oh, yes, Miss Diaz, Toro is not bad at all. He used to be friends with Wally, but they had a falling out some time ago. He didn't want to have anything to do with Wally, but Wally kept coming back. Toro hated being called by that name. His real name is Pedro. Wally is the only person that calls him 'Toro' and he hates that name all the more. Wally was a nuisance. He kept bugging Pedro about doing something together, but Pedro thought it was stupid; he wanted no part of it. As for you, Pedro thinks the world of you. But he's embarrassed because he is so behind. That's why he asked me to tutor him, so that next year when he takes the course again, he'll be ready for you."

Maria left sometime in the early afternoon, after having spent about three hours at the hospital. She promised she would come back the next day, but Elena told her she was going home in the morning. "Good," said Maria, "will I see you in school next week then?

"Maybe... I hope so." Elena responded.

After the hospital, Maria went to her parents for a change of pace and for some of her mom's good home cooking. She spent a quiet evening there. They watched a Spanish movie from 1954 that her parents had seen ages ago. It was still a favorite: "Marcelino pan y vino," (Marcelino Bread and Wine). The movie was just what Maria needed to end that day, something pure, innocent and touching.

The movie is about a little boy, Marcelino, who is raised by friars in a Franciscan monastery where he had been abandoned as a baby. He is sweet, but full of childish pranks. The monks adore him and spoil him. One day, when Marcelino is about six years old, he starts visiting the attic. There he has found a new friend with whom he talks regularly. His friend is wounded and seems emaciated and hungry. Marcelino takes pity on him and brings him food every day. It is Jesus. One day Jesus comes down from his cross to sit on a chair and talk to the child. The monks cannot figure out who is stealing the bread and wine from the pantry. One monk suspects it is Marcelino; he follows him and confirms his suspicion. Marcelino is, indeed, taking bread and wine to the attic for his weak and hungry friend. The movie is a tearjerker. Marcelino falls asleep on a chair by the crucifix and never wakes up again. Clara, Maria and even Pablo cried after the movie.

Z   Z   Z   Z   z   z   z

38. GUILDA

That Saturday evening Maria was asleep by 1 a.m., exhausted by all the day's doings. She made the usual rounds through the lobes of her dome, letting everybody know that she was in and that she would be holding court in the conference room. Her dream denizens started filing in and getting seated. There was so much to talk about this evening. Sasha, as usual, began the commentary with a snide remark.

"Boy, go to bed with dogs and you get up with fleas. Your students, Wally and Toro, are real sweethearts. Hope they catch that creep, Wally, soon."

"I'd rather not talk about that mess. I loved the movie about Marcelino," said Maria Luisa. "Let's talk about that instead."

Maria herself was indifferent. She would just as soon let the girls talk about whatever they wished while she descended some 20,000 leagues under oblivion to forget the world and soak in the deep rest of a simulated death.

"Do you all realize that it's been twenty-five years since that movie came out? The child actor that played Marcelino must be in his thirties. I bet he is handsome," said Sasha.

Then Maria spoke to clear up something that still bothered her about Thursday's attack. "Before we get carried away with Marcelino, I would like to tell you what's on my mind about Toro and Elena. I am still puzzled about a few points in this sordid affair. First, why did Toro think that Wally had taken Elena to that house at West Palm Beach? How did he know that he would take her there? Had Toro and Wally discussed this previously? Was Toro in on the rape and then changed his mind at the last minute? As far as Elena knew, he just popped into that house out of the blue. This doesn't compute for me. Also, why did Wally and Toro have a falling out? I've always thought of them as two dirty peas in a pod. I am convinced that they both had a hand in that nasty note about the angles of the dangles. Elena was no help this afternoon because she was not clear on many things. She told me all she could, but the poor thing is as lost as I am. I'm going to see Toro tomorrow at the hospital. Maybe I'll get some answers."

To judge by the girls reactions, the subject of Toro and Elena did not engage them. They were eager to talk about something else.

"Okay, let's talk about *Marcelino pan y vino* now," one of them blurted out enthusiastically. That started it all. They were eager to discuss that movie. "Wasn't that a darling little boy in the movie? He was so cute! I understand the child actor won a prize at a film festival for his performance," said Maria Luisa.

"That's true. I wonder what happened to him…child actors often have miserable adult lives."

"Mom just adores that movie. She must have seen it ten times, three times in the last few days," said Maria Eugenia.

"I know. Tell me about it," said Maria. "She has been on my case to watch it for at least two weeks."

"Did you like it?"

"Well yes, of course! Who wouldn't? It's so clean and pure, and so, so saccharine. But Mom loves it more than I do. To her, it is not just a religious fantasy, but a veritable miracle. I also think she was using the movie to lure me into religion. It's her way of saying: Look at how beautiful faith can be. The love of God just permeates that movie in such a sweet way. Lately, she has been leaning hard on me to go to church with her. Last night, she really applied the pressure for me to spend the night there. If I had, I would be going to church tomorrow morning. No thanks."

"Let's face it," said one of the Marias, "Mom's secret wish is that you become a nun."

"Well, I think she is concerned about my safety in this evil world. What happened to Gwen and now to Elena just exacerbates it all. She is very concerned about the school where I teach. She'd love for me to teach in an all-girls catholic school."

"Just think, you could be her little Marcelina in a nunnery. Wouldn't she be in heaven then?" added Sasha.

"I don't quite agree with all of this," said Libby. "Yes, she is concerned about your safety, and does want you to go to church, but for a different reason. I think she just wants you to get married. If you became a nun, you couldn't give her grandchildren, and she wants that even more badly. I think the reason she wants you to accompany her to church is so she can show you off. It's her way of looking for a husband for you. It's the decent way, the safe way of fishing for grooms, not like Gwen's way. Every time she sees young good-looking men in church, she wonders if they are single. And she wonders where you are. How will you ever meet them if you're not there? She despairs for all the missed opportunities."

"There's some truth to that," added Maria Luisa. "But you all go to extremes with this business of marriage and convents. Religion is a big concern for her, but not to the extent that she wants you to become a nun. That's an exaggeration. Her concern is your mind and the state of your soul. She takes you to be weak in faith, and this bothers her. She worries about your spiritual wellbeing. She doesn't know what you believe in. She assumes that you believe in God, but she doesn't hear you say it. She never hears you pray. She suspects you're on your way to becoming an agnostic like Dad. And one is enough for one family. Besides, Dad is a man. You're her little angel."

"Well, enough of this," said Maria. "Does anybody want to know what I think and what I wish? Well, let me tell you. I certainly don't want a nunnery, and I don't want church on Sundays, either. But I do want a husband. I want to meet Prince Charming somewhere soon. It doesn't have to be in an exotic fancy place. I will gladly settle for one right here in Miami. But soon! The real question is: should I start going to church if, as Mom thinks, that's a good way of meeting the right guy? Logically, I must admit she may have a point, but I can't get around to accepting the idea."

"What about meeting Prince Charming at the Louvre in Paris?" Sasha asked. "By the way, did you see Kenneth Flynn? Wasn't he gorgeous?"

"Glad you brought that up," began Maria with a serious tone. "That reminds me. I was so mad at you I could have killed you all. That little cameo appearance by Kenneth was awful! You showed him so far away that I had to strain to recognize him. And then, you whisked him away. I chased after him, screaming, but he was gone. Don't ever do that again! Don't tease me like that! That's the sort of impish thing I would expect from mean gremlins that hate me."

"I'm sorry, Maria. I really am," said Imogene. "We weren't trying to tease you, or to be impish, I promise you. Keep in mind that the subject of the workshop for that night was heavy philosophical stuff about the afterlife and what not. We had very little time, and we had worked so hard on those darn triptychs, trying to distill the essence of Don's talk into visual capsules. Kenneth Flynn was just meant to be the sweet taste that clung to the memory of those triptychs so you would recall them and think about them. But when you started chasing after him in the dream, we realized that the dream had gotten out of hand, and that we needed to keep the dream rolling a little longer. We would have integrated him somehow, but you jumped the gun and woke up too soon. The reason we made him disappear was that, frankly, we were stalling for time. We were playing it by ear; we hadn't figured out how to include him in a reasonable plot. We'll do better for you next time, I promise. We owe you one."

Out of the corner of her eye Maria saw Dr. Broca, who was sitting on a chair far back in the room, nodding his head with a grin on his face.

"Dr. Broca," Maria called at him, "I can read that smile on your face. It's saying: Don't be hasty storming out of dreams… you could trip up."

"I didn't say anything," said Dr. Broca sheepishly.

"No but you thought it. And you're right, I admit it. But how was I to know the dream wasn't over yet? What was I supposed to do, sit around and cry? But let's not dwell on this anymore. All right Imogene, I accept your apology. Take your time the next time. And remember, where Prince Charming is concerned, give me all night. I got time. May I make a suggestion? Take two nights if you must, one to plan the dream and the other for the dream itself. I don't care if I don't dream one night. You just make it a nice long dream, the longer the better. It doesn't matter if I only remember the last five minutes," said Maria.

"Would you like a dream like the one with Leonardo in Buenos Aires?" asked Libby all excited. "We could get you a get-together like that with Kenneth in the Louvre or on the Eiffel Tower, or wherever you say in Paris."

"*Oooh, la-la, mon Dieu. C'est si bon, ça sexy bon, bon,*" said Sasha trying to sound French, clapping her hands with excitement.

Maria was embarrassed; her blood rushed to her skin. She was trying to come up with a response to Libby's suggestion when she saw Guilda barging into the room like a runaway truck. Guilda was, without a doubt, the most despicable component of Maria's psyche. Everybody was scurrying to one side trying to get out of her way, hoping Guilda was not after them. They feared her as one fears a plague, or a rabid dog on the loose. And Guilda was the one gremlin that Maria had not yet met face to face. Maria did not know whether to run for cover and close her eyes in fear, or to stand her ground and dare to see what this ogre was up to. In the end, she looked, and she saw for herself how horrible Guilda was. She bore no resemblance to Maria whatsoever. She was ugly, brutish and Amazon like. She carried tasers, whips, knives, and ropes. Maria had only seen shadows, and intimations of her before, and she had only heard rumbles coming from her. Of course, she had also felt from time to time her electric bolts lashing at her, her kicks, her pinches, her pulls and twists. To Maria, Guilda was like the deranged relative, the monster sister that lived hidden in the basement of the residence, and that the family never mentioned out of fear and embarrassment. Guilda was more than a dungeon monster. She had an official function and a position of authority that came close to being an aide to conscience herself. Guilda often played quasi-institutional roles; she was arresting officer at times, bounty hunter, interrogator, inquisitor, torturer and executioner. What was certain was that whenever Guilda did surface, she often brought pain and suffering. Maria had heard that she also took various forms, all of them horrid. Sometimes she was a dog, a vicious mean dog like a Doberman. When she assumed different human forms, she chose figures such as a medieval torturer or a Gestapo officer, often depicted with their related equipment. Tonight, she was wearing the leather and studs outfit of a punk motorcycle gang member.

Maria saw Guilda run across the room, headed straight for Libby. She was pushing furniture aside and running over people. Along the way she shoved Imogene aside, knocking her to the floor. But it was Libby that she was after. Libby tried to make a run for it, but she couldn't get away. Guilda got hold of her. She grabbed Libby's right arm and twisted it behind her back while at the same time, she wrapped one of her fat hairy arms around Libby's neck in a suffocating choke. Then she applied pain. Gilda was a six-foot, 260-pound behemoth of a woman. She was butchy, like a Russian peasant, a babushka with a face like a Mack truck.

The strange thing was that while Guilda was working over Libby, it was Maria that was feeling the pain in her own flesh. Maria tried to speak, but she could not; she tried to scream, but she only managed to make muffled sounds from the strangle hold. Her scalp hurt, as if her hair was being pulled. She felt nails digging into her. For all intents and purposes, Libby was only a reflection of Maria's actuality.

"What did I do? What's this all about?" Maria would have asked if she could have articulated a question. Guilda, somehow, caught the question and answered it for her.

"This is for Buenos Aires, you bitch. This is for Leonardo; this is for making plans with Kenneth in Paris; and this is for not going to church, for your atheism, your agnosticism, and for your soulless butt, you slut. You'd better get thee to a nunnery, or I'll tear you a brand new one."

Right about then, conscience finally appeared, and this was merciful, for otherwise Maria and Libby would have been crushed and smothered. Once again, conscience had taken the form of Janet Reno.

"All right, that's enough now, Guilda!" said Janet Reno, as she grabbed hold of her. "Let her go. As for the rest of you, let's declare a moratorium on sex and religion for the rest of the night. Come Guilda. Let's get back to the dungeon."

Guilda grunted and walked out of the room like a gorilla, huffing and puffing, with Janet Reno a few steps behind her. There was silence in the room again. Everyone was waiting for conscience to leave and take her monster out of sight before saying anything. As soon as they were gone, Maria got up and slammed the door shut behind them. Then she looked at everybody and gestured that she had something to say to them. She was collecting her words, thinking of how best to put it. All eyes were on her. Then she spoke.

"I want to set the record straight on one thing here tonight," began Maria, pausing for dramatic effect, timing her silences to get everybody's undivided attention. "Hear me now and hear me well... I have never... I repeat: NEVER! ...never been to Buenos Aires in my entire life! Is that clear? What's more, I don't know any man by the name of Leonardo…and that's a fact. What we have witnessed here tonight is an outrage, a most grievous injustice. That's all I want to say."

Having said that, Maria stood quietly, gripping the chair to release her tension, almost in tears. Maria Luisa approached her and embraced her, patting her on the back to calm her down. Others followed suit. Maria acknowledged their kindness and thanked them. Then Libby approached her, looking as if nothing had happened, as if she hadn't been touched, while Maria, herself, felt as if she had been through a war.

"We know it's not your fault, Maria," said Libby. "You didn't deserve that, but it is an old and long story that goes back to the Old Testament. Let me see if I can put it in perspective for you. You were used as a sacrificial lamb in an ancient game that is more like a war between primeval forces. I, as you already know, stand for temptation and carnal pleasure. Guilda is guilt, shame and recrimination. The human species is the arena in which we play and fight. This has been going on from time immemorial. You were not the real culprit. You didn't really do anything that deserved punishment. I'm the one that she was after."

"Ah, yes, sure, but I was the one that felt the pain and suffocation, not to mention the humiliation," replied Maria. "I was the one that felt her dirty fingernails piercing my skin; and I was the one that had her hair pulled."

"Oh, yes, yes, I know," said Libby calmly. "That's true. That's the way it goes. She goes through me to get to you. The irony is that she can't hurt me no matter what she does to me. I'm here to stay. I've been around for a long time. I go way, way back—back to the Garden of Eden, back to Adam and Eve, back to the lure of the apple, back to original sin. I came into being when sexuality was made part of the human condition. I thought I had free rein, but I was wrong. Guilda also came with sexuality, but as a constraint, to keep me in check. She was made part of the taboos of human sexuality. I have to emphasize the word 'human' because there is no such constraint in the sexuality of other animals. There are no age limitations, no gender restrictions, no family taboos with the lower species. Everything goes, from pedophilia, pederasty, polygamy, adultery, infidelity, to incest. You name it. It's a free-for-all there. There are no Guildas in the world of dogs and cats. But where humans are concerned, Guilda is part of the shame that dates to the covering of the genitals with fig leaves."

Maria had a puzzled expression on her face. "I need to ask you something. Is Guilda involved in other situations that do not involve sex? I think I've run into her before in other contexts."

"Oh sure, sex is not the only taboo. You could have run into her when you felt recrimination for anything, not just sex. Where do you think you met her before?"

"I am thinking. It's coming to me now. How could I have missed this? Yes, yes, I am sure of it now. She was the nasty manager at the restaurant Dream-R-Us, the one who taped my mouth shut, the one who ridiculed me, the one who orchestrated that whole humiliating episode with the cake blowing up on my face."

"Bingo! You got it. That was our sweet Guilda," said Sasha.

"But here is what's strange about that," added Maria. "There also, I didn't really feel responsible for any of the infractions I was accused of. I felt like I was railroaded, falsely accused. Was I used then also? I couldn't believe I could have been so stupid. I am not as greedy as the person in that dream. I am certainly not so inconsiderate as to ask for all the cakes to go. Who made me do that?"

"It wasn't me," said Libby, "…that's not my department."

"Right here," said Imogene, raising her hand over her head.

"And me, too," said Professor Quixote, coming forward.

"You too? Brutus Quixote?" Maria asked incredulously.

"How else could we have conveyed to you the unreasonableness of your request to take all the dreams of the night with you? You wanted to wake up in possession of all the deliberations of your mind while asleep. You wanted a record of the thinking processes of your mind during sleep, not just the dreams. You wanted the sorting and the weighing of what is and is not important to remember. You wanted it all, remember? You asked us to sneak it all into a dream that you could take out. Now, I know you weren't trying to cheat. You were making an innocent suggestion, out of ignorance of how things worked. But that's how you learn heuristically," explained Professor Quixote.

"Amazing! I'm feeling shame all over again," said Maria blushing. "If I understand you correctly, we learn during dreams by being recriminated for crimes we did not commit but merely thought about. We're shown the bad scenario and then we're pilloried for seeing it."

"It's worse than that," added Sasha. "Instead of telling you not to go there, they actually take you there and then punish you for being there."

"Yes, all of that is true. But remember, what you get is only a facsimile of the punishment, not the real thing. No bones are broken; no blood is shed. But the lesson is taught and learned."

"Did I once say or write there was no schooling while we slept? I think I need to revise that," said Maria.

Maria felt the sense to move on, to go on to other things. But there was no need for Maria to physically go elsewhere. People started shuffling around, leaving the room. In a few minutes it was almost all clear. Dr. Broca was one of the last to leave.

"Well, how about it, Miss Diaz?" he said as he went by her. "Do you think the witches and gremlins have lived up to what they promised you? Do you think you're getting your money's worth now?"

"Oh, yes, yes, Dr. Broca. I've gotten everything I hoped for, and then some. It hasn't always been fun, but it's always been worth it."

"Good, good, I'm glad. Good night."

"Good night, Dr. Broca."

Maria then made herself comfortable on a sofa and prepared herself to enjoy some quiet time.

Z   Z   Z   Z   Z   Z

39. MARCELINA

This evening's episode, including Guilda's intrusion, still had to be incorporated into a dream to-go. The girls at Dream R Us went to work on it and came up with a dream in which they turned Maria into Marcelina. This was her Sunday morning dream.

Maria was around fifteen years old. Her mother was leading her by the hand against her will towards an austere Gothic convent with daunting stone and granite walls. Its steeples rose eerily like mountain peaks that scraped the sky and looked threatening. Maria resisted every step, dragging her feet.

"Mamá, no quiero ir, no quiero. No me dejes aqui." (Mom, I don't want to go, I don't want to, don't leave me here).

Clara would try to comfort her, telling her that it was for her own good; that she would become a lady there; that the nuns would teach her everything she needed to know to become a good catholic woman and eventually a good wife. They were met at the gate by a couple of nuns who took them to the office of the mother superior along corridors that were deserted and interminably long. The mother superior's office was also a stately hall that reminded Maria of Dracula's private chamber in a Bela Lugosi movie; it was dark and sinister. The mother superior was sitting at her desk at the far end of the long chamber, and standing beside her was another nun, big and tall. When Maria was close enough to recognize the faces underneath the wimples, she knew instantly who they were. The mother superior was Mildred Colson, and her assistant was Sister Guilda.

Clara chatted with the two nuns as if they were the nicest people, irritating Maria. Her mother could not see through their pretense, their hypocritical smiles, their feigned sweetness. "We will take good care of her. She will soon get used to the convent and she'll be very happy here." Maria wondered what would happen after her mother left, saying to herself: "God help me! What hell is this I am in?"

After Clara left, Maria was led to her quarters, a room for four girls. Her roommates were three strangers that looked like younger versions of Libby, Sasha and Elena. It did her heart good to meet the girls. At least she was among peers once again. Perhaps she would survive the place after all. The girls wore drab gray uniforms which Maria did not like.

The dream fast forwarded through several days, showing scenes of life in the convent, from the daily routine in the morning to turning in at night. Her days began with reveille, then prayers; breakfast, more prayers; mass, more prayers; classes, more prayers; lunch, calisthenics, and soccer, then vesper prayers; supper— blessings and prayers before eating; then study hall, which was followed by the final night prayers. This she did day after day until, by the end of the first week, she reached the verge of a nervous breakdown, and she exploded in sobs.

"I can't take any more of this," Maria told the girls. "I'm going nuts. I'm either going to escape from this hell hole or die trying. This is insufferable."

It was then that Libby took her into her confidence and told her that there were ways to survive the tedium. But she would have to learn to beat the system.

"This place will drive you to madness; they go out of their way to rob you of life's simplest pleasures. But it's up to you to steal them back," she began. "Therein lies the key to your sanity and your happiness. They force you to bend the rules and break the law. The trick is to not get caught. When you get good at it, as Sasha and I have become, every infraction you commit and get away with will be a victory; every apple that you eat that was forbidden will taste better than any apple you ever had in the outside world. Every transgression that you can get away with will be like a gift you give yourself and it will fill your heart with joy. You'll have to learn to beat the system. It will be your salvation."

While Maria had never been a boarding student in a convent, she did attend two all-girl catholic schools run by nuns in Guayaquil,

Ecuador, when she was eight years old. That experience provided real memory for this dream and gave Maria a good immersion into the ambience of catholic girl schools. The first school was called La Providencia. Maria was miserable there. She hated it so much that she cried and complained to her parents daily. They saw fit to take her out. But then they put her in La Immaculada, another Catholic school for girls run by nuns. As far as Maria was concerned, she went from twiddle-dee-dum to twiddle-dee-dee. One was just as bad as the other. What saved her from the fate of religious schooling was coming to the U.S. Her parents also investigated catholic schools in Miami, but fortunately for Maria, the laic schools were closer and happened to be more convenient.

The experience in those catholic schools planted the seeds of heresy in Maria at a very early age. She struggled with religion for many years, but by the time she was in high school she had hardened to her own position which was: I can't swallow this. I just don't believe. When she lived with her parents, she went to church on Sundays. But her heart was not in it. To this day, Maria and her mother do not agree on religion, and this is a major reason that Maria chooses to live apart. Clara lost the power to inculcate religion into her daughter long ago, but she does not recognize her failure, or she refuses to accept it. She hasn't given up on a lost cause yet.

At the convent, in her dream, Maria did not recognize Libby and Sasha for what they were, as parts of her own character. They were simply peers. Elena was pretty much who she was in real life. Maria felt protective towards her and wanted to shield her from the influence of the other two. She did not encourage Elena to beat the system. That sort of thing wasn't for Elena, who was docile, innocent, and who took things in stride and went with the flow of authority. She did not have the temperament to be rebellious and did not have what it took to enjoy beating the system. Maria was afraid that if Elena tried it, she could get hurt.

"What is it that you hate so much about the convent, Marcelina?" Elena asked her once in a sweet, innocent way.

If Maria had answered honestly and told her what was on the tip of her tongue, she would have said: "The excesses! The prayers without end! The tyranny of it all! The oppression! The extreme boredom!"

But when Maria reflected on the innocence of Elena's question and when she considered that Elena might not understand, it would be cruel and counterproductive to tell her. She simply said: "I miss home."

Libby and Sasha, on the other hand, were pros at resisting and defying the order of things just so they could feel alive and human, just so they would not feel like praying machines. They had stashed away a few items of forbidden material and their collection was growing. Some items, such as the pen-size flashlights, were used for reading under the blankets after lights-out. Libby had licentious literature ranging from the risqué and mildly pornographic to hardcore. She had the book "Little Birds" by Anais Nin, the diarist of porno fantasies, and she also had a couple of Playboy magazines. Libby usually tore out the jokes from the magazines and gave them to Sasha who treasured them. Sasha had no books as such; she had handwritten notes from material on the premises that she had copied. It turned out that she had the nose of a bloodhound when it came to finding lustful literature, and she did not have to go far to find it. There, within the walls of that austere and prudish convent, she had found a treasure trove of lascivious literature. It was under the nun's noses, but Sasha was protected by the nun's little minds. Take Shakespeare, for example, under that respected name you could find a mother lode of prurient verses. There were the narrative poems "The Rape of Lucrece," "Venus and Adonis," and the play "Cymbeline." Sasha could read these works with impunity, confident that she could get away with it because nobody would question the propriety and high class of a book entitled: "The Collected Works of Shakespeare." Sasha boasted how on one occasion Sister Guilda did catch her reading it and had made inquiries. Sasha just blinked her eyes innocently and showed her the cover. The nun, impressed by that, gave her a pass and went on.

Sasha was dynamic; she was creative; she brought life, laughter and joy to the girls, and also education. She had memorized entire verses from Shakespeare, and she loved to recite them to the girls, explaining to them the context and the background, as in this account from "Venus and Adonis."

"Venus, as you all know," she began, "was the goddess of beauty and of love. But she was also a horny goddess. And she had a bad crush on Adonis who was the most handsome and most gorgeous hunk of a man among mortals. You can imagine how special he must have been for no less a goddess than Venus herself to fall head over heels for him, a mere mortal. But Adonis was not interested in love. He was a nature boy that just loved the outdoors, the hunt, and the woods, and so he rebuffed her. Venus followed him around, always trying to seduce him, saying things about nature and the woods that she knew he would like. Listen, for example, how she turns herself into a pasture here and turns him into a deer, how she invites him to roam and graze over her:

"Fondling," she saith, "since I have hemm'd thee here
Within the circuit of this ivory pale,
I'll be a park, and thou shalt be my deer;
Feed where thou wilt, on mountain or in dale:
Graze on my lips; and if those hills be dry,
Stray lower, where the pleasant fountains lie."

The girls loved it, especially the way Sasha acted it out. They hung on every word as she recited it. The next day they would go to the library to read it for themselves. Sasha had prepared precise directions where to find it, volume and page number. In the meanwhile, the girls were eager to know how the story ended. "What happened between Venus and Adonis? Tell us, Sasha. Don't leave us hanging like this."

"Nothing happened," said Sasha. "The dumb jerk died in the hunt, killed by a boar."

Shakespeare was not the only author who had a halo over his head and a reputation that absolved him from any suspicion and who could, therefore, sneak his salacious verses past the nuns. Other such authors were in the Bible itself. Sasha had mapped a route to its treasure troves, to "Susannah and the Elders" and to "The Song of Songs of Solomon."

For Sasha it was the search and the hunt for this literature that were fun and fulfilling. She could be seen going about her business, outwardly innocent, while really searching like a dowser for forbidden underground water. Unlike Libby, for whom sex was very compelling, Sasha mostly looked for love and romance. The literature she read was neither indecent nor obscene, although it was prurient and would have been forbidden had the nuns read it. From The Song of Songs, she would recite these lines from memory:

Oh, that you would kiss me with the kisses of your mouth
For your love is better than wine,
Your anointing oils are fragrant,
Your name is oil poured out
Therefore the maidens love you
Draw me after you, let us make haste.
...I am my beloved's, and his desire is for me,
Come, my beloved, let us go forth in the fields
And lodge in the villages;
Let us go early to the vineyards,
And see whether the vines have budded
Whether the grape blossoms have opened
And the pomegranates are in bloom
There I will give you my love.

Maria was awed by Sasha's ability to memorize so much. "How do you do it? It's incredible. You are amazing."

"Ah, Marcelina, let it never be said that there is no education when the lights go out, when we are tucked away in bed, when we are under our blankets and under darkness. For if the mind wishes to learn, it will find a way even in the dark of night, even while we sleep."

"But how and when do you memorize the poems?"

"I copy the poems long hand at the library because it is too risky to use the Xerox machine. Then I go over the poems during lights out, before falling asleep, hoping I will have dreams about Venus lying on the grass while a faun grazes nearby, and Adonis comes from behind the pomegranate blossoms. But when I really, really, memorize them is during prayers. It's my antidote to the words of prayers that I learned years ago and that now I am compelled to voice again and again like an automaton, like a broken record, forty times a day in tortuous repetition. If you read my lips then, you will notice they are not in sync. My mind is elsewhere. That's how I learn my poems and keep my sanity."

Elena admired Sasha's daring at the library but feared she could get caught one of these days and she asked her: "Aren't you afraid that sister Guilda will go past the book cover someday and want to know exactly what—in the Bible or in Shakespeare—you were reading? What would you do then?"

"I would recite the verses to her, leaving out the juicy parts," replied Sasha. "I would warn her: Behold! For it is written, whosoever banneth the reading of this book shall incur the wrath of God."

"Yes, but that wouldn't apply to Shakespeare. She could be onto your tricks and evasions," continued Elena. "What if she made a move to hit you?"

"Well, if it came to that, I would tell her what I tell any woman who is bigger than me: 'I'm not afraid of you… Bigger dykes than you have tried and failed. So, why should I be afraid of you?' And that, my dear Elena, is called chutzpah, spitting on the face of your aggressor when you have no better weapons."

"What's a dyke?" Elena wanted to know.

Before they could explain that to Elena, the girls heard the announcer going down the hall, as was the custom every night, letting everyone know that it was time to get to bed. "Five minutes to lights out. Five minutes!"

The girls scrambled, trying to get ready for bed in a hurry. Sasha, always the clown, cried out frantically: "Oh, my dildo, my dildo! Where is my dildo? Where did I put it? I can't go to bed without it."

"Her what?" asked Elena. "What is a dildo?"

"She means her pocket flashlight to read in bed," Maria explained.

"But why does she call it that?"

"Because she is just being silly, just being Sasha."

Libby called Maria aside and spoke to her sternly. "Listen, Marcelina, you'd better tell her what it is, or she could get herself in trouble. She is liable to go to Guilda one day and ask her for batteries for her dildo."

"Oh, my God, you're right!"

Libby had been truly prophetic in anticipating trouble on that account because it came to pass that Elena did get herself in trouble over a dildo, and it was a real one.

Elena was aware that she was an ingénue, that she was years behind the others in being savvy and she did not want to be a drag. She wanted to catch up with them and be like them. Perhaps, if she were able to contribute to the stash of forbidden things, she could gain in their esteem. She had a cousin by the name of Toro, and she had begged him to bring her some material, poetry, magazines, anything that was risqué or funny in a salacious way. He brought her tabloids from the supermarket showing aliens with watermelon heads; a baby with horns, the product of a man and nanny goat; and fat people in bikinis. He also had a piece which he considered to be racy poetry. Elena wondered if the girls would like it.

"Okay, Sasha, add this to your collection," announced Elena. "This is from my cousin Toro. It happens that he has a crush on his math teacher—a very beautiful woman that he idolizes named

Maria. He goes to class only to see her. He doesn't understand a word she says in class; it's all about theorems, lemmas and corollaries. The only math he can understand is in these lines: *The angle of the dangle is equal to / the heat of the meat / divided by the mass of the ass.*"

"Prrfff!" Marcelina sputtered in contempt, "I hope he didn't tell you it was original because it is the most hackneyed doggerel known to soldier, sailor and high school sophomore."

Sasha, however, played with it. She repeated it and savored it. "Hmm, it does have a nice cadence though…good rhyme pattern, too. And yes, it does conjure up a sexy image, albeit a very vague one."

Libby liked it. She drew imaginary curves on the air with her hands, trying to picture them. "I see the dangle, yes, oh yes, I see it, and the mass of the ass also. Nice. Tell your cousin to add more verses. It's too short. But he's on the right track."

"Well, I think it is stupid," Marcelina said emphatically. "I've tried to see if it has any mathematical significance, but I can see none, none whatsoever! It is all drivel. Rubbish. It doesn't make sense."

Elena was disappointed that her contribution was not the hit she had hoped for. So, the next time she wrote her cousin, she escalated her demands, asking him outright: "Get me a dildo."

In her mind, that would top anything the girls had ever come up with. "It is one thing for them to talk about dildos," Elena thought to herself. "But it is quite another to see a real one and hold it. I'll bet they have never even seen one." She was intent on wowing them. She imagined that Libby would appreciate it the most. She might even buy it from her. In any case, she would earn enough credentials to be inducted into the group of anti-puritans and be given recognition for beating the system.

The news of the device spread through the convent fast. Within a few days, everyone knew about it. Some of the girls, including Marcelina, were not amused by it. In fact, Marcelina was downright disgusted and scared out of her wits to have such a hot potato in their room. Her concern was Elena's safety now. She had to get rid of it. She had to spread the word that she never had one, that it had all been a hoax, a lie. The sooner that thing disappeared the better off everybody would be. Elena herself regretted having gotten it and was game for getting rid of it now.

But it was too late. One evening Sister Guilda came barging in, heading straight for Elena even though it was Libby who had the dildo in her hand and who was playing with it, juggling it in the air against her flashlight, throwing them one after the other.

Guilda was like a bulldozer, knocking things and people out of her way. She pushed Marcelina aside, making her fall, and then she grabbed Elena in the same way that she had wrestled Libby previously, pulling Elena's right arm behind her back and putting a choke on her neck while at the same time pulling on her hair. The strange thing was that Maria felt the pain in her own flesh, as if Guilda were doing it to her. This is empathy taken to the extreme, Maria thought. Sasha, for her part, was enjoying the scene as if it were a circus act. "Watch your tough love, Sister Guilda. Don't overdo it! You're bear-hugging her to death."

Guilda meanwhile was listing the litany of Elena's sins and punishing her for them. "This is for the Playboy; this is for Anais Nin; this is for Shakespeare; this is for Adonis; and this is for the whatcha-ma-call-it."

Marcelina could take no more. She went to the closet and grabbed a broom and beat Guilda with it repeatedly, saying: "I've beaten bigger butches than you for less than this…Take this, and this, you brute!"

Sasha was on the sidelines, applauding, egging on the fight, and saying: "Bravo, bravo, Marcelina. You go, girl. Sock it to her."

The last blow to Guilda's head actually broke the broomstick in half. But amazingly, it seemed that Guilda didn't feel a thing. Maria could not understand that. It was as if she had swatted her with a feather. It was all so bizarre, but the laws of physics didn't seem to apply here. Nothing made sense.

The Mother Superior, Mildred Colson, showed up around this time. She separated Guilda from Elena, saying: "All right, that's enough now. Let her go. Come, Sister Guilda. Let us repair to our quarters. I will deal with them tomorrow." Then they left, Sister Guilda grunting like a gorilla, huffing and puffing, with the Mother Superior a few steps behind her.

There was silence in the room. Marcelina got up and slammed the door shut behind the nuns. Then she looked at everybody and gestured that she had something to say to them. She was collecting her words, thinking of how best to put it. All eyes were on her. Then she spoke.

"I want to set the record straight on one thing here tonight," began Marcelina, pausing for dramatic effect, timing her silences to get everybody's undivided attention. "Hear me now and hear me well... Elena does not own the book by Anais Nin. She has never... I repeat: NEVER! ...never read it. She has not read Shakespeare's "Venus and Adonis;" and she was not juggling dildos while she was being beaten up. What we have witnessed here tonight is an outrage, a most grievous injustice. That's all I want to say."

Elena approached her and embraced her, patting her on the back to calm her down. The other two followed suit. Marcelina acknowledged their kindness and thanked them.

Marcelina had a strong uncanny sense of déjà vu, like she had dreamed this dream before. The scenes, the dialogues were familiar almost word for word. And she could anticipate what came next. She wasn't surprised when Libby explained that this was a morality play that went back to the Old Testament, back to the Garden of Eden, back to Adam and Eve, back to the lure of the apple, back to original sin, back to the first covering of the genitals with fig leaves. She had heard that before. She remembered that Sasha would follow next by addressing the unfairness of it all. And, sure enough, she did.

"This is weird," said Libby, "but it has its logic. There is method to the madness. Think about it. These dreams not only take you to the forbidden place, but they let you enjoy the sin briefly. You get a taste of the forbidden fruit. How else could virtuous people, such as Mother Theresa, ever know what the sin was about? Sister Guilda then comes along to make sure that you don't develop an appetite for the sin. She punishes you and lets you know what it will cost you."

It was time for lights out. Once again, the nun that heralded the coming of bedtime passed by the corridors, making her rounds, crying out: "Lights out in five minutes! Lights out in five minutes!" The girls got in their beds and not long after that Maria woke up with another dream to jot down in her dream diary and with another nugget of the sleeping mind to analyze.

z Z Z Z Z Z z

40. INNER ECHOES

On Sunday morning, while the Marcelina dream was still fresh on her mind, Maria wrote copious notes in her diary, all by longhand. Then she went to the computer and wrote distractedly, as if someone were driving her hands and her fingers on the keyboard, as if she were taking dictation rather than composing thoughts. These were the lines she typed.

I am the voice that whispers
In the womb of your subconscious
The fantasies that you dismiss as silly.

I am near you, and yet so far apart,
So intimate, yet almost a stranger!
I am part of a soul we both share.

We meet without touching
Like shadows on the screen of our dreams,
Our silhouettes eclipsing past each other.

Like strands of the same braid entwined,
We're spirit and specter of the same psyche:
Id and ego, character and intellect.

You, the mathy one, teaching by day
Using up all the hours of our Mind
On job, on duty and on banausic chores.

While I wait all day for the night,
For the depth of sleep to emerge in dreams
To speak of love and poetry.

You wish to see me? Stand in front of a mirror

And look into your eyes. I'm waving
From the depth of your pupils.

Dreams are a waste, you say.
Nothing useful comes out of sleep.
Then tell me: who wrote this?

Maria typed the above lines absent-mindedly and did not dwell on them. Her fingers walked through the keyboard as if she were a robot. The piece virtually wrote itself. As soon as she finished writing it, she had breakfast, then finished the house cleaning chores that she had started the day before. By 3:15 p.m., she was at the hospital in West Palm Beach to see Toro.

Z   z   z   z   z   z   Z

41. TORO'S CONVERSION

Maria entered Toro's room timidly, tiptoeing, not wanting to wake him in case he was asleep. She stood by his bed silently for a moment while he looked at her with his eyes half open, not knowing whether he was dreaming or awake before a mirage. How beautiful she was! How impossibly wonderful to have her there, so close to him, a phantom of loveliness! He wanted to do nothing, nothing that could spoil the vision or perturb the dream. He would have remained that way for hours, except that Maria spoke.

"Hello, Pedro. How are you?" Maria asked when she saw his eyes were open. "I hear that you forgot to duck."

Pedro was beside himself, unable to speak coherently. "Hi, Miss Diaz! What are you doing here? What's up?" he said as he tried to sit up.

"No, no. Please don't exert yourself. Please don't move. I'll only be here for a couple of minutes. The nurse said it'd be all right to visit you, if you were up to it and if I kept it short."

"Oh, yeah, yeah. No problem."

"I promise no theorems and no corollaries, okay?" Maria said, trying to be cheerful. "I just came to see how you were doing and to thank you for saving Elena. That was a brave thing you did, quite commendable. And we are all very grateful."

"Nah, that was nothing. I blew it. I let him get away. If it hadn't been for Elena, Wally would have killed me. She's the one who saved me. She's the one that got him on the run."

"But she wouldn't have been able to do that if you hadn't come to her rescue."

"Maybe... I dunno...How's she doing?"

"She checked out this morning. I think she's on the mend and will probably come to school sometime next week. How about you? When do you get out?"

"I don't know. But it won't be tomorrow or the day after."

He seemed groggy to Maria. Perhaps, she thought, he was

under a lot of pain killers. He did not seem to be in condition to talk for long. He had grimaced in pain once.

"Are you in pain?" she asked him. "Can I do something for you?"

"The pain comes and goes. But I'm all right. You don't need to do anything for me, except just stay with me a bit."

Maria stood by quietly, unable to think of anything to say next. He was content with just seeing her. Then he broke the silence and told her something that had been pent up inside him and was driving him out of his mind. "Miss Diaz, I have something to tell you. Could you give me five minutes?"

"Yes, of course."

"Some time ago I had a dream about you, Miss Diaz, and I'd like to tell you about it. It would mean a lot to me."

Maria did not say anything. She did not encourage him, but she didn't refuse. She just gave him a look of silent resignation.

"It's not a bad dream, Miss Diaz. I promise you. Nothing dirty... In fact, just the opposite, something beautiful happened in that dream and it changed my life for the better. I owe it all to you. I learned more from you in one night than years' worth of Geometry. You were like a goddess to me, like a special angel sent to save me. I never knew dreams could be so powerful. Several times I wanted to come see you in school about it, but I never had the nerve. You would have refused me. So, coming here today is like a dream come true for me and I can't waste it. I have to tell you about it. It's now or never."

Maria, who had been standing all this time, pulled up a chair from the wall to his bedside and sat down, thus signaling that she would hear his dream. He, in turn, asked her to lower the height of the bed and to raise the head so he could sit up and see her better while he talked. She complied.

"It started off as a bad dream. So, let me get past this part quickly before you turn me off. I had kidnapped you—okay? — and I had taken you to the same house where Wally took Elena last

Thursday. I had you all tied up and blindfolded. I had done this because for the longest time I had had a crush on you. It wasn't sex I was after. You have to believe me here. I was curious about you, but you were out of my reach. There you were a smart and beautiful woman who could have her pick of men and was still single and alone. I wondered: What does it take to earn your love? Who do you have to be? A prince…? A King…? I just wanted to ask you these questions. I wanted to be somebody who could talk to you freely, who could be near you. I would have changed places with your pet; I would have been your servant, your pillow, or anything, just to be able to get to know you. Because I knew that would never happen, I had no choice but to kidnap you.

"But, shoot, I couldn't kidnap nobody in real life. Somehow though, my dream fairies heard my prayers and made it happen in a dream. Finally, even if it was only a dream, I was with you and I could talk to you. As I said, my intention was not to rape you. I didn't want to bring you harm and, above all, I didn't want to do anything that would make you dislike me or hate me. I just wanted for you to become my friend, like in the movie 'Tie Me Up, Tie Me Down' with Antonio Banderas. Did you ever see that movie?"

Maria nodded.

"For what it's worth, just so you can relax, I never in the entire dream undressed you, or touched you in a bad way. Very early on, I had to uncover your eyes because you had recognized my voice and there was no point in blindfolding anymore. Then I discovered that you were made of steel, and you had such spunk. It was incredible. You feared nothing. I couldn't threaten you with anything. I was supposed to be in the catbird seat, but you took control of the situation. You managed to turn the tables on me. I know it is silly to ask you, because you weren't really there, but anyway, just for the record: how in the heck did you manage that? You had a strength I had not counted on. You could stand up to a hurricane and you had nothing but contempt for me. That hurt me deeply. I talked tough, but I was really disgusted at myself for offending you. I did threaten to rape you at times, but it was just tough talk to regain my authority. I won't bother you with the details now. What is important is that you know how much that dream meant to me because it taught me a lot--a lot about myself. I learned that I was not capable of hurting or raping anyone, least of all you. Rape was not my game. 'Know thyself,' I understand, is something of an eleventh commandment. But how does one come to know oneself? Then it hit me. I've come to know that dreams help on that account. It seems weird, but it is true. You can learn much about yourself from a dream! Has that ever happened to you?"

Again, Maria nodded demurely with feigned aloofness, but inwardly she was crying out: Oh, I can't tell you how many times—and very recently, last night, in fact! She still remembered her Marcelina dream.

Toro continued. "Here's what happened in that dream. I blew it badly by talking tough and threatening you with rape. Instead of crying and begging for mercy, you took me to task. You turned the tables on me. You shamed me. You told me off. You acted as if you didn't care about what happened to you, and I wasn't expecting that. I remember that at one time you told me:
'I have only one last request, if there is any decency left in you. Please blindfold me again! I don't want to see your face. Duct tape my mouth because I have nothing else to say to you. And then, go ahead and get it over with. But kill me first before you rape me.'

"It was like slamming all doors in my face. Such guts! Such nerve! It made me feel like dirt. You called my bluff. You put your head on the chopping block, but I couldn't kill you, and I couldn't rape you. I don't know if you were just acting. But if it was acting, I got to tell you, your performance deserved an Oscar. You were fantastic! There was nothing else for me to do at that point but to untie you and to let you go free. And so, I did. But then came the best part, the part I will never forget for as long as I live.

"Once I set you free, you grabbed me by this arm with both your hands and told me: 'Thank you, Toro. Thank you. I knew you weren't as despicable as you make yourself at times. There is some decency left in you…'

"You were so nice to me. You said it so sweetly that I wanted to cry. Even to this day, I feel your finger marks on my arm from the way you squeezed it as you thanked me. Those finger marks remind me of your kindness towards me. For one brief moment I felt in my heart that you liked me, that you thought well of me. I will always treasure that moment."

"And then what happened?" Maria asked.

"I offered you a drink. You accepted—a beer, I think. And then I woke up."

"Where do Wally and Elena fit into all this?" Maria asked.

"The dream had both good and bad aftereffects on me. I felt that feeling, like when you are at war with yourself, what's the word for that?"

"Ambivalence?"

"Yeah, that's it. I felt ambivalent. The macho man in me, Toro, was at war with Pedro, the decent guy in me. Toro was disappointed that I came out of that dream empty handed, with nothing. The squeeze in my arm, which meant so much to Pedro, meant nothing to Toro. Toro felt cheated. He wanted a dream rematch with another ending. Pedro, on the other hand, was happy with the dream as it was. In the end Pedro won, but not at first.

"The following day, while I was under the spell of Toro, I saw Wally and told him a made-up version of the dream. I just ad-libbed and heaped lies upon lies. Supposedly you got drunk, you became willing and wild, and you loved it. I enjoyed telling it at the time. In my mind, thinking as Toro did, it sort of evened the score and made up for the defeat.

"It was soon after that that I began to change. Guilt began to eat me up. The lying and the bragging just gagged me. I was sick of myself, and I hated myself. Here was a guy who couldn't rape you but could lie about you and turn you into a slut. When I saw you in class, it was more than I could bear. I had wronged you and I wanted to come and apologize to you, but of course, that was out of the question. How could I? You knew nothing. Then, when I saw Wally, my regret was even greater. The fact he enjoyed the lie made it more disgusting for me. The guilt ate me up.

"I tried to correct the situation by telling Wally that the dream had been a lie. But that did not make any difference to him. He liked the original dream, even if it was a lie. I told him that I was sick and tired of the damn dream and did not want to be reminded of it. I never wanted to talk about it anymore. I told him I didn't feel that way about you anymore, that I didn't lust for you, but he didn't believe me. I started avoiding him, wouldn't talk to him. But he had become obsessed by the stupid dream and there was no going back with him. To make matters worse, he started talking about carrying out the kidnapping and all. That's when I got really mad at him and told him I wanted no part of it, and no part of him. I was through with him. I told him to get lost and leave me alone. I didn't want to be his friend anymore.

"He wouldn't give up. Last Monday I finally blew up and let him have it. I beat the hell out of him. Didn't pull any punches. I wanted him to believe that I was serious, that I was sick of him and was breaking up for good. I cut his lip and bruised him bad; I think he got the message. I could tell he was mad at me this time. I suspected he was planning his revenge. I just didn't know where or when. I realized it last Thursday, when I looked for Elena in your office and didn't see her there. I knew something was fishy. I inquired around and when I was told that they had seen Elena get in his car and drive off, it hit me like a bucket of iced water. I burned rubber and raced to that house."

"Why was it so odd that Elena got in the car with him?" Maria asked.

"Because she doesn't really know him, and she doesn't like him. She started tutoring me in Math, but only on one condition: that I didn't bring him along. He wanted to come, just to cut up, but I told him this was serious. He resented being left out. He didn't like Elena either. She was boring and square. He must have given her some line to get her to go with him."

"He told her that some students were giving a party for me, and they were going to honor me with a present," added Maria.

"After that dream I took the first steps to change my life. I became aware of the rut I live in. I could see my future and I could see myself as a grease monkey or a burger flipper. And I didn't want that. I'm sick of the idea of growing up to be nobody. I've got to get off this rut. I'm not dumb; I'm capable of a lot and I'm going to improve myself or die trying. But do you know what moved me to think this way the most? What drove me to pull out of the mud and reach for the sky was you! Or someone like you. You stood for something to aim for. I asked myself: what would I have to be to have a chance to reach someone like you and not be shot out of the running from the get-go? And then it hit me. It was education. It was so obvious. Education! It was right before me, like the road to the Promised Land, and I was taking detours to nowhere. Then I got on track. Overnight education became my goal. I didn't want to waste another day, so I got started right away. But I couldn't come to you since I was so far behind; I have too much catching up to do and I didn't want to waste your time. I felt embarrassed. I went to Elena instead. Maybe she could help me get ready for you next year."

Maria, who had been quiet throughout the whole visit, was eager to speak. She wanted to encourage him on his quest, and she wanted to offer to help him. But she didn't have a chance to say it. At that moment several family members came into the room: Pedro's parents, brother and sister. She was introduced to everyone. They were most appreciative that she was there. It was crowded in the little room and Maria had spent a long time there, so she stood up, said goodbye, and started to walk out of the room. From the door she looked at Pedro and saw a sad expression on his face. After all he had told her, she had said very little. There had been very little reaction from her. To leave like that didn't seem right. It was cold and unresponsive to his confession, the outpouring from his heart.

So, she moved towards him, as if she had forgotten something. He deserved a more personal adieu than a wave from afar. She walked towards him to give him something very special. When she was close enough to touch him, she grabbed his arm with both her hands and let her fingers retouch the indelible traces she had left there in a dream. As she squeezed his arm, he recognized immediately the significance of her gesture and his heart rejoiced. He remembered the intensity of her gratitude in a facial expression that was as beautiful as a sunset. He had asked himself a million times: what would I give to see that same expression for real? What would he have to do to earn it? Would he ever achieve it? And now, his wish had come full circle in a dream come true.

"Get well, Pedro, so you can make all your dreams come true, and so you can move towards that distant star that shines in your horizon and which can be yours. She's waiting for you. I will help you reach it. I will be waiting for you with Euclid and Pythagoras. Take care."

Z z Z z Z z

PART VIII: THE FOLKS

42. DAD

On her way home from the hospital, Maria stopped by her parent's house for a few hours. She told them she had been to see her other hospitalized student, Pedro, but she did not go into details.

Maria showed interest in her mother's cooking and took notes on making flan and *pan de yuca* (cheese biscuits made with tapioca flour). Shortly after they finished dinner, the family got an unexpected and most pleasant surprise: Maria's brother, Paco, called. He was her only sibling—four years younger than she—and had just arrived at his naval base in Virginia after being in the Mediterranean for several months, where he had visited several countries in Europe and the Middle East. Maria could not stop calling him a 'lucky dog' out of pure envy for all the places he had seen. She was so anxious to go abroad. When they finished talking, she turned to her father and asked him about his travels.

"How about you, Dad, what countries did you see when you were in the military?"

"Not as many as Paco. I was in the army, and I was mostly stateside. I did see Hawaii and the Philippines and, of course, Viet Nam—which was nothing that would appeal to you—at least not the way it was then. Aside from the military, as you know, your mother and I went to Ecuador, Peru, Chile and Argentina recently."

Maria pressed her father to tell her more about his background. She enjoyed hearing the history of her family and tracing the comings and goings of her parents before she was born. It put her life in better perspective. She had a general idea of their past, but there were gaps and fuzzy periods. Her father had come to the U.S. in the mid-50s as a teenager to learn English; he had stayed with relatives in Miami. One thing led to another, and he ended up staying longer. In fact, he finished his junior and senior years of high school in Miami, graduating in 1956. He piddled and drifted for two years, working odd jobs here and there as an aimless youth, not knowing what he wanted. He thought about returning home, but he was not ready. Except for finishing high school and learning English, he had not achieved anything yet. So, he joined the U.S. Army when he was twenty in 1958 as a means of finding himself. At least for the next four years his destiny would be decided. Then in 1962, not knowing the turns the world would take, he re-enlisted for another four years. He was sent to Viet Nam in 1964. He had heavy fighting around Danang in 1965, where he was gravely wounded. The remainder of his time in the army was spent in hospitals convalescing and recuperating. He left the Army in 1966. By then he knew what he wanted, and he had the means to get it. The GI Bill helped him get through college, so he got a degree in business with a major in accounting. Now he could go back to Ecuador.

He was at the top of the world in late 1970 when he returned to Guayaquil as a U.S. citizen and with a college education. He had youth and he was full of dreams, everything seemed possible, and there was so much to do. As a desirable eligible bachelor, he had the time of his life. But he soon fell in love with Clara Alvarez, a young woman from a respectable, middle-class family. Things developed fast. They married in 1972, and in less than nine months their first child, Maria, was born on September 11, 1972. Their second child, Francisco—or Paco to the family—was born in 1976.

At first life in Guayaquil was thrilling. But in time, Pablo Diaz realized that he had changed too much to fit in his former country anymore. Ecuador, he decided, was not in his long-term future and it would certainly not be in his children's future, if he could help it. He had become too Americanized and just didn't fit well. He was constantly confronting attacks on American imperialism, and unrelenting criticisms of American foreign policy. He was sick of having to defend the Viet Nam War. The war itself had been less traumatic to fight than the aftermath of criticism and harangue which came in a constant barrage. In fairness, Ecuador was not the only place where he had encountered carping about the war. He had also caught indifference and hostility over the war in the U.S. The wonder was that he lasted ten years in Ecuador. In 1981 he returned to the U.S. for good.

Maria asked her father to recount the army years and the army life. As she heard him, she had a wistful abandoned expression on her face as if she were transported in time. Her parents, who noted her strange, trance-like mood, thought she was reliving vicariously his experiences. They were, therefore, very surprised when Maria blurted out something that revealed what had really been going through her mind during those silent pensive minutes.

"Dad, since you know the military," she began, "let me ask you something. What prospects would there be for somebody like me, with a Masters in Math, in the army?"

Clara nearly had a fit when she finished hearing the question to the end. "What? Are you out of your mind, Maria? Why on earth would you ask such a question? *Ay, Dios mio!* What has gotten into your head?"

Pablo was surprised also, but not as shocked as Clara. He knew Maria would not like military life and would never last a day, because army life would be ten times more hellish than a bad day at her high school. He took her question for what it was: idle curiosity. Perhaps it had traces of something else as well. As he heard mother and daughter carry on, he couldn't help but be amused at his women folk. He knew that Maria enjoyed pushing her mother's buttons at times. Part of the fun was Clara's unfailing and predictable exasperation.

"I'm just considering all my options, Mom. I'm just curious. In a minute I'll give you equal time and let you recommend a good catholic school for girls where I might teach."

Clara shook her head dismissively, not taking her daughter seriously and went into the kitchen saying: "I think the flan should be cool by now. I'm going to serve it."

"Ah, the flan, yes! That gives me a better idea!" began Maria again. "Forget the military, Mom. And forget the convent. I will go to Paris and become a chef! Did you hear that, Mom? A chef, I said."

Clara came back from the kitchen to respond to that and with some indignation reminded her daughter: "You are already a teacher and a mathematician, Maria. Or are you going to throw all that away? What has come over you?"

"Actually, they do need good cooks in the army. Soldiers have to eat, you know," added Pablo. "They will send you to cooking school. But your mother is right. You're already a teacher and a mathematician; so, what gives?"

"…Nothing gives, Dad. It's just that we heard from Paco, and he's just been to all those wonderful faraway places; you just told us how you had been halfway around the world before you married, and here I am on a Sunday night, a school night, I might add, with a full week ahead, getting ready for the drag... That's what gives."

Maria left for her apartment soon after that, leaving her parents, especially her mother, in a puzzled state. Pablo was a little intrigued, but Clara was full of apprehensions. All she could do was utter mumbles of: "*Ay, Dios mio,*" in recurring gasps and sighs.

Z   Z   z   z   z   Z   Z

43. Girl Talk

Maria could raise questions and stir a hornet's nest of doubts and provocations and then walk out of her parents' house leaving them befuddled and bewildered, as she had done earlier this evening. But she could not do that to the girls of Dreams R Us who were able to give Maria her comeuppance. When they came out of the woodwork of her subconscious, they sometimes worked her over till they got to the bottom of an issue. They could explore her innermost feelings and extract confessions that put her soul through a wringer. Unlike her relationship with her parents, who could not corral her, she was a captive of her psyche's inquisitors. The rules of the game were turned; then it was Maria who could not escape.

This late Sunday night, or early Monday morning, they had a lot to talk about. There was Toro and his other half, Pedro. Everybody was curious as to where that was going. Then there was that persistent restlessness of Maria of recent times, that wanderlust, that longing for something else, for another life, for another job, for another career; and there was that yearning for companionship, for love, for an ineffable need in her heart which she could not specify. Sasha was the first to speak.

"Thank you for letting me use your computer this morning, Maria."

"Oh, sure, don't mention it. What did you use it for?"

"Don't you remember? I wrote a poem, 'Inner Echoes.'"

"No, I haven't seen it. What was it about?"

"Maria! Shame on you! It was about me talking to you, crying out for recognition. I not only used your computer but your own hands and fingers."

"I'm sorry. I'll look for it tomorrow... first thing... I promise."

This was not the first time that Maria could not recall having written something that she found on her computer. She often found fragments of essays, lines of poetry, cryptic verses, embryonic thoughts that left her wondering: When did I write this? What was

I getting at? Sometimes the lines seemed out of character—as if another person had written them. Sometimes she would delete the literary snippets on the spot. But more often she would leave them to gestate, to grow roots and hopefully tap into a lode of wisdom that would make sense later.

Next to speak was Maria Luisa, the quiet mathematician, who commented on Maria's reticence at the hospital, saying: "You were quiet this afternoon, Maria. You said very little at the hospital. Did you know that?"

"I know," acknowledged Maria, "I mostly listened. It was awkward. But I don't know him that well and I wouldn't have much to say. It was a good thing he talked, because he cleared up a lot of questions that had been whirling in my mind since yesterday."

"How are you going to deal with him when he comes back to school? Do you think he will come back as Toro, or as Pedro?"

"Interesting question… I don't really know the answer to that. I was moved and touched by his apparent sincerity. That's why I went back and held his arm, trying to recreate the moment when his vision of me had been so inspirational. It seemed like the right thing to do. But I don't know how things will play out from here. Of course, I'd rather he would come back as Pedro."

"You would!" said Libby critically. "I think you got a Jekyll and Hyde on your hands and there will always be a Toro inside of him; don't kid yourself. As for me, I don't mind Toro; I would just as soon deal with Toro as with Pedro. I kind of like the idea that students are following more than just the curves and lines of Geometry on the board. When I think about Toro's stares undressing me, I don't mind it at all; I love to bask under his scorching gaze singeing my skin; I love to know my presence has stirred up all that testosterone that is charging the air like an inflammable fume about to explode into passion. I must confess that I was a little turned on by his account of things when he mentioned the dream he made up about Maria being 'drunk, willing and wild.' Can you all picture that? Can you see Maria with her hair down, ready to rumble the way Toro envisioned it? That must have been something. Unfortunately, we heard none of it because Pedro got on the way and suppressed it. Oh, I wished he hadn't done that. I was dying to hear the pubic details. By contrast, when Pedro had the floor, he actually made me sick at times. When he gave you all that sanctimonious pap about never undressing you or touching you in a bad way, I could have puked, and I wanted to kick his wimpy butt."

"Yes, I would expect that from you, from my own Mr. Hyde in 'hyding'," said Maria. "It's a good thing I can keep you under wraps and under control in the real world, or I'd have the reputation of being a good-time floozy by now."

"Okay, Maria, but now you listen to me," said Libby in a stern tone. "You're not going to be able to keep me suppressed much longer. I am going to do all I can to break loose and take control of our body one of these days. You have kept me in chains for far too long. To still be a virgin at age 26 is overdoing it. It is sacrilege, in my book. You're way past due. How much longer are you going to wait and keep your precious little treasure intact and zipped up?"

"…Until I get married, what else?"

"Oh, come off it! When will that be? You can't be serious. Even Mom and Dad didn't wait that long!"

"What? What are you talking about? Where did you get that about Mom and Dad?" demanded Maria.

"Put two and two together, Dummy! They were married in March of '72 and we were born on September 11. What does that tell you?"

"That tells me simply that they loved each other; that mother knew she had found the right man; and that she knew they were going to get married. Under these circumstances having sex before marriage is not all that bad; it's just twisting the calendar a little. You are also losing sight of another important fact here. Mom was a virgin for the man she ultimately married, and that's important."

"Wow! Do you realize what you just said? If I understand you correctly," concluded Libby, "you are saying that you would do it before the wedding day, if you thought the man that you did it with was the man you were going to marry. Do I have that right?"

"Yes, I guess so."

"Well, well, well... then, at least we are making progress. Bravo! Bravo! You're moving in the right direction. You've now moved the date from the wedding night to the marriage proposal. Good for you! Even so, that is still too long. Marriage is so far on the horizon that we are talking about pie in the sky in the sweet by and by."

Maria became exasperated and protested: "What is it that you're driving at, anyway? What would you have me do?"

"I would have you loosen up, Maria! I would have you live. I would have you discover sex, once and for all, with Tom, Dick or Harry!"

"What do you have in mind, playing the field a la Gwen Wingate?"

"Yes, but not the way she did it. She was too stupid. She was a disaster. She got the worst of all possible worlds. She had sex but didn't even know it. She didn't know with whom, where or how, and didn't even enjoy it. That is definitely not the way to go. That's like getting the calories, the fat, and the indigestion from a cake you don't remember eating, because you were sleepwalking when you stuffed it down. She could have gotten a sexually transmitted disease. I think you have far more sense than she. What happened to her need not happen to you."

Maria stood up and waved her arms, gesturing a time-out. "I must interrupt you here, Libby, for a very important announcement. Now hear this, all of you! Let me have your undivided attention please. I want to go on record with a dream injunction. Please do not, and I repeat, do not. Please do not elaborate on that metaphor of stuffing cakes while sleepwalking. Resist the temptation, even if by some bad luck the metaphor should apply. I'm tired of having cakes I can't eat, and I don't want indigestion for cakes I ate while sleepwalking. Is that clear?"

"Oh shucks, you spoiler, I was just working on it, trying to decide whether to make it cheesecake or carrot cake," said Sasha.

Then Maria walked around saying: "And there's something else... I would like to set the record straight on another matter." She held her words as she paced the floor for effect. "As to the over-extended period of my virginity, I have something to add. It may come as a great surprise to you but get this: I don't disagree with Libby. I am not a prude. Or, if I have been one, I don't want to be one anymore. I, too, want to live. I want to enjoy life. What do you think this restlessness that I've been feeling lately is all about? I want to change jobs; I want to travel; I want to give full vent to this wanderlust that burns in me like a chronic fever. And yes, to get to the point at issue, I do want to discover sex, with or without marriage. Yes, I do, I do. So, there! I've let it all hang out. What more can I say? The problem is that I don't know how to go about it, and I don't want to be a skank either. I wouldn't know how to act like one if I wanted to."

"You leave that to me," Libby interrupted. "That's where I come in."

"Thanks," Maria continued. "I do need your help there. I'm curious about sex, but I'm also afraid. How do you make it happen? It should be so easy for a woman. She should be able to get up one morning and say to herself: today is the day. And sure enough, without further ado, she should make it happen! God knows, at times I have fantasized about taking matters into my own hands and running down the street with nothing but a robe over my naked body; grabbing the first man that came along the way, flashing him, and then offering him my virginity, telling him: 'This is your lucky day, my friend. You just won the virgin lottery, and I am the big jackpot.' But, of course, I know that's just too direct; that's just a silly fantasy. That's not the way to do it for a dozen reasons, not the least of which is that it simply might not work. Just as people sometimes fail at suicide, virgins can also fail at giving away their treasure. Wouldn't it be something if the first guy that came along was gay, or impotent? What would I do then?"

"Maybe, you'd better take some Viagra along, just in case," added Sasha.

Libby was ecstatic. She approached Maria saying: "Maria, this is wonderful news. I can't believe my ears. Much as we are not supposed to have any secrets between us, I must say I am surprised. I didn't know that you had these flights of fancy. It never occurred to me that you could have been suffering, poor thing. I want to give you a hug."

Their silhouettes merged, just as Sasha had described it in those lines of "Inner Echoes" that said: "we embrace without really touching, like shadows in the screen of a dream, our bodies eclipsing past each other."

When they disengaged, Maria commented: "There are more things in the caverns of this mind than we ever suspected. Like the moon, each of us has its dark side. That's why we have these sessions, to get to know each other better."

"Well, good, this is wonderful!" Libby continued. "The important thing is that you now are receptive to opportunities. You won't necessarily go to bed with the first guy, but you won't rule it out either. You'll play it by ear. You have just opened a new vibrant phase of your life. Watch for a tinge of roses in the air from now on. *La vie en rose* has begun!"

"Well, I don't notice anything different just yet."

"Give it time. Give it time. You've taken the first step. You have just issued your emancipation declaration and broken free from the restraining commitment you had made to yourself that only a husband-to-be could be a potential candidate for sex. You don't need to rush into things. If whoever you meet doesn't cut the mustard, you pass him over and remain virgin. It's okay to take your time and be discreet. The important thing is that when you fail to have sex, let it be for the right reasons. Saving yourself for your wedding night is definitely not it. You've been doing that through all these wasted years already."

"Fine. So, what do we do now?" asked Maria.

"You have to do your homework," said Libby. "This is the beginning of the rest of your new life. Now that I have the green light from you, we will work to make it happen. Let's set a deadline for ourselves. It is almost mid-April now. Let's say that within this millennium, before next December, we shall have known carnal pleasure with a real man, enough of dreams and such. But to achieve this, you may have to change your habits and create opportunities. You may have to start going to church on Sundays."

"What? Am I hearing this right? I would never have expected it from you, Libby. It seems that you're changing Mom's tune from: 'Go to church to get married,' to 'go to church to get laid.' Is that it?"

"Well, I did borrow a page from her book," conceded Libby. "That's probably how she caught Dad. She has a good point, you know... if it worked for her, why not you? I must confess that right now I am out of ideas. It's all happening too fast. But we must start somewhere, and the church has possibilities. I am going to keep my eyes and ears open for every opportunity that comes along. You need to circulate and be more proactive about meeting people. Right now, you are too lonely, too isolated."

"I will try. But there is something else that I'm still uneasy about. I don't know how to put it. Let me start by saying that I was very flattered by Pedro's high esteem of me. To be revered that way is nothing short of exalting. He made me feel like a goddess. You asked why I was so quiet, Maria Luisa. Truth is, part of the time he was talking, I was on cloud nine. My feet were not on the ground. My problem is that I just don't see the beauty he perceives in me. I don't see myself as being that beautiful. I can't imagine what he is looking at. He must be in awe of Math, or my accomplishments, or my character. I don't know. He must be confused. I see myself as plain. In a lineup of ten women my own age taken randomly, where men are asked to choose their favorite, I would never come up Number One, or Two, or even Three! I think I might be 6th or 7th runner up. That's how I feel."

The room roared in protest and disagreement. "No, no, no, Maria! I disagree most vehemently with that," said one. "You are dead wrong," said another. "No way! You are blind!"

"Actually, your self-confidence is low," said Libby. "We are going to have to work on that. In my book, with a little touch here and there, you could be a knockout."

Sasha spoke for all of them when she said: "Nothing we say here can possibly carry as much weight as the words of someone external to us; so, let me remind you that it is Toro, Pedro and Elena that have placed you in a high pedestal. Elena worships the ground you walk on. She thinks you are beautiful and tries to emulate you. As for me, I could compare you to a summer's day. But thou art more lovely and more temperate."

"Thank you, thank you, Sasha. That was sweet."

Z   z   z   z   z   z   Z

44. GUAYAQUIL

It was perhaps the accounts of her father when he was young that inspired Maria to imagine how he had met her mother. Also, Maria had been hearing so much talk about church on Sundays in connection with catching husbands, that it conjured up sunny mornings full of love in the air. She could think of at least two tangos that captured this spirit and celebrated that unique time of the week: "Voces de Bronce," (Bronze Voices) and "Flor de Alhelí," (Alheli Bloom). Both tangos speak of that idyll when young people meet and fall in love after Sunday mass. She could almost hear the *Voces de bronce, llamando a misa de once* (the bronze church bells, calling to eleven o'clock mass).

Maria still had vivid memories of Guayaquil as a child. She remembered the cheerful, sunny and festive Sunday mornings when the family went to church. She could remember the cathedral on the avenue *10 de Agosto* across from the park Simon Bolivar and the parish church San Francisco on the main boulevard *9 de Octubre*. The streets leading to the churches were like fair grounds, always full of people milling around, walking leisurely, and passing the time away, meeting friends, seeing strangers, doing business. There were parishioners, vendors of all sorts, beggars, street performers, jugglers, clowns, musicians and—so she was told— invisible pickpockets also, plying their magic in front of everyone, but unseen. Above all, there were children dressed in their Sunday clothes. The dress was definitely part of the euphoria! Being gussied up in her crisp, pink Sunday finery gave her the feeling of floating on air, lifted by the vanity of wearing her sartorial frills, the ribbons and laces, the spotless shiny shoes and the impeccable white socks.

The vendors peddled all sorts of ordinary things, whatever they had, and that meant anything from pencils, batteries, and toothbrushes to rubber bands, screw drivers and balloons. It was a wild assortment of wares in a chaotic market that was full of rhyme, without reason whatsoever. Maria, being a child, was attracted to the vendors with the sweet nibbles: the fruits, pastries and candies, and above all the ice creams. The place had a joyful, cacophonous jungle sound. Everyone was making their own music, singing their own song out of sync with the rest of the world. Maria enjoyed the way the vendors barked their wares; this was part of the bizarre character of the place. There was, for example, the alliteration of the candy seller: *Chiclets, chocolates y chocolatines*; the repetitive twangy chant of *a tomar helados, a tomar helados, de coco y leche, de coco y leche* (get your ice cream; get your ice cream, of milk and coconut, milk and coconut), and the rhyming cry of *Ajonjolí de maní,* a sweet concoction of spicy peanuts. Beside the vendors' barks, there were other things—uniquely Latin—that Maria would hear on the street but could not understand. These were the wolf whistles, the doggerels and verses—*piropos* they called them—that Romeos felt irrepressibly compelled to tell pretty women. Some were florid nonsense, but others were lewd and downright raunchy double-entendres, not fit for a child's ear.

This was the setting for Maria's early morning dream. She was a child again, about six years old, playing games with other children on the plaza leading to a church entrance. Suddenly, a car stopped at the curb to let out three young women in their early twenties. Her mother, Clara, was one of them. How young she looked! And how pretty! She made Maria feel so proud of her. Clara did a little dance on the open square in front of the church, and then she started taking off her clothes in striptease fashion. First, she took off her jacket and hurled it with a flare at one of her friends. Then she doffed her skirt, and then her shirt, until she came down to her walking shorts and a tight T-shirt. She was now dressed for hiking, or mountain climbing, or cathedral steeple scaling.

"What is she up to?" someone in the crowd asked.

"I think she's going to scale the church and get up to the belfry."

"Why doesn't she walk up the stairs?"

"Because this is a stunt. This is something the young ladies came up with, in response to the priest's continued complaint that not enough men come to church anymore. Only women and children, that's all he ever sees. The girls promised to fix that."

Clara was just beginning to clamber up the outside walls, pulling herself up on a rope. Her beautiful body strained and stretched, swinging a little to the sides till she stopped herself against the wall. Her legs would spread open at times as she would swing to another position, drawing men's stares like magnates to her body. Maria, who was playing on the ground with Sasha, would hear moans of desire from the men. "*Ay, ay, ay!*" one would emote while another one would whistle. One man, in particular, who was standing nearby, staring lasciviously at her mother, sighed plaintively, almost in pain, these words:

"*Ay mamacita, no me mueva tanto la cuna que me va a despertar el bebe* (Hey, little mama, don't rock my cradle so bad, you're gonna wake up the baby).

At first Maria took the words literally and she looked around for a cradle. There was none. Then she looked up to see if the man was holding a baby. But he wasn't. There wasn't a baby in sight. Then she figured it was something figurative like a double-entendre, something dirty that she didn't really understand, but which she knew, intuitively, had to be bad and demeaning of her mother. Maria got up and went in search of a big rock, with malice in her little heart, mumbling to herself: "Just you wait mister. I am going to fix your cradle." She returned with a half of a concrete block that she could hardly carry. When she was back in front of the man, she dropped the block on the man's foot with all her little might. But, amazingly, much to Maria's disappointment, the man didn't budge at all.

Sasha, who had been following the proceedings, said matter of fact: "He didn't feel a thing. He can't hear us or see us."

"But why?" asked Maria, with anguished disbelief.

"Because we haven't been born yet," responded Sasha.

"Oh, that's right. I forgot."

The little girls played around on the ground, soiling their fancy Sunday dresses, watching people look at their mother-to-be doing her acrobatics. Then Sasha nudged Maria and pointed excitedly at a man, saying: "Look, look, Maria, there is Dad."

"Dad? Where?"

"He is the man that's talking to Mom's friends over there," said Sasha as she pointed to a dashing young fellow wearing a white suit and a Jipijapa hat—better known to Americans by its misname, Panama hat. Maria could hardly recognize him for all his youth and debonair good looks. The girls saw the man go into the church only to reappear a few minutes later on the belfry, waiting to help Clara into the window. He pulled her in, and then he took off his hat, bowing with a cavalier's flair, in a gesture of great gallantry as if introducing himself to her. She smiled coyly. Then they both waved at the crowd below that was applauding, whistling and carrying on as if they were watching live theatre. It was a scene of romance in the making, pregnant with the promise of an embrace or a kiss, which the crowd demanded. People were cueing them in, cheering them from below, some crying out loudly: "Give her a kiss, you dope! Whatcha waiting for?"

The crowd got only waves from the couple on the belfry. The couple was soon rescued from the clamoring crowd by the appearance of another couple at the church doors, who stole the show. It was a wedding couple, just coming out of the church into the sunlight. People opened a lane through the crowd to let them pass. The bride was beautiful in her dress, glaringly bright and white, and her groom dressed in black. They stopped for a few pictures, and then the bride tossed her bouquet over her shoulder. It flew through the air, as if carried by a magic wind over 100 feet to the belfry where Clara was still standing, looking down at the wedding party. Clara reached out for the bouquet and caught it.

Maria loved the dream. It had an enduring charm that lasted through the morning. She thought of it several times, relishing the memories from childhood, and savoring the message of the dream.

"Hm. Very interesting… wonder if my parents really met through the church. Maybe I need to start going to church on Sundays."

Z   Z   z   z   z   Z   Z

45. MOM

Elena was absent from class on Monday, but she came to Maria's office after school to share with her what had happened over the weekend. On Sunday the police had contacted Elena to tell her that Wally, who had been on the run, had been caught. Even his family did not know where he had been. He was lame and in pain with a cracked clavicle from the blow that Elena had given him with the crowbar. On Saturday a patrol car had seen him driving erratically and had tried to stop him. A high speed-chase ensued, and Wally lost control of the car, flipped over twice, and ended up in one of those many canals of Miami. Now he, too, was in a hospital in South Miami in very serious condition, with a broken back and a good chance of becoming a paraplegic or quadriplegic for life.

On a happier note, Maria also received on this day a box full of books from June Hampton-Valverde, which was more than just a delightful surprise; it was a reaffirmation of friendship from someone she admired. Maria had expected to receive the books someday, perhaps weeks later, but to follow through, as June had done, so soon, showed an exceptional commitment that Maria appreciated enormously. She opened the box and read June's brief note: "For Maria: Welcome to the world of Spanish Literature. *Cariños*. June." The books and the note brought back memories of a wonderful party. Now she had her work cut out for the following months. It would be challenging, slow reading for her, but she looked forward to it. One book dealt strictly with Spanish authors; another dealt with Latin-American writers, a third book was mixed, Latin American and Spanish literature. A fourth book was a compilation of short stories by Julio Cortazar and a fifth was a small book of verses by Alfonsina Storni. This was a new direction for Maria, and she was very excited about her project. She browsed through all the books that afternoon, thinking to herself that perhaps she might even take a course over the summer. Then she called her mother to tell her the news. Clara was also delighted that June had remembered sending them.

While they chatted on the phone, Maria remembered the dream with which she had awakened this Monday morning. She made a point to ask her mother how she had met her father.

"Why do you ask?" Clara wanted to know.

"…Because I've been thinking about the two of you. Ever since last night when Dad was telling me about his military years and his college years, I've had you both in my mind. It occurred to me that I heard next to nothing about you, about things from your side, your background or how you met him. Then last night I had the silliest dream. It was ridiculous but really was funny. I could picture you both, and I saw how you met."

Clara was delighted to hear it. How sweet that she should dream about her parents when they were young. But what was funny about it? What was so ridiculous? She was curious to hear about the dream. "So, tell me. What happened?"

"Well, you met outside church, before Sunday mass, in Guayaquil."

"*Si, si. Así fué*," Clara concurred. "What else did you see in your dream? What church was it? Do you remember?"

"Don't get your hopes up, Mom. Dreams are not that faithful to facts. The church could have been a hybrid of three churches in Guayaquil—with parts of a fourth church from Miami. Dreams change structures and warp time and place. To make matters more complicated, I was cast as a six-year-old in the dream. Can you see the illogic of that? That's just crazy. I couldn't possibly have been there. I wasn't born yet. But dreams are like that. What I am sure of is that it was Guayaquil, because it had all the craziness, all the weird doings of uninhibited people being themselves in the streets, without caring about what others might think. I could see the people, the vendors, the beggars, and pickpockets carrying on, making noise, using bad language, dancing around, and so on."

Clara was amazed at Maria's memory. "I am surprised you remember Guayaquil so well. You were only eight when we left. Tell me one thing: Was I alone?"

"No. you were with two young ladies, friends of yours."

"Esto es increible! Could you recognize either one of them?"

"Mamá, stop it! Of course, not! I didn't know your friends then."

"It's just that one of them could well have been Patricia Alvarez, Azucena Valverde's younger sister, whom you do know, because she was at the party where you met June. We went out together often in those days."

"Well, maybe …it could have been her, now that you mention it. I only vaguely recall your friends."

"Now think hard, Maria. Are you sure we haven't talked about how Dad and I met before? I can't believe you would have learned it strictly from a dream."

"I assure you, Mom," Maria responded, "you've never told me how you met. I did not know this."

"This is fascinating. Tell me more."

Maria thought that Clara was making too much of the dream, ascribing it magical powers and approaching it too credulously, checking for consistency in the slightest details. For Maria, the only important issue was whether her parents had met in church, and they had. As far as Maria was concerned, her curiosity had been satisfied, and she wanted to change the subject. But Clara loved this sort of thing. She was superstitious; she liked to believe in the power of the bizarre and she was eager to learn more.

Mother and daughter were galaxies apart in the way they thought. Maria was the logical one, the skeptic, the questioner, the challenger and debunker of myths; she put up barriers, she filtered ideas critically, while Clara bought on impulse. Clara was an incorrigible romantic who embraced every fairy tale with loving arms and who was willing to accept claims as true, without examining them critically. She believed in miracles, in legends, in ghost stories, in myths, and, of course, in received religious doctrine. Mother and daughter often clashed. Just a couple of days earlier, they had had disagreements as to whether Clara really saw the attack on Elena and

Pedro in a dream. The attack took place on Thursday, April 15, Tax Day. But Clara's nightmare took place in the early morning of April 17th, two days later, when Maria called her to inform her that she was going to the hospital at West Palm Beach to see Elena. Maria pointed out the difference in the dates to her mother. The dream could not possibly have been a prognosticator. Then she added with a touch of sarcasm: "A true Calpurnia would have raised the alarm before the event."

Clara was completely baffled by that statement. "Who the devil is Calpurnia?" she asked with great exasperation. But Maria was in a hurry and left without explaining. She drove off for West Palm Beach, leaving her father to do the explaining. Pablo told Clara that Calpurnia was Julius Caesar's wife and that she had foreseen his death in a dream. Calpurnia tried to keep Julius Caesar at home; she begged him not to go to the Senate on the Ides of March. But he went anyway and was assassinated.

That Saturday morning Clara responded with some irritation: "Where does Maria get all this stuff? Sometimes I think I don't understand my own daughter. She talks in circles around my head."

"Well, this is kind of well known," answered Pablo. "But Maria probably gets it from reading Shakespeare, who immortalized the story with his play, Julius Caesar."

"I don't know about all that. I am not as cultured as you two. All I know is that I am very unhappy about Maria living where she does. I don't like those apartments. And I don't like the school where she teaches. There isn't a week that goes by that I don't wake up because of some nightmare involving Maria's world. First, I dreamed about Gwen and then I dreamed about these students of Maria. I don't care if it wasn't before the fact. That doesn't really matter. I'm not trying to have a good batting average at predicting events with my nightmares. I am just trying to warn Maria that where she lives and where she works is not safe, and it worries me to death. I would just as soon be wrong every time, as right only once in predicting that she was a victim of foul play."

Pablo comforted her: "I share your concerns, dear. They bother me too. Maybe she should switch to another school or change jobs altogether. I know Maria is very stressed about her school."

"I am also worried that she has no religion," added Clara. "I don't know where that leads to, but I don't like it. It scares me. When she comes for dinner tonight, I am going to insist that she watch *Marcelino Pan y Vino* with me. I want you to check on the VCR and be sure that it is in working order. I've got the tape already. It would make me so happy if she would go to church with me on Sundays."

"*Y dale que dale*... (there you go again) ...You don't give up on Sunday church, do you?" Pablo said good-naturedly.

All this was a flashback to last Saturday. Returning to Monday afternoon, Maria was still on the phone with her mother, although she was ready to finish the conversation. "Mom, I have to go. I'll miss my exercises if I don't leave now."

"Ah, *si, perdona*. But you haven't told me what was so silly about the dream in Guayaquil yet. All my dreams about you are nightmares about rapes, beatings, and violence. Your dreams are happy and funny. Tell me more. What was I wearing? What was Dad wearing?"

Maria knew then that she had to at least go into a few more details. So, she began by telling her mother that her dad was wearing a white suit and a Jipijapa hat. Those details transported Clara as if she were before a miracle, before an ESP sort of revelation. She was beside herself with awe. This was another big score on the tally sheet she was keeping about Maria's dream.

"*Ay, Dios mio... ¡Esto es increible!*"

Maria, for her part, did not attach much significance to the fact; after all, she had seen a picture of her father dressed that way in an old family album, and it was quite likely that her memory had borrowed that image to lend authenticity to her dream. In addition, that outfit was very common among men in Guayaquil; it was practically a Sunday uniform.

"What about me? What was I wearing?" asked Clara.

"Now it gets silly, Mom. You came wearing an overcoat which you flung off in strip tease fashion. You danced around a bit, made a couple of turns, and then you took off more clothes, handing them to your ladies in waiting. You then shed your shirt and your skirt, and you got down to your walking shorts and a T-shirt."

"Goodness! Now this is ridiculous. As you know, I've never worn shorts in my life! Never had any! I wouldn't do that strip-tease stuff for nothing in the world. That couldn't have been me. Are you sure it was me? Oh, this is too much! But then what happened? Tell me more."

"Then you grabbed a rope and started to climb the church tower to the belfry."

"Oh, this is too much! Me, an exhibitionist? Me, climbing a church steeple?" Clara was guffawing now. Maria spared no details. She told her mother everything, including the bit about the man who had been ogling her lecherously and had said to himself: 'Hey, little mama, quit rocking my cradle so hard, you gonna wake up the baby.'"

"*Ay, que vulgar*! Now I really believe you were in Guayaquil."

"…You want to know what I did to him? I grabbed a big concrete block and dropped it on his foot. Unfortunately, he didn't feel a thing because I wasn't supposed to be there. Remember, I hadn't been born yet."

"Now I can see why you love to sleep so much, till noon on weekends!" said Clara. "With dreams like this, who needs movies? How do you manage it?"

"Well, believe it or not, you had a lot to do with this dream, Mom. You were not only the star of the show, but the producer, the great force behind it. It all has a simple explanation. You've been trying to get me to go to church on Sundays; you've been trying to hook me on religion, you showed me that saccharine movie *Marcelino pan y vino,* and I asked myself: why? The answer, in part, is due to your concern for my religion, or lack thereof, but partly also, because you see Sunday Mass as a social event, like a place to meet people, and maybe even catch a husband. It was only natural that I should put two and two together and ask: Hey, maybe she knows whereof she speaks. Maybe she caught Dad that way. So, the dream was really a question. Is that the way it happened? But Mom, seriously now I really, really, must go. I'll talk to you later. Let me run. *Chau.*"

Clara relayed the conversation to Pablo, point by point, missing nothing. But when it came to the fundamental question: did they meet in church? Pablo's recollection was different. "We met at a party."

"You are wrong. It was before Sunday Mass. But promise me this: please don't tell Maria otherwise. Let her keep the sweet version of the church."

z z z Z z z z

46. ABORTED CONFESSION

The lobes and quarters of Maria's sleeping mind were changeable like a Hollywood lot that led to different sets. Besides conference rooms and auditoriums, besides university halls and school corridors, it also had libraries and other sites of a world that could handle anything. This evening, after so much recent concern over the church, her cerebral digs were transformed into something dark, gothic and austere. She found it eerie and frightening. Tonight, she was in the halls of a priory. It was poorly lit and quiet. Maria approached a seminarian receptionist.

"Good afternoon. I'm looking for Father Quixote. Could you...?"

"He is hearing confessions right now."

"Oh, super! That's exactly what I wanted to see him about."

Maria walked across a courtyard and entered the church. Several people were kneeling on the pews, praying away the penances imposed by their confessor. Others were standing against the wall in line, waiting their turn to confess. Maria stood behind them. They were grandmotherly types with a scarcity of sins; to judge by the short time it took them to tell their sins and molt the soiled skin of their souls.

It had been so long since Maria had done this that she was now quite apprehensive. It did not go well. The priest did not help. He exacerbated her discomfort by asking her questions that put her on the spot.

"How long has it been since your last confession?"

Darn! He would ask me that! Maria told herself. She had forgotten that priests usually began by asking that. Maria swallowed hard and she answered honestly: "It's been years, Father."

"How many years?" he pressed.

"I can't remember, Father."

"Well, try to remember. Has it been three or four, or more?"

"More..."

"What was that?"

"Maybe ten, Father."

"I can't hear you. Speak louder. How many years did you say?"

She could hardly repeat it. "About ten, Father."

"Have you been going to church all this time?"

"On and off, not regularly," she said sheepishly, almost inaudibly, her embarrassment and discomfort increasing unbearably.

"Have you been going to another church then, a non-Catholic one?

This inquisition was going so badly; she was so mortified that she walked out of the confessional and ran out of the church. When she got out on the street, she woke up, panting on her bed. The clock by her bedside table read: 2:37.

It took a while for Maria to get settled and fall asleep again. When she finally lost consciousness, the denizens of her sleeping mind saw fit not to disturb her. They left her in that nebulous interlude of calm where she did not dream, where she did not even think, where she descended to oblivion and basked in a dark peace that was almost blissful. They even dispensed with having her fall asleep at the auditorium, as she often did. Instead, they came to her bedroom and materialized around her bed. Sasha sat at the foot of her bed with Maria Luisa on the other side. Libby sat on a chair nearby, Imogene on another, and Professor Quixote stood by the head of her bed. Suddenly Dr. Broca also came into the room, syringe in hand, and gave Maria a shot of some sedative. "You don't need to worry about waking her up now. You can talk as loudly as you want. She'll be out of reach for a while." Then he left.

"I can't believe she was going to confession," Sasha remarked. "Does anybody have any idea why she did that?"

"I think she wanted to have a heart-to-heart talk about religion," responded Professor Quixote. "She wanted to confide her deepest feelings on the subject, but she never got there. She didn't even make it to first base."

"That's because you ran her off with all those questions," said Libby, adding: "I wouldn't have lasted half as long as she did."

"Oh, but that wasn't me," responded Prof. Quixote.

"Well, Maria thought it was you. She asked you. Who was it then?"

"It must have been conscience impersonating me. But it doesn't matter. I would have asked her the same questions. It's what any priest would have asked her. She needs to come to terms with the reality of her estrangement from the church. Lately, she has been going through great stress, struggling with her conscience on this account."

"But I thought she was all through with that," said Libby. "I thought her religious conflicts involved only Mom, especially about mass on Sundays."

"No, there's more. A lot more," added Professor Quixote. "Let me be blunt: Maria is a closet atheist. And it is not easy to come out. You don't just divulge it to the world with a proclamation. There are always doubts, and you don't want to offend your dear ones unnecessarily. So, you keep your beliefs to yourself, avoiding confrontations, postponing revelations. Her mother is a problem, of course, but not the most important… Society at large is a bigger problem. Maria's real struggle is accommodating her philosophies to the world around her. How does she fit her convictions into her daily life? That is not easy. Religion binds us in many ways. It is ingrained in the fabric of our lives and governs what we wear and what we eat. The theological bindings are the easiest to cut, and Maria is already free of those. But the cultural ones are more problematic. These involve consuetudinary habits –sacraments such as Baptism, weddings, funerals and other rituals. It is these rituals that are giving Maria problems. Although she has been adjusting her beliefs to the real world for some time, she still has many unresolved issues. There are many implications that she must take one at a time as they come up."

Imogene, who was anxious to settle an issue, interrupted the professor to ask him: "Don, is this going to be a time when we give her a free pass and not have a dream?"

"No, not necessarily," he responded. "I would suggest that you rerun it exactly as it happened so it serves as a warning of what she might expect if she should entertain the idea of going to see a real priest sometime."

"Good! I think we can manage that easily."

Then Maria Luisa wanted to ask something. "Getting back to Maria, tell me: what exactly is her problem? Could you be more specific? Why should the church be bothering her now? What has come up to disturb her?"

"It has to do with this business of going to church on Sundays. As you are aware, this has come up several times in the last few days. Even Libby, of all people, suggested it. At first the idea made sense to Maria, and she liked it in principle. It would make her mother happy and—who knows? She might even find a husband. So, why not? It seemed worth a try. She was all set for it. But when it came time to do it, she just couldn't do it. It tore her apart."

"But why?" the girls asked, all in unison.

"…Because it made her feel like a hypocrite! The idea of lying so she could catch herself a husband nauseated her. The thought of using the church for her expediency, as a steppingstone, was tantamount to prostituting herself. It was not fair to the church. I should add, Maria respects the church enormously, even if she does not believe in most of its tenets. And last, but not least, it would not be fair to the man she would meet in church this way because it would have been under false pretenses. Sunday Mass was but one issue. There were more insuperable issues.

"The further down the road she looked, the more knots and untenable situations she found. One such problem was a church wedding. How was that a problem? For most people it is not. But in Maria's case, she feels she does not deserve that ritual. Church weddings are beautiful –if your heart is in it all the way, if you are a true Catholic, and you don't do it just for appearances, for the pomp and ceremony, for friends and family. Maria cannot be superficial about that. Maria is torn between doing what she feels is right and what her family would like. She would love to be a good sport and do it for her mother's sake. But she doesn't want to get deeper into living a lie just to make her mother happy.

"Then, another knot she saw as she looked further down the road was even bigger. How would she deal with the religious upbringing of her children? This is so difficult that many people find it easier to stay in the church whether they have faith or not, for the sake of their children. But to Maria's way of thinking, this is just perpetuating a lie.

"There is more to the church than just beliefs and tenets. The church is woven into the social fabric of our lives. It is difficult to go without a church, when so many of our customs involve religion. Maria is very honest. Social expediency is not for her. In Maria's way of looking at things, either she would embrace religion fully and sincerely and become a full Catholic, or she wouldn't. There is no in-between on this issue. But if she couldn't embrace the church, then she would have to give up the perks and the social events sponsored by the church. It would be the honest thing to do."

"How do you know all this?" Sasha asked him.

"Hey, are you asking me, her father confessor? I know what's in Maria's heart, even before she thinks about what stirs there. If I had heard her confession, she would have gotten around to talking about this, just as I have described it. I would have agreed that you shouldn't stay in the church just because it is socially convenient. She would have also asked me if there was some compromise, some way of being true to the church and to her own beliefs. But I would have told her that the Church wouldn't accept such a compromise."

"From what you say, it appears that Maria is in a sort of limbo. She has not broken with the church, and yet she is not in it. How likely is it that she would go back to the church?" Maria Luisa asked.

"I think that's very unlikely. Mentally, she is an agnostic through and through. But emotionally, she has not grown the hard carapace to be able to profess her true beliefs openly. This takes time, and it is not easy. It's a lonely fight. It is she against the world."

Z   Z   z   z   z   Z   Z

47. COLUMBINE

On the morning of Tuesday, April 20, Maria was awakened twice by the same bad dream. The first time was at 2:37 a.m., but she forgot about it. The second time, it was impossible to forget. She sat up in bed out of sheer embarrassment, mortified to death by a confession that had gone bad. The priest had given her a hard time. She aborted the confession by running out of the church, waking up abruptly several minutes before her alarm went off. The dream makers had used the same episode of her mind at night –a nightmare, really –and had replayed it around wake-up time so she wouldn't forget it and so she would heed its warnings.

That morning her mother also awoke, alarmed by a nightmare. In Clara's case the nightmare was a frightful shocker in the same genre as a horror movie. In fact, her nightmare borrowed freely from Stanley Kubric's "The Shining." For a change, Clara's dream was anticipatory and strangely coincidental with events that would unfold later in the day.

As in the movie, Clara's dream took place somewhere out West. Supposedly, Maria had been invited to go for a job interview at an elite private boarding school. Clara had gone along to keep her daughter company, but also to see the West, since she had never been further west than Florida's west coast. Still, for all her curiosity about the West, in her heart of hearts Clara would have preferred that the trip had not come up. She was very unhappy that Maria had even considered the job. She hoped and prayed that things would not work out, or that Maria would turn down a job offer. She couldn't bear the thought of Maria moving that far away from her.

Clara was, therefore, delighted when she learned that Maria had not liked the principal. "He is another Mildred Colson," she had told her mother. "I don't trust him. I can't put my finger on it, but he is odd and creepy. He scares me a little." Clara would have flown back that same day, but Maria had to follow her commitments to the end and stay another day. The following morning classes were out, and Maria took her mother on a leisurely tour of the grounds of the school. As they walked through the halls of the empty building, looking into the classrooms, Clara would see strange things that frightened her, and in a cold sweat, she would press Maria's hands very hard.

"Mom, you're hurting me," Maria complained. "What's the matter?"

"This place gives me the creeps! I can feel death all around. I've been noticing all sorts of weird things."

"Don't exaggerate, Mom! What have you seen? Where? Show me."

"In the classrooms we just passed I saw two skeletons carrying on."

"That's probably the biology lab. It's very common to have skeletons in those classes to learn human anatomy. They could have been swinging in the wind."

A few minutes later they went past another classroom and, again, Clara was horrified. Maria noticed it and exclaimed: "*Mami, estas pálida*! What is it this time?"

Clara could hardly speak; she stuttered that she saw a headless young man writing on the board the words: **red rum**! "What does that mean?"

"If you read it backwards that spells: **murder**," answered Maria.

Maria had had enough. She turned to go back to the classroom to investigate for herself. She didn't go far, because at that moment they heard the roaring sound of an avalanche of water, crashing and spraying against the walls. They soon discovered that it was not water, but a river of blood, and it was just turning the corner at the end of the hall—just as in the movie—and it was rushing towards them. Maria and Clara ran ahead and got into the first classroom they came to, closing the door, to get away from it. As the river passed, blood slithered through the bottom of the door onto the classroom floor. Clara and Maria got up on top of the school desks to escape the blood. They made their way across the room towards the window, stepping over desks, anticipating that the river of blood would bust through the door and drown them. At the window they would either hang from the window ledge or jump.

Clara was so distraught that she woke up Pablo. It was a few minutes after six in the morning. She had had a few bad nightmares in the past; they always seemed to involve Maria, but none had been as gory and as horrifying as this one. Neither she nor Pablo could go back to sleep after that. Clara recounted the dream for Pablo in full detail, leaving nothing out.

"We were trapped. Our only way out was through the window, but it was a long way down from the second story. That river of blood was after us. It was only a matter of time before its force would bust the door open. I just had to wake up."

Pablo tried to calm her. "You've been worrying about Maria too much lately. On the one hand, you want her to quit her job, but not if her next job will take her far from here. This is your mind's way of bringing up the conflicts about jobs concerning Maria. You don't like it where she is, but you wouldn't want her to move far."

Clara disagreed with Pablo's explanation. "No, no, no! It's not about jobs. That's the least of it. Of course, I would prefer that she didn't leave the area, but if she did, I could live with it. I would want what was best for her. This is much worse. This is about evil. This is a warning about a more sinister danger that she is in. This had demoniacal implications that really scared me."

"Oh, for God's sake, what are you talking about?"

"Tell me, Pablo, when was the last time you saw Maria go to church? When was the last time you saw her pray? When was the last time you heard her talk about God? She always ducks out quietly when I bring up matters of faith, or we end up arguing."

"So what? What's wrong with that?"

"I hate to say it; I can't even bring myself to pronouncing the words that might apply to her because they are so hurtful to me."

"Well, say it. Spit it out. Say what the hell you are driving at, once and for all. Say it! Tell me what's so wrong with Maria."

"She has no God. She is a heretic, an atheist."

Pablo dismissed it as trivial. Clara, for her part, had expected his nonchalance. Even so, she could not understand how he could be as dismissive of something as grave as that.

"Is that all? Oh, that's nothing," Pablo remarked. "There are worse things than being an atheist, if she happens to be one. I may be one myself."

"I thought you would say that. You are so cavalier about it. You think it is such a natural thing, like there is nothing wrong with it, like there are no costs involved in denying your creator's existence, in being ungrateful, and abusing His kindness. It's ingratitude in the extreme and God could punish you for it."

Now Pablo was furious, but he restrained himself and measured his words. It was too early in the morning to be arguing about something so complex, something that demanded more energy than he could muster at that early hour. Besides, they had argued about this many times in the past, always in a futile and unproductive way. He didn't want to go through that again and merely said: "Don't worry about Maria. She'll be fine. Worry about yourself. You have more problems handling your beliefs than Maria has handling her lack of beliefs. Your beliefs are the problem. They are irrational; they create tornadoes of fear that feed your nightmares; they have the potential of driving you to the edge of madness, if you don't watch out."

They did not talk anymore after that. They both went about their morning chores quietly, keeping their thoughts to themselves. It was a few hours later this day, April 20, 1999, that they all learned of the massacre at Columbine High School in Littleton, Colorado. Thirteen people were killed, twelve students and one teacher-- not counting the killers who committed suicide after their killing spree. The number of wounded was more commensurate with war casualties—with an ambush or mortar attack in a war zone—than with a high school. In all, twenty-eight people were wounded. It was a blood bath of horrific proportions, motivated by no reason other than pure malice, wanton murdering by random shooting. The whole country became glued to the TV, riveted by the horror. Clara pictured the river of blood running in her dream as she watched the news on TV.

Clara insisted that she and Pablo should go to Maria's apartment that evening to be near her. Talking to her on the phone would not be sufficiently comforting, and Clara feared that Maria would not want to get in her car and drive to their house. So, they went to Maria's. Clara needed desperately to hug her daughter after such a long, bad day that began with a horrible nightmare and a torrent of fears and questions that were still unresolved. Inevitably, the connection between Clara's nightmare and the Columbine massacre came up. Maria, wisely, reserved judgment on the matter this time.

Z z Z z Z z Z

PART IX: PIVOTS AND TURNS

48. Churros y Chocolate

It was after 10 p.m. when Pablo and Clara dropped Maria back at her apartment after an exhausting evening in which they discussed nightmares, massacres, wars of good and evil, and religion. Earlier they all needed a respite, a change of pace, so along about 9 p.m. they piled in the car and went out to a Spanish restaurant for *churros y chocolate*. It was a refreshing outing that cleared their heads and calmed the stress of the day. Yet, despite being tired of the Columbine massacre, both Maria and her parents could not help getting another fix on the subject and when they got home, they turned on the TV for the latest developments.

The massacre was not the only thing they discussed at the restaurant. Maria's job was the other important item of the day. Of course, the two things were related in Clara's mind. As far as she was concerned, schools were just too dangerous. First it was rapes and stabbings, and now this. Maybe Maria should leave teaching all together. Why couldn't Maria quit that job and look for something else during the summer? If need be, she could move back in with her parents to save on expenses. Maria kept her options open, adding only that if it came to that she would add one condition. Her mother should not pressure her about religion or going to Mass on Sunday. Maria might accompany Clara voluntarily from time to time, but it would be strictly as a gesture of goodwill, since it meant so much to her mother. Clara accepted Maria's condition and could not wait for her to move in.

Later that evening when Maria began to dream and she found herself in the conference room of brain central with the girls, Sasha said, pouting: "Must we always meet like this in this semiofficial setting? This is so drab."

"Well, this is what it is. Where else could it be?" asked Maria Luisa.

"I don't know… I just wish there was something else and I do have another place in mind. Could we go back to the Spanish restaurant for *churros y chocolate?*"

"But it's closed now and, besides, we can't eat anything…"

"Leave it to me," interrupted Imogene. "I'll fix it."

Then by a snap of her fingers, the conference room turned into the restaurant. "Voila! There you have it… Happy now?"

"Oh yes, yes, this is much nicer. And we have it all to ourselves."

"Yes. But don't forget where you really are," admonished Imogene. "We've only changed appearances, but behind it all, it's still brain central. Now, as to *churros y chocolate*, who is stopping you? Just ask any of the Marias walking around to bring you some. But don't overdo it. You can get sick here also."

With that, Imogene left to join Ram at another table. Those two were always together, perhaps because they were at the beck and call of the others. Every time somebody needed memory, Ram's forte, or anytime someone needed the imagination, Imogene Natien's domain, they called on them. It seemed that it was at any moment, incessantly. They often had to go together to bridge the lapses of memory or stretch the lapses with imagination. They never rested. They were the most servile functionaries of Maria's sleeping mind.

Maria stood up to look around the restaurant. It was full of familiar faces. Behind her, in a distant corner, she could see Dr. Broca and Professor Quixote at a table. Abe Lincoln and Janet Reno were at a large table with other people she could not quite recognize. Maria sat in a booth beside Sasha, facing Maria Luisa and Libby.

The girls were never at a loss for words, but tonight they seemed to be operating under an implicit injunction: no talk about religion, massacres, or good and evil. Food was also out of the question tonight because Maria was under some discomfort from the *churros y chocolate* she had had earlier. She wished Sasha had chosen another place to meet instead of a restaurant, and she was quietly praying that Sasha would not order *churros y chocolate*. The very thought of that made her gag. This dessert was too rich; it consisted of deep-fried flour strips powdered with sugar and cinnamon; the chocolate was a cup of very thick cocoa. It invariably upset Maria's stomach. Maria was, therefore, pleasantly surprised—and relieved! —when Sasha ordered hot tea instead. The other girls ordered nothing. Hot tea was precisely what Maria would have fixed herself had she been awake. Even in her sleep she craved hot tea to settle her tummy. It was as if Sasha had read Maria's innermost yen and granted her what her tummy was desperately craving for. Maria watched as Sasha sipped her hot tea and savored it vicariously. She could feel the warm salutary liquid as if she were drinking it herself and, ah, it was so good; it was just what the doctor ordered! Now she understood why Sasha had wanted to go there. She felt so much better.

Libby suddenly broke the silence by asking Maria a question which left everyone puzzled.

"So, Maria, will you be going to the hospital tomorrow to see Toro?"

"No, I have no such plans. What brings that up? Why do you ask?"

"Stop being coy with me... you know why I ask."

"No, I don't know why you ask. I haven't the foggiest."

"Well, you should reconsider. I wish you would…"

Sasha and Maria Luisa were following the exchange, turning their heads from one side to the other as if following a ping pong match. They didn't have a clue as to where Libby was headed, but she had gotten their attention, and they were curious. The volley of questions upon questions seemed to be headed somewhere.

"I think you must be referring to Elena's visit today. Is that it?"

"That's exactly it!"

"What was that about?" asked Sasha. "I missed that."

"Elena came by my office again today to tell me that she had gotten word that Pedro was not doing well. He had taken a turn for the worse," said Maria.

"I'm sorry to hear that. I guessed I missed that also," said Maria Luisa. "Are you going to see him, then?"

"I don't think so. It's not my place. If I did go, it would be to keep vigil over a very sick person to whom I am not very close. His situation calls for a close family member at this point, someone like his mother, not a distant friend."

"She has a point," noted Maria Luisa. "I wouldn't go either."

"Yes, all that is true, but it's only the half of it," added Libby.

"It's back to you, Maria. What's the other half?" asked Sasha.

"Tell us." Demanded Maria Luisa.

"No, let Libby tell you. She seems to have all the answers and is just using me for a prop. I really don't know where she is headed with all these questions. So, tell us all, Libby. Let's finish this game of cat and mouse, once and for all."

"Okay, fair enough, here it is. You all remember when Maria went to see Pedro… She stopped at the nurse's station briefly to inquire about his room. What you may not be aware of, but I certainly was, was that before the nurse could answer, a young doctor who had been standing nearby and who had been looking at Maria admiringly, said: 'Room 207, straight ahead.' Maria, always trying to be aloof and proper, answered curtly with a simple 'thank you' and moved on. I wanted her to smile, I wanted her to look into his eyes and find a way to prolong the conversation, to say something like: 'Oh, you're so kind. Are you his doctor, by any chance? Is it all right to visit him for a short while?' But no, that was not to be. She practically stiffed him and went on. I didn't press for Maria to flirt a little then, because at that time we had not yet established our current working relationship, and she had not appointed me as her advisor in all matters concerning men. But a lot of water has run since then, and it is time for Maria to start being a little coyer around men. She's got to be always on her toes, looking for opportunities and making things happen."

"Do you remember all that, Maria?" Sasha asked her.

"Yes, I do. It's pretty much as Libby says."

"And was he handsome?" asked Maria Luisa.

"Oh, yes, as I recall, he was very handsome."

"Very handsome…? Is that all? That's underwhelming it," interrupted Libby. "He was gorgeous! He was a Prince. And guess what! This is the best part yet. Do you all know that he called Elena today? To put this in perspective, even Elena was surprised that he called her, supposedly to inquire about her, to see how she was doing. Heck, he knows she is fine. He released her from the hospital himself! What he really wanted to know was more about that 'pretty young lady' that had visited her on Saturday, and who had also visited Pedro the next day. 'Was she a relative?' he inquired. I think the man is desperate to know more about Maria; I think the man is smitten!"

"WOW! Maria, this is exciting!" exclaimed Sasha, rubbing her hands with excitement.

"Oh, yeah! Wow!" added Maria Luisa. "What do you say, Maria?"

"Well, I think that Libby tends to put her own spin on things. She forgot to mention that the doctor was concerned about Elena's possible infection. It so happens that a staph infection is what is racking Pedro right now. As I understand it, these infections can be very serious. Sometimes they are resistant to antibiotics, and in those cases they can be deadly."

"The staph infection Pedro has may well be true, but I think it is a stretch as far as Elena is concerned. I think the doctor used it as an excuse to find out more about Maria. I think he is interested," said Libby.

"I'm beginning to see your point more and more," added Sasha.

"So, what are you going to do? Will you go to the hospital tomorrow or not? You'll have to admit, Maria, that his inquiries about you change the complexion of things," said Maria Luisa.

"Not so fast." said Maria. "I can't just go there willy-nilly— or, as Mom would say, *calán-calán, tulún-tulún.* What if the man is not there when I go? What if he is there, but he is busy? What if he is married? Then I will have wasted a lot of time and made a fool of myself."

"Good point!" conceded Libby. "We'll have to think of something."

The girls thought for a few minutes, and then Maria Luisa announced: "I've got it. I can think of something that would work, but we would need Elena's assistance, and it may even require that she lie."

"That's no problem. What have you got?" asked Libby.

"Suppose Elena were to call the doctor tomorrow morning saying that she didn't feel well, and she was concerned. She wondered whether she could come and see him in the afternoon. Her teacher, Miss Maria Diaz, would accompany her and would be driving her over. If he agreed to see her, they would have an appointment with him and would not be taking any chances about making a trip for nothing."

"Brilliant!" exclaimed Sasha. "I love it! We'll get Elena to develop a fever overnight."

All the girls thought it was a good plan and were fully behind it. Only Maria still had reservations. "What if he is married? she asked.

"What if he is not?" retorted Libby. "Stop being so careful! You can't go through life lining up all your ducks neatly in a row every time before you shoot. You must venture and take risks. If he were married, you would have wasted a dollar's worth of gas and a couple of hours of an empty afternoon going. You must think positively about these things and follow your leads to the end. There is a good indication that he is not married. Would he have been making inquiries about you if he were? I say: go for it!"

Sasha and Maria Luisa picked up on Libby's exhortation and raised it into a chant which they accentuated percussively by pounding on the table with their fists as they intoned: "Go for it. Call Elena. Go for it. Call Elena."

"All right, all right, I will!"

"Good girl! Now tell us: do you know his name?"

"John Shiller."

"John Shiller, what a pretty name, it rhymes with thriller," said Sasha.

Sasha would have continued finding other words that rhymed and making doggerels, but Professor Quixote and Dr. Broca stopped by their booth on their way out. "What are you ladies up to? Planning a good intellectual uplifting dream, I hope," said the professor.

"Oh, yes, Sir. We are working on a special, the best ever!"

"Run it by us when you get further along."

Z   Z   z   z   z   Z   Z

49. RUBICON

The next morning Maria was full of trepidation as she debated whether to call Elena. She didn't want to do it. Her heart was still not in it. Then she felt a rush of encouragement as she thought of Shakespeare's lines: *There is a tide in the affairs of men, which taken at the flood leads on to fortune.*

She picked up the phone. She called Elena. She was awkward about it. She beat around the bush and threw hints about Pedro's wellbeing and about Elena's stitches and discomfort. Fortunately, Elena read between the lines and picked up on the main point, which was that Maria wanted her to go to the hospital. If Elena could get an appointment with Dr. Shiller, Maria would be glad to take her to West Palm Beach. That was good enough for Elena, who would have done anything to go on an outing with her favorite teacher.

Meanwhile at school Mildred Colson was frantically calling meetings, calling people, talking to the press, and agitating about security in schools because of the Columbine massacre. That item continued to dominate the news; it was all everybody at school talked about and Maria was tiring of it already. She suspected that Mildred Colson had her own ulterior motives for churning the matter so much. Being the political animal that she was, she knew a good opportunity when she saw it, and would use the incident to reconfigure her budget, to make speeches, to be noted and to position herself in a leadership role that would serve her well in her future political life. When Elena called Maria about 11:00 to let her know that she was all set to go that afternoon, it was difficult for Maria to force herself to go see Mildred Colson about being excused at 2:00 after her last class, but it was a formality she had to observe, and she swallowed hard to do it. To Maria's surprise, Colson denied her request. She pulled rank and demanded that Maria attend a meeting that Colson had scheduled for 2:30.

Maria was convinced that the meeting would be of no real value, that it would be all show. Her presence would contribute nothing. Maria felt that the principal insisted on her attendance only to exert her self-importance. It was strictly an ego trip. When Maria suggested that she had a pressing personal problem that was very important to her, Colson simply upped the ante and threatened that Maria would regret it if she was not there. That really irked Maria. She regretted having asked. But now she was caught in a vise. What should she do? Should she cancel her commitment with Elena just so she could attend Colson's meeting? Or should she simply not show up at the meeting and let Colson be damned?

Maria quit her job. In one fell swoop she extricated herself from Mildred Colson's stranglehold, from the stupid meeting, and from the school all together, and she got the freedom to proceed as planned. She wrote a brief letter of resignation and personally handed it to Colson. She will not be coming back next year, and she will not be attending that meeting.

In one minute of resolve she ended months of timidity. She felt free, emancipated; she felt new, invigorated. Her spirit soared high to the sky. Who cares if she will be unemployed come September? Today she didn't care. Today nothing would worry her. She had taken a new course for her life. Everything from this day on would be an adventure.

On the way to West Palm Beach Maria asked Elena how the call went with Dr. Shiller. She wanted details. What did she tell him? What did he say? What were the exact words exchanged? Maria got the distinct impression that Elena had botched it, that the doctor might think that Elena had called about Pedro's staph infection, and that she was coming on his account. He might not even be there.

"Did you tell him that you were coming because you were concerned about your own wounds, your own infection?"

"Well, sort of."

"Oh, Elena, I'm afraid that he might think you are just coming to visit Pedro, that's all. There is no reason for him to be expecting you."

"No, I think he said Pedro is not taking visitors."

"Well, that's better. Did you tell him I was coming?"

"Ooops! Sorry. I'm not sure I did. I think I forgot."

"Maybe that's just as well. It doesn't matter."

Maria was never comfortable with the idea of having Elena lie to the doctor and pretend to be sick. She did not make the purpose of the visit very clear to Elena. Also, she did not spell out details or reveal the fact that her true intention was to meet the doctor. She had not been conniving enough about the whole scheme. In fact, she did not know how she managed to call Elena in the first place. Someone somehow had put her up to it. If things had gone awry, she could not really blame Elena for it. Maria's own involvement had been halfhearted. She, therefore, resigned herself to the possibility that she had made a trip for nothing. She abandoned hopes of meeting the doctor. For this reason, when they arrived at the hospital, Maria did not bother to go up with Elena. She waited in the main lobby on the first floor.

Time went by slowly as thirty or forty minutes passed. Maria had given up on meeting the doctor. As soon as Elena came down, they would just go home, and that would be the end of that. She was stunned, therefore, when she saw the doctor approach her with Elena. Maria felt an electric shock go through her body, a strange current of fear, incredulity and excitement.

He extended his hand, introducing himself, saying words that were music to her ears. "Miss Diaz, I am John Shiller. I am so glad you came. I've wanted to meet you in person. You have two students that speak nothing but high praises about you. I had to come down."

"Thank you. I am glad to meet you, doctor. Elena speaks very highly of you, too. I am glad to know that she and Pedro are in good hands. By the way, how is he doing?"

Pedro was not well. His situation was serious. He had had quite a struggle with his infection, and the battle was not over. But there was hope. In all, they talked for five or ten minutes. The conversation ranged over all topics, including the Columbine massacre. It was all non-personal talk, but it was all part of the obligatory social formatting that people must go through on their way to becoming friends. Maria was a little apprehensive about taking up his time for too long; she feared that at any moment his beeper would go off and he would have to rush off. The encounter was brought to its polite conclusion with proper decorum. They shook hands and said goodbye, without promises and without commitment. Fate would have to do the rest.

Maria and Elena left the lobby and walked out of the hospital. The doctor went to catch the elevator. As he waited for the elevator, the doctor could still see them through the glass walls, walking out into the parking lot to their car. Soon they would disappear, and he had nothing to connect him to Maria. Every step she took carried her farther and farther away. That wasn't right; anguish rushed through him. It dawned on him that he could lose her forever unless he did something. She could disappear into oblivion very easily. On the other hand, he could just as easily cling to her; he could plant a seed to build upon. When the elevator arrived and opened its doors to take him up, he did not take it. He realized that by going on that elevator he would shut her out, perhaps for good, and they would walk out of each other's lives. That's all it took for him to decide. He rushed out of the hospital after her and cried out: "Miss Diaz. Miss Diaz." Maria stopped and turned when she heard him. She could see him coming towards her, and told Elena to wait for her, as she walked towards him to meet him.

"I have a favor to ask of you," he began. "I am new to Florida. Would you believe that as close as we are to Miami, I have only been there once? I hear that Miami Beach is quite lovely. I thought, since you are from there, that maybe I could ask you to show me around and be my guide. As a token of my appreciation, should you accept, I would like to take you to dinner the same day. Of course, since I don't know the area, it would have to be a restaurant of your choice. Is this possible?"

Maria looked at him smiling, almost laughing, and thinking

about what to say. In a few seconds she just blurted out what was in her heart, saying unabashedly: "I thought you'd never ask." He couldn't contain his elation and hugged her impulsively, muttering: "Oh, thank you, thank you."

"It just so happens," said Maria, "that today I resigned from my position at school, and I have nothing else lined up for a next job. Being a tour guide seems like a nice new venture for me. And I certainly like your terms."

At that point his beeper went off. "Gosh, I have to go. And I don't even have your telephone number."

"Don't worry, I'll call you," said Maria.

"Don't forget. I'll be waiting for your call."

zzZ   zzZ   zzZ

50. LOVE STRUCK

Maria was love struck. She was in another world. On the drive back to Miami she had to try to get her feet back on the ground and get a hold of herself while driving on I-95. She tried to talk with Elena about other things. But Elena had seen the fireworks between them, and she could feel the forces of their magnetism. She was dying to know more. What happened in the parking lot? Why did he come back out? What did he tell her? Maria tried to change the subject, but Elena pleaded. Curiosity was killing her. Finally, Maria agreed to talk if she could keep it short.

"Okay, here it is. I have a crush on him, Elena. I have a humongous, wonderful crush on Dr. Shiller, and I think he has a crush on me, too. When he came out of the hospital after me, it was to ask me for a date, and I accepted. By the way, you need to give me his telephone number, because I don't know where to call him. He doesn't have my number either, and the date cannot take place until we can coordinate time and place. We want to meet—oh, yes, we want to meet—but we need to work out the details."

Elena still wanted more, the exact wording, everything. How did he ask her? And then what did she say?

"I will tell you later. I promise I will give you a word-by-word account, but now I need to talk about something else because I need to cool it; I don't want to be too emotional while I drive—not in this horrible traffic. Here is something to change the subject. Did I tell you that I resigned from my job today? I won't be coming back next year. I'll teach till the end of this term in May, and that's it."

That certainly changed the subject for the rest of the trip. Elena was devastated, on the verge of tears, and she kept asking: why? Was there any chance that she could change her mind?

"No. I have crossed my Rubicon, Elena. Do you know what that means?" Elena shook her head, confessing ignorance. Maria explained: "There are times in life when you must make an irreversible decision. There's no turning back after that. Julius

Caesar made such a decision when he crossed the river Rubicon. After that he couldn't reverse the consequences and war followed. Well, today I made my critical decision when I resigned."

Maria dropped off Elena and then she backtracked north again towards her parents' house. Normally, she would have saved herself the wear and tear of so much driving, but this was not the sort of news she could deliver by telephone. Her parents would appreciate hearing it in person. Besides, such a marvelous day called for celebration.

Her parents were just finishing supper and—fortunately for Maria, who was very hungry—there was plenty of food left. Maria was all chipper when she barged in. "Uhm, what are we having, Mom?"

"*Estofado de pollo*," (chicken stew).

"…and Dad, do you have Champaign? Pop it out now, I have great news! Just kidding, wine will do fine."

Maria's parents had known she wanted to quit, but they hadn't expected it so soon. What had precipitated her decision? Maria told them in two words: Mildred Colson. She recounted the day's development, telling them that she had agreed to take Elena to the hospital. She left out the part that she had instigated Elena's visit to the hospital so she could meet the doctor. Perhaps, someday, at an appropriate moment, she would tell her mother the rest of the story. For now, she would let matters stand as they appeared—she had met her new beau naturally, by a fluke of fate, without pulling any strings, without scaling any cathedrals to the belfry. They had met briefly once and made good impressions on each other. One thing led to another, and now he had asked her out.

Then Maria received a barrage of questions from her parents for which she had no answer. How old is he? Where is he from? What sort of doctor is he? When can we meet him? All Maria could say was: "Mom! Dad! I just met him today, for God's sake."

Suddenly, as if she had just thought of something that was long overdue, Maria got up from the table, leaving her supper—her plate still half full, her salad still untouched—and she called the hospital. It was the only number she had; the one Elena had given her. She knew he would not be there, but perhaps they could help her locate him. She had wanted to do that for hours. Now the only thing stopping her was her supper, but her supper could wait.

"Is it an emergency?" inquired the nurse at the hospital.

"You bet! A desperate emergency!" Maria responded.

"What's the nature of the emergency and who shall we say is calling?"

"It is a matter of life and death, and my name is Maria Diaz. If you cannot put him through directly, I will give you the number where he can reach me. I'll be waiting for his call."

Then Maria sat down to finish her supper. Her parents were dazed and fascinated. Pablo translated for Clara the part about "a life and death emergency," which she had missed. "*Es de vida y muerte*," he whispered to Clara, feigning gravitas.

Maria continued eating her supper. In between bites she said: "With any luck, you will have the answer to some of your questions from the horse's mouth himself before the night is over." As it happened, Maria did not have time to eat much more of her supper because the phone rang within five minutes, and she took it in the bedroom. It was him.

"Hello, this is Dr. John Shiller. May I speak with Miss Maria Diaz?"

"This is she. I'm so glad you called. How are you?"

"I have thought of you incessantly since you left, wanting to call you but unable to, wondering how we could ever connect, hoping you would remember, and now you've called, answering my prayers. How am I? I am in heaven, just knowing that you're there. And how about you?"

"Same as you. I've had you so much in my thoughts, anguishing over the fact that I didn't have a way to reach you. By the way, let's do something about this right now. Do you have paper and pencil ready? I am going to give you my apartment number. The number you just called is my parents'. I'm at their house now."

They exchanged telephone numbers. He gave her several: that of his office, the hospital, his apartment, and his cellular. What power those numbers had! The lovers were still apart; they were still strangers to each other, but because of those telephone numbers, they had now closed a circuitry that connected them. Now, because of those numbers, they could always find each other, no matter where they were. Those numbers had the power of keeping them only a dial away. The next thing for them to do was to be together in flesh and bones. He spoke to that.

"I have half a mind to get in my car right now and fly over to wherever you are. How I would love to see you tonight! But I know that cannot be. Could it at least be tomorrow night though?"

"Yes, tomorrow evening would be lovely."

"As my tour director, I hope you don't mind if I change the order of the arrangement agreed upon this afternoon and that you allow me to remunerate you in advance for your touring services by letting me take you to dinner first. Maybe we can do the touring some other day, like on the weekend. Will that work for you?"

"Well, yes, Sir. We do have a policy of honoring such requests—but only in very special cases, from very special customers. Under the circumstances, this would be most appropriate for tomorrow. Shall I book you for dinner tomorrow, then?"

"Yes, most definitely! Now, if I may, another question. Do your bylaws allow for me to call my tour guide by her first name?"

"We insist upon it. We will not have it any other way, Sir."

"Maria, I love your name! I'm sure you know the lyrics to the song from West Side Story, Maria. *The most beautiful name I ever heard. Maria, Maria, Maria! Say it softly and it's almost like praying.* I never dreamed I would meet a Maria as lovely as you that would make me feel as if those lyrics were written especially for me, to express the way I feel now."

"That's sweet. Well, you know something? I love the song also, but I never personalized it until tonight. As far as I was concerned, it was sung for another Maria, not me. Tonight though,

I love my name! You've made me feel as if the lyrics were meant for me."

"Oh, Maria, I could talk to you all night… Do you mind if I call you later? I have to go now. At what time do you usually go to bed? Would ten o'clock be too late?"

"Absolutely not! I'll be waiting."

Maria returned to the dining room where her parents awaited news. She was done with supper. "Well, what do you know?" her mother asked.

"I know that my name is Maria, that it is the most beautiful name he ever heard. That's all I need to know for now."

He did call her later that evening. They talked for almost an hour. Among other things, they made arrangements of where and when to meet the next day.

Z   z   z   z   z   z   Z

51. MUSES

The girls at Dream Central waited anxiously for Maria to show up. If they could have had libations there tonight, the chamber would have been awash with Champaign. There was so much to celebrate. A live man had entered the scene, and love was in the air.

But there were also distant rumbles of a gathering storm and there was uncertainty in the air. Maria's world was changing, and it wasn't clear in what direction. For at least one of the girls, the day's developments did not bode well. An era was coming to an end, and she could feel its melancholy undercurrents that dampened the blithesome spirit of the day.

"You were wonderful, Maria," said Libby. "I'm proud of you. I think you got your man, although for a while I thought you were going to blow it. You were very wishy-washy with your instructions to Elena. It's a miracle that it all worked. You gave me a fit when you decided to stay in the main lobby of the hospital downstairs. I thought you were out of your mind. But in the end, you pulled it off, despite your fumbles. There is no doubt about it; he is smitten by you."

"Oh, Maria, he is head-over-heels in love with you," said Sasha.

"Congratulations, Maria! I'm very happy for you. He seems like a wonderful guy," said Maria Luisa.

"Thank you, thank you all. It's been a great day. You were so right to push me to take Elena. I couldn't have done it without you. I'm glad you persevered. But what do you think of the other top news item of the day: my resignation?"

Sasha spoke first. "It's funny how fate precipitates your decisions and forces you to order your priorities. Your world unravels before your eyes. The trip to the hospital triggered your confrontation with Colson, which led to your resignation, which set you free to pursue your dreams, which led you to your first date with John. So now you're in love and happily unemployed. Who could ask for anything more? You've done it, girl. Way to go."

"I am a little concerned," said Maria Luisa. "After the euphoria of your new freedom simmers down, reality is going to impose itself and present you with some sobering bills. Right now, you haven't even begun to think about what you are going to do to get another job. Pretty soon you are going to have to go into the market and start to line up something for August. Have you thought that you may have to move? What if you found a job away from the area, away from mom and dad, and, above all, away from John?"

"Oh, Maria Luisa, don't be so pragmatic. This is not the time to worry about such things. She has at least four months at full pay. Let her enjoy her free-wheeling days before the going gets tough," said Sasha.

"It's not just the economics of the situation that bothers me," continued Maria Luisa, "I feel a cold wind blowing and it is bringing something sad and uncertain, something that I can't quite put my finger on. It is something a little ominous that reminds me of the nostalgia of the passing of an era. But, ah, never mind; it could be just me. Don't pay attention to me. You all have a party. Don't let me spoil it for you. I must go now. I still have a lot of work to do for the next dream that's been assigned to me."

Maria approached Maria Luisa and hugged her. "You sound to me like you need a hug, *Marilucha* (an affectionate diminutive for Maria Luisa). Just so you know, I don't worry about being unemployed, at least not yet. I'm trying to enjoy it before trouble hatches, as Sasha suggests. It will probably get painful later, but I get paid through the summer months, and that's a long time. After that, who knows? Maybe I'll mooch from Mom and Dad. Cheer up. Today has been a day full of wonderful promises. I see nothing but blue sunny skies ahead."

Maria Luisa left. The other girls chatted for nearly an hour about the date the next day, about John, and about various things. Sasha was the last to leave. She stayed behind because she wanted Maria to hear a poem she had just written.

"It's not really a poem," she allowed. "It's really a doggerel. It's my latest contribution to our series on sleep. I call it 'The Alarm Clock' and it's chockfull of rhyme. Listen!" She reads.

The Modern Alarm Clock
He is electric these days
And works in quiet ways.
His ticking has been muffled,
So as never again to ruffle
The sleeper's calm.

Gone as well
Is the obnoxious bell
That used to ring
Like a bee sting
In people's ears.

Now the digits glow
In a continuous flow
Of phosphorescent lines
That morph in pantomimes
Upon a screen.

You may now sleep
Soundly and deep.
Feeling free to unwind
With peace of mind
'Cause he's in charge.

He has a battery pack
Around his back
That will prevail
Should the power fail.
He thinks of everything!

And there is no harm
In sleeping past the alarm.
Just press a button on his head

And linger longer in your bed.
He'll call you again.

But don't be a glutton
With the snooze button,
For if you overdo it
He will make you rue it
Yes, he will.

He can take once, or twice
But three times is no dice.
He's an ogre by the third buzz
And he'll raise an awful fuss.
Up, up and away.

He'll scream in your ear
Ever so loud and near.
He'll give you a panic attack
That will bolt you off the sack.
He'll sic guilt on you.

"Oh, Sasha, that's cute. I like it. Very clear ideas, overall. Good rhymes. But you know me; I strive for other things in a poem besides rhyme. The only thing I can think of in criticism is that the meter is irregular."

"I know. I know. I'm still working on that. I have another one, especially for you. You are always saying that I am incapable of writing anything without rhyme. Well, this one is made to order just for you. It has very, very little rhyme. I call it 'The Transnighter.' Can I read it to you?"

"Yes, by all means, do. But what the devil is a transnighter?"

"Oh, you know, a person who hasn't slept for over 20 hours, a leftover from yesterday who struggles in a new day trying to keep up with the rest of the world, stretching his leash on wakefulness to the limit."

"Gotcha! I know exactly who you mean. I've been there before. Go ahead. Let me hear it." Sasha then reads.

The Transnighter

Awake for over twenty hours,
I am from Planet Yesterday
Trespassing on Today.
I'm tethered to the past
While I stretch my leash
On wakefulness to its limit.

Time runs amok for me
The clocks now fold
As molten metal in Dali paintings.
My bearings lost, I now confuse
Sunrises with sunsets
And morning meals with suppers.
My tastes are all mis-flavored in a warp of time.

So many things are wrong.
The morning air is much too fresh.
Instead, I long to breathe
The mellow and warm recycled air
Of my own breath upon my pillow.

I'm a shipwrecked time traveler
Marooned in a forbidden day
A fish out of water that gasps
And longs to reach the sea of sleep.
A lone hitchhiker on a road
Thumbing for a car that will not come
Thumbing for a bed to take me home.

"Ah, that's more like it," said Maria. "I love the last two lines."

"But those are the only two lines that rhyme," said Sasha.

"That's why. You should put more rhyme in it."

"Maria, you are a pain!"

"I am teasing you, Sasha. You and I both need to coordinate more on our poetry. You need to make a rhymer out of me, and I need to turn you into a non-rhyming verser."

Sasha left, carrying her poems, and Maria was left alone with her thoughts. She was moody and contemplative tonight. She did not want to go down into a dark interlude of oblivion just yet. She sat quietly in broody meditation thinking mostly about the girls, especially those that were closest to her, her muses. They were all so different. Maria could see very clearly their spheres of influence. They really were like special sisters. She thought of each of them one by one.

Maria Luisa. Something is bothering her. I think I know what it is, but I hate to bring it up. She lives on the right side of my brain; she is the embodiment of my mathematical proclivities; she is the source of my fascination with analytical challenges; she inspires me to reason, to create theorems, to engage in mathematic problem solving. I have been very close to her for years, perhaps even more so than the others, but I fear that we are drifting apart, and I think she senses it. She feels the pull of other forces drawing me away from math, and thus, away from her. I can read what is on her mind. What if I found a job in an area not related to mathematics? How long till I left mathematics altogether? What would become of her then? She could become obsolete, useless, rejected as words that wither in the brain for lack of use.

I fear the distancing has begun. I can remember things I've done that she would have noticed with some pain, as when I canceled the subscription to my last math journal. Never mind that I couldn't read it! Never mind that the journal was over my head, that the articles were so esoteric, so abstract, and so hard to read that I didn't understand them. I was wasting my time and money subscribing to that journal. And all for what? What good did it do me in the rat hole where I teach? I was getting nothing out of it.

Still, it was another step away from math and another step away from her. Then there was the time when I snuffed out the idea of going for a PhD in math. She would have loved for me to go into higher mathematics. I had considered that for a while, but it was so futile, so impossible. It was a hopeless pipedream I had entertained, until I finally came to my senses and drove a stake through it. I was so upset when I made the decision. Now I can see how that must have hurt her. I tore to shred all the brochures from graduate schools that I had been considering. I remember I cleaned out my desk, my drawers and my shelves and threw them all in the trash. Good riddance! This is just too expensive, both in terms of money and effort. It's not worth it. Let's move on to other things. How it must have hurt her!

So, it's been coming little by little but surely… and now today, I quit my job. Poor Marilucha! I hate to hurt her. I don't want to abandon her, and I don't want her to feel rejected. I must let her know that Mathematics will always have a special place in my mind. She is an ineradicable part of my intellect. I will always keep it alive as an avocation, and Marilucha will be enthroned as one of my most cherished and most special muses.

Sasha. Then there is Sasha. Where did she hail from? A few months ago, I didn't even know Sasha. I was not aware that she was a part of me. Yet, we've become so much closer lately. She is a rising star on the left side of my brain, a hemisphere that has been gaining power and influence over me. I read more and I write more. I've developed a greater appreciation for poetry and literature. Words and letters are becoming my tools and weapons of choice more and more. I sense that Sasha and I will be collaborating very closely this summer. I have so many ideas and I plan to write a lot. Oh, my God! I just realized something –could it be? Could Marilucha be jealous of Sasha? I am sure she has noted the realignment. I can see where this, too, would have hurt her. This is all so amazing! How uncannily similar is the world of the subconscious to the real world, with its rotation of people, with friends that come and go, with clashes of personalities, with political alignments! Yes, even here, especially here, man is not an island.

Libby. What about Libby? Oh, Libby, she is something else. She has been pivotal for the last few days. I'm comfortable with her and I no longer fear her. I hope she no longer resents me for being a virgin for so long and keeping her in chains in the dungeon for so many years! Poor Libby! She has helped me mature and has instilled a confidence in me that has made me feel stronger, a full woman. But Libby has another interesting facet. For all that she is bubbly, energetic and sexy, she makes me ponder transcendental thoughts that point to the transitory nature of things. Man's ultimate destiny may be death, but his penultimate destiny is aging—sexlessness. What will the years do to Libby, I wonder? Because I am young, we have a great affinity. But will it always be so? Most assuredly not! Fifty years from now I will see Libby across a wide rift that is as big as the Grand Canyon. We will be more distant. Youth, beauty and carnal desire will have waned by then. Old people, I understand, remember sex, but their memory lacks fizz. It is worse in men, of course, poor things. It was Anatole France—I seem to recall—who referred to the decline in libido as 'the first death.' I wonder how Libby will appear to me then. Will she still be young? I wonder if her youth is ageless?

Ram. Ram, sweet Ram, oh Ram, my faithful dog, my loyal colt... we have traveled so far together, through the meandering byways of my mind. You have gone along where my whims would take me, traveling to places that I can no longer recall—places that only you know the way back to. And yet, for all that you've seen and heard, you are not judgmental like that busybody, Conscience. You are the rearview mirror of my life; you help me find the lost souvenirs that I treasure. Always solicitous, always helpful, you fetch the facts my mind requires, and you bring me the memories my heart desires.

Professor Quixote. What about PQ? I would never call him that to his face, but it's sort of cute for Professor Quixote. He intrigues me. I need to have a long chat with him one of these nights. I am not quite sure where he fits in all this. Is he an alter ego, or is he an oracle? He is distant. He comes and goes. I can always count on all the others to be here, but not him. He is not as permanent as the others; he is more independent, and I can't quite understand his role here. But he is kind and helpful to me. He is my mental beacon. When I look ahead; when I ask myself where I will be intellectually ten or twenty years from now, I just look at him and I see me going there. It's amazing how much I think like him already!

Dr. Broca. He plays the role of a medical functionary and is strictly professional. He doesn't get involved in personal chicaneries like the girls, but he doesn't fool me. He knows everything that's going on, but he plays his cards close to his chest, like a *mojigato* (a prudish hypocrite) and he acts like he knows nothing like a *mosca muerta* (a fly that plays dead), but he stings.

It seems that my little coterie here is like what one encounters in the real world, at the office, at school. How sad that it is only during sleep that I can see them. I can't recall having seen any of them while I was awake. And yet, they are as much a part of me while I am awake as when I am asleep. Why is that? Perhaps it's just as well. What would the world think if I carried on with Libby, Maria Luisa and Sasha in plain daylight? I suppose some people do talk to their muses during the day, but they are known as 'loonies' and they live in insane asylums. We owe our sanity to the fact that we can keep our two lives separate, that only at night are we able to remember what happens in both worlds. The implicit protocol is: Keep your hidden voices to yourself. The world has enough problems handling you. Keep your unseen creatures to yourself, the likes of Libby, Sasha and Marilucha. There are too many people in the world as it is. If you insist on traveling with your subconscious retinue, we will be forced to accommodate you in a loony place.

And yet, how curious! It is a fact that strangers often search for the hidden parts of us. They want to know how you get along with your inner constituents. Who are you really? What lies beneath that semblance? They want to know what sort of genies, fairies or monsters you have. People search for the skeletons in your closet, for your talents, your predilections, or your dislikes. A man, by his nature, will try to size up a woman, probing for the Libby inside her, trying to lure her out. He will push her buttons, searching for sex and passion, but instead of Libby, he might awaken Miss Prude, who will come at him like a mad hornet. When we look at people, we are attentive to all the nuances of their demeanor. We scrutinize their tone, their gestures, waiting for the signal from deep inside that would betray their true nature and reveal traces of Mr. Hyde in Dr. Jekyll's semblance. Ah, but here comes one of my own now, my quiet stinger. I see Dr. Broca coming this way with a syringe in hand.

"Hello, Maria... time for your shot before a special dream. I hear you are having a blockbuster tonight. This will rev up your dream engines."

"Aha! So that's how you do it. I suspected as much about you."

"Yes, and now you know all our secrets."

"A lot of good it will do me. I won't remember them tomorrow."

"Sweet dreams!"

Maria began to feel drowsy and lethargic. In a few minutes she was dead asleep.

Z   z z   Z   zz   Z

PART X: HEAVENLY DAYS AND NIGHTS

52. Maria Luisa's Heaven

The shot that Dr. Broca gave Maria never failed to do its magic. It relaxed her; it made her oblivious and it recharged her dreams, enlivening their colors and sounds. This morning, she would be treated to Maria Luisa's rendition of heaven. Imogene had gone around asking the girls if anyone was ready with a dream of heaven for Maria. Only Maria Luisa was. She was the steady one, the punctual one, and she had hers ready.

The scene of Maria Luisa's dream opens in the cabin of a cruise ship. Maria is there sitting at a desk, looking out the window. The sky outside displays a panorama unlike anything she has ever seen on earth, for here the planets are much larger—like giant billiard balls, three times bigger than a full moon—with painted designs in vivid hues that shout out their colors in the silence of space. The colors of the planets change before her eyes; they are in a state of flux, unstable—like orange wishing to be more gold than red, and greens tending toward blue. Space was alive, looking more like a family of celestial bodies out on a Sunday morning outing than an agglomeration of suspended masses in gravitational equilibrium. Maria could see the rings around the Saturn-like planets, discs of porous layers of star dust. She could count several satellites orbiting busily around their respective planets, like squirrels chasing each other up a tree. The heavens were active, playful, and joyous. The sky was warm, hospitable, full of things, busy and interesting. Although she was alone, there was no sense of isolation because she could hear people around.

People were not only on board the ship but, oddly, outside the ship as well. Out of her window she could see bodies floating in space like astronauts on a spacewalk, drifting slowly, inching towards the ship. This did bother her and prompted her to begin to ask questions. What is this? Where am I? And where am I headed? I wish someone would tell me.

As if someone had just read her mind, the answer to her question came in a sudden announcement over the intercom system.

"Ladies and Gentlemen: this is your ferryman speaking. Let me have your attention please. We know you are wondering where you are, where you are going, and how you got here. Here are your answers.

"First, this is not what it appears to be. This is not a love boat, or a cruise ship, or a liner. This bubble-looking craft is a ferry of the afterlife, making deliveries of souls to their final destination."

There was a loud gasp from the passengers as they heard that. The reaction was so strong that the ship yawed and shook. The speaker continued. "Please, please, watch those gasps, ladies and gentlemen, because when all of you heave at once as you just did, you can really rock the boat.

"Where are you going? It could be heaven, or hell, or places in between, depending on your situation. That will be decided after you have been registered and processed.

"How did you get here? You flew in—same as those people you can see out of your window, looking like they are floating in space. They are the new arrivals. The sky is dotted with them. There is no pattern for their arrivals; it's all helter-skelter. They show up as they die.

"Finally, a lot of you are thinking that you are not dead because you have no recollection of how you died. Well, death is an unpleasant subject. We are sparing you the details at this point. You will have a chance to go over all aspects of your entire life, including its end, before long. By then you will have gotten used to being away from the world you knew; you will have accepted that there is nothing you can do to change anything; you will start accepting the fact that the living world is all in your past. If you forgot to turn off the stove, or the water tap, that's the least of your problems. Now look out of your windows and notice the flock of souls that is just leaving the bubble all in formation, looking like geese following their leader on their flight south. You'll be flying out like that in due time. These are the souls that have already been judged and processed and are being sent to their destination. You might ask: do they know what their destination is at this point? And the answer is: negative. They do not know where they are headed yet. But I can tell you one thing. I would bet they all think they are going to limbo or better; otherwise, they wouldn't be staying in formation. As they say, hope springs eternal. Some of them will start getting hints when they feel the air getting hotter and the sun looking bigger and bigger. Well, okay folks. That's all I have for now. If you have any further questions, you can turn on the TV in your cabin for an interactive individual consultation. Enjoy the rest of the time with us and good luck on your destination."

What a character, Maria thought… a real sweetie. I would not want to ask him anything. I bet he was a hardboiled drill sergeant back on Earth and they gave him this job to make him do penance. I just want to find someone I know, somebody I trust and can talk to, but, of course, it would have to be someone who was dead already. Who do I know? Much as I would love to see Mom and Dad, I would just as soon not bring them here yet—not before their time. I really can't think of anyone at this point. I'll just have to go looking to see what I can find.

Maria went down the hall and along the way she passed a classroom. It was full of men, all of them academic types and of another age—mostly of the eighteenth and nineteenth century, to judge by their dress. They were listening to a presentation by a woman who seemed of the current century and who seemed oddly familiar to her. The board was already full of mathematical symbols and notations. Having come late to the presentation, Maria was lost. But she was curious. She stopped to watch. She could not hear what the woman was saying, and what she was writing left her just as clueless. What she saw was a hodge-podge of long, inscrutable and intricately concatenated mathematical expressions being charged up for an imminent big bang of meaning. The woman wrote her equations with the intensity of a virtuoso making music at the piano.

There was bravado to her logic. She was inspired, excited, and absorbed in the intellectual art that only mathematics can impart. A logical drama unfolds which leads to an inevitable conclusion, a climax that lights up worlds. When the woman finished the mathematical coda of her rhapsody, she got a nice round of applause from her audience and as she took a bow, she caught sight of Maria on the hall.

The stranger seemed delighted and surprised to see Maria. She acted as if she had seen a long-lost friend. The woman waved and signaled for Maria to come in and join them. But Maria was shy, confused and reluctant to intrude. To Maria's surprise, the woman then came rushing out to meet her.

"Hi, I am Marilu Zaid, and I know a fellow math teacher when I see one. You have math written all over your face. I know we've met before, but I can't remember where."

"…Nice to meet you. My name is Maria Diaz."

"Well, isn't that something? Your name, Diaz, is like mine spelled backwards, Zaid."

"Yes, it seems like we are twins of sorts. I am a high school math teacher, but I didn't think it showed. Anyway, you look very familiar also. Would you happen to be from Buenos Aires?"

"Why, yes! I am *bonaerense,* but how did you know? Was that where we met?"

"Oh, I seriously doubt that. I've never been there, except in dreams and movies."

"Well, that will work. You could have seen a video of one of my lectures. Whatever the case, I'm glad you're here. You must have just arrived. So, let me tell you that you have come to the right place. Please come in. Let me introduce you to the people here. You would not believe who we have here. This is la crème de la crème of the mathematical world. Look at them! Let's see how many you can identify. Who do you recognize?"

"Oh, gosh, I don't know. None of them look all that familiar to me except, perhaps, let's see… that old gentleman on the right.

Something about him rings a bell. Could he be Karl Friedrich Gauss by any chance?"

"Yes, exactly! What made you recognize him? Was it the halo of the Fundamental Theorem of Algebra that hovers over his head like a ring around a planet? Or was it the Normal Probability Distribution that bears his name and gives him a certain bluish glow? Whatever it was, you really got his number right away! But name another. Who else do you recognize?"

"I don't know, really. Any of the others would be just wild guesses on my part. That very young looking fellow on the first row towards the left seems out of place among so many old men. I would guess he is Evariste Galois, the French mathematician who laid down the beginnings of Group Theory."

"Yes, yes, absolutely so! You are right again!"

"I once wrote a poem about him. I was so touched when I learned of his short life. A genius cut off at the early age of twenty-one in a duel. How stupid! How sad! He wrote his legacy on the last hours of his life that night. I would like to meet him, but not just yet. Oh, my goodness, I think I recognize another person also, the man to the right of Galois. Is that Sir Isaac Newton? God, he is handsome! But he looks too young to be Newton."

"You are right again. You are doing great. Let me tell you who some of the others are. We have Laplace, Lagrange, Euler, Fermat and Fibonacci. Isn't it fabulous? Come in and meet them."

"Did you say Euler? Show him to me. Where is he? I think he is one of the greatest mathematicians of all time, and certainly one of my favorites!"

"He is the one with the baggy clothes and that funny looking hat that looks like a sleeping cap."

"I didn't realize he was so old."

"Well, he is old, and he isn't. Appearances can fool you here, because people can choose to be at any age they want. They can wear any age the same way as you grab a sweater or a hat when going out the house. Sir Isaac Newton often chooses his youngish, thirties look—true to his reputation of being a little vain—but, as I'm sure you know, he actually died in his eighties. Euler, on the other hand, doesn't seem to care about his looks or his age. And neither does Gauss. I have seen Gauss as a child and in his twenties. They have videos of virtual reality here that you wouldn't believe. They can reproduce history, recapturing the moment of creation of a particular development in math so you can see how things really happened. This is so wonderful. Think about it. Here we can finally get to the truth of things. As you know, there are many legends that grow around the lives of great personalities. Some of these are true and some are not. But here you can see the unadulterated reprise of the real thing. These reality replays also help to settle controversies. All these people are great friends now, but in life they were embroiled in polemics, in accusations and counteraccusations that dealt usually with plagiarism. It is one of the foibles of human nature to be suspicious, especially in matters of invention and creativity, and people are prone to suspect foul play rather than accept the possibility of independent coincidental creation. A case in point is the controversy over who invented the Calculus: Leibnitz or Newton? The fact is that the state of science was on the edge of discovery. There was no plagiarism. Both mathematicians developed calculus independent of each other. But Leibnitz could not accept it to his dying bed. And there were other contributors to the Calculus. There was Lagrange, and, of course, your friend, Euler."

Maria did not know whether she was in her Seventh Heaven or on Cloud Nine—fascinated as she was by all she was hearing. She was aware of the controversies because practically all mathematical texts have at least a historical footnote on this subject.

Then Marilu continued. "Let me tell you of one historical re-enactment that I found delightful. I am sure you are familiar with the oft recounted story about Gauss when he was five years old. The one where he startled his first-grade teacher when he came up with the answer to this problem: find the sum of the integers from 1 to 100. The teacher had given the kids this assignment to keep them quiet, as they had gotten a little rowdy. If they didn't finish it by the time the bell rang, they could work on it overnight and bring the answer the next day. Well, the story goes that in a matter of minutes, little five-year old Gauss blurted out the correct answer: 5,050. Is this anecdote or fact? It is fact, of course. I never doubted it. But the re-enactment demonstrates his thinking process, his intuition, his creativity and his genius. You see this kid line up the numbers 1, 2, 3, up to 100. Then he enters the numbers again in descending order in another line underneath: 100, 99, 98, and down to 2, 1. Then he adds the two lines together, pair by pair, and notices that they always add to 101, thus: 101=100+1=99+2=98+3, etc. He then multiplies this result by 100 because he is basically adding 101 by itself 100 times. The result is: 10,100. But this result should be twice the result he is looking for, since he used two lines of numbers. Therefore, divide by 2 to compensate for the doubling and he gets his final answer: 5,050. This is the sort of thing that they recreate for you here. I have also seen Gauss in his twenties when he was working on the fundamental theorem of algebra for his PhD dissertation. But come on in and talk to these great men yourself. Come in and meet them."

"I can't now. Can we do that another time? I just as soon watch from here and have you tell me about them."

"But why? What's the matter?"

Maria had difficulty expressing her complicated feelings.

"Really, tell me. I can't believe this. I would have thought you would be rushing to meet them like a groupie after an autograph."

"There was a time when I would have done that," Maria said. "At one time I would have been there licking their feet and the ground they walked on. For me, mathematicians were demigods. There was a time when mathematics itself was sheer poetry and art. I saw such beauty in it, in the alignment of its symbols on the page. A set of equations involving multiple integration looked like a forest of tall slender stalks flanking a country road. A system of partial differential equations appeared to me like a field of tulips and daffodils all aligned in rows. The ideas behind them were just as awesome. I had such great hopes; I had ambition; and I was committed. In fact, up to a couple of months ago I was still thinking of going for the priesthood in math, studying for the PhD. But then I lost it. I came to the realization that, at 26 years of age, I was too old for it. I've wasted too much time during the last three years in that jungle of a school where I teach, and I've forgotten so much. I find it harder and harder to keep up with the journals. I don't think like a mathematician anymore. I've lost the touch and the inspiration."

"Oh, nonsense! Don't say that" interrupted Marilú chiding her. "Being washed up at 26, shame on you, that's just ridiculous!"

"Math is like music," continued Maria, "you have to start early—when you are still a child—and you have to have that special gift from the gods, which I don't know that I ever had. Talent is not enough if you want to go far in math."

"I could not disagree with you more, Maria. You don't have to have perfect pitch in music to be a great musician, and you don't have to be a Euler or a Gauss to be a great mathematician. The only thing I would concede is that you do have to work at it to keep up with it. Even if you are a little rusty, it will all come back to you with a little practice. Ambition, inspiration and commitment will follow once you apply yourself. But, hey, all that is irrelevant, now. Do you know why?"

"No, I have no idea."

"You're forgetting a very important thing. You are not home anymore. Here you have all the time in the world. You could go for five PhDs. You are out of the rat race. There's no pressure to publish or perish here; there's none of that nasty competitiveness; there is no urgency to earn a living so you can keep body and soul together. On earth, people slog along to earn a living, often putting the wishes of their heart on the back burner, postponing them for that time during their golden years, when they are retired, when they are finally free to pursue them. This tops that. This is the real thing, and this is heaven forever. This is the retirement of all retirements. This beats it all."

Maria beamed up at that. "You are so right! I had forgotten where I was. This is very exciting. I can see the possibilities. You've just given me a new lease on math, and I'll take it. So, come on, let's go into the pantheon of the gods of mathematics. I'm dying to meet them."

With that the two of them walked into the room and Marilú announced: "Gentlemen, I would like to introduce a sister-at-heart, a fellow math teacher, someone who is like my other half. She just arrived. You'll be seeing a lot of her for at least the next decade or so. Here is Maria Diaz."

She got a warm round of applause; then Maria went around the room, shaking hands with each of them. She was in heaven. But not for long. The alarm clock went off a few minutes later and brought her back to earth. It was time to get up, time to face the real world and a new working day. And what a day it would be. Tonight, she would have her first date with John.

Z z Z   Z   Z z Z

53. First Date

Maria Luisa's heaven lingered through the morning with a sweet after taste that put Maria in a joyful mood. She did not feel bubbly, or particularly cheerful, but she felt a sense of peace and serene contentment. Everything was right with the world. It was as if she breathed the perfumed air of a faraway paradise, and for her the world smell of roses. From time to time, she would picture the vivid splendor of the planets of heaven, or she would recall one of her idol mathematicians and she felt as if she had really visited heaven. But as the day wore on and she thought about her date with John later that evening, she felt as if she was caught between two heavens. As the hours passed, her date with John became the dominant fascination and for once the universe was upside down because it was the real world that felt like heaven's promise.

By noon, not even that beautiful dream about heaven could have competed with the euphoria of her real life. The anticipation of her first date with John had an immediacy and intensity that was more compelling than a fantasy or a dream; it could trump even heaven for sheer bliss. And she had to get ready. There was so much to do. What should she wear this evening? How should she fix her hair? What would they say to each other when they first met? Surely, they wouldn't just shake hands. God forbid! And yet, they couldn't just kiss, either. It wouldn't be proper. And yet, before the night was over, there was no question they would kiss. The question was when, for how long, and how often. Ah, don't rush things. Be natural. Don't be too demure or too forward. Maria felt so lucky to be alive on this day, so happy, with so much to look forward to! The cup of love was about to be filled, and she couldn't wait to drink from it. She would not waste a drop. Today was the beginning of a wonderful chapter in her life.

She had chosen the Dadeland Mall as their meeting place. It was practically a straight shot with no complications for him, and it was not far from her apartment. The instructions she had given him were simple. "Take I-95 and stay on it till it dead ends," she had told him. But he had balked at hearing that. She had to repeat it to him.

"I thought I-95 went all the way to Key West." he protested, unable to accept the fact that a major highway that traverses the east coast of the U.S. all the way from the Canadian border for over a thousand miles, would simply peter out ignominiously and come to an end in the middle of Miami without fanfare. In any case, he was looking forward to seeing that point. "How does a great road come to an end? How does it just peter out? I must see that."

Maria had teased him over his sensibilities. It showed a side of him that she liked. "What a romantic you are. I like that in a man… to feel so much for the ending of a road. But I hate to disappoint you. As you will see, I-95 will come to an end, not with a bang but with a whimper. There is a little sign that simply says: I-95 ends.' And that's it. That's all you get. Before you know it, the big I-95 has run into US-1, which is another venerable road of long standing. It also traverses the East Coast, and this one does go all the way from tip to tip, clear to the end of Key West, and it has the distinction of bearing the number '1.' Think of that! Maybe that should inspire you. Of all the federal roads in the country, this is the one that has the unique distinction of being 'number one,' the one and only, the first of the first. And yet, for all that, do you know what people around here call it? They refer to "US-1" as: 'Useless-1.' Oh, well. Anyway, take a right to Kendall Drive and you'll soon come to the mall. I'll be waiting at the front entrance at 6 p.m."

This was one day when her working chores became welcome distractions. She needed distractions to take her mind away from the anticipation and help her keep her sanity. Several colleagues stopped by to wish her well. She accepted graciously—wondering how they knew—all the while thinking that it was about her date with John. She had forgotten about that other momentous change in her life. People were wishing her well for her having resigned from her job.

Maria didn't tarry around school on this day. As soon as she was free to go, she left for her apartment to get ready. She made a quick call to her mother to fill her in on the developments. She took a shower and dressed. It was a cool day for Miami. Spring gave its blessings to the day. She selected a skirt and blouse outfit of beige and white, simple and classic. She tried a different hairdo but decided against it. She preferred the natural look as she usually wore it. She wanted to look real, comfortable and casual. But it would not have mattered what she wore, because she would have looked stunning to him in anything. He wore his standard suit and tie, but by any other attire he would still have been her Prince Charming.

He was the first to spot the other. He caught sight of her as he drove in, before he ever parked. She was waiting by the entrance as she had told him, looking in another direction, not even aware of what car he was driving because she had forgotten to pin down that detail. He was, therefore, able to walk from behind her and surprise her. When he called out her name, he startled her and caused her to lose her balance, but because he was close enough to her, he was able to catch her and embrace her. The encounter could not have been better executed if they had planned it. They were thrust into each other's arms for a close and warm coupling, if only by accident.

"Sorry, I didn't mean to startle you," he said apologizing.

"Oh, I startle easily. Anyway, welcome to Miami."

"I thought this was Miami Beach." he said puzzled.

"No, Miami Beach is actually an island, over that way," she corrected, pointing in its general direction. "You have to cross a causeway to get to it. We will go there on our extended tour."

They continued to play on that motif of tour guide and tourist with which their relationship had begun. It had served them well so far and was still useful. Their relationship was still so new that it was still covered by a crust of formality, with layers of ice that had to be chipped away tactfully and civilly. The pretense of a tour service was a convenient means for them to communicate and break the ice. They played it to the hilt.

They walked around the mall aimlessly for a few minutes looking for they knew not what. Then Maria said: "There are restaurants here. We could find a place here if you would like. But I thought Coconut Grove is more special. It's not far from here, so why not let me take you there instead."

"You are my guide. I'm in your hands. I will go with you anywhere, to the ends of the earth if need be."

"Good! You'll be easy to please then."

They left his car at the mall and went in her car to Coconut Grove, an old classy area of Miami full of restaurants and shops. They walked around looking for a restaurant that would be suitable, quiet and private where they could talk and get to know each other. There was so much they needed to know about each other yet. Both were mature enough to recognize that they shouldn't rush things, that they had to be prudent and get to know each other first. The strong attraction of love at first sight had to be tempered with good manners and mutual respect. They knew that love, like a lazy river, sooner or later, would reach its rapids and rush wildly all over itself… but all in due time.

When they were finally seated in the restaurant, looking at each other, thinking of what to say next, Maria realized that she was in one of those private moments that she had so anxiously dreamed about, where she could get to know him better. Maria returned to the tourist-and-guide skit again. She pulled a note pad out of her purse and a pen, as if she were going to take official notes.

"I hope you don't mind, Sir, if I conduct a little business," she began. "Management requires that we gather certain data from our clients—routine sort of things, you know. Some of the items I can fill out for myself by just looking at you. For example, I am looking at the block for 'eyes,' and that's easy. I would say it is blue, azure as the sky. Then we have 'hair' and that is also easy. It is a very bountiful crop of straight blond. But that is about as far as I can go on my own. There are other things that I'm going to need help on. For example, age."

"Thirty-two," John volunteered.

"How long at current address?"

"A few months."

"Profession, I know, doctor… but what kind?"

"Surgeon. Thoracic surgeon."

"Hm, that explains why you were assigned to Pedro Santoro. Very interesting. Let me see, something else I see here, a little bit more complicated: marital status."

"Single," he answered.

"Is that just a recent condition, or has it always…?"

"I was married for about three years. I have now been divorced for almost two years."

Maria nodded her head several times. The skit was being most revealing, most effective. She continued pretending that she was filling out a form, looking for blank boxes and said in a low voice, whispering to herself: "Let's see, what else is there? Sex?" The minute she uttered the word, almost inadvertently, she blushed, regretting it, but it was too late to take it back.

"Hungry," he said, as if replying to her question. There was a brief, awkward silence. To relieve the embarrassing situation, he asked her: "Are you hungry?"

"A little."

He then took the reins of the inquiry, saying: "Of course, you know, what's good for the goose is also good for the gander. Does your management permit the customers to ask questions of its guides also?"

"Naturally! Certainly! We are most fair minded. By all means, proceed when ready. Would you like paper and pen?"

"No, thank you. That won't be necessary. I will also dispense with what is obvious. I have your hair down as a flowing, luscious cascade of straight black strands, and your eyes as mesmerizing black magnets that draw me helplessly. I could look at them for hours even though I have had them memorized for days. But let me see, what are some of the other less obvious things that I need help with …age?"

"Twenty-six," Maria replied tersely.

"Marital status?"

"Single for all my 26 years."

"Current attachments?"

"None."

"Sex?"

Maria looked at him for an instant, not knowing exactly what to make of his question, and then she responded with a single word: "Virgin."

Her answer took his breath away. He raised his eyebrows, puzzled, wordless. Maria noticed his expression and asked him: "Is there a problem?"

"No, not at all. It's just that I am incredulous, like finding something too good to be true. It is so rare, so unexpected these days."

"You are not displeased then, are you?"

"No, heavens no, not displeased, but maybe thrown a little off balance."

"I guess that's understandable. You are probably asking yourself why, wondering what's behind it. I, for one, am ambivalent about it, not necessarily proud of it. While I am not exactly ashamed about it, I don't want to flaunt it either. I think it may send false signals about me."

"Such as?"

"That I am prudish; that I consider it a treasure, something that I have guarded all these years and that I will keep intact till the night of my honeymoon. That was never my intent. I am more curious about life and more venturesome than that. It just so happens that no one has ever come along to make it worthwhile. I suppose you could say that I am very picky. I would concede that. Still, all in all, I wouldn't say I have any regrets about it, either."

"The more power to you, Maria. I think it is admirable. I respect you and I like you even more for it. But here is another question that comes to my mind on the heels of this. Are you Catholic? And are you very religious? Does that have something to do with your virginity?"

"Hah, you would think so, wouldn't you? I can see where you're coming from on that. But, no, my virginity has no connection to religion. It is, in fact, a paradox that confounds my irreligiousness. I was raised Catholic, but I am not a practicing one. I have a mother, however, who is Catholic enough for both of us. If you only knew how much she tries to get me to accompany her to church on Sundays. And the funny thing is that I would like to go for her sake, I really would; I would love to give her that satisfaction, but I cannot do it. Religion is not something we should engage in for the sake of pleasing others. I have not been to church in years. I am a hard-core agnostic. I will someday face a serious problem when I am close to getting married, on account of my mother, because she will insist that I marry in the church, but I will not. Another serious problem I will face in the future is when I have children. I will be inclined to see to their religious education in a laic sort of way, as a cultural and historical dimension of their upbringing. That is an awesome responsibility. Fortunately, this is not an urgent issue. I have time to resolve it. For the children's sake, but only for their sake, I may find it necessary to join the church for a while. Now, let me ask you the same question. Where do you stand on religion?"

"Oh, it is not that important in my life, either. I, too, have not been to church in years. It is not something that I think about very much. My parents were Lutheran, and they raised us in that church. They still go to church, but it is more out of habit, out of social decorum, than out of faith. But I am a little intrigued by your attitude about religion. I detect strong conviction in your words, and you seem adamant."

"Well, that goes with the territory. As you get to know me better, you are going to detect strong conviction on a lot of things. As it concerns religion, it is difficult to be brief. The night is not long enough to do justice to the subject. But it comes down simply to a lack of faith. I don't believe in 90 percent of the claims of the church, and, unlike millions of churchgoers, I cannot dismiss this disbelief, I cannot subsume it as an insignificant thing and go to church anyway.

I am not political enough or diplomatic enough for that. I don't care what people think. I feel very strongly that if you believe, then you should give your all to your religion. But if you don't believe it, you shouldn't pretend. For me, religious ceremonies, prayers and rituals are acts void of conviction, like going through hoops, and they bother me enormously. I have tried to go to church for appearances sake, to please others, only to be torn apart by a sense of hypocrisy that I find unbearable. That's all there's to it. There's nothing sinister, like being abused by priests when I was young, or things of that sort. In fact, I admire the abnegation and dedication of the catholic clergy, their vows of celibacy, their vows of poverty, and their work for the poor, for the misbegotten, for the sick and abandoned. This real commitment speaks of something truly admirable, which is true faith, and which I revere, even if I don't have it."

They began to feel much closer to each other. Layers and layers of wrappings fell off, exposing the real person, especially Maria. For John, Maria was a brave new world. He felt like the explorer who thought he had discovered a new island, but the island turned out to be a vast new continent. Maria was not a simple creature, but she was frank and forthcoming, easy to get to know. No matter how long it took to know her well, he was up to the task. He knew she could be a lifetime study, and he was willing to embark on that quest. In his heart he knew, even that night, that she would become his wife someday.

The rest of their dinner was not all serious talk. There was bantering and joking also. He filled in the major traces of his life for her, telling her about his siblings. He had an older brother, William, a lawyer; and he had a younger sister, Catherine, a chemist, married to a biochemist. His father was a business executive; and his mother had been an English teacher. His parents, now both retired, lived in Savannah, Georgia. He grew up in the Midwest, around Chicago. As to his short marriage, it had been a mistake from the start. Alice, his ex-wife, was a beautiful woman, but unsure of what she really wanted in life. Whatever it was, it was not a family, or marriage, at least not to a doctor. She was a dilettante, a free spirit with ambitions to becoming a star in the theater. Last he heard she was going to drama school in New York City. She was not ready to settle down.

Along about 8:30, John and Maria grew tired of sitting and needed to walk and to be outdoors. They left the restaurant and walked the streets of Coconut Grove. He kept looking for a secluded nook where they could whisper, caress and maybe even kiss. They walked across a street on the excuse of examining a Banyan tree more closely. These trees are native to India and Miami has a lot of them. They are huge and exotic. John's real purpose was to see if there was a nook behind it where they could hide. But there wasn't. Still, he kissed her anyway. They stood there partially covered by the Banyan tree, kissing passionately and with abandonment. He could not hide his feelings any longer. He declared his love for her. He told her how he had gone around in a daze, longing to see her again, from the first time he saw her. He told her he had counted the hours and minutes waiting for this encounter. He told her he would continue counting the minutes till their next encounter, because he was madly in love with her. He was totally bewitched by her. Maria confessed the same, that she had never felt so drawn to anyone before. Whatever her feelings were, whether crush, infatuation or love, it was a wondrous thing that, for all its blessedness, also hurt a little for its intensity, for its constant unrelenting need to be near him. They would have stayed longer under that tree, but Maria was apprehensive. She was not at ease there. She was also a little cold and had borrowed his coat. She tried to think of other places, but all the places she considered safe would probably be crowded, while all the places she considered cozy and quiet would most likely be unsafe. "It is up to you," he would tell her. "You are my guide. I'm in your hands."

"Okay, let's go back to get your car, and then you follow me. I know another place not far from here that is warm, private and safe."

He did not object or make further inquiries. He went along, not knowing, or caring where she would take him. He became curious only when they parked their cars and noticed that it was the parking lot of a condominium. When he got out of his car, she told him where they were.

"This is my apartment. But don't get any ideas. It is an invitation for coffee, for privacy, for seeing how I live, for sharing my taste for things, my music, my décor, and my pictures. No men except my father and my brother have ever been invited. Do you think you can handle it?"

He was wordless for a minute, pacing around her, trying to collect his thoughts. Then he grabbed her by the shoulders with both of his hands, as if preparing to lecture her.

"Maria, I am honored that you invite me, and I thank you. I can assure you that I am a gentleman and that I would do nothing to jeopardize your respect for me. But I do have problems accepting any preconditions, not only because I am a man, and men will be men, but because I am—whether you know it or not—your future husband. I know this in my bones. If I haven't asked you to marry me tonight, it is only out of respect for your intelligence. I don't want to be dismissed as a fool who takes marriage frivolously and proposes on the first date. It seems so ridiculous, so uncivil. But that's what my heart is clamoring for. So, instead of proposing, I will tell you what I know will be a fact in a matter of months. Mark my word; you will be mine and you will be my wife. We will be married to each other in a matter of months. Oh, yes, I will propose to you formally; you can count on it. I will ask you in the next few weeks for sure. We will do the engagement ring, we will follow protocol, and I will do whatever you ask me to do. Have it your way, but you will be mine. Play hard to get. Refuse me even. But I will persist. You are special to me. I will not let you get away. I love you. So, I make no promises concerning what may happen upstairs tonight. Our destinies have entwined already and lead to the inevitability of our eventual marriage. If you tell me to leave now, I will do so without hard feelings, and I will call you again tonight, and again tomorrow. I am prepared to wait till our honeymoon, if you ask me. I hope you won't, but if you do, I will insist on a condition of my own. I will then insist that we schedule the wedding as soon as possible. Now, can you handle it if I come upstairs, or would you like us to go somewhere else, or would you like for me to leave now?"

Maria said nothing. She extricated herself from his grip, and then she took his hand and led him towards her apartment, murmuring *Che sera, sera* to herself.

Once inside the apartment, she gave him a full tour, skipping nothing, assuring him: *Mi casa es tu casa*. She showed him her things, her books, her music, even her closet. He, for his part, was glad to see her place, the more the better. "I want to place you in my mind in your own setting so that I can picture you when I call you, where you are and how you are."

"Let's open our lives to each other," she said. "Let there be no secrets between us. Before leaving the subject of marriage for the rest of the night, I do want to make one comment. I am glad you've brought up the subject and I feel flattered and honored that you want to marry me. I do believe you are sincere, and I trust you. Since you haven't really proposed, I can neither accept nor refuse, but if you had proposed, I would have given you a big tentative 'yes.' Now let's leave that subject for another day. Tonight is too soon. These things must follow their course and we need to know each other more."

"I agree completely," John remarked. Then he looked at his watch. It was almost ten. He had told her that he needed to leave by 10 p.m., by 10:30 at the latest. He had surgery in the morning, and she had school—it was Friday. He had a thoughtful expression on his face, as if he were considering options. Maria watched him and started to giggle. He tried to snuff out her giggles by holding her tightly, but she started to laugh harder.

"What's so funny? What's the matter?"

Maria kissed him and caressed his face gently, saying: "Please don't think it's about you, or anything you said. Please forgive me." Then she started to laugh again. He was patient but was becoming a little irritated.

"Okay, okay. So, it's not about me. Then tell me what it is."

"It's a joke I remembered," Maria explained. "When you said you had very little time and you looked at your watch, I wanted to say… (And she laughs again) … I wanted to say: well, I am showing you my apartment as fast as I can."

"I don't get it" he said. "What's funny about that?"

"The joke is about a traveling salesman who comes to Miami and picks up a woman in a bar. Soon they are dancing, and while they are dancing, he drops a hint, whispering in her ear: honey, I only have one night in town. To which she responds: 'well, I am dancing as fast as I can.'"

John laughed a little. "That's cute," he said. "But you must have a funny bone to laugh about it as much as you did. Well, it's just as well. On that sobering note, I think I'd better go. Goodbye, Giggles. I will call you later."

Now it was Maria who was concerned. "Well, you don't have to rush out so suddenly. I haven't even fixed you a drink. I am sorry, John. I think I blew it with my giggling. How silly of me. It's like I threw cold water on your evening. I really am sorry."

"Don't feel bad. It has nothing to do with your laughing. It is really me, and it is something you should know. It's good that this has come out at this point. I need to warn you that being married to a doctor entails some hardships. You will be married to me and to my profession. At times my responsibilities will be in bed between us. Being married to a doctor is anything but romantic. I've often wondered if medicine didn't do in my previous marriage. I am sure it didn't help. I am very committed, Maria. I have to be."

"I understand; I can imagine it must be very trying at times. It will be hard for me, yes, but I am up to it. I can see how your obligations can exact a very heavy price on your life, but I will stand by you. Don't worry about me. I will help you bear that cross."

"Glad to hear it. You can consider this to be the first of many such intrusions on our happiness. There will be many more. But I think that true love can withstand the interruptions and intrusions."

"I agree and I'm willing to give it a go, John. You are worth it. You deserve all my love and support. I am glad we cleared this up because I was beginning to feel bad about my giggling, as if it is my fault that I've been a virgin all this time. Do you know that I once had a nightmare about my virginity? I dreamed that I wanted to get rid of it and I went out on the street wearing nothing but a robe, totally naked underneath. I was going to flash the first man that came along and tell him that he had just won my virginity lottery. 'Hello, Sir, congratulations!' I was going to tell him. 'You've just won my big jackpot.' Then I stood there alone in the street unable to trap even a fly, feeling totally rejected. A few minutes ago, I was beginning to feel that way again."

"Have no fear. I also have a confession to make. A few minutes ago when I looked at my watch, I was contemplating staying here all night and ravishing you two or three times. Then I would drive to the hospital directly from here. But I wouldn't have slept a wink, and I owe it to my patient to be in better shape tomorrow. I decided it was a sensible thing to do. So, I'd better go now. Can I call you later after I get home?"

"Absolutely! I won't be able to go to sleep if you don't call."

They kissed and embraced. It was hard to say goodbye. They dragged and shuffled their bodies to the front door, unable to let go. Then he stood apart and told her: "I have a couple of special requests before I go. First, I want to address your virginity and congratulate it on getting a reprieve for another night. But I also want to put it on notice that its days are counted. Your whole body should be on notice that I am lusting for you. I am leaving your house now, so, have no fear. Your virginity is safe. But and this is my final request, let me at least see you and touch you before I go. I am dying to see more of you."

He proceeded to unbutton her blouse and expose her breasts. Maria stood unresisting, helping to undress actually. He caressed her breasts and kissed and sucked her nipples. Then he kissed her lips, muttering 'I love you' several times. Finally, he raised her skirt, reassuring her all along not to worry.

"I'm leaving. Don't worry… I promise you... I just want to see what I must live for."

He then lowered her panties, and he knelt before her, coming face to face with her dark bare bush, which he rubbed against his face as he kissed and squeezed her thighs. Her hips, her buttocks and every fleshy curve his hands could hold had the touch of love incarnate. Then he stood up. When he was face to face with her, he continued to kiss her lips, but all the while pressing her Venus mound and probing its contour and crevice.

"Ah, Maria, you are irresistible. I love you passionately. I can't wait till the next time. But now I must go. Thank you, thank you for everything. I love you so much. Goodbye my love." And true to his word, he rushed out the door.

Z   z   z   z   z   z   Z

54. First Date Commentary

That passionate farewell left Maria befuddled and bewildered, turning in a whirlwind of unfulfilled passion, battered by conflicting emotions. Her giggling continued to mortify her. She wished John had finished what he started and not left her in the unresolved state she was in, full of questions, full of doubts, full of unrequited desire. Oh, John, what you do to me, and what you don't do to me, just drives me crazy!

So many major barriers down! No vestiges of forbidden zones between us! And yet so far away from consummation! You left me standing denuded, like a plucked duck on a platter. Did I do something wrong? Was it my fault? Who won? Who lost? I only know that it was wonderful and that I loved it. I liked your timing, your gradual pace for devouring me in stages with such masterful control. I could recall that scene repeatedly, when you raised my skirt. I trembled with the strangest sense of trepidation. Where is this going? Now I can't get enough of that scene, and I replay it like a movie clip that loops over and over on itself. Then you surprised me. I am astounded by your strength and self-control. How could you reach the gates of heaven and then walk away? Such incredible fortitude! You have shown me a side of manhood that I had never imagined; it challenges all my previous notions, confusing me. Such willpower, such self-control and such commitment are incredible. John Shiller, you are no ordinary man and you're most definitely my kind of man for being so inscrutable, so mysterious and so mischievous. I love you more and more, your naughtiness, your curiosity, your raw carnal touch, your roaming probing fingers, and the desperate search of your thirsty lips when they explore my most sacred parts. Ah, you were magnificent.

We are entering a brave new world, you and I, a world which is exciting and scary at the same time. If this foray into intimacy—which wouldn't even qualify as foreplay for being so brief and unconsummated—if this prelude to sex, this fooling around, this wild voracious imbibing of my body could be as powerful as it has been, then I can't imagine what the real thing, the whole thing, orgasm and all, would be like. It must be so incredibly overwhelming as to be virtually lethal. It boggles my mind.

It was around midnight when John called Maria to say goodnight. It was way past his usual bedtime, but he was already in bed, ready to turn his lights out. It had been a wonderful day. He told her he loved her, and he was sweet and loving, but he kept it short. They smacked kisses over the phone and hung up.

Maria was circumspect and respectful of his wishes, and she put her own needs and desires aside, deferring to his need to get a good night sleep. Left to her own devices, she would have talked on the phone for hours. There was so much she wanted to say to him, so much she wanted to ask him. She did manage to tell him that she admired his fortitude and his willpower, but she warned him that he had freed a wild and horny cat in her, a tigress that would be waiting for him.

"You are talking like a fiery Latin woman, and I love it," he said. "Sex can be so grand. It is the nearest thing to a human atomic explosion, especially when there is love. Watch for the mushroom cloud and hold that thought. I can't wait till the day after tomorrow."

"Nor I."

Maria was left in a state of anxiety that normally would have kept her awake for hours. But she had learned much about controlling her mind by now, and she would be able to go to sleep. You just don't toy around with thoughts that can keep you awake. Tonight, she relaxed by reading magazines which kept John, and sex out of her mind. When she did begin to dream around 2 a.m., the girls at dream central were anxiously waiting for her. They had turned dream central into one of the bars of Coconut Grove and had a table all to themselves.

"There she comes! Look at her bringing in the sunshine!" exclaimed Sasha as she waved for Maria to join then. "We are going to start calling you 'Libby II' because you are looking more like her every day."

"*Hola corazones*," (hello dear hearts) said Maria.

A waitress almost stumbled unto Maria but managed to maneuver out of a collision just in time, saying: "Watch it, Tigress!"

Maria was miffed by that. My, she's sassy and insolent! Where does she get off calling me that? I ought to report her for being too familiar.

"Oh, come off it," said Libby. "There are no strangers here where you are concerned. The whole world knows by now what a tigress you've become. But you're still a virgin tigress. Don't forget that. And you've got a lot to learn still."

"It's been quite a night. Hasn't it?" Maria acknowledged.

"We have a lot to talk about. You've given us a banquet to feast on."

"Wow! I'll say. Above all, I am astounded by his self-control. He must be an exceptional man," said Maria Luisa.

"I know! Wasn't that something?" Maria agreed. "Such self-control is scary. John must be one of those demigods with complete control of mind over matter, one of those people whom I envy because they are able to be fast asleep within five minutes of putting out the light."

"I guess the question is: Would you call the episode a success or a failure?" asked Maria Luisa.

"Well, she kept her virginity, for what that's worth. A prude would score that as a success," said Sasha.

"I think it was an utter failure," said Libby.

"Well, you would… that's nothing new," added Sasha.

"What do you think, Maria?" asked Maria Luisa.

"The truth is that I didn't want to keep my virginity towards the end. So, I managed to keep what I wanted to lose. I suppose you could call that a failure."

"Yes, but John didn't know that you wanted to give it away," said Sasha. "So, it doesn't count as a failure."

"How do you think John feels about it?" Maria Luisa asked.

"Ah, that's the question that bothers me," replied Maria. "I really don't know. Is he disappointed? I hope not."

"He shouldn't be! I don't think he's keeping score like we are. I think he loves you, and that's what matters. There'll be other times," said Maria Luisa.

"Bravo! …Something positive for a change. I like that."

"Oh yes, there will be other times," said Libby with a sardonic tone. "Oh yes, he will come back for more. But don't kid yourselves, the night was still a failure, and unless she learns from it, she could blow it again. Maria lost a golden opportunity to act out her lottery dream, the one where she serves herself as the big virgin jackpot. She had a live man on his knees, drooling at the mouth, yet she lost him. The woman who gets that far and doesn't lose her cherries, and doesn't get her man, is a damned fool."

"That hurts, Libby! Don't be unkind," protested Maria Luisa.

"Well, she's right," conceded Maria. "I feel as if I have acted out the curse of my virgin nightmare in real life now. I stand naked and rejected."

"Cheer up! The war has only just begun. That was just a skirmish. There'll be more battles," said Sasha.

"I also feel like I am in a crucible, or under a microscope here… as if I were being dissected alive."

"Calm down," said Libby. "You should be used to this. This is just your usual nightly postmortem of your day's failures… nothing new."

"Well, I for one," began Maria Luisa, "do not feel that you are to blame for John's untimely departure, although I do believe something went wrong during the evening."

"Maybe John has erectile dysfunction," noted Sasha. "Maybe he didn't have an erection after all. Do you know for a fact that he did?"

Maria gave Sasha a nasty reproaching look. "Oh yes, he had one. I could feel a hard lump poking me. That was not an issue. But I also want to make another thing clear right here and now. Get this straight all of you. I did not go after him. It is not as if I tried to seduce him and failed. You seem to have forgotten that it was he who initiated the monkey business, not I. Moreover, he did it knowing that he wouldn't finish it. In fact, that is why he succeeded in undressing me. He kept assuring me that he was leaving. Not to worry. Nothing is going to happen. I'm on my way out. That was a good line he used. I don't think I would have acquiesced without these assurances. He was a clever rascal. He dropped my defenses with that line."

"Yeah, and your panties too," commented Sasha.

"Quiet you…you've been like a little terrier yipping at my feet all night tonight."

"Actually, Maria, you still have a lot to learn about men and seduction," said Libby. "I demoted you by a couple of grade levels tonight because of that laughing and giggling episode. That sort of nonsense has got to go. I was so mortified when you started that. Laughing like that is an anti-aphrodisiac, a veritable counter agent to Viagra, a turn off that can have disastrous consequences. Next time, grit your teeth and suppress those giggles!"

"Do you think that had something to do with John's leaving?" asked Sasha.

"No! I wouldn't go that far, although it probably didn't help. I think the main reason he left was because of his commitment to his job and his patients. He is a very responsible and sensitive man, but I also think he is something of a perfectionist. He wants to have things just right, and it wasn't in the cards for him tonight. He didn't want to rush through it; he was willing to wait for perfection. His timing is good. Think about it. He is well set up for the next time. He has broken off all the big chunks of ice and melted the rest of what was left. He's got you good and primed. Next time he can be in like Flynn in no time at all. What I would like to know is why you thought of that silly joke at such a time."

"I suppose it was because John looked at his watch, sizing up how much time he had left. I could hear the little wheels and cogs in his brain spinning and calculating. I couldn't help but connect with that joke. That's what triggered it. I still think it is funny… (Imitating) *I am dancing as fast as I can.*"

"Well, try to stay in control. Let the thoughts come as they will, but you try to stay on top of the situation. Don't let your laughter rain out your love making."

"Oh, it's no big deal, Libby. He got over it. And on that note, good Ladies, if you'll excuse me, I am going to retire to my cabin. I'll stop by Dr. Broca's office on my way down for a shot before another episode of the heavenly saga. By the way, Marilucha, through all this I had neglected to tell you how much I enjoyed your dream about heaven. I loved the orrery you conjured up with those colorful planets dancing in space, violating every principle of gravity that Sir Isaac Newton ever laid out. Those planets were doing orbits designed by a choreographer rather than an astronomer. And where did you get that nut on the intercom system? He was a trip. But, of course, the highlight was meeting Newton, Euler and Gauss. That was most inspiring. By the way, who is next in the series?"

"I am," said Libby, flashing fire out of her eyes.

"I have only one request. See if you can fit John in it. It wouldn't be heaven without him, you know."

"Have no fear. He is in like Flynn."

Maria left. On her way out she thought of something else and started to turn back, when she bumped onto the same waitress again. They both looked at each other and laughed this time. Maria asked: "Are we the klutzy twins or what?" The waitress responded, chuckling: "Shall we dance?"

When she returned to the table where the girls were, Maria gave them another charge. "I am still looking for Professor Quixote. Haven't seen him in ages! If you see him, please tell him that I think he is hiding from me and that this is beginning to worry me. It is not urgent, although it is about life and death, about the waste of memory in our lives. He'll know what it is about."

"It sounds deep to me," said Sasha. "Maybe that's why he is avoiding you. Give him a break."

Maria stuck her tongue out at her; she pivoted and went out.

Z   Z   Z   z   Z   Z   Z

55. LIBBY'S HEAVENLY FIESTA

Later that same night Maria was treated to Libby's dream version of heaven. It began at the hospital in West Palm Beach, and it reprised the memory of that afternoon when Maria took Elena to the hospital. Maria was alone in the lounge waiting for Elena to come down. She was impatiently reading one magazine after another, flipping pages without absorbing anything. She was getting restless when, suddenly, she saw Doctor Shiller approaching, but this time without Elena. In her mindset he was still a stranger. They hadn't met yet.

"Hello, I am Dr. Shiller. You are Miss Diaz, aren't you?"

"Yes, I am. Where is Elena? Is something wrong?"

"No. She is fine. In fact, she is so well that that's the reason she could not come. She is not allowed here. She belongs on earth with the hale and the living… She is not ready to come here yet."

"Oh, I am sorry to hear that, although I suppose I should say I'm glad for her sake. It's odd—isn't it? —deciding whether she is lucky for not being here. I do think she is still young and deserves more years down there. But thank you for coming to let me know. Nice to meet you, doctor. I've heard so much about you from Elena and Pedro. How is Pedro by the way?"

"He is not well. He is in bad shape, fighting a severe infection with no antibiotics to help him. All the ones we've given him are ineffective. He is fighting alone with nothing but his own inner resources. It will be a miracle if he pulls through. I would not be surprised if he showed up here anytime."

"I am so sorry to hear that. Both are so young."

"They think very highly of you, you know. They praised you to the skies… Just from hearing their praises, I must have said something like, I was dying to meet you…They must have taken my wish seriously, because next thing I knew, here I was."

Maria laughs. "Oh, you do exaggerate, doctor. But it is a strange coincidence. I also came here because of them to meet you.

It's fate, I suppose."

"We were destined to meet in heaven, it seems."

"So, it seems. But is this really heaven?"

"Yes, I think so. What else could it be? If you are here, then—as far as I am concerned—this must be heaven."

"There you go again, exaggerating…"

"Since you've been here longer, Miss Diaz, perhaps I could prevail on you to be my guide. I know nothing about this place. I know no one. Could you show me around?"

"I'll be glad to, but I must warn you, I am also new. I think I've been here a couple of times before, but it is very vague in my mind. I don't know when it was, or for how long. One time I think they were having a mathematical convention here. I am not very familiar with this place either. I have no friends or family here. What I do remember is that this place is stunningly beautiful in parts, but behind its cheery appearance, there is also eternal coldness. I have felt drafts of loneliness here that were so hurtful they could frost bite you. Thank God you are here. Maybe we can stick together. You are my only connection to anything real."

Dr. Shiller took her hand and pressed it, saying: "Count on me. You are also all I have. By all means, let's stay together. You be my guide, and I will be your protector."

"Thank you, doctor. I feel better already. Shall we go and explore then?"

"By all means, but before that, could you please call me John? Let's drop the formalities."

"I agree. That's a good first step. Please call me Maria."

They walked through a long corridor, casing out the place, looking for someone they could talk to. He suggested stopping for a drink somewhere and talking to the bar tender, because they usually had good leads. Besides, he could also use a drink.

Suddenly, in front of them they saw something drop from the ceiling. It was large like a human-size butterfly that wafted gently to the floor. It was, in fact, a woman, a Eurasian beauty, who unfurled her large wing-like cape as she levitated herself downward. She then hung her cape across the corridor as a provisional wall blocking further passage down that corridor.

The lady pointed to her name tag that read: Li, as she introduced herself. "I am sorry for coming down like that and startling you. I was running a little late, but I caught you just in time. You were headed the wrong way, going into a restricted area full of engines, pipes and wires. Anyway, allow me to introduce myself. I've been sent to welcome you and to guide you. My name is Li B. Dhoh."

Maria was the first to speak. "We are delighted to see you, Li. We had been trying to find somebody, an employee, a representative, an official, anybody who could tell us something about this place. We are so lost. We don't know where we are. We don't know why we are here or where we are going. There is so much we would like to ask you. Believe me, you were just heaven sent."

"You poor dear souls, I know what you are going through. I'll explain everything to you if you promise to relax. Don't be in a rush. You have time forever here. Everything will be all right. Now hold on while I take us all to a place where we can talk."

Li placed herself between them and put her arms around their waists and said: "Okay, hold on! Here we go!" Then they moved swiftly through the corridor as if riding on air. They came to a central atrium. There they floated upwards for a couple of levels. From all appearances, they were on a huge cruise ship. They continued sliding through another corridor, until they came to a bar with large windows all around. Li placed them on a table close to the window. The view was spectacular, with huge colorful planets rotating all around, which Maria recognized. "I've been here before," she announced.

"Well, here we are," said Li. "Let's get you a drink and make ourselves comfortable, shall we? What is your pleasure?"

"I don't know… er, Water?" said Maria nonchalantly.

Li kicked the leg of Maria's chair jokingly, saying: "Oh,

come on. Water! No, no. That is not allowed here! We do not serve just water, unless you want it as a chaser. It is sacrilege to have only water! You will have to have something with a little zip, mild perhaps, something fruity maybe. I know just the thing. Let me welcome you with a specialty of the house, with our compliments." She then signaled the bar tender with two fingers.

To the amazement of John and Maria, a glass cylinder rose out of the ground next to Li, bearing their drinks. "Wow!" said Maria and John in unison when they saw their drinks. Then Li handed them their glasses, and with the flair of a Flamenco dancer clicking her heels, she made the cylinder disappear beneath the floor again. Li excused herself and said she would return shortly to answer their questions.

They sipped their drinks and chatted for a few minutes. The effect of the drink was immediate. It replayed their memory of the last few days, from the day they met in fast mode, up to the time when they were at the restaurant in Coconut Grove. The memory trip immersed them in the same feelings of love they had sensed before. Both felt again that insatiable longing for each other. Maria could recall driving on I-95 with Elena by her side. She could remember saying: "I have a humongous, wonderful crush on Dr. Shiller and I think that he has a crush on me too." They both remembered their conversation on the phone later that first night, and they remembered meeting at the Dadeland Mall, then going to the restaurant in Coconut Grove. But that's as far as it got. They did not go across the street seeking refuge behind a Banyan tree where they kissed for the first time. Their fast recollection delivered them to the edge of the oasis of love with their thirst for kissing and caressing still intact, still not sated.

When Li returned, Maria asked her: "What was in that drink? It has raised me to a higher level of heaven; we're riding high here."

"This has got to be at least the fifth level of heaven for me, maybe even scraping Seventh Heaven," added John.

"I am so glad to hear it, because when you came here, you

had just met, and you were still in introductory mode. There was too much formality to go through, too much ice breaking to be done. Rather than let nature take its course, which here could mean years, it was better to rebuild on something beautiful that you already had. So, we just fast forwarded your memory to bring you up to a more recent time in the very recent past. It's just your own true feelings. We haven't altered anything or added anything. Thanks to that drink, you are no longer strangers," said Li.

"We noticed. We've come from strangers shaking hands, to two people in love. Look at us now. We are like two trees, seemingly apart, standing side by side, but with their hidden roots intertwined and playing footsy."

"Well good. Are you ready for me to answer your questions about heaven now?"

"Oh, no! I totally forgot about that. Who cares about that? It doesn't matter to me anymore. How about you, John?"

"I could stay like this forever, in blissful ignorance..." said John dreamily, leaning against Maria.

"Do you know how I feel?" Maria asked. "There is an Italian song that expresses exactly the way I feel, but you probably never heard of it."

"What's its name? Li asked.

"I am not sure about its title."

"Can you sing a line or two for me then?"

"Okay, you asked for it." Maria cleared her throat, preparing to sing. "Here goes." She then sang it, looking at John as if specially addressing the lyrics to him.

Che m'importa del mondo, quando tu sei vicino a me
Io non chiedo piu niente al cielo se mi lascia te.

John applauded vigorously, saying: "That was wonderful, Maria. You shouldn't have stopped. You have a beautiful voice. I loved it. Now tell me what it means."

Maria translated: "What do I care about the world when you're near me. I ask nothing else from heaven if it lets me keep you."

"That expresses my feelings exactly, too. How about it, Li? Do you know the song? And can you get it, since Maria won't sing any more of it? I would really like to hear the whole thing."

"Oh sure, I know that song. It is by Rita Pavone, and I can get it for you. Nothing is impossible here. I will play it for you now." Then Li pulled out her cellular and punched some numbers, as she made a signal to the bartender. The song then began to fill the air, as if Rita Pavone herself were there with full orchestra and chorus. All of them sat quietly listening to the song. John and Maria held each other's hands in a tight squeeze. When the song finished playing, they asked Li to replay it.

After the song played for a second time, Li asked them: "Are you ready with your questions about this place now?" But John and Maria were still absorbed in the lyrics of the song.

"Well, I'll tell you anyway. I'll answer what everybody usually asks, and I'll keep it short... Am I dead? That's the first thing they want to know. And the answer is: not necessarily. You could have had an accident on earth. Things could have happened so fast that you are not even aware of it and have no recall of it. Your bodies could be in shambles, hanging on to dear life by a thread, but you don't know it. People down on earth could be hovering around your bodies, thinking that you are in a coma, half dead to the world. Meanwhile your spirits are here, in limbo, waiting for the powers that be to decide about your fate, whether you will live or die, and if you died, whether you will arrive at the pearly gates, or at the other place. But if you are not to die, you will wake up on earth somewhere—amid the rubble of an accident, or in a hospital bed, or in your bed at home. In that case, this could be nothing more than a dream, and you won't remember all of it. So, Carpe diem! Live it up. Will that do it for now? Anyway, if you do have more questions, feel free to ask them."

John had a question. "Why is this bar so empty? Where are the rest of the people? Are we the only ones?"

"Do you want people?" Li asked them, "then, here. Look

around you!" All suddenly the bar became covered with tables, full of diners, like a crowded restaurant. Maria and John looked around the room in amazement.

"Just so you know," Li began again, "I could have a party to your heart's content. I could bring in here anyone you liked, anyone you wanted me to have at your party, living or dead, stranger or not, personalities of the past, or of the present, relatives, and friends—whatever."

"Amazing! Incredible!" John exclaimed repeatedly. "I am awed by all this. Is it providential magic, or is it advanced science fiction technology? How do you do it?"

"It's a little of both. Would you like me to share some of my secrets? Look over in the mezzanine above the bar. You'll see some people there manning the controls. When you told me that you wanted to see people, I turned on the phone so they could hear your request. The floor of this deck is like a moveable stage. It happens that the deck below us is a restaurant. To materialize the restaurant on this deck, I just give a signal to rotate the stages. One of my colleagues there, Imogene Natien, I don't know if you can see her from here, is a super whiz at fashioning things like these and running the controls that make them happen. Captain Kirk beaming up Scotty has nothing on us! Believe me!"

They looked intently behind the bar. It was dark. Just then someone turned on the lights in the control center so the crew could be seen. Imogene was small. Her head seemed big in proportion to her neck and her petite build. She had a headset on, and she wore large dark rimmed glasses. She waved and smiled when the light came on. Next to her was a Hindu fellow whom Li introduced as Ram. He was behind a camcorder recording the proceedings. He, too, waved at them, continuing to peer at the back of the camera all the while.

"Well, now. You have nothing else to do but enjoy yourselves before dawn. You have the power of all our magic at your disposal. Your wish is my command. I can refill your glasses.

I can bring you food. I can play music for you. Request whatever you like. I can have live musicians playing for you, your favorite tenor, your favorite group. Just name it. Or, if you prefer privacy and intimacy, I can clear everybody out and make myself scarce."

"Oh, Li, you are absolutely wonderful," said Maria. "I am so glad we ran into you. You have been extremely helpful. You have clarified so much for us already; you have made us feel comfortable. More than that, you have turned this place into a palace of fun. Please don't go away. Could you stay a little longer and visit with us?"

Li looked at the control center and gave a signal. "Sure. I'll be delighted to join you for a little while. If you still have more questions, fire away." Li then pulled up a chair and sat with them. At the same time, she looked at a spot on the floor and with her right hand signaled it to come up. Up, up, up! The glass cylinder rose bearing a drink, and she reached for a glass of sangria for herself.

"Tell us about yourself," said Maria. "Who are you? What do you do?"

"Okay, I will tell you. But I hope you don't mind if I use music to express myself." She stood up and made a signal to the control room. A young woman came to the middle of the restaurant where there was a small stage. The lights dimmed and a spotlight shone on the person on the stage.

"Ladies and Gentlemen, as part of your entertainment tonight we are pleased to have Miss Li B. Dhoh, who will sing Mimi's aria from Puccini's *La Boheme.* Li changed the lyrics to suit her story.

> *Si, mi chiamano Li B. ma il mio nome e Maria.*
> *La mia storia e breve. A tela o seta ricamo in casa e fiori...*
> *Son tranquilla e lieta ed e mio svago far gigli e rose.*

There was a small screen in front of each place at the table which translated the lyrics Li was singing. Maria pointed it out to John, so he followed the meaning of the aria in English. It read thus: Yes, they call me Li B, but my real name is Maria. My story is brief. I knit and embroider flowers; I am quiet and easy, and I love roses.

When the aria finished, Li joined Maria and John, who were incredulous and excited. "That was magnificent, Li. You are a professional diva. Who did you sing for back on earth? La Scala? Or the Met?" asked Maria.

"Bravo! Bravo, Li!" said John. "We are honored to have you at our table."

Li thanked them, but she also kept shaking her head and smiling, indicating that there was a trick to it, that things were not what they seemed.

"Don't tell us you lip synched it," said Maria. "You couldn't have!"

"Nope! I didn't lip synch it. I sang it, fair and square. That was my voice you heard. You probably think I am a showoff then— that I was on an ego trip or something. But that's not true either. The reason I sang that was to make a point. I am trying to tell you how things work here. On earth, talent and genius are sparingly given. Often those that have them waste them.. They don't work at developing themselves and perfecting their talents. Well, here you can be all that you can be. You are here for an eternity, and you have time to work at perfecting yourself and fulfilling your ambitions. There is no reason not to. You don't have to toil just to keep body and soul together. You are basically retired. You work only in the endeavors of your own choosing, and you can reach perfection in anything you truly value and make up your mind to conquer. Also, fame is not what it was on earth. And speaking of fame, notice some of the people around you."

John and Maria were incredulous, stunned. "You know," said John, "I was going to ask you about them. I couldn't believe what I was seeing. I thought I was just imagining. Is that Marilyn Monroe over there sitting next to Andy Warhol and Errol Flynn?"

"Absolutely. They are the real thing. And did you see Elvis and Albert Einstein? You may not be able to recognize some people at first, because you are used to seeing them old, but they may be young here because they can choose to be any age they want. I think Einstein is in his 30s here."

Maria and John looked around, trying to recognize more celebrities, nodding to each other, pointing at people as discreetly as they could. Oh, did you see so and so? No, where? Oh, and did you see Sir Winston Churchill with his cigar over there?

Li was amused to see them rubber necking like tourists in the Big Apple. She also had something else in mind. "John, did you play a musical instrument back home? Or did you ever study music as a kid?"

"Well, yes, I dabbled at the piano a little. I took piano lessons in high school. But, gosh, I haven't touched a piano in years."

"Would you like to know how good you can sound here? Would you like to play in front of this audience?"

"Heavens, no! Are you crazy? That's the farthest thing from my mind. Why would you even ask such a thing?"

"Because this is a party, and at a party you have fun. This is a heavenly fiesta, and we have only just begun. Everyone will have to do something. I just did my thing. Now, I should tell you that you get beginner's luck on your first three performances—we call it providential dispensation. After that you must work at developing your skills just as you do on earth. If you put your heart into what you do, and if you concentrate, heaven will take care of the rest. Now, if you would prefer to do something else like juggling, or acrobatics, or singing, or dancing in lieu of the piano; that is perfectly all right also. So, don't be afraid and don't be shy. Be a sport. Give it a try. What have you got to lose? I give you a few minutes for you to concentrate on the piece before we announce it. Were there some pieces you struggled with when you were a student? Is there anything in particular you would like to play?"

"No, frankly, I'd just as soon you give me some suggestions. What would you like, Maria? Name me one, maybe I know it."

"Do you know 'The Man I Love,' by Gershwin?"

"Yes, but I couldn't play that."

"Oh, yes, you could," asserted Li. "If you know the piece at all, it will come to you. And if you concentrate and put your heart in it, you will stun us all."

Li began singing in a whisper, softly carrying the melody of its lyrics. "I tell you what…I will join you on stage. You start if off as a piano solo, give me a short intro, then I will join you with the lyrics."

"How can I possibly refuse? Where is the piano?"

Li gave one of her usual signals to the control room, and suddenly a Steinway concert grand descended gently from the ceiling onto the stage. When the piano was secure on its place, a young woman came on stage and introduced the next performers.

"And now, Ladies and Gentlemen, it is our pleasure to introduce Dr. John Shiller, who will show us what else besides surgery he can use his hands for. He will be accompanying Li B. Dhoh in 'The Man I Love' by the Gershwin brothers, George and Ira."

John walked across the room to the Grand Steinway. He sat before it for a few minutes, wringing his hands and concentrating. Then, he lunged forward and broke the silence with the rich beginning chords. As agreed, at one point he nodded to Li, who had been standing by the piano, to bring in Ira's simple but powerful lyrics. It was one of Maria's favorites.

> *He'll look at me and smile*
> *I'll understand*
> *And in a little while*
> *He'll call my name*
> *And though it seems absurd*
> *I know we both won't say a word.*

The audience gave them both an enthusiastic long round of applause. As he made his way back to the table, John shook hands with people along the way, hugging some of them. Maria was waiting for him with open arms.

"That was wonderful, John. That's one of my all-time favorite songs. I've been humming it in solitude for years, waiting for the man in the song to appear. I never expected that he would materialize from the song itself as he played it. You were magnificent!" said Maria.

"Thank you. Thank you. But did you see how many people I stopped to say hello to? And here we thought we were alone a while ago. I couldn't believe how many friends and relatives were here." He continued looking back and waving at some of them after he sat down.

A few minutes passed and then suddenly Li and John each grabbed one of Maria's hands. She knew what that meant. "Oh no, no," said Maria as she lowered her head on the table. "I don't know what to do! I can't play any instrument, and I just wouldn't dare to sing. Please, please, I beg you. Don't let me make a fool of myself."

"Yes, you can sing, I know you can. You have a beautiful voice," affirmed Li. "But if you don't want to sing, that's all right. Then you can dance for us Maria."

"Dance, you say, that's worse. That's out of the question. I don't do solo dances. No way!"

"Well, we can get you Fred Astaire or Gene Kelly if you liked."

"Yes, I bet you could. Well, thanks, but no thanks"

Then Li counter offered: "Well all right, I tell you what. Let me go change into a suit and then let's do a tango, you and I. A little bird told me that you love tangos. Come on, don't look at me like that. It will work out fine. You'll see."

Although Maria still showed some reluctance about the prospect, she put up less resistance to this suggestion. Li stood up. "Don't worry. You'll do just great. I promise." Then Li looked at the control center and raised her hand above her head as if giving a signal, saying: "Okay Imogene baby, tube me on down." Then she entered a glass cylinder and disappeared under the floor, saying to John and Maria as she left: "I'll be right back."

"Oh God, what have I got myself into now?" asked Maria.

"You'll be fine with Libby. Don't worry," John assured her. Li returned wearing a dark suit over a white silk blouse and a white scarf in lieu of a tie. Her hair was fully collected now under a Fedora in true Buenos Aires Porteño fashion. As she approached the table where Maria and John were waiting, she took a bow and flicked the rim of her hat signaling that she was ready.

"Wow!" exclaimed Maria. "I guess you are ready to tango. You look stunning! Well, guess what, it happens that I just had two big swallows of John's drink, and I am ready too. What shall we dance to?"

"You choose. It's your call."

"Can we maybe do a medley of a few favorites like La Cumparsita, El Choclo, and Danzarín perhaps?"

No problem. Nothing was a problem there. Even as they walked to center stage the plucking of bass fiddles began pulsating, followed by the virile sensuous melodies of the strings and the bandoneon intoning the strains of La Cumparsita. Maria and Li began erect and stiff, with parsimony of movement, with slow and distinct steps which they executed with elegance and simplicity, so unique to the tango. Their legs were like straight long fountain pens, their shoes like pointed writing tips that sketched over the floor a series of choreographic statements. It was like a warming up and a teasing, as if their body language asked for directions: shall we go forward or backwards? Neither, let's slide to the side. This scant routine of slow, hesitant movements followed by resolute steps soon led to a crescendo of physical dexterity that culminated in a fast workout of turns and kicks, to an entanglement of legs, to jumps and sittings. Maria would jump to a sitting position on Libby's extended leg, anchored for catching her. They danced as one, as if they had practiced all their lives, as if their bodies were governed by a single brain. Maria loved it, thinking to herself, in all my dreams I never thought of tangos in heaven. And yet, if it weren't for this tango, this wouldn't be heaven.

The last note of "Danzarín" came to an end on a collective peak of breathlessness. Neither the orchestra, nor the dancers, nor the audience could have stood another note of music. They were all about to burst, as if straining on the last gasp of air within a climax. The musicians wiped their brows; the audience broke into a din of applause, of shouts and whistles, while Maria and Li stood frozen for a few long seconds, holding the position that signified the final choreographic exclamation mark of their dance.

Then they made their way through the audience, shaking hands, embracing some, and kissing others. Maria was delighted to see so many people whom she recognized. She sincerely relished seeing them there, except for Mildred Colson, who astonished her. Maria would not have invited her if she had had the choice. The two of them were inherently and congenitally anti-magnetic. To Maria, the principal was a humorless, competitive woman who vied for all the things which had no value in Maria's scheme of things. Her presence stirred ambivalent feelings in Maria. The instant she saw her, she felt a surge of embarrassment. Instinctively and by force of habit, Maria's submissive half wanted to apologize for her performance. But her rebellious half wanted to gloat. I don't know what you might have thought of my dancing. I don't care. What matters is that the rest of the people liked it. I got a great ovation. I was good. And I loved it. Don't you forget it!

The principal sat alone under a restaurant umbrella, but her table was unlike any of the other tables around. Maria became almost indignant when she recognized it. It was in fact the principal's usual desk. How out of place, and yet how fitting, she thought. As she approached it, the principal led off with a very restrained applause in slow motion which served as her perfunctory congratulatory gesture. Maria responded in silent body language, by smiling broadly while fluttering her right hand to say something like "hello, goodbye."

Then Maria moved on and came to another table which also stirred mixed feelings.

"Mami, papi!" exclaimed Maria as she saw her parents. "What are you doing here?" She rushed to them and put herself between them so she could hug them both simultaneously. It was a great relief from the previous table. Then she kissed each one and moved around the table so she could face them. As she did so, she stepped on her father's foot. The old man let out quite a howl. What was that? Maria thought as she looked under the table for an explanation. Then she saw his naked toes wiggling about, trying to shake off the pain. Her father was barefoot. His pajama bottoms stuck out below the hem of his trousers. Then she noticed that he only had a T-shirt under his blazer. He was unshaven. He looked a sight. She was disappointed by his appearance. How embarrassing Maria thought as she looked around. "Daddy! What's with you?" She asked him. "Mom, why did you let him come like that?"

"I was in bed minding my own business," Pablo responded sheepishly, "when your mother called me, all excited, to watch something. 'It's Maria, it's Maria your daughter' she said. I thought you were on TV. But it turned out to be here. Well, all I can say is that at least this time my pants are zipped. That ought to count for something, shouldn't it?" With that they all had a hearty laugh. Maria sandwiched herself between them again and hugged them.

"What the heck, it's my party. You can come any way you like. The main thing is: did you like my tangoing? That's what matters."

"*Estuviste esplendida!*" said her mother. "We wouldn't have missed it for the world. But neither one of us could remember where you learned to dance like that. We couldn't think of when you might have picked that up."

"Oh, I've been shadow dancing the tango for years, Mom. The thing is, I always stopped when I heard you coming, but this time you caught me in *fragranti*."

"Well, you were wonderful, dear. But go on now. See your friends. Don't worry about us."

As Maria left, she bumped into Li again. They both smiled and looked contentedly at each other. Then Li spoke in a hushed dissembled mode. "Maria, be careful. There could be trouble. Don't look now, but at the table directly below the Control Center there is an obese Brunhilda stuffing herself. That's Guilda. She is bad news. Most of the time you are safe from her because she is either busy eating or sleeping. But when she is out on the prowl, look out! She is the Gestapo."

"But why should I fear her? I've done nothing wrong!" asked Maria.

"It's not what you've done, but what you might do. The night is young; you are in love; and men will be men. As far as I am concerned, that's what makes this more heavenly. But Guilda doesn't think so. Don't let her inhibit you and ruin your fun. But be careful."

Libby gave Maria a pager. "Here. Take this. I must go back in. If you need anything, just let me know with this." And she left. When Maria joined John, he was ecstatic about their performance. "Such elegance of movement, such body poetry! You were both magnificent!"

Z   Z   ZzZ   Z   Z

56. Between Heaven and Heaven

Maria got up feeling cheerful that morning. This was the second consecutive night that she had dreamed about heaven, and she had felt that Heaven had been, indeed, divine. This dream had been lavish with magical props, with make-believe wonders, with the demonstration of the limitless possibilities of the imagination, and the display of futuristic things to come. Music played in her heart and put her in a dancing mood. She went to work that morning thinking of tangos and humming "Che Me Importa del Mondo." During her coffee break, even her friend Karen noticed that she was bubbly and full of songs.

"You seem so happy today. What gives?" asked Karen.

Maria felt happy on so many counts that she didn't know where to begin.

"There's so much, Karen, so, so much… I could say it's the freedom… resigning from this place. I could say it's John; I could say it is love. I could also say it is heaven because, incidentally, I had a dream about heaven last night. So, I suppose, the truth is that it is all of the above."

"You are so lucky to be so happy. They say luck begets luck, and it appears that you're on a roll. Well, don't forget to rub off a little on me. But now tell me about heaven. Did you die to get there? And wasn't that sad?"

"Funny you should ask that, because it was such a bizarre experience on that account. The dream danced around the issue of death. We were never sad. It was all tongue in cheek. My dream was more like a parody of heaven. John was in it, of course, as you might have guessed. He started saying things that hinted at heaven while undermining the role of death. He would say things like: 'I am here because I said I was dying to meet you. Somebody heard my prayers. Next thing I knew, here I was.'

Then I would say: 'Oh, how you exaggerate.'

Then he would say something like: 'If I am here beside you,

this must be heaven. What else could it possibly be?'

Then I would play along and say something like: 'I, too, was dying to meet you. I suppose this proves we were destined to meet in heaven.'

That's how we acknowledged the issue of death, with a lot of silly banter. There was nothing sad about it. We both laughed about it, even in the dream."

Karen laughed, and begged Maria to tell her more of this cheerful dream, asking: "Were you drunk during this dream, by any chance? What were you on? You're not making it up, are you?"

"No, I assure you. There was this Eurasian lady by the name of Li B. Dhoh who was our guide. She just descended out of the blue, like a butterfly."

"Libido?" Karen interrupted in disbelief.

"No," Maria corrected as she spelled the name out. But it was then, for the first time, that Maria realized that the woman's name was a homonym of 'Libido.' Was that deliberate? Maria wondered. That seemed to be another one of the pranks perpetrated by the dream.

The coffee break was too short for further dream elaboration. They agreed to have lunch together and talk some more about the dream, which gave every impression of being strictly profane and hedonistic. Heaven was a pampering paradise.

But by the time they had lunch, the magic of the dream had faded. Maria was not as cheerful as before. The real world had imposed itself in the interim, reminding her that she had resigned from school, and that she had nothing lined up, reminding her that her life was about to change in important new directions that she hadn't even begun to contemplate. Could she even picture where she would be in August or September? Everything would not be rosy. The realization of so much uncertainty began to bother her a little.

Karen noticed the change in Maria. She tried to get Maria to tell her more oddities about the dream. Maria complied but without gusto. She rushed through the scenes.

"What happened since this morning? Did you have bad classes? Were your students rowdy?" Karen asked her.

"No, just the opposite. It was very quiet in my classes because they were taking a test. But while I sat there monitoring the exam, my mind wandered, and I had time to meditate and think about a lot of things. I've been living on holiday these last few days, but now reality has come calling and I feel disoriented and insecure. This job, bad as it is, has at least given me a routine, a coming and going every day. But now it's as if I'd rung the bell for the bus to stop and I find myself in the middle of nowhere. John has talked about marriage already. I think we will probably marry before the end of the year. But then what? Marriage solves some problems for me, and it answers some questions, but not all. Being a housewife is not enough. My life ahead seems blank and undefined. I need a vision of my future, and I have none. I should be making plans, but I haven't even started to think.

"I do not fear the future, mind you. I think I will be happy. The question is: happy at what? Should I continue to teach? Should I reconsider the PhD in Math? At one time I had thought of becoming an airline stewardess, just so I could travel and see the world. Traveling is something I want to do. Maybe I could still do that for a few months before getting married. But would I put John on hold while I did that? That doesn't seem right. If he had not come into my life, I probably would have tried flying. Perhaps there are ways of incorporating travel while being married to a doctor.

Karen broke in. "You are something else, Maria. One minute you have the world by the tail. You are riding high, and then you lose it. But I understand it all. It makes perfect sense. It's all very normal. You are going through a lot of changes in your life. Take it all one day at a time, one step at a time. And don't worry. But you do need to prioritize. Some of the things you mentioned are minor. From where I sit, I see this: First, you have love; then you have freedom. Financial security does not seem to be far behind. What else could possibly worry you? Everything else beyond that you can easily work out. Things will fall in place."

"Thanks, Karen. It's so good to talk to you. You just keep on rubbing off your common sense on me. You are the good and pragmatic Sancho Panza to my moody and chimerical Quixote. You anchor me to the ground."

Later that evening Maria went to her parents' house and told them about John, but, of course, only the parts that she could share with them comfortably. She did not mention that they had talked about marriage. She did not mention that he was divorced. She just stated the basic facts: that he was thirty-three years old, that he was a surgeon, that he hailed from the Midwest, and that they were very much in love. But it was still too early to bring him by. Perhaps in a week or so he could come for dinner. Clara, of course, couldn't wait: the sooner, the better.

That night, around 10 p.m., John called her, and they talked for nearly an hour, filling in the parts of their lives that were still lacunas to the other, becoming better acquainted, learning of their tastes, of the things they liked.

"I dreamed about us last night," she told him. "We were at a fabulous party. Guess where! In heaven of all places, you and I!"

Then, in what seemed like a non sequitur, like an abrupt change in subject, she asked him: "Do you like music, John?"

"Oh, yes, I love music—all sorts of music from Jazz to classical to opera."

"Do you play an instrument by any chance?"

"I took piano as a kid, but I don't have time for it now."

"What about languages?"

"I struggle with them. I like them, but they don't like me."

They talked about travel, about literature and about everything that came into their minds to better know each other. He liked to travel, but it was a luxury he had no time for—except for professional conventions. But potentially, there were opportunities for travel both domestically and internationally in medicine. As far as Maria was concerned, he passed all her questions with flying colors. There was no disappointment. The last thing they discussed was the agenda for the next day. Tomorrow, Saturday, will be the day for the tour of tours. He would be at her apartment by 1:30, and the rest of the day would be theirs. They would have plenty of time to really get to know each other and to make history.

Z   Z   Z   z   Z   Z   Z

57. STEALING FORBIDDEN DREAMS

That evening Maria had trouble going to sleep for all the anticipation of the next day. It was around 2:30 a.m. when she finally joined the girls at dream central, and she wasted no time looking for her mentor.

"Where is Professor Quixote?" was the first thing Maria asked with some impatience. "Please get him for me right away. And, Ladies, please understand, I don't want to be rude, but he has priority tonight. I have been trying for days to have a talk with him. I have so much to ask him. You can stay, if you like; I am not kicking you out, but I need him urgently and I need to talk to him at great length."

A few minutes later Professor Quixote entered wearing a Spanish helmet of the 16th Century and carrying a lance. "*¿Me habéis llamado, mi Dulcinea? Os he oído, creo, desde las tinieblas de mi mazmorra,*" he intoned in Castilian Spanish. ("Hast thou called me, my Dulcinea? I have heard thee, I thinketh, from the darkness of my dungeon)."

"Oh, Professor Quixote, I'm so glad to see you. There's so much I want to talk to you about. I am coming to a crossroad in my life, and it feels as if I were approaching the edge of the earth. Suddenly, I am confused about my own beliefs. I am not sure that the earth is round anymore. I have doubts about things that I thought I knew for certain."

"Such as?"

"Such as whether heaven exists and whether there is life in the hereafter, such as whether I should have a church wedding or not, such as whether I should pursue further studies in math, and if not in Math, then in what? And finally, above all, whether there is a way to come to terms with this constraint that drives me to insanity, this inability to communicate with you during my wakeful hours; this stupid waste of a precious opportunity to learn and to grow that gets squandered in oblivion every night because we cannot remember what transpires in the sleep interludes of our lives."

"Ha! I knew it would come to that. You are as tenacious as a Rottweiler. You just haven't given up on this obsession, have you? You still want to steal away the forbidden dreams of your wee hours."

"Oooh, I like the sound of that!" interrupted Sasha. "Listen to that: 'Stealing Forbidden Dreams'! It has the cachet of a best-selling novel. Don't you think?"

"Maybe so, but it is not factually correct," Maria noted. "I would not call it stealing because I have never conceded my rights to any of these deliberations. These so-called 'forbidden dreams' belong to me. If I can't have them, it is only because of a technicality, because of a shortcoming in memory transference. We've been through this before. I think the upshot of that awful nightmare about the cake I couldn't take out was about this issue. For technical reasons of memory capacity, I could not take the totality of these dreams, but only their essence, their gist. What I'm really asking for is a better mechanism for relaying this gist. The dribs and drabs that I have been getting in my regular dreams are too few and far between. It is too difficult to get much out of this system; it is most inefficient."

Professor Quixote interrupted her to ask her: "Have you been analyzing your dreams carefully, Maria? And have you been entering them in your dream diary as you agreed to do?"

"Do you want the truth? The honest answer is no. I don't have time for that. That process turned out to be much harder than I thought, and I can't continue it. There's got to be a better way."

As usual, Sasha was the one to break in with unsolicited advice and unwelcome observations, saying: "Yes, but don't forget, Maria, that you're going to have a lot of free time on your hands in a month or so when the summer-break starts."

Maria said nothing, but she felt like kicking Sasha for suggesting it. She was about to tell Sasha that in that case she should write the diary herself, but Professor Quixote intervened.

"You are right, Maria. There's got to be a better way. And, fortunately, there is. I have also been thinking about these concerns of yours and I believe I've found an answer to all your problems. What I have in mind will solve them all, your concerns about your future and your communication with us. I think we can tie it all together very neatly."

Maria was incredulous. "Oh, my God, then tell me. I am dying to know. Except that, wait! What good would it do for you to tell me now? Have you forgotten that I won't remember it tomorrow? How will we get around that?"

"I am aware of the problem, but there is a way. Trust me."

"Will I remember all this tomorrow? How…?"

"No, you won't remember this tomorrow word for word; I can't promise you that. What I propose is creating a force that will generate a strong current of thoughts. It will be like an intellectual gale that will blow constantly. Your mental weather will change. You will be absorbed in a consuming project. It will be like a jet stream of ideas, like a hurricane, like a mistral that will sweep through the fields and byways of your mind. Over the long haul, you will not know what ideas came from sleep and what ideas came from wakeful hours, because they will have eddied and churned together through all your hemispheres. Your ideas will have all melded together and will be stored in a permanent indestructible medium that will outlast your lifetime itself. They will last even after you are dead. Of course, this will come to pass, provided you follow the plan I suggest."

Maria was excited and impatient. "Then please tell me. Let me have it right now. Give it to me plain and simple."

"Okay, I will give it to you in one word: write."

"Oh, come on! Don't overdo the succinctness. I am missing something here. Write what?"

"Write your diary and read it!" Sasha volunteered.

"Oh, be quiet, Sasha."

"No, don't shush her. She is not far off the mark. Writing is the key. It need not be a diary per se, although that wouldn't hurt.

Write essays, write short stories, or write a novel, but write. Put your thoughts into words. The important thing is that you get in the habit of listening to your mind and putting the thoughts into sentences and paragraphs. Choose your form, choose your style, but write. Writing is the only way that you can salvage these interludes when you are awake. You will make us come alive during your conscious hours when you write."

Maria was still unconvinced. "I would love to believe you, but I guess I still don't get it. I cannot picture how writing is going to make you come alive during my daylight hours."

"It's easy. Dream while you are awake. Imagine! Write about us, about these interludes. Start with last January when you first began coming here. Do you remember the early episodes?"

"Well, yes, I do. I remember them now. But I won't remember them tomorrow when I am awake."

"At the risk of sounding like Sasha, you will remember them better if you read your diaries. In those days you were recording the number of hours you slept each night, and you were appalled that you went to school with only three or four hours of sleep. You were an avid reader of the mysteries of the mind at night; you were obsessed with the subject, and you wrote quite a bit about it. I have here some of what you've written, and there's even more in your diary. What is not in any of your writing, at least not yet, is that you came into this building one night looking for answers to the mysteries of sleep. Insomnia hounded you. You were looking for gremlins in your brain, 'the witches' you called them, the demons in your subconscious that kept you awake at night against your will. Over the coming weeks you got to meet those witches and gremlins, and they turned out to be none other than Sasha, Libby, Maria Luisa, Dr. Broca and Yours Truly. We've come a long way. Look at us now; we are one big happy family. But back in January, you were going to wring our necks if you ever caught us. Well, here we are. Don't wring our necks, just write about us instead."

The professor continued. "I remember that you were

astonished when you did the arithmetic and discovered that over a period of sixty years you would sleep twenty years. Imagine twenty years of your life unaccounted for! Twenty years wasted! You couldn't get over the waste and you were going to do something about it. So, you embarked upon a quest to salvage those years. You would push back the darkness and steal those years from oblivion. You would squeeze awareness out of every hour of your existence. If that isn't a noble cause worth writing about, I don't know what it is. In my opinion, you have found your challenge. Tell the world about your dual life, about the characters that populate your dreams. Show them what the dark side of the moon is like by writing about these interludes."

Maria agreed in principle. She had no problem with the idea. What troubled her was her memory.

"Okay, I agree that these interludes would be wonderful to write about. But how can I write about them when I don't remember them when I am awake. How can I write about the dark side of the moon if I can't remember having been there?"

"You imagine it!" said Prof. Quixote.

Sasha burst in with a suggestion. "Yeah, I have a great title for it. Call it: Postcards to myself from a place I can't remember having been in."

"I like that," said Prof Quixote. "It catches the contradiction of the situation…"

"I'm not crazy about it. It's too long," said Maria.

"Then call it simply: Interludes of the Mind at Night," suggested Sasha. "Or, better yet, "Dialogues of the Sleeping Mind.""

"Besides," continued Maria, "how do I bring back the pictures and sounds from the dark side of the moon. How will you help me? Will you slip me a tape of the proceedings surreptitiously?"

"There you go with that tape again. You put too much stock in memory, Maria. That tape would not solve your problem. It would help, but only a little—less than you think. Memory isn't all that important. The imagination is infinitely more productive and, often, after you start writing, memory will come on board to help. Memory alone cannot put order in the chaos of facts you get from history. Memory plays a role in writing, but it is not the only one, nor even the most important one.

"Suppose you had your tape recorder, and you were able to record these hours. You flatter us by valuing so highly what we say and do here. If you had that tape and played it through and through, you would be disappointed to find how little was significant. Out of an eight-hour sleep there might be two or three hours with gems of wisdom. But there would also be a lot of chaff, a lot of waste, blank moments and inane discussion. What do you propose? Would you sit through eight hours of daylight to go over what you heard during the night while you slept? That would be squandering more time, throwing good hours after bad hours. You would satisfy your curiosity, but at a very high cost on time. You would increase the proportion of your life devoted to sleep, which is precisely what you decry and call a waste. Is it worth it? I don't think so.

"The better way is by using your imagination in creative writing. Here is how it works. When you write, you think, and when you think, you inject blood and oxygen into our lives. You lure us with the aroma of your thoughts. We will come drooling to see what's cooking. You won't be able to see us or hear us as you do now, but we will be there kibitzing, trying to contribute to your thought processes. I will be there playing devil's advocate, questioning you, making suggestions and helping you think. Sasha, also, will be objecting to a word, coming up with a better one, or suggesting a quirky metaphor, or recasting a sentence into a more poetic structure. You'll have to fight her off the keyboard. Don't forget we are real; we exist night and day, 24/7; we are always involved in your life, but we are invisible only during your conscious hours.

"Don't put so much stock on memory, Maria. Loosen up! If writers were to write only from memory, you would eliminate a lot of literature. Fiction would be emasculated. Fantasy would be restricted, confined, crippled, asphyxiated! Creative writing is the art of dreaming while awake and putting it all on paper.

"Now here is one more oddity that you will discover when you write about these sleep interludes. Believe it or not, memory is indistinguishable from imaginings when you write about dreams. Suppose you were recounting a dream while awake. Suppose the dream involved abstractions, complicated arguments. The deeper you analyzed, the greater the chance that you will be making things up, that your memory will morph into imaginings. But here is the clincher: so, what? Who is keeping score of what is what? Who could argue that what you are writing is not accurate? Who could say that things didn't quite occur the way you told them? How could you, yourself, be sure of what is memory and what is imagining? A thought is a thought, whether you recalled it or imagined it, where dreams are concerned. When you open the faucet of your mind to recall your dreams, the pipes behind that faucet have already crisscrossed and mixed memory with imaginings. In sum, don't worry about remembering your dreams, just make them up. Create them while awake. But don't be surprised to learn that what you thought you were creating was really memory that was being dictated by the likes of gremlins like us from the dark side of the moon.

"The human brain is a juggler. It juggles balls of memory and imagination, and it confuses them while they are up in the air. Don't worry about which is which. Just don't drop them and keep them moving. Tell your story. Tell how sleep changed the way you thought, how it altered your beliefs. Write about the treasures you found in these interludes. Wax poetic on the nuggets of forgotten moments, on the oases that you found in the sands of your Sahara. I want to read you something I have here, something that you've written. Listen to your own words.

> *Conscious life monopolizes memory.*
> *All our remembering goes to our time awake.*
> *Our hours sleep are shut out. Those hours,*

Which were private, solitary, and secret to begin with,
Are, in addition, cursed to be forgotten.

No matter how many people populate our dreams,
In the end the cast reduces to a plurality of one.
All the roles in every act and every scene of our dreams
Involves only the myriad fragments of 'me' and 'I'
No one can remind us of dream scenes we may have forgotten
No one can correct our dream accounts in the re-telling
Because nobody else was, in fact, there.

"Well, that's not quite true. We were there. And we will help you recreate it. Notice that I didn't say: help you remember. We will help you write. We will help you rescue those hours that seem dark and empty. But let me go on. You wrote much more.

How like an open book is our life awake!
It touches others and is touched by others.
There are witnesses who can affirm what we did do
And who can contradict us if we make false claims.
Who beyond us witnesses our dreams?
Sleep and dreams fall through the cracks of memory
Like drops of rain onto the sands of life's Sahara.
What became of those feats that no one witnessed?
What purpose was served by those uncorroborated episodes?
The epic escapades and the cowardly retreats,
Those dialogues with other voices within ourselves,
Those morality plays where conscience upbraided the libido
And which we managed to conveniently forget by the next
day?
What was the point of all that?

For some mysterious reason
Dreams seem to be written either with invisible ink,

Or self-destructing ink for short duration.
Sleep memory evaporates
With the dawn of our awakening.
And yet…and yet …is the life we lived asleep really a waste?
A part of me cannot accept that.
There must be a hidden value in this apparent waste.
And I must find it.

"Did you want something to write about? Well, there you have it. Think about how much you have learned these last three months. I can't believe it is all wasted. Don't let it be. Write a little every day! Go about your business and do what you must do but come back and write. Write as if writing were the key to happiness which, in your case, I think it could be. Take care of your husband, of your children; take them to school; take them to soccer; but while they are gone, come back and write. You don't need a job to keep busy. Writing about your life at night can be your mission and it can keep you busy. You don't need to go for a PhD to be intellectually engaged, writing can be a worthwhile challenge.

"When you think about it, Maria, a book is someone else's equivalent of that tape you wanted to wake up with. A book is a distillation of hundreds of hours of ideas, ideas that were thought during sleep and during wakefulness. A book embodies the words and thoughts of that author's own Sasha, Libby and Maria Luisa. But the author didn't just quote them. Rather, they dictated lines to him. Writing is the closest you will come to reliving these interludes while awake. It is what you've been looking for, but with one major difference. As you write, you will be able to keep your thoughts and save them in your computer files, the entire proceedings of these sessions: my lectures, Sasha's sassy interruptions, and Libby's pleas for free love. You can even print it all! So, write, I can't emphasize it enough."

Everybody was quiet, attentive to every word of the professor. He had them in a trance. Maria, too, was digesting his words and considering their implications.

"Yes... ah, yes... I'm beginning to get the general idea ... why didn't I think of this before? It's so obvious now. I like it. I like it. Yes, I do. I see your point. It's a brilliant idea. The more I think about it, the more I see how it works, how it connects all the loose ends that were bothering me. It will be time consuming but also gratifying. And I can see how it could bring us all together, how it could let me have the benefit of your mind and your input. This is very exciting. I believe it can be done. Count me in. I will most certainly give it a try."

"Good. That's the spirit. Just don't get stressed about it. Pace yourself comfortably. Think about what you want to write and then hit one key after another. A book of a thousand pages begins with a single word. Once you get going, your book will absorb you. Your mind will draw freely from its reservoir of thoughts, not knowing or caring where the thoughts came from—whether from sleep or conscious meditations. Your ideas, your plot, and your novel will expand within your brain night and day when you are not even aware of it. Count on it. It will grow like a seed that extends its roots in the underground of your mind, unseen at first, unmindful of what belongs underground and what belongs above ground, of what belongs to consciousness and what belongs to the subconscious. The seed will transcend barriers and one day will break ground and sprout in broad daylight into the open air to soak the sun rays of your wakeful hours. When you see its stem, its leaves and petals, you will forget about its roots. But what is taking place beneath the ground is also serving, keeping the plant alive in its own imperceptible way."

While the professor was speaking, Maria was trying to recall the times when she had written something. Surely the professor, Sasha, or Maria Luisa would have exerted their influence. The question was: could she recall their intervention? She could not picture them, but at the same time, she could not imagine that they were not present. Like the roots of the professor's metaphorical plant, they would have been working in silence and unseen, even as their influence was strangely palpable. Oh, yes, she could feel their influence and she could almost picture them and hear their suggestions. In the case of Maria Luisa, it would have been when Maria worked on mathematical projects such as handouts for her students, explanatory notes to herself, exercises and exams. Maria Luisa's criticisms would have been firm, but also gentle. Maria could almost hear her say: That proof is okay. It will take you there. But it is awkward; it is a little forced. It lacks elegance. It doesn't flow. Rework it. And Maria would start anew, trying to satisfy the silent unseen critic in her. On poetry, it was Sasha that surfaced unmistakably. Sometimes it was her humor, her irrepressible sassiness. But it was always that restlessness, that compulsion to tweak things, and that penchant for the quirky, that marked Sasha's undercurrents. Professor Quixote came through in her correspondence both personal and professional, when she had fought City Hall, or a utility company; when she had to write term papers in college—whenever she had to zap the reader with cutting logic a la Zorro, with snappy blade work.

"I have one more question for you, Professor Quixote. Do you think I have what it takes to be a writer? Do you see me as a writer? What makes you think that? What sort of a writer do you think I will be?"

The professor paced around for several seconds, weighing his words. "Let me answer you by telling the type of writer that you will not be. You will never be a sportswriter. Sports do not interest you. You don't even have the lingo for that. Nor will you be a porno writer, much to Libby's chagrin. You neither have the interest nor the dirty vocabulary for that. I could go on like this. Next, I would eliminate politics. You will not be a political commentator because politics also bores you. But that still leaves a whole world of possibilities. In the mathematical area you could write textbooks with your own spin. You've expressed dissatisfaction with the material that you have had to work with. Most books don't go into the cultural evolution of mathematics. The students learn lemmas, and mathematical abstractions in a vacuum, devoid of history and circumstance. Well, here is a chance for you to do something about it."

"Oh, yes, yes!" exclaimed Maria Luisa excitedly as she got up from her seat and got closer to Maria, pressing her shoulders in an unrestrained show of exuberance which was unusual for her. She was most enthusiastic about the project. "There is a lot we can do together, Maria. I have lots of ideas. That is a wonderful project. Oh yes, please, please, keep it in mind."

Professor Quixote continued. "While still in the mathematical area, you could explore the history of mathematics, going into the lives of the great mathematicians, bringing incidents and anecdotes that will show not only their humanity, but other revelations that will help explain certain aspects of their work. It is intriguing to me, and immensely fascinating, to think of the way the Calculus developed at the time it did, touching so many minds at the same time, like an idea desperate to be born and seeking anyone who would sire it. It must have been in the wind, in the atoms in the air. How is it possible that men living so far apart geographically—men like Newton, Leibnitz, and La Grange—could be thinking along the same lines at that point in time? Remember that we are talking about a time when there were no telephones, no radio, no faxes, no trains, no cars, only horse and buggy transportation. There was ambition, vanity and jealousy—humanity is humanity—but there simply wasn't the means to play dirty. Or was it there? We touched a little bit on this during Maria Luisa's dream version of heaven, when you met with all the greats briefly. This could be another project to investigate and write about."

Sasha interrupted again. She was all excited about a story she considered germane to the discussion. "Your mention of Galois brings to mind a collaboration--more like a confrontation, really-- that Maria and I had when we worked on a poem about him. Maria was so touched by the circumstance of his untimely death that she cried. The poem began well, but Maria got carried away with the rhyme pattern. She used words like night, light, might, write, quite, kite, bright and fright to excess. She would have thrown in the kitchen sink, if it had rhymed."

Maria shot back at that. "Yes, and I remember that it was your fault. You had dared me to write two lines that rhymed. You thought I was incapable of it. You were goading me on, and I wanted to prove you wrong. Then the poem took a life of its own and got away from me. I couldn't stop the momentum of the rhyme bright, light, night, fight, tight. It got longer and longer. It became a challenge to write a whole poem with that rhyme scheme. The irony is that I really don't like rhyme that much. Sasha is the great rhyme maker. It just goes to prove what bad influences can do."

"Maria don't blame me for your failures. I won't be your scapegoat. You liked your one-track rhyme, and you were proud of it. I was the one that was critical because, much as I love rhyme, one can overdo a good thing."

"Yes, I overdid the rhyme, but it was only to spite you. You drove me to it. You want rhyme? I'll show you. Now I am not sure whether I like it the way it is anymore. You are to blame for its excessive rhyme pattern."

"Ladies, ladies, you are going to come to blows here," intervened Prof. Quixote. "Let's settle down. You have aroused my curiosity about this poem. May we see it?"

At that point, the large monitor on the wall suddenly lit up with the poem's lines.

Galois (1811-32)

The price for an immortal site
Among the stars is never slight
Fate often exacts its cruelest bite
From those who reach that height.
On this score one need only cite
The story of one young and bright
Evariste Galois on his life's final night,
A story which has seen little light

> *Beyond the mathematically erudite.*
>
> *Fate must have been the perfect Shylock that night*
> *Demanding every ounce of flesh that was his right.*
> *Poor Galois had no choice but to requite*
> *The full measure of his genius in a single night*
> *Rushing to write in the few hours before daylight*
> *All that that he had thought and someday might*
> *Express as a dying swan sings his final rite*
> *In the desperate grip of a mortal plight*
> *He must have struggled to put in black and white*
> *The brainstorms raging in his mind before twilight.*
> *To leave in theorems the legacy of his insights*
> *Unknown even to his renowned mathwrights.*
>
> *That night there would be no distractions, no delight*
> *In boyish musings, in mathematical mental flight*
> *No wonderings about the catenary bight*
> *Of the string of a high-flying kite*
> *No equation for the orbit of a fleeting meteorite.*
>
> *That night there wouldn't be even time for fright.*
> *Despite the fact he knew he would die outright*
> *By the break of dawn's first light*
> *In a choreographed stupid fight.*

Professor Quixote remarked, "It's not bad. I like it. Maybe the two of you can come together and change it to your hearts' content some day. The one-track rhyme pattern doesn't bother me so much, because it does seem to flow with a nice cadence, and it does tell a story. It is not strained, in my opinion. But I would like to ask Maria one question that is germane to our previous discussion. So, tell me, Maria, were you sleep or awake when you wrote that?"

"I was awake, of course."

"Awake? Really…? And you were arguing with Sasha about a rhyme pattern while awake?"

"Maybe we discussed it over subsequent nights, and I remembered the discussion the following days when I wrote it. I couldn't have written it in my sleep, that's for sure."

"Well then, I rest my case," said Prof. Quixote. "This clinches the 'how' that you were looking for—how we can come together when you write. Whether you were awake, or sleep doesn't matter. What matters is that you collaborated. The poem is what it is because of your differences and influences. It seems that you two can make beautiful pearls in broad daylight while irritated at each other about rhymes. Carry on…you're doing great."

Maria was dumbstruck. "Well, I'll be... You all make a great point."

"I also liked the poem, Maria," said Maria Luisa. "It captured the pathos of the last night of Galois' life and made me feel how utterly unfair fate can be when it deals humans such bad hands. I am glad Galois was among the mathematicians you met that night in heaven. I am also delighted that you have quit your job because I look forward to working with you. Just remember, when you're not writing poetry with Sasha, I would love to work with you in math related subjects."

"I will definitely keep it in mind, Marilucha" said Maria as she hugged Maria Luisa. "I want you all to know that I consider these hours of my life a hidden treasure. You enrich my existence and double my joy. I also want to tell you that I love you, all of you, even you Sasha—even though we lock horns as much as we do. I can't say that I miss you when I am awake, because--as you know well-- I'm not allowed to remember you. I suppose it's just as well because if I could remember you, it would be sad as one remembers a deceased loved one; I would not be able to really see you or touch you. Missing you would be so hurtful that I would cry buckets of tears through my days. I can see the logic of providential design in this."

"Good," said Professor Quixote. "Are we all done then? Are there any other questions?

Maria Luisa responded. "Yes, I have a question. I've been meaning to ask you: what did you think of our renditions of heaven?"

"I am so glad you brought that up," interrupted Maria, "because I have several questions for Professor Quixote as well. I can't quite reconcile my denial of an afterlife with my dreams about heaven, especially since I enjoy those dreams so much. How can that be?"

"Good question. I'll give you my thoughts on the matter, but you must think about this while awake and write about it. Not many people write about the conflicts in their beliefs, and that is why they are so confused about where they stand. Everybody should be required to do this, if nothing else, because it makes them think. When you write about beliefs that trouble you, you are forced to dig, to examine, and cross examine. You mature philosophically. Writing opens communion with your heart and your mind. It is like talking to yourself. It is the best way to know yourself."

"Can we take a break? I can feel another long lecture coming—one that is really deep. I move we adjourn for an hour or so," said Sasha.

"I second that wholeheartedly," said Libby, who hadn't said a word all night. They all left.

Z   Z   Z   z   Z   Z   Z

58. HEAVEN REVISITED

Everybody took a break from the long discussion on writing. The girls talked about going to Coconut Grove.

"Anywhere but Churros y chocolate," Sasha interdicted.

Maria stayed alone and repaired to darkness and quiet. When they returned, Professor Quixote was reminded by Miss Dili to pick up on the topic they had left off before the break.

"We were talking about heaven, Sir," she reminded him.

"Ah, yes, heaven," said the professor wistfully. "But where in heaven were we?"

"Should an atheist such as Maria be dreaming about heaven?" Sasha offered. "And if so, should she be able to enjoy it? Does her enjoyment betray her beliefs?"

"That came later," Maria Luisa corrected. "First, I had asked him about our renditions of heaven. Did he like them? My version was so different from Libby's. How can heaven be heaven when it varies so much by individual?"

The professor paced the floor deep in thought. "These are all excellent questions. I'll take Maria Luisa's question first about heaven's diversity. Does it vary by individual? Yes! Absolutely! Why so? …Because Heaven is not cast in steel or granite. It is fluid. Imaginary. It is not a place that anyone knows from experience. It is fictional and as such it is malleable, capable of being molded to the heart's desire of each imaginer. People elaborate on what others have imagined and refashion it to their liking; they add their own touches and their own coloring because heaven leaves a lot of room for personal touches.

"Heaven is like a cold spot inside the sun, a paradise that you can reach only by dying. But it does have common characteristics which are shared by various religions and cultures. Let me have you think about these for a minute. Could you name the common characteristics? And which of these would you say is the most important?"

There was a long silence in the room as the girls thought of an answer. The professor paced the floor, allowing time for the girls to cogitate on the issue. But the minds of the girls were sluggish tonight. The thinking wheels turned lazily. Everyone was stalling, as if waiting for someone else to come up with an answer. Sasha was the first to break out of the impasse and clear the air by saying: "I give up. I think we have a rhetorical silence here. We're all just waiting for you to go ahead and tell us what in due time we won't be able to stop you from telling us anyway. So, please let the poor pregnant pause give birth without further delay."

That perked up everyone. The girls howled over Sasha's petulant remarks. "Fair enough," conceded the professor, good-naturedly. "Your bluntness is, as usual, most disarming, Sasha. Well, I'll get to the point before you put me in the rack."

He paced a little more, collecting his thoughts and then he said: "In my opinion, the most important common characteristic about heaven is that it is Everyman's concept of perfection. It is ideal, but it lacks specificity and leaves room for personal ideation. So rare is the concept, so sublime, that we presume it is saturated by everything good, by purity, virtue, and bliss. There is no poverty there, no famine, no drought, and no imperfection of any sort, no diseases, no pain, and no unrequited love. You breathe happiness. The air is suffused with love and joy forever. It is the Utopia of all Utopias, the entelechy of all entelechies, the fulfillment of all the secret longings of the human heart. Its common essence is the figment of the impossible. It is the enigma that only death reveals.

"Because heaven is ultimately personal, heaven can be static in stagnant minds, or it can be dynamic in free thinking minds. In the stagnant minds, heaven is a nebula that has not changed in a thousand years. For these minds, the heaven of 999 A.D. is the same as that of 1999 A.D. In this category are the ascetics, the ultra religious, the monks and nuns who live in another world from the rest of us. But I am also thinking of non-religious people whose minds also happen to be impervious to change. These are primitive people such as nomads, aborigines, tribal people, and the Taliban, who are wrapped up in stultifying traditions. For these people, the centuries will come and go, and the world will pass them by while they continue to adhere unchangingly to the views of their most remote ancestors. These people have another characteristic in common with the people of the cloth. They have no aspiration for freedom and happiness on this earth. They eschew physical comfort and material well-being here. Their life is rustic, harsh and brutish, but they brook it because they are more focused on the promise of a nebulous better life after death. In some cases, this belief in the promise of heaven is so extreme that they have little regard for life in this world. The infatuation with the promise of heaven makes some of them fanatics to the point they lust for death. For these people, martyrdom is a ticket to heaven.

"Then we come to the other extreme and consider people who are content with this world; who are free and free-thinking; who are happy and who enjoy life. They are in no hurry to die. Life is good, but it can always be improved; it can be made a little more heavenly right here on earth. These people have an eye on the future and are always eager to try new things, new technologies. They are the first to reap the latest crop of new inventions and modern ways. They are what we would call *noveleros* in Spanish, *avant guardes* in French, fad-chasers, hip, with-it sort of people. For these people, heaven is the glamorization of the impossible; it is a carte blanche for the imagination. I was most attentive to your tricks in describing heaven in your dream series. There were interesting differences between Li and Marilu. Li went for the future, showing us the whiz of the latest technology, while Marilu went for the past, for the vivification of history, for intellectual delights. She used very few props, nothing more than a room full of great mathematicians engaging in serious shoptalk. Now, I am not passing judgment on which was better, or which view I prefer. As a matter of fact, I liked both dreams very much. Heaven could be spiritual and intellectual. It need not be all razzmatazz.

"Both of you invoked time travel. Good thing you did, because time travel always conjures up flavors of the impossible and whiffs of the unreachable which is, incidentally, another one of the characteristics of heaven. I can't emphasize enough how important the sense of the impossible is to heaven, that's why I think of it as a cold oasis within the sun. Heaven, like a distant better future, invites you to conjure up what is impossible now, but may be real some day. Heaven is the outer limit of human dreams.

Looking back through history, you will see mankind reaching out for heaven through its dreams, through its visions of the yet unrealized but feasible possibilities. But fantasy is tantalizing as long as it remains impossible. When fantasy becomes doable it loses its magic; it becomes déjà vu. For example, one of those perennial dreams of man through history has been flying. Not for nothing, angels have wings and epitomize this ideal as something you'll be able to do in heaven. Man has envied the angels and the birds from time immemorial and has tried to emulate them, only to fail. In an earlier dream, you all had Maria cavorting in the sky to the tune of the song 'Volare.' From the early Greeks we have one Icarus who got off the ground but flew so high that his wings melted by getting too close to the sun. Even Leonardo da Vinci added his efforts to the lore of flying. As long as man failed at it, flying remained a chimerical quest, a stab at reaching for heaven. But when the Wright brothers succeeded in flying, even if it was for only a few seconds, they turned fiction into fact, and fantasy into science. From then on, it was only a matter of perfecting aviation to get us where we are. So it was, also, with Jules Verne's trip to the moon in the 1800s. That quest became history in 1969. These human successes pushed us closer to that outer boundary of heaven that hovers like a ceiling over our dreams.

"I was amused to see Li's mode of transportation. She pushed flying beyond all limits. She rode on a cushion of air, powered by will. Remember when she grabbed John and Maria by the waist and took off? That is so far out that it is several millennia away. It is off my radar screen. However, other things in her bag of tricks are already doable, such as dispensing with a waiter to take your order and bring you your drink. Heck, ATM machines and banks chutes already do that sort of thing, although it hasn't been applied to bars, as in Li's case. Other things are in the works right now, even as we speak. For example, Steve Jobs of Apple Computer is working on something that will be called an 'iPod' and will hit the market very soon. Also, Larry Page and Sergey Brin—virtual unknowns now—are working on a web search engine that will revolutionize information sharing in just a few years. It will be called 'Google' and it will become a household word. Within the next three years you will be able to get any song from the internet. The lyrics will come by way of Google and the music by way of iTunes and your iPod. What Li was able to do will become déjà vu very soon. And that's not all. The performance of Rita Pavone will be reproduced visually as well, through something called 'You Tube' which will also become a household world. The advances over the last century have been phenomenal, but they are getting old. It is these frills that I just mentioned, these developments that are just budding, that are so titillating now, and that were examples of heaven's tricks in Li's dream. We are spoiled by living in an age where stunning advances keep coming out at a rapid dizzying pace. We come to expect change, innovation, and progress to improve the quality of our lives. Will it ever stop? That's very unlikely. Heaven will always be above us, challenging us to reach it, and in the process, forcing us to come up with better things that make life on earth a little more heavenly. Now let me see, did I cover all the issues?"

Maria raised her hand. "I have a question. Is death one of the other universal features about heaven? Does it always have to come up, even in dreams?"

"Absolutely! This is, indeed, another prerequisite. No death, no heaven. It's as simple as that! Death is the ultimate barrier that ensures the other prerequisite, impossibility. Death is the abyss between us and heaven. Death is at the gate of heaven. Li's and

Marilu's heavens recognized the need to acknowledge death, and both invoked Maria's demise in some fashion. In Maria Luisa's case, it was through that obnoxious announcer on the intercom system who ferried souls from limbo to heaven. The implication was that if you were on that ferry, then you had to be dead. In Libby's dream it was by a tongue in cheek acknowledgement. It's a wonder it worked, because Maria and John merely paid lip service to the subject. They did not dwell on death, but they felt obliged to make oblique references to it, piling clichés upon clichés. For example, they said that Elena was not able to join them in heaven because she was too fit and healthy. Maria was in heaven by virtue of having caught John. And John managed to get in because he had been, as he put it, dying' to meet Maria and so on. Death is the ticket to get into the heavenly show."

Maria was shaking her head, still bothered by something. "Well, death still gives me problems," she said uneasily. "It raises a contradiction. How can I entertain thoughts about heaven when I do not believe in an afterlife? Why don't I wake up on the spot? Why am I fooled into believing such fantasies, even in dreams?"

"And enjoying them to boot," added Sasha.

"The reason is that during dreams about heaven, death is a dramatic prop. It is like the token money in a game of Monopoly. It is fake money, but it gives you the illusion of wealth and, above all, it enables you to play the game. Dream death lacks gravitas and for that reason it does not interfere with your bedrock beliefs. It suspends these beliefs temporarily so you can enjoy the dream. Why not? For example, you may not believe in UFOs, and yet you may enjoy a science fiction movie about them; you may not believe in vampires, but you could be delightfully scared out of your wits by a Bela Lugosi or Christopher Lee flick; you may not believe that animals can talk and carry on as humans, and yet you may enjoy a funny cartoon with Daffy Duck and Bugs Bunny. Life is full of myths and fantasies. Look at Halloween; look at carnivals, and Christmas. There are all sorts of fictitious worlds populated by legendary idols,

Superman, Wonder Woman, fairy godmothers, leprechauns, Donald Duck and Mickey Mouse. No adult believes in these fictitious worlds, but they are entertaining and there is nothing wrong with indulging in their fantasy. Heaven falls in the same category as Santa Claus and Bambi. It's innocuous family fun.

"Anyone can dream about anything under the sun. That goes for atheists dreaming about heaven as well. But there is an important qualification to bear in mind: don't make dreams your master. When we dream, we suspend our critical thinking. We adopt fantastical beliefs temporarily to enjoy the show. There is nothing wrong with this. But you should gravitate back towards your beliefs of long standing when you wake up. The dream will have gotten out of hand if it ends up confusing you and changing your bedrock beliefs, if it causes you to have doubts. In your case, this will happen if you start believing there is an afterlife, and if you feel uncomfortable with your philosophies. In that case, you could have a problem. You could be changing in a fundamental way. Your values and your faith could be in flux. Perhaps religion is the best thing for you. People do change their faiths and their religions, you know. There's nothing wrong with that. But for all of us here, our beliefs are well set, I think. Surely you don't have any problems with your fundamental beliefs, do you?

"Absolutely not!" replied Maria firmly.

"Fine. That's that then."

"Ah, Professor Quixote, this is one of those times when I wish I had had a recorder and could save every word you said. You have clarified so many things and have dispelled so many doubts, so many troubling ideas that were entangled in my mind. I feel much better now. How I wish I could save your words. I don't know if I could ever recapture them on my own."

"Yes, you will. Don't forget, we have a mental bond that makes us part of the same mind. My thoughts are your thoughts, my beliefs, your beliefs. You are bound to find them when you invoke them, and you invoke them when you write. The beliefs are already part of your intellect, part of your value system. You need only summon them and try to articulate them in words. They will practically write themselves."

"I seem to recall Ram telling me the same thing once."

"A poet may not remember his own poems word for word, but if he is sincere when he writes he cannot change his values and his beliefs anymore than a zebra can change his stripes or a leopard his spots. He will know what he stands for, and he'll be able to articulate his philosophies, albeit in different words."

Maria looked sheepishly at him, trying to make excuses for not starting on her writing project right away. "Tomorrow I will not be able to write because I'll be touring John."

"Well, Sunday then, or Monday," said Prof. Quixote.

Z   z   z   z   z   z   Z

59. LOVE BURST

There was no dream this morning for lack of time. Sasha was told to hold her dream of heaven for another day. The discussion about heaven had dragged on for too long. Besides, Maria would have no time for dreams this morning. This was the day when John would return for the full tour. From the moment she got up she was frenetic. John would be there in the early afternoon, around 1:30, and she still had no concrete plans for the day, what they should do or where they would go. She had several ideas, but she still had not whittled them down to a specific plan. Her mind flitted between one possibility and another, unable to decide on anything. Where should she take him first? It would make sense to start in nearby places such as Coral Gables, or Little Havana. Had he ever drunk coconut milk out of a coconut—she wondered—or had he ever had sugarcane juice freshly squeezed from the cane? All these things they could have on *Calle Ocho*, the hub of Little Havana. Had he ever tried fried plantains? But it had better leave those for some time when her mother could make them at home. There were many possibilities and her mind flitted about them like a bird jumping from branch to branch, incapable of deciding.

But the thought to which she invariably returned—if only briefly because she did not like to dwell on it for long—was sex. When would they do it, if they did it? She tried to think of other things; she told herself not to fret about it, but her thoughts always returned to that. Perhaps they should wait till evening, till such a time when she was good and ready. Maybe she should meet him in the parking lot and not let him get out of the car even. She should hop right in before he ever parked and say: "Okay, let's go and start the tour." That would solve the problem or at least postpone it. There were so many places to go. There was Vizcaya... such a lovely, enchanting place, but it could take all day, and it was too far. She straightened out the apartment; she vacuumed and dusted; and she cleaned the bathroom till the faucet fixtures glittered like brand new and the porcelain and the tiles had sheen. She loved bathrooms that were impeccably clean and antiseptic. Beauty and sparkle were one of her manias, and she thought John would appreciate it.

I wonder if it hurts… I wonder if that detracts from the woman's pleasure. Should she start it? Or should she let him make the first move? She was too nervous to be in the mood. Oh, stop it! Enough now! Maybe nothing will happen…better put on a tape and dust some more. By 1 p.m. she couldn't stand the anticipation anymore and she called her mother just to distract her mind and help pass the time away, but her mother was out shopping. She talked only briefly with her dad.

A wild idea ran through her mind, goading her to do something seductive and naughty. Why not greet him at the door wearing a robe and a towel over her head, as if she were running late and had just come out of the shower? Somewhere back in the recesses of her mind there was the faint memory of a dream that suggested that. She could then spread out the robe and flash him, announcing he had won the big jackpot. Forces inside her were urging her to do it, daring her. She was tempted to do it for a moment, but she soon quelled the idea with disgust. No, she would not do that. That was the sort of thing one sees in B movies or in bad dreams, she told herself; that was something she did not feel comfortable doing in real life. It was not for her and that was final.

She was fully dressed when John finally arrived some ten minutes late, which seemed like hours to her. It was a moderately warm day in the mid-80s, and Maria wore a white chambray summer dress under a light linen blue shirt. She had put on her walking shoes, low-heeled pumps, in case they toured on foot. As far as she was concerned, he was coming to be toured, and she was going to give him a tour. Of course, if fate in its wondrous ways led them casually, without forcing the issue, into other pursuits, she could live with that as well. *Che sera, sera.* For starters, however, she would go deadpan with no funny business and nothing skanky.

John, on the other hand, had other things in mind from the

moment he came in. She met him at the door to her apartment. They greeted each other warmly with hugs and kisses. Then she asked him if he was ready to go on the tour. He replied: "A tour of you, yes." She blushed and changed the subject. She asked if she could serve him a drink, but he declined.

"Well, then, I'll have one," she said, getting away. "Are you sure you won't change your mind?"

"No. I'll just drink from your lips."

John was very perceptive. He realized immediately that she was nervous. He did not press the issue anymore. This was all too abrupt for her. He simply could not pick up where he had left off the night before last, even though she had been properly primed then. Too much time had elapsed in between. She was uneasy and needed to be cajoled and humored. A good man shouldn't swim against a woman's tide, he told himself. It's better to go with her flow, even if she is lost and doesn't know where she is going. Such are the idiosyncrasies of femininity. Little did he know that there had been a struggle within Maria herself. Two of the girls from dream central, Libby and Sasha, had pushed for the skanky, vamp demeanor, but Maria Luisa and Maria had prevailed.

Maria went behind her kitchen counter and served herself a diet coke as she talked about places she could take him. But he interrupted her, asking her a question that denuded her and mortified her.

"Maria, you wouldn't be having your period, would you?

"No. I am not," she said blushing.

"Sorry I had to ask. I noticed you are nervous today. I think you are dying to get away. I think you feel trapped in you own house. You would love to walk out of here into the madding crowds this very minute so you would feel safe and at ease. I think I scare you out of your wit today. So, here is my suggestion regarding this situation. Could we go some place nearby where we could walk around for a while, and then come back and rest for a bit before going out again?"

Maria beamed. That was a splendid idea. She emptied her coke on the sink. It was mostly untouched, proving that the drink had been just a prop which she no longer needed. She was relieved and extremely appreciative of his understanding. He knew just what to say and what to do to make her feel at ease and to inspire love in her. Already she was feeling much better about him. They went to *Calle Ocho* (8th Street) where she introduced him to freshly squeezed sugarcane and to the Latin ambience. They also stopped for a cup of Cuban coffee. John was amused to see how small the demitasse cup was. "This is good for only two or three sips at the most," he said jokingly.

Maria explained that that is the way Cubans like their coffee. "The word for coffee in Spanish is *café*," she began. "There is an apocryphal story about it. Someone made up an explanation for each letter of the word as if it were an acronym, which it is not. Supposedly, the 'C' stands for *caliente* (hot); the 'A' for *amargo* (bitter); the 'F' for *fuerte* (strong); and the 'E' for *escaso* (scanty). That is why you get a thimble's worth of potent, unsweetened extract. I certainly drink it this way, without sugar. But the Cubans have put their own twist on the 'A'. For them, the 'A' must stand for *azucarado* (sugary), because they are very generous with the sugar."

"Yes, this is extremely cloyed," John agreed. "It's almost like the liquor '*Tía Maria*.' But I'm with you. I'll drink it the way you do, without sugar. It just goes to prove what I've observed again and again when I'm around you. The more I know you, the more I agree with you, the more affinity I find between us, the more I like you, and the more I love you."

"I feel the same way. I love you more by the hour it seems. I am sorry if I acted strangely. I guess I was nervous, and I can see why you asked me if I was incapacitated. I am glad we came out. I feel much better."

The outing had, indeed, done wonders for Maria. She was in a different mood. She was more herself, less inhibited, more affectionate and more smitten by love. A song kept going through her mind that made her feel like dancing, and she kept humming it. She couldn't wait to get home to play it for John.

"This song makes me feel so happy and carefree. I will play it for you as soon as we get home. I have never heard such panache and defiance in a song. The woman is so in love, she is telling Heaven it can keep all it's got, so long as it lets her have him. Nothing else matters. Who cares about the world out there… for her, Heaven is just the two of them."

The song that was so exhilarating—to the point of being intoxicating—was Rita Pavone's *"Che me Importa del Mondo,"* (What Do I Care About the World). It was the same song she had heard in Li's dream of Heaven. It reprised her dream of that party in Heaven. As soon as they got back to her apartment, she played the song. The music now drew sensual kinesics in Maria that would have been impossible an hour earlier. She moved, half dancing, expressing in body language the paean to a free spirit that the song inspired. John loved watching her. That song had injected fire in her veins again. She was ready for love making. They played the song one more time, until they became catapulted to heights from which there was no turning back. They loved and loved for hours, till the afternoon faded into dusk, till it was dark, and the surfeit of love gave way to other necessities of living again, like going out to eat. When Maria came out into the night air she felt as if she had been reborn into full womanhood and was a complete human being for the first time in her life. They went to Miami Beach for dinner that evening. Then they came home and loved again. He spent the night there and a good part of Sunday. They were two independent bodies with their hearts fused into one by love.

Z   z   z   z   z   z   Z

Part XI: A Final Dawning

60. THE REST OF 1999

The months flew by for Maria as she became busy with her new life. She didn't begin to work on her novel about the dialogues of the mind during sleep until late December. By that time, she was already married and seven months pregnant.

In the ensuing months since she met John, she had become much happier. She dreamed as much as before, but she remembered less. Her focus was on the real world. She had become less introspective. Quitting teaching had done wonders for her temperament. She used her free time to become better informed and more concerned about the world. She read the newspapers and news magazines more thoroughly, and she expanded her set of information sources. She watched more TV, but it was the informative programs like "60 Minutes," "Nightline," "This Week," "Meet the Press" and "Face the Nation." It was as if her sleep characters Maria Luisa, Sasha, and Prof. Quixote had been replaced by real commentators such as Tom Brokaw, Cokie Roberts, Sam Donaldson, and George Will. She remembered having dreams in which the TV celebrities, and not the girls, played a role.

She did keep a diary, but her entries showed very little analysis of her dreams. For the most part her diary was a calendar of activities, doctor visits, appointments, and social gatherings. When there was commentary in her diary, it was only about life in the real world –nothing about the mind at night. From time to time, events in the news would impact her emotionally and she would write a few lines. Such, for example, was the case with the untimely death of John F. Kennedy, Jr. in July of 1999. Although Maria did not know him personally, she grieved his loss because he was an icon bigger than life, Prince Charming, a handsome creature who, as an immortal demigod, wasn't supposed to die. His untimely death was unbearable, especially at such a time, so soon before the end of the millennium. She felt as though she and he had been running together as members of the same generation, but he had dropped out and could not make it to the next benchmark, to the end of the century, to the start of a new millennium. He had been so near it, just beyond the bend, but he was cut off before reaching it. His death nullified so much of what one expects from life. It awoke her from the false sense of immortality that the young inadvertently profess. Although she did not remember it, she must have had long discussions with Prof. Quixote around that time.

Another event that caught the attention of Maria and made it into her diary occurred in November —and right in her own backyard. The eyes of the world were focused on Miami when a little boy by the name of Elian Gonzales took to the sea with his mother, escaping from Cuba, trying to reach the U.S. Here, also, fate played out an incredible human tragedy. There was a mishap at sea and the mother perished off the Florida coast. Somehow, the little boy held on to a raft and survived the journey. Fortunately, he had relatives in Miami; so, despite the loss of his mother, there was a redeeming element to his odyssey. But there was one complication. Elian's father, who had remained in Cuba, demanded him back. The trouble was that, in the meanwhile, the Cuban community in Miami had assumed the role of surrogate mother for the little boy and held on to him tenaciously. They would not give him back, no matter what. The controversy flared into an international political incident that pitted the rights of a father against the dreams of a mother who died trying to reach the U.S. shore, trying to give her child a future here. Janet Reno, who was the U.S. Attorney General at the time—and who happened to be from Miami—was called upon to be Solomonic in deciding whether the child should stay here or go back to his father in Cuba. Maria, who had already seen Janet Reno in her dreams as a surrogate for her own conscience, followed this story devotedly daily. In her heart of hearts, Maria wished Elian could remain here, but she admired the unpopular stand that Janet Reno took and applauded the firmness with which she carried out her decision that Elian should be returned to his father.

The pages of her diary earlier in the year, especially the

entries for that week in late April when Maria first made love, were full of commentary about heaven—the ethereal Heaven with the hedonistic touches of a heavenly party, and the real one in Miami. That time unfurled a golden period that turned her life into a whirlwind of joyous days. Nothing untoward happened then. One good thing came right after another in rapid succession. John met Maria's parents the following week and a mutual admiration society was established. John liked Clara's cooking and encouraged her to be sure and pass her culinary talents on to her daughter. Pedro Santoro finally overcame his infection and came out of the hospital. There was a round of parties for Maria before school ended. After school was out, she often went to West Palm Beach. It was the thing to do to save John traveling time. On several occasions she spent the night in his apartment. By May, they were already living together as a loving couple, and both wanted to formalize their relationship as soon as possible because by June they had learned that Maria was pregnant. Maria then started looking for a house to buy in West Palm Beach. Those were busy days.

In late May another memorable and momentous event took place. John took Maria to Savannah, Georgia, to meet his parents. That also went very well. His parents loved Maria, and Maria, in turn, embraced them warmly as her future in-laws. There was a bonus surprise on that visit. It was the city of Savannah itself. Maria loved it. Had she known Savannah was as beautiful, as unique and exceptionally charming as it was, she would have visited it many times. She looked forward to coming back again. John suggested half jokingly that they should move there, since she liked it so much. He was taken aback by Maria's unequivocal, quick and enthusiastic response. She was game. Nothing would please her more.

The church wedding was still a problem. As expected, Clara was hurt and disappointed by Maria's resolve not to have a church wedding. She continued to press the point, hoping that Maria would change her mind, but Maria stood firm. They had a quiet civil ceremony in July and then, as man and wife under the law, they had two big receptions. The reception in Miami, which was Maria's concession to her mother, was the bigger of the two, because in addition to the Valverde clan, it drew out of the woodwork friends and relatives that Maria did not know she had. Of course, her own friends from school days such as Karen Powers, Elena, and Pedro Santoro had a special place of honor. The reception in Savannah was more family oriented and brought out John's siblings and their families. Maria was delighted with all of them. A fresh new life was starting on the dawn of a new millennium. She couldn't ask for anything more.

As for the honeymoon, Maria would have loved to take a month-long honeymoon, but John could take off, at most, ten days. He left the choice of where and when entirely to Maria. She didn't have to think very hard. It was hot as blazes everywhere in Florida, but in the southern hemisphere they were in full winter. So, they went to Buenos Aires for four days and three days to Rio. Rio was fun, delightful and memorable. But Buenos Aires had a special attraction for her. It was the fulfillment of a wish upon a star that had come due. It beckoned her with an irrepressible pull. She heard the fleeting passages from tangos rising from her dreams and she was drawn to their source. Buenos Aires was inevitable. It was her future finally knocking at the door of her present. She loved Buenos Aires, and she came back loaded with tangos.

Z   Z   Z   z   Z   Z   Z

61. SASHA'S HEAVEN

Sasha's dream, which had been scheduled for one of those days in late April when Maria was enjoying a festival of heavenly dreams, had to be postponed because on the night when it would have been shown Maria had asked for an extraordinary session with Prof. Quixote. She had many questions for him, she felt unsettled, nervous, eager to get a hold of her new life. That was the night they discussed so many things: writing, the nature of Heaven, whether an atheist had a right to even dream of heaven. Above all, this was the night when Prof. Quixote exhorted her to write. It was a way of summoning the spirits of the night and keeping in touch with her lost world. Writing could become more than just a new intellectual endeavor; it could even become a new career for Maria. All this left no time for Sasha's dream. Circumstances conspired against Sasha. By the following night, Heaven was déjà vu. It would have been the third dream in three consecutive nights. This was also a period when the real world asked for nothing from Heaven, when life on earth was a whirlwind of bliss as it was, when Heaven had an address, and it was home in Miami. Each day was like a cup that ran over its brim with happiness. That was the week when Maria felt the ebullience of her youth at its maximum, when she discovered the intense gratification that sex can bring when it is exalted by love. Heaven could wait.

Sasha bided her time and waited for the appropriate moment. That moment came some time in December when Maria was reading Shakespeare. She was deeply immersed in his verses and moved by the power of his words, having just read *Hamlet* and being midway through *Romeo and Juliet.* She could not stop gushing with admiration. Every page was a delight for all the similes and metaphors that rang so true. Shakespeare's virtuosity was phenomenal. His use of tropes and rhetorical tricks was masterful. His poetry was eternal. Above all, Maria was mystified by his prodigious vocabulary, which was like a parade of roses for her. The sense and sound of his words, the ease with which he used them, their appropriateness, the number, and variety were of no mortal, but of a god! Where did he ever get so many words? How could he keep them viable, at the tip of his tongue and on call for when he needed them? His active vocabulary was beyond the norm; it was double or even triple that of an educated man. And then there was his prolific output, which also defied credulity. How could he find the hours in one lifetime to write so much? No wonder scholars were always coming up with theories to explain it, claiming that it was someone else, or that it was several others using the same name. Language aside, it was the humanity of the man that impressed Maria the most. He must have covered a lot of worlds—both in a geographical and figurative sense. How many languages did he speak? His worldliness and his knowledge of mankind seemed timeless. He knew the pompous man, the pedant, the ambitious, the avaricious, the murderer, the jealous, the schemer, the liar, the true and loyal, the feckless, the virtuous, the brave and the wise. Nobody escaped him. Without a doubt, Shakespeare would be one of the personalities in the whole world and for all time that she would wish to meet. He would be her pick for the most interesting human being to visit in Heaven.

That was all Sasha needed to spring into action with her dream. It opened with Maria on a plane bound from Miami to Savannah via Atlanta. She was, supposedly, going to look for houses in Savannah.

Strange things began to happen in the flight. As they approached Atlanta, the pilot made an announcement that seemed a little odd. It was something to the effect that those passengers who were headed for Athens should proceed to the head of the plane to be dropped off. Maria, who happened to be reading Shakespeare at the time, did not pay much attention and thought they would make a quick stop in Athens, Georgia—site of the University of Georgia and not far from Atlanta. But a few minutes later she heard an even more bizarre announcement.

"And now, Ladies and Gentlemen, from the golden age of

Greece to the grandeur that was Rome at the time of the Caesars. We will be making our next drop-off in the eternal city around year zero."

Maria was perplexed. She knew there was a town by the name of Rome, which also was not far from Atlanta, but the pilot had ruled that out when he made it clear that he meant Rome, Italy--and in a bygone era. Maria called the stewardess for clarification. The stewardess was a perky and lithesome young woman whose name tag read: "Sasha."

"What's going on?" began Maria. "I know there is a saying in Georgia that even after death, you must go through Atlanta. Whether you go to Heaven or Hell, you still must go through Atlanta. But are we doing this in reverse order now, going through every place on earth first before landing in Atlanta? Also, could you clarify for me what the pilot just announced about the date being year zero?"

Sasha smiled and sat beside her. "I think we need to talk."

To Maria, Sasha was a perfect stranger. She bore a certain resemblance to Audrey Hepburn, boyish, thin, and charming.

"We are traveling in time," Sasha explained. "We just left the Athens of about 300 B.C. Next, we will be coming up to Rome at about the time of Christ. And if you are thinking that you're dead and on some sort of voyage to Heaven, no, you are not dead. This is not really the afterlife. I know you don't believe that. This is simply a dream, the fulfillment of a wish you expressed once upon a time, and which you have re-expressed many times over recently."

"What wish was that?"

"That if you could travel back in time and meet one person from the whole of history, you would love to meet Shakespeare. There were so many questions you wanted to ask him. Isn't it exciting? We are going to fulfill your wish. In a few minutes, after we leave Rome, we are going to proceed at warp speed straight for London in the Elizabethan era. We have arranged for you to have an interview with Shakespeare."

Maria kept shaking her head in frustration. "Normally, I

would be delighted, but this is so weird that I am more in a state of shock. There is so much I don't get yet. You say: 'we have arranged an interview…' Well, who is 'we'?"

"Good question… we are your mind, your conscious and your subconscious, but mostly your subconscious right now. We are not an airline, and this is not really a plane. This is your brain all made out to look like a plane, so you can imagine that you are flying and going somewhere. Please try to relax and try to enjoy your dream. Ask questions, but don't overdo it, because dreams are fragile and shatter with too many questions. I will try to be as forthcoming as I can, but I must warn you, we are under a time constraint. By your look I can tell that you are wondering about me. Who am I? Have we met somewhere before?"

"Yes, you read my mind implicitly."

"Well, Maria, the fact is that I am a part of you; I am part of your intellect and part of your psyche. You see me every night, but it is usually in sleep interludes that you do not remember. Only rarely do I appear in dreams that you can keep when you wake up, and tonight is one of those nights. I am going to see to it that you remember this dream, believe me!

"Although you do not remember me now, you and I are very close. We've been through a lot together, especially this year. There are enough adventures for a novel. And this is what makes this so, so sad, that you remember none of it; that I have to introduce myself to you, as if I were a total stranger, after all we've been together. We are like sisters, Maria. But I sit here beside you, remembering everything, while you remember nothing. It's as if you had come up with Alzheimer's and suddenly knew nothing about me. You shut me out. You don't even recognize me. It's so sad, I could just cry."

"Let me ask you something, Sasha. I know you said you are part of my intellect, but where exactly do you fit in my mind?"

"My purview is literature and poetry and involves language in general. What's more, I am always on duty. Of course, during your conscious daylight hours I'm present only in a silent, nonvisual way. You don't see me then and you don't even hear me. We communicate telepathically without articulated words. But as your minion of language, I am always awake when you write. I am your editor, your literary critic. I am like a mirror that helps you don your words and adorn your thoughts in language. I think of myself as your poetic muse, your own resident Erato."

"Oh, Sasha, I don't know what to say. This is so odd. I want to say I am delighted to meet you, but that would be so inappropriate given what you just told me and that you are a part of me. I feel like a prodigal sister returning after a long exile. I almost feel guilty."

"It's not your fault. You can't help it. It's nature's way."

"Would you mind if I ask you a few questions? Please don't think I am testing you. I am just curious. Name some of the poems I've written."

"Let's see. There is 'The Transnighter,' 'Insomnia,' 'Pelagic Voyage,' 'Of Life, Death and Sleep,' 'Nightmare,' 'The Bed,' 'The Alarm Clock' and 'Drowsiness.' In fact, there is an entire series dealing with sleep and dreams. In addition, there are some Sonnets, a few songs, and a whole series of verses about words. Then there is one poem with the longest, repetitive rhyme pattern in the English Language, 'Galois.' But, above all, there is one poem which binds us, which has special significance for us, and which I wrote entirely by myself--although, of course, you typed it for me. I used not only your computer, but your hands and fingers. I was trying to reach you then. I was trying desperately to communicate with you across the great divide between conscious and subconscious to tell you that I existed, to ask you to remember me. The poem was 'Inner Echoes.' Do you remember it?"

"But, of course, I remember it. That poem has always intrigued me. Oh, Sasha, this is amazing! Incredible! It's all beginning to come back to me. Although I still don't remember everything about our relationship, I feel a great kinship with you. You know, it is funny you should mention 'Inner Echoes,' because I would get the strangest feeling every time I saw that poem. I couldn't remember having written it and I couldn't figure how it got on my computer. Worse still, I couldn't think what I was trying to say. Is that weird? The poem eluded me. What was I getting at? It was, indeed, as if somebody else had written it. And now I learn that it was you...'I,' as it were, writing to 'me.' Oh, Sasha. There must be a name for this curse we live under."

Sasha and Maria were both clasping their hands tightly as they spoke. Then Sasha elaborated on the subject. "Well, you know, this sort of thing is common. It happens to poets quite often. They write words that come back to baffle them. The English poet Robert Browning was asked once what he meant by a particular poem, and he replied: 'I thought I knew at one time, but now God only knows.' It's natural that you should feel that way about that poem because it was written from my perspective, not yours. I was decrying the fact that we are so close and yet so distant. We are separated by an abyss between the conscious and subconscious in the human mind. Sadly, I am more aware of you than you are of me. We are close, so close to each other, like twin sisters. But it is all in a world that you cannot always recall. When you are out of that world it is as if the camera that records the action had no film. When you awaken, you go into the bright lights and forget me. I become invisible. You forget all those precious hours we shared together as sisters.

Sasha continued. "A poem of yours comes to mind about this curse. The lines went something like this: Our wakeful hours distill themselves into ingots of recall, into dew drops of remembrance, to form the reservoir of our memories. The water molecules rise to the air; they evaporate into a mist that turns into clouds which will condense and return as rain, or snow, or sleet, or drizzle in a perpetual effluvium which is tantamount to memory recall. When it rains within your brain, it is really your past life that returns in a glorious monsoon that drenches you in recall. You recapture what you thought was lost and that is when you really sing under the rain with joy. But where, alas, do our sleeping hours go?"

Maria interrupted her at that point, saying: "And then I

remember what I replied. Those sleeping hours fall, alas, on the sands of our Sahara like droplets of dew to be evaporated under the sun and swallowed by the scorching sands of oblivion."

"Ah, yes, but you didn't drop things there," continued Sasha. "You became convinced that those hours were retrievable, and that you would find them if you had to dig through the sands of the dessert and squeeze the moisture out of the sand. That is when you decided to go looking for those hours. You made it your quest. You became analytical during your sleep hours. You took half of your consciousness to bed with you. You wanted to be a spy, stealing secrets from the night to bring to broad daylight."

"How well you know me, Sasha. It's uncanny. But tell me more about my lost world of sleep. Are there others?"

"Oh yes, dozens. We are a big happy family. This whole plane is full of us. I am only one of your muses. There is Libby—short for your libido—and there is Guilda your guilt dog, and there is Maria Luisa, your Muse of Mathematics, and a host of clones that represent your instincts. There is Imogene Natien—can you figure out what she represents? And there is Ram, and many, many more. There is even a new one whom we are just getting to know. Her name is Maria Clara. Poor thing, she is klutzy. She may become the future Julia Child or Martha Stewart of your mind, a new culinary muse, but she has a long way to go. She emerged out of the blue when you developed an interest in cooking after you got married. And there are others that come and go and make cameo appearances."

"Do they all look the same? Are they all clones?"

"Not at all, Ram is Indian or Pakistani, but in any case, male; he does not look like you. He morphed himself into that name, I suppose, from the acronym for Random Access Memory, which describes what he does. I understand Ram is a common Pakistani name. I wouldn't be surprised if he popped up anytime now. He is monitoring time and memory for me very closely tonight. He needs to let me know how the memory meter is running. There are two more males: Dr. Broca and Prof. Quixote, who are part of your alter ego and are elderly gentlemen. You are close to both, but especially to Prof. Quixote, who guides you in matters of philosophy and beliefs. As to the girls, do you know what? It just occurred to me; you should be able to remember them because you've had take-home dreams featuring them. Let me see if I can make you recall."

"Oh, this is so exciting."

"Do you remember a dream set in Buenos Aires? It took place in Maria Luisa's apartment. It was X-rated. Poor Maria Luisa was turned into the spinster of *"Nunca Tuvo Novio"* while your libido, personified as Libby, gave lessons in seduction. She had sex with a medical student, and you almost came to a climax as you watched them. Do you remember that?"

"How could I forget? The details of the dream are fuzzy, but I will never forget it because I almost lost my virginity while dreaming."

"All right, if you can remember the women of that dream, you can picture Libby and Maria Luisa. I think Libby was sending you all sorts of messages in that dream. Of course, you've had many more dreams involving them. They do change names and appearances. In fact, in another dream about Heaven, Libby appeared as a Eurasian beauty and called herself Li. This was the dream where you kept playing Rita Pavone's '*Che me importa del mondo.*' You were with John. Do you remember?"

"Yes, yes. I remember the dream, but I can't picture Li. Let me ask you something else. Do we get along with each other, or is there a lot of fighting between us?"

"There is fighting. Libby and Guilda come to blows because, as you can imagine, Guilt and the Libido are not only incompatible, but deadly enemies. As for the rest of us, for the most part we get along beautifully. But we do have our differences. When you and I have words, it is usually about poetry. You accuse me of using too much rhyme, which you don't like. I accuse you of not using it enough. I believe you wrote 'Galois' to spite me, to show me just how much rhyme you could write, and you over did it. I, in turn, wrote 'The Bed' to show you that I can write a whole poem without a drop of rhyme. The poem describes every aspect of a bed that you can think of. By the way, Libby didn't like it. It was flawed, from her standpoint, by an unforgivable omission. She is so transparent. I could see right away what she objected to and, I must admit, it was a major omission for a bed.

"What did you leave out?"

"Take a guess."

"Sex?"

"Exactly."

"How could you? Why?"

"I didn't think sex was important there. You don't have to be encyclopedic. Sex would have detracted from the major theme, which was sleep. Sleep is the big mystery of life. That poem is part of a bigger work; it is only a tile in a big mosaic of sleep. There was a time when you devoted a lot of time to the world of the mind at night."

"This sounds very interesting. I am fascinated by sleep. Tell me more about it."

Sasha suddenly turned pale, as if she had just remembered something terrible. "Oh, my God, Maria, I just realized something. We are running out of time. What is even worse, we are running out of memory as well. We are up against that curse you have decried so many times yourself; the damn memory constrains of the dreaming mind. How many times have you cried and pulled your hair in despair about this unfairness of nature. It is so frustrating."

"Get hold of yourself, Sasha. You are not making sense. You forget that I don't remember, and don't know what you are talking about. What unfairness?"

"That none of this will be remembered! Your memory receptacle for carrying dreams into your consciousness is very small. This dream is about to exceed the limit, and I haven't even begun to tell you half of what I wanted you to remember. Anything you dream beyond this point will start taping over what you have already dreamed, erasing me and everything we have discussed."

"But that's ridiculous!"

"That's the way it is. That's the unfairness you've lamented and there is very little we can do about it, except play tricks to try to fool nature. And, oh, speak of the devil, oh no, it's sooner than I thought! Look over there! I see Ram already coming out of the cabin to give us bad news."

Ram stood in the middle of the aisle, as stewards are wont to do when they demonstrate the safety features of the plane. He made gestures, pointing to his watch, then to his head, twirling his hands about, nixing out something, drawing Xs in the air with his arms and ending with a gesture of timeout, which he accentuated by a feigned slit to his throat.

"What was that about?" Maria asked.

"What I just told you. We are entering the time for Shakespeare's dream. We are about to land in London. That means that all this is kaput now. You will remember none of it tomorrow. You will forget me. The only thing you will remember is what you are about to dream from this point on, and that will be the upcoming interview with Shakespeare."

"Then in that case, the heck with Shakespeare. Let him wait," said Maria. "I don't want to lose you. I'd much rather retain what you have told me. Tell me more or rerun the dream if you have to. Tell the captain to keep going, I don't want to land."

"Do you mean that? It will mess up their plans, but it will help me enormously. Let me go see what I can do."

Sasha went up to the cockpit. There was arguing and shouting. Ram was very upset with her, but Sasha came back looking victorious.

"We caught it just in time. I told you there were tricks to get around nature's constraints. They agreed to my suggestion, but reluctantly. Even so, we are going to have to do some odd things so you can walk off with most of what I've told you. Also, this may get a little wild and scary towards the end. Are you up to dreaming dangerously?"

"Whatever you say, I'm game."

"Okay, then. Relax now. We'll have up to five or six minutes. Let's make them count. I'm sorry we won't get to talk to Shakespeare because I, too, wanted to ask him something. I've developed a theory about him. Perhaps some other time we shall have the Shakespeare dream. There's so much I want to ask him. The especial connection that you and I have—that of muse and poet—is common with other writers. In particular, you can imagine that Shakespeare, of all people, must have had one. But Shakespeare did us one better, much, much better! I believe that his muse was actually made of flesh and blood, and it was actually separate from him. Even so, it was uniquely intertwined to him. It was, in fact, another human being, an identical twin. Can you imagine the possibilities? If, in addition, they had mental telepathy, then anything was possible. Only such an arrangement could explain Shakespeare's superhuman accomplishments. He could lead two lives! The twins—Bill and Will—must have communicated with each other constantly, maintaining the information in their brains up to date. They could share all sorts of experiences, real as well as sleep experiences. Their bodies could have worked in shifts giving them an immense advantage. While one rested the other went about performing the physical tasks of life. Bill would tune in to Will's dreaming mind from time to time and jot down what was happening if it seemed important. Thus, they got to keep their dreams. Their lives were so much fuller because it included their sleeping interludes—the very thing you've been trying to rescue from the sands of your Sahara. They were able to keep the time wasted in sleep to a minimum.

"That, of course, is not the case with us. This is the sort of thing you tried to get around. But nothing can be done about it. This is part of the human condition. Only Shakespeare beat it! This is what I will ask him when I meet him in a dream. Where is your twin? Would you be Will or Bill? But never mind. Back to us.

If you only knew the schemes that we came up with to

salvage your sleep interludes. You tried stealing from those forbidden dreams by wrapping them inside the allowable dreams. The trouble was that the package was too large for the wrappers. I came up with a wild idea myself once. What if I were to wake you up several times during the night so you could transfer your dreams onto long term memory bit by bit? In between naps you would have been able to write them on your computer. The trouble was that we hadn't solved the problem of how to wake you up. Nightmares could do it, but they would drive you crazy. Also, you were not too happy about the idea of sleep interruptus through the night. Those were just fanciful schemes. The only thing Prof. Quixote thought would work was writing. He really believed that if you became a writer, you could keep your lost world.

"How?" Maria asked incredulously. "Writing what?"

"…A novel. We even had a couple of titles: "Adventures of the Mind at Night," or "Stealing Forbidden Dreams." He thought that when you wrote, you would summon all of us: your logic, your intuition, your imagination, your memory, your ego, your libido, your conscience, your intellect and your muses. We would all be there contributing, even though you couldn't see us. I didn't believe it would be as easy as Prof. Quixote thought. I think you needed more of a push from us. And, incidentally, this is the reason for this dream. I wanted to remind you that one night during one of those long sessions, you agreed to write the novel. The idea was that as you wrote, you would come to know us, and we would populate a world of fiction as rich and varied as any in the real world. That is what you would find under the sands of your Sahara. You would show the world that those hours were not wasted, and you would lead the way into the grottos and caverns of the mind. Well, the truth is that months have gone by, and you have written nothing, except a few verses related to sleep. We all know you have been busy. You've started a new life. You are happily married. Your life awake is so engaging that you have forgotten us. We are very happy for you, don't get me wrong. We don't begrudge you that. Prof.

Quixote keeps reminding us that that is what really matters. If we cared for you, we should leave you alone. In time, perhaps, you will get around to writing about us. But I wanted to make one last-ditch effort to remind you of your promise and to let you know where things stood."

"Don't feel badly, Sasha. I am glad you told me. I do want to keep the communication open with all of you and I will write. I am sorry that I have not kept my promise. But I'll try again, especially if I can keep this as a reminder. How much of this will I remember tomorrow?"

"Most of it since we are not going to meet Shakespeare. But let me check with Ram."

Sasha went back to Ram's station near the cockpit and engaged in technical consultations and discussions with him. Once again, she came back very encouraged and enthusiastic, giving Maria some thumbs up.

"We have to act fast. They are going to allow me to implement a fantastic idea that will help you remember us when you wake up. Are you ready for it?"

Sasha led Maria to the cockpit, telling her that she had a great surprise for her. When they got to the cockpit, Prof. Quixote and Dr. Broca were already standing up waiting for her. "Hello, Maria," they both intoned in unison. Maria cried tears of joy as she hugged them.

"I feel as though I've known you forever, even if my recollection is very vague. I feel so close to you all. I love you. Ah, you must be Maria Luisa. Don't tell me you are the navigator also. That figures, for a mathematician. You resemble me even more than Sasha."

Maria went around hugging them one by one, saying something personal to connect with each of them.

"Ah, you must be Libby. I looked for you in Buenos Aires during my honeymoon."

"And did you find me?"

"Everywhere… in every tanned beautiful young woman I saw in Biela by the Recoleta, or in Calle Florida, or in Puerto Madero, or in San Telmo. You really get around."

Then she came to someone who, for a minute, she could not identify because she did not resemble her at all. She was petite and with a disproportionately large head for such a thin body. She wore short, boyish hair and big dark-rimmed glasses that made her look artistic. "Ah, Imogene, how could I ever miss you? I could have picked you out blindfolded. But I do remember having seen you in brief cameo appearances. You are responsible for the most beautiful dreams I ever had, dreams for which you should have won Oscars."

Behind Imogene, standing by the galley wearing an apron, was someone that Maria had never seen, but who bore a striking resemblance to her mother. If Maria had had a sister, that's what this young woman would have looked like. Her hair was auburn light like her mother's, and she had the same body build. The apron also gave away her identity. "Hello, Maria Clara. What's cooking?"

"You wouldn't want to taste it," said Sasha.

As Maria looked towards the back of the plane she saw several people looking towards her, and she recognized Janet Reno, Abraham Lincoln and Mother Teresa. Instinctively, she knew what they represented, disguises for her conscience. Just ahead of her was a big burly Amazon of a woman who was fast asleep and snoring like a lion. That'd be Guilda, she thought to herself.

"Come on. Let sleeping dogs lie," said Sasha as she led her back to her seat. "We need to get moving."

Sasha installed Maria back in her seat and turned on the monitor. "I've asked Ram to replay the scenes that he recorded earlier. Look at these till we land. It will freshen what transpired here a few minutes ago."

Maria saw herself listening to the pilot's announcement about Athens and then about Rome at year zero. Then she fast-forwarded till she saw Sasha joining her. She could fast-forward and replay certain segments, then rush again, reliving the minutes of the last hour, committing them to memory as if she were cramming for an exam. Suddenly the plane started to rattle, toss and shake, freefalling at times as if it had encountered serious turbulence. Seconds went by that seemed like hours, with no let up on the rough ride. Luggage started falling from the overhead compartments. Then the plane began a precipitous downward spiral, out of control, and Maria for the first time thought the unthinkable. We are going to crash. I'm going to die. Instinctively, she put her hands on her belly saying: "My baby, my poor baby…I never even got to see you…"

Z   Z   Z   z   Z   Z   Z

62. New Millennium

It was 6:12 a.m. when Maria woke up from that nightmare crying: my baby, my baby, alarming John, who thought she had had a miscarriage. Maria assured him she was all right; it was just a nightmare. She had been on a plane that was breaking apart, falling and about to crash, when she bailed out just in time.

She couldn't have given him any more particulars that morning because she wouldn't have known where to begin. The dream was too complicated to explain. It involved so many characters, so many memory constraints and such a long history. Maria herself did not grasp its full depth. She needed time alone to analyze it and waited till after John left for work to give it her full attention.

When Maria closed her eyes, she could still picture Sasha's image entreating for Maria to remember her sleep world and to write about her family there. Maria had drifted away during the last few months, and Sasha had made one last ditch effort to connect with Maria and remind her of her other family. Sasha reminded her of the promise to write about them. All the people on that plane were her inner world, characters waiting for an author to give them life. As Maria thought about them, she could feel them as palpably alive within her as the baby she was carrying. She was swept by gales of recall that awakened very deep feelings for them. The memories brought back joy of the times together, the fights, the arguments, the sharing of life. And although she could not remember everything, she could imagine it, because she felt it very strongly. It was as if feelings within her materialized into inklings of memory which then her imagination clarified in living colors. Oh, thank you, thank you, Sasha. Thanks for the visions, even if I nearly had a heart attack living through that virtual plane crash. Maria could understand its purpose. Everything about the mind during sleep made sense to her this morning. The near crash was meant to wake her up abruptly to ensure she would remember the dream. As the minutes passed, she remembered increasingly, and more clearly.

The writing of this novel began that morning. It took her ten years to write about the experiences she lived during 1999. Maria had folders on her computer dealing with sleep, which she designated with the letter 'z'. She had z-Poetry, z-Essays, and z-Notes. Everything was Zs. But this day she started a new folder which she called "z-Novel." She resolved this morning that she would mark the end of each chapter with a string of seven Zs.

Ideas were spinning vertiginously in her head. Thoughts were coming so fast that she gave up trying to write them. Instead, she sat back and closed her eyes to better grasp the mental flashes and the bursts of memory. She pictured scenes, characters and episodes of forgotten nightly interludes in a caravan of visions that covered months. Ideas connected so logically one to the next that it was as if she were rewinding her life at high speed, living a fantastic dream while wide awake. On this morning, the primeval amalgam of ideas that was churning desperately in Maria's mind, wrote itself into a novel in no time at all and took the form of a virtual book. She held the inchoate virtual manuscript and turned its pages like a fast-turning rolodex that fanned out its plots and subplots and the breath of its characters into the air, which she then inhaled deeply into her lungs and into her blood. She read over one hundred thousand unwritten words this way, by just unfurling the pages of her virtual book and blowing their meaning into the air.

In this perusal she saw herself walking to the abode of her mind at night. It was like the attic of a building up on a hill, full of things, full of relics, full of mystery and wonder. The custodian was an old doctor who gave her a tour. "This is the place where you will know yourself," he told her. "This is the home of your mind at night." Then he opened doors, and she met endearing characters whom she felt she had known all her life, and a world came alive.

In a very real sense, the writing of this novel began that day. It took her ten years to finish the manuscript. She wrote other things in the meantime; she became involved in other projects; she traveled; and she had two children. But no matter what else she did during these years, Maria always came back to this work because, aside from the personal and biographical aspects, there were aspects of sleep which, she thought, were human and of universal interest. People would associate with the stories. The workings of her mind at night would hit familiar chords in people who would recognize the modus operandi, the kibitzing, the digesting and regurgitating of the day's events. Ah yes, that happened to me too, people would say. I, too, have felt the beat of a world alive in me but unseen. I have also felt the influence of unremembered debates upon my conscious hours, imbuing me with that sense of conviction when I told myself: enough now! I have heard enough. No more tedious arguments! My mind is made up and I know what I must do. Then I forgot all about it. But when decision-time came into the real world I was ready with resolve and courage that I didn't know I had.

For Maria, sleep afforded another view into the world, into humanity. She could see the seams of the fabric of her life, the woof and warp. Sleep afforded another perspective of the human psyche. She could see intertwining threads that formed the fabric of her beliefs. During sleep she could examine beliefs at length, and she could see the raw materials of those beliefs.

True to something that Prof. Quixote had once told her, the world of sleep would come alive for her when she started writing about it. But it would not be memory that spearheaded the telling. It would be introspection and imagination. This morning, as if to make the point, something, or someone within her, brought up a specific issue for analysis. It said: "Maria, you don't need to go too far to find a vivid example of how dreams influenced your actions while awake. Take John, for example, your husband. How did you meet him? Do you remember that day in April? Think about it."

Maria recalled it was April 21, the day after the Columbine massacre, the day when she had an altercation with Mildred Colson and quit her job. When she met John later that day, she was happily unemployed. She was intoxicated with feelings of freedom and adventure. He came into her life at an optimal time.

"Yes, yes, all that is true. But think about earlier that day. Why were you taking Elena to see the doctor? Was Elena sick?"

"No, I don't think so."

"Then why take a healthy girl to the doctor?"

Maria thought deeply about that morning. She remembered that she woke up feeling pushed to do something she didn't want to do. She didn't have the resolve for it. Then some inner voice prodded her, and she distinctly heard these Shakespeare lines: *There's a tide in the affairs of men, which taken at the flood leads on to fortune.*

That's how she found the gumption to pick up the phone. She cajoled Elena into making an appointment to see Dr. Shiller. She remembered feeling like a general before a battle, with all her troops standing by waiting for her order to execute a battle plan that had been amply debated. There was a hush in the morning air as everyone waited for her word. Then she raised her arm and gave the order: Forward, march! She still remembered that deep inside there was much trepidation and some reluctance. In fact, had she hesitated much longer, she would have lost the nerve.

She couldn't remember the debate that led to that. But on the night of April 20, the day of the Columbine massacre, she had gone with her parents to a restaurant where she had ordered churros y chocolate. Could they have discussed it then? They discussed many things but not that. It wasn't her parents.

It was much later that she inferred that it must have been the girls at dream central. She could hear drumbeats, thumping and clamor that became louder and louder and which materialized into a vision. She reconstructed a dream, and she could picture Maria Luisa, Libby, and Sasha. They were pounding on a table in unison and chanting: "Go for it, call Elena! Go for it, call Elena!"

Maria acquiesced just to make them stop. "Alright, alright, I will!" Then the next morning, she felt committed, as if she had given her word in a meeting she couldn't recall. She also remembered that later that day she had an opportunity to cancel the trip to West

Palm Beach when Mildred Colson blocked her plans. But by then, she was full of fight, and she went for broke. The job be damned. Colson be damned. Forward, charge! She resigned. Then the loom of history began to weave its tapestry.

This morning Maria understood that her novel would need to be fashioned with inspired recall, with memory inebriated with copious help from her imagination. She would be dealing with an elusive world, without tapes or videos, but rich in allegory and symbols, which she would have to decipher.

z   z   Z   Z   Z   z   z

63. PUBLISHING THE MANUSCRIPT

One evening in early 2009, when the manuscript was all written, Maria went to Dream Central and told the girls that the great undertaking had come to an end. The manuscript was hot off her printer.

"Well, ladies, here it is," she said. "Except for some revisions here and there and some editing, this is it. Here is the masterwork we've all been waiting for. Here is the account of our world. We come alive in these pages. Whoever reads this will know the accounts of our nights together. Our story."

The question in everybody's mind was: yes, but how do you get it bound, printed, and marketed? Now what's the next step? Nobody had any experience with publishing. Maria herself had investigated the publishing process and had been frustrated and discouraged. First, you must search for a literary agent because no publisher would give you the time of day as a new author. But finding an agent was equally impossible. She would have to write a query letter, which was a pain. It was more difficult to write than the novel itself. The entire process promised only long delays and innumerable rejections. Maria would just as soon train for a marathon as do that. She thought she would self publish it, but even then, she did not know with whom, or how to go about it. She wanted to consult Prof. Quixote on this. Maybe he would read between the lines and recognize that her consultation was really a plea for help on the next step. Perhaps he would offer to help. The book was entering a phase about which she knew nothing. There were, also, other very basic and personal decisions that only she could make. Paramount among these decisions was the author's name. Should she use her maiden name, Maria Diaz? That wouldn't apply now as she went by Maria Shiller. It seemed silly to worry about such minor things; nevertheless, the nuances of the name bothered her.

"What about Maria Diaz-Shiller? What's wrong with that?" Sasha asked.

"That sounds logical, except that a good portion of the novel took place in 1999 when I was Maria Diaz. The novel is about me in that year—not in the years since."

"Well, that does it then. You are out of options. You need a pseudonym."

Maria nodded in agreement, as she had considered that option earlier and found it appealing. The girls were excited because searching for a pseudonym meant that a naming game would be in play, and they loved that sort of thing. Maria Luisa, the statistician, suggested a random process.

"Why don't we just pull up twelve or fifteen letters at random and fashion a name out of them?"

They played the game, opting only for ten letters instead of fifteen. As it happened, the first sample drew a preponderance of consonants, Ks, Zs, Ws, and Cs.

"Good grief, Maria, you're going to sound Polish with those letters."

"Yeah, like Dr. Broca," Maria commented.

"Broca doesn't sound Polish to me," said Sasha.

"That's because it isn't… Broca is not his real name."

"How come we all call him that? What is his real name, then?"

"You know," Maria began to explain, "he was the first character of this dream world I ever met. It was very early on when I first came here some ten years ago. He gave me a tour of the great dome, our home-sweet-home. At some point I asked him what his name was, and he gave me something that sounded like Polish gibberish to me: Kcz@Jt&wichX. It was a contorted concatenated cacophony of consonants. I didn't ask him to repeat it because it wouldn't have made any difference. Spelling it would have made it worse. So, I took to calling him Dr. Broca. It seemed fitting for this place, and he didn't seem to mind. It stuck."

"I wonder if he is really Polish…" said Sasha wistfully.

"Isn't it amazing that after all this time we still don't know much about each other. The mysteries of this place continue rising out of the nooks and crannies. It's incredible."

The postman entered the room at that moment, delivering the day's mail. He greeted the girls courteously. "Hello ladies. Here's the mail. Have a nice day."

"Hola, Mario, what you got there for us?" said one of the Marias, as she took the bulk of magazines and envelopes and flipped through them. She made a face of recognition as she picked up the magazine with beefcake on the cover. "This has got Libby written all over it. Here, take it." Then she came to an issue of Scientific American and said: "Maria Luisa, of course." And there was a cooking magazine which left no doubt as to whom it might belong. "Maria Clara, where are you? On second thought, Sasha, would you please take this to her? I am afraid that if we call her, she'll abandon her sizzling pans and boiling pots and have an accident."

She was puzzled when she came to one magazine, *The Economist*, because it rang no bells for her. She could not guess to whom it might belong. "This one eludes me. I can't imagine anyone here reading this. I'll have to look at the label. It's addressed to E. L. Albán. Who is that?"

Nobody seemed to know. "Maybe the postman made a mistake," said Sasha.

"No, it's got the right address... Dream Central."

They all looked at how the name was written, in case they missed something when they heard it pronounced. "It has an accent mark over the last 'a' so he must be Spanish," someone noted. Maria, also, got up to see for herself.

"Very interesting…" Maria mused as she looked at the name. "I have a strange suspicion. I think I know who he is, but let's ask Ram. He would know."

Ram was summoned and he came right away. When the question was put to him, he answered without the slightest hesitation: "That's Prof. Quixote."

"Just as I had suspected," said Maria. "This is very odd, and it gets more and more interesting. We have here one more proof of the mysteries of this place and one more living victim of my nicknaming zeal. I seem to recall that it was I who started calling him that during a meeting. He had presented an algorithm for putting order in the chaos of sleep. Poor thing, I thought then. This is quixotic. It doesn't stand a chance."

"Was it like devising a logarithmic algorithm for the arithmetic of alga growing rhythmically on a log in a sea of dreams?" asked Sasha.

Maria ignored her. "He was charging at windmills. Nobody took him seriously. Imagine that: to put dreams in order! To arrange chaos into a system! Pshish! The name, Quixote, seemed to fit him."

"That also goes to prove that what you name someone around here seems to stick. I bet you christened all of us. What I want to know is: how did I wind up with a name like Sasha? Did you run out of Maria combinations?"

"As I recall, you named yourself. I asked you once to identify yourself when you were trying to sound like the Wicked Witch of the West, and that's what you gave me. But back to Prof. Quixote. He is a big puzzle. Who is he, really? He is not like the rest of you girls—parts of me in human form. He is distant, male, older. He is like a guest, a visiting scholar with an independent mind and, I suspect, an independent body of his own. He exists in real flesh and blood somewhere, like Janet Reno. He performs a function here but is not a part of me. Is he here now? I would really like to talk to him."

"He hasn't been here in months," said Ram.

"Maybe he died," said Maria Luisa.

"Oh, dear God, I hope not. Then again, what difference would it make? Would death stop him from making appearances here? Abraham Lincoln has been dead for ages, and he comes around. Janet Reno is in Washington, not here, but she manages to make a presence here."

Then Imogene spoke. "This suggests to me that we—Sasha, Libby, Maria Luisa, Ram and myself—are your real core. We are the ones that will be with you until you die, because we really are a part of you. The others are transitory and symbolic entities that come and go. They perform a function, but having fulfilled their purpose, they move on."

"What was his purpose then?"

"He helped you through your doubts when you were philosophically weak, when you had doubts about the afterlife, when you were confused about your responsibilities to God, and when you wondered whether as an atheist you had a right to dream about heaven. Above all, he gave you a mission in life when he headed you towards writing. And now you have just turned in the manuscript of your first novel."

"I just hope he is not gone, and I hope he will come back. I am not through with Prof. Quixote yet. I need him more than ever. It makes a lot of difference whether he is dead or not. I need him to run errands for me."

"Maybe he is through with you, with us. He turned you into a writer. You wrote your book; he accomplished his mission."

"I hope that's not the case, Sasha. Let me consult Ram about something. Oh Ram, dear good old Ram, could I prevail on you to do one more miracle? Could you please see to it that he gets this manuscript? I would like to send a note with it."

"I'll try. Where is the note?"

"I'm going to write it now."

"You could just dictate it to me, if you'd like."

"Okay, here goes."

Dear Prof. Quixote… No, no… scratch that… Dear Professor Albán: Thanks to you, I have at last finished the work on sleep. I have written it from the standpoint of a third person, someone who followed my comings and goings through the real world and through the world of dreams; someone who knew me intimately, as you do. I didn't think of it this way before, but it is clear to me now that I must have been writing as if I were seeing it from your perspective. I did not use the first person.

"Ram! You are not taking notes. You're just standing there."

"I don't need to take notes. Don't you remember who I am?"

Maria acknowledged with a smile. "Of course, how could I forget!" Then she continued dictating.

I would like to ask a favor of you. Could you please read the manuscript and tell me what you think? Please feel free to make any changes you see fit; after all, this is as much your work as mine. I feel so strongly about this that I have one more request. I have decided to go with a pseudonym, and I could think of no better name than E. L. Alban, if you would allow it. Also, could you write the first chapter for me? I know you don't like prefaces and prologues. You once told me that nobody ever reads them. I would like so much to have words from your own mind and your own pen, and I think chapter 1 would be appropriate.

I can't remember when it was the last time we talked. So much has happened...September 11, the wars in Afghanistan and Iraq, Islamic terrorism. Have we talked about these things? There could be another novel in all this, but I couldn't do it without you. Please, please come back. I miss you. Affectionately, Maria.

PS I haven't got a clue on how to proceed from here. Literary agent? Self-publish it? I despair thinking about all that. I don't want to deal with that. As you know, I don't need the money. If the book depended on me to see publication, it could just die on the vine. But if you think this has merit and deserves an airing beyond a shelf in my house, I would be most grateful if you ran the ball to a touchdown. I am passing it to you. Catch! I suspect that you are more than a figment of my dreams. I would bet that you have connections in the real world, although we never talked about this. When it comes to selling this, it is I who is the useless insubstantial one. I feel as if I were just an actor, cast in a dream, a dream in the theater of your mind. Please help me and my sisters come alive in the real world. Love. Maria.

"Did you get all that, Ram?"

"Would you like me to play it back for you?"

Ram read the entire letter very fast without missing a single word. Maria stood by watching him in awe, staring at him. He was a phenom. He reminded her of Srinivasan Ramanujan, the mathematical savant that could make complex calculations in his mind. His pupils would emit sparks of light. His hair would glitter as if he had shiny sequins that spangled as they caught electric charges from his brain. Maria couldn't help but wonder to herself whether he was a humanoid, a robotic structure of her brain in anthropomorphic form that handled her memory.

"What time is it?" Sasha asked.

"It's 4:30 in the morning. Why do you want to know?"

"Because I can just picture Professor Quixote," said Sasha. "Maybe it is just my imagination, but I see him very distinctly, far from here in a different time zone, six hours later, as in Madrid, Spain. It is 10:30 in the morning there. It is a bright and sunny day, and he is walking leisurely on Calle Preciados midway between La Puerta del Sol and La Gran Vía, breathing the fresh morning air. The pedestrian walkway is abuzz with people. There are Marias everywhere, real ones, live ones. He is ogling at all of them, and he is thinking of us. They remind him of us. He misses us. Maybe we'll get a postcard from him soon."

Maria Luisa spoke, articulating another thought about Professor Quixote that had just crossed her mind. "Has it occurred to you all that Professor Quixote could not be dead because if he were, we would die with him? You just said it, Maria. You expressed a thought of profound implications when you said: 'I suspect that you are more than a figment of my dreams. I feel as if I were just an actor cast in a dream in the theater of your mind.' All of which raises the inevitable question: whose mind is this anyway? Here we thought we revolved around your mind, Maria, but you are just another one of us—another Babushka within a series of Matryoshka dolls. And he is the biggest babushka of us all."

Sasha jumped in, asking: "Oh, Maria Luisa, who but you would ask what only a child would dare blurt out?"

"Let her answer," Maria Luisa pressed. "So, tell us, Maria, what do you think about all this?"

"Oh, I don't know… you've asked a bunch of questions at once. What is life? What is fiction? What is real? Who am I? Who are you? Who is Professor Alban? But if, as you suspect, he is the biggest Babushka of us all, that is not such a bad thing and here is why.

"If Professor Quixote is the head over all our heads as you suggest, we would all owe our lives to him. He dies; we die. He lives; we live. And happily, we're all alive, hurrah! But also, he would have had total power over us. He could have turned us into miserable perverts, into psycho serial killers and what-not. Thank God he is not onto that stuff. Instead, he has crafted his ideal of a woman in me, and for that I am very thankful. He's done very well by us. I am so, so happy to have come of age and to have lived a double life in two decent normal parallel worlds. My life has been an idyll, like a blissful fairytale. I wouldn't change any part of it. Of course, you also have benefited by surfing on the wave of my good fortune. Finally, let's not forget my last bonus, which is: I don't have to go through the jungles and minefields of the publishing business to take this manuscript to print. It is his baby now. He's got it with my blessing. I'd love for him to put his name on it and be in full charge of things from here on!

"So, in short, Marilucha, I see no negatives. I don't feel weirdly fictional, like a freak, like an alien woman who escaped from the nether world of night's oblivion. I am just an ordinary woman with the usual human foible of limited dream memory. My psyche flourishes in my dreams into blossoms, who are none other than the beloved sisters of my very own elite sorority. You, too, are not freaks. You are universal. You exist in the soul of every human being. There are millions of Marias out there. And they all have their own universe, a world such as ours. The difference is that they haven't been written about as we appear in these pages. But they all have their own stories. A toast to us all."

Z   z   z   z   z   z   Z

www.ingramcontent.com/pod-product-compliance
Lightning Source LLC
Chambersburg PA
CBHW021330310726
48971CB00001B/64